Despite being unanimously projected to go first overall in the upcoming NHL Draft, Noah Anderson wants nothing more than to get the Draft over with so he can escape his dad's unrelenting criticism and establish himself outside the rivalry he's never tried to fuel.

Alex Valencia can handle getting picked second after a guy touted as the next Gretzky—but he can't wrap his head around the fact that Noah is the one friend he can't make.

When the draft lottery all but guarantees they'll play for rival teams, Alex accidentally walks them right into a loser-buys dinner competition, ensuring their relationship remains a point of interest long after the season begins.

Opposites in so many ways, neither Alex nor Noah expect a relationship built on the begrudging acceptance of a challenge made on live television to become so deeply important to them. But as the line between chirping and flirting blurs, they both must decide how much they're willing to sacrifice to play in the NHL.

# PROVE IT

DO OR DIE, BOOK ONE

*STEPHANIE HOYT*

A NineStar Press Publication
www.ninestarpress.com

# Prove It



First Edition, February 2024

ISBN: 978-1-64890-723-4

Also available in eBook, ISBN: 978-1-64890-722-7

CONTENT WARNING:

This book contains sexually explicit content, which may only be suitable for mature readers. Depictions of homophobic attitudes .

*For all the rivals who fell in love.*

Oh, mama don't you cry,
USA hockey is do or die.

# Chapter One

THERE'S A NOISE to Noah's left. He expects to see his dad, annoyed and ready to tell Noah every way he should've done better, how he's never going to make it in the NHL if he keeps hiding from all his problems instead of facing them head on. He's gearing up for another blow to this lackluster eighteenth birthday when he glances over at Alex Valencia walking down the row toward him. For a fleeting second, Noah's relieved he doesn't have to face his father yet. Then Alex takes the seat next to him and the image of hats flying to the ice after Alex scored the game winner for the United States flashes through his mind and irritation floods through him.

"Come to gloat about your buzzer beater?"

"Does that sound like something I'd do, Anderson?"

Noah drags his attention away from the Zamboni smoothing over the ice to find Alex smiling at him. Which isn't unexpected—Alex has the opposite of a resting bitch face—but this smile is different from any

Noah's ever received. This one doesn't match the earnest incandescence Noah has never understood, but now expects from Alex.

Noah's shocked by how much he hates it. Even more so when he admits, "No, I suppose not."

He wouldn't say he's an expert on Alex's smiles—they barely *know* each other—but he's seen enough to recognize the transformation. A second ago, it was subdued, a little tight, but now he's grinning, loose and broad enough to dimple his cheeks. This one's real and Noah has an inexplicable, yet familiar, desire to press his thumb to Alex's tan skin and measure the depth of his left dimple—always a little more pronounced than the right. Noah's stomach twists and his heartbeat ratchets up—he can't afford to still have these thoughts.

Hockey is already a parasitic environment, but being attracted to the one guy he can't escape is another level of hell entirely. No one, from his dad to the reporters covering their international matchups, can shut up about how Alex would be the clear first overall if Noah wasn't in his draft class and if anyone could upset the predictions, Alex's strength and size might give him the edge to do it.

Which...fine. Whatever. Noah can't fix his height, but he can get stronger and if he has to measure himself against Alex, who truly *is* phenomenal, to know he's trying hard enough, then so be it. And maybe, if Alex weren't gorgeous—with his perfect smile, perfect cheekbones, perfect jaw, perfectly silky-smooth hair—Noah wouldn't hate it so much. But Alex *is* stunning, and every time someone mentions his name, everything Noah wants but can never have flashes before his eyes.

Which, for the record, isn't Alex.

Noah might not know Alex, but after years of crossing paths, he's pretty confident he's too much for all of Noah's anxieties to handle in large doses. Alex is loud and vibrant and always moving. His personality draws people in and keeps them, and he seems to thrive off it. Alex is everything Noah isn't and nothing he wants to be around.

Noah wants the freedom to fall in love, to live without the pressure to blend in—constantly worried someone can tell he isn't straight. Noah doesn't want Alex, but Noah looks at him and his chest aches for what could be if he liked girls, if he didn't care what people thought of him, if hockey wasn't such a toxic environment. He looks at Alex and he *wants*.

Not for the first time, Noah hopes they get drafted to different conferences. He's not naïve. He knows their first matchup in the NHL will be a big deal regardless of where it happens, but only playing twice a year should mitigate the fuss. If Noah's lucky, their so-called rivalry will fade into the nonexistent thing Noah wishes it already was.

"Why're you here then?" Noah asks.

"Wanted to say happy birthday."

Noah's pulse skyrockets and his stomach swoops under Alex's unwavering attention. He sounds so genuine, but Noah narrows his eyes. "How do you know it's my birthday?" Alex averts his gaze and Noah nearly laughs. "Was someone gloating about my birthday loss?"

"It might've come up."

Noah snorts. "And what—you found me out of the kindness of your heart?"

"Who said I was looking for you? Maybe we both wanted some quiet and when I saw you sulking, I thought, 'Must suck to lose on your birthday—lemme go cheer him up.'"

Noah arches an eyebrow. "There's no way you don't thrive in post-win chaos."

Alex tilts his head to the side, mouth slanting in a tiny grin. "You've got me there."

Noah purses his lips. He doesn't understand why Alex keeps seeking him out. The first time, it was understandable. Enough scouts had hyped up the two of them facing off in the u-17 Challenge that Alex doubling back in the hotel lobby the night before their game wasn't unexpected. Despite years of hearing how good he is, Alex saying he looked forward to playing Noah *because* he was so talented still threw him off. He's never taken praise well, but Noah couldn't even stumble through a thanks for Alex's earnestness.

Noah was embarrassing and rude and, despite Alex finding him after every tournament to tell Noah how well he played, he never adapted. Alex's attention gets under Noah's skin, their interactions leaving him restless and unbalanced, unsure of how to act.

"You had a good game," Noah says, hoping he can avoid Alex complimenting him if he does it first. "Keep any of the hats?"

"Yeah, can never have too many."

Noah turns back to the ice as his traitorous mouth twitches in a smile. "Of course."

"Even found a Canadian one in the mix."

Noah snorts. "Sure you did."

"Look."

Noah does, right in time to catch the black cap Alex was wearing moments before. Noah flips the cap over to find the Hockey Canada logo and absolutely doesn't laugh. "So much for team loyalty."

"We've learned a valuable lesson here tonight."

Noah can't help himself. "Oh, yeah? What's that?"

"Hatties outrank patriotism."

Alex's smile is sunshine bright and if this were Julien, Noah might even smile back. But Noah refuses to let his guard down around Alex, no matter how tempting he always makes it. He and Alex aren't friends. They never will be.

With nothing more to say, the silence stretches between them. Then Alex stands and taps Noah's forearm. "Keep the hat."

Noah meets Alex's gaze. His smile is soft, guarded maybe.

He attempts his most winning smile; he's certain it falls flat. "If we meet in the final—you're going to lose."

Alex walks down the row backward, grin turning sly. "Better wish for it when you blow those candles out tonight, then."

"Don't worry. I won't need to."

Alex tips his head back in a loud, honking laugh. Despite how ridiculous he sounds, Noah has to push down the warm flutter in his chest—hopefully for good this time.

# Chapter Two

ALEX WOULDN'T SAY he's superstitious, but when they go into the gold medal game against Team Canada, he's quietly thankful he only *implied* his team would win while Anderson straight up said it.

It doesn't matter in the end. Anderson was right.

When both goalies are hot, Alex's lone goal in the first can only get them so far. With two minutes left in the game, the puck hits Anderson's tape and time seems to slow. Alex's chest constricts as Anderson's pass connects with Thorn's stick right in front of the net. Thorn beats Beaver by a hair's breadth. The puck squeaks between the bar and Beaver's glove for the go-ahead goal that leaves Team USA racing against the clock.

He doesn't come away with another eleventh-hour goal to tie it up; Canada wins and Alex's stomach bottoms out, heart hollow and defeated.

Beaver has tears in his eyes as they skate back to the bench. Parse still has his helmet on as he rests his head against the boards. Ben drops his hand to Parse's neck and squeezes, but Parse doesn't even move. Alex wants to ignore the celebration going on around him, but his eyes sting from the forlorn slump of his teammates and Alex hates that more.

He turns away right in time to see Thorn lift Anderson off his skates in a hug, their flushed faces lit up in victory. Thorn sets Anderson down and before Alex can look away, their eyes meet. Alex's heart aches, but he still musters a smile. Anderson blinks, excitement flickering to surprise before he nods at Alex with a timid smile that makes Alex's stomach lurch.

Then Ben's at his side, pulling him into a hug, and time passes in a blur—medals and anthems, subdued post-game media scrums, and a silent bus, heavy footsteps as they pile into Parse and Beaver's room to pass whiskey between one another while they sulk.

The crushing weight of failure becomes too much with them all pressed together in one hotel room and Alex escapes to the roof, the thrum of alcohol in his blood convincing him the cold might shock the sadness away.

It doesn't.

But Anderson startles at the opposite end of the rooftop when the door squeaks open, and that cuts through it some. Alex joins Anderson at the railing and bumps their shoulders together. "While I'd never complain about getting a moment alone with Canada's golden boy—"

Anderson makes a dismissive sound.

"Oh, come on. Acknowledging the masses think you're God's gift to hockey won't hurt my feelings."

Noah wrinkles his nose. "You're no hand-me-down."

Alex grins, chest swelling. "Don't hurt yourself there, bro."

Anderson scowls, but that's par for the course and Alex won't let it deter him. He kicks the sole of Anderson's shoe. "Seriously, shouldn't you be off celebrating in a sea of red and white? Why're you up here?"

Anderson narrows his eyes. "Why're *you*?"

He asks Alex some version of this every time they interact, and Alex never has an adequate answer. He gets under Alex's skin though; makes him want to work a reaction out of him, leaves him aching for a sign he isn't taking this rivalry so damn seriously.

"Rooftop's a pretty good place to sit with your failures after losing, don't you think?"

Anderson rolls his eyes. "You didn't even bring a scarf." His gaze drops to Alex's hands. "Or gloves. You're not prepared for sulking."

"Oh, this is nothing."

Noah scoffs. "Yeah, okay. Aren't you from—" He takes a beat, eyebrows knitting, mouth pressed in an impossibly thin line. He blows out a sharp breath. "—a non-traditional hockey market?"

He doesn't think Noah means to be funny, but Alex cackles regardless. "I can't believe you used 'non-traditional hockey market' as a geographical marker."

"But aren't you?"

"Texas forever, baby."

Noah doesn't smile, but there's a tiny upward slant to his mouth when he looks back out over the city that keeps Alex there after the silence turns tense. He would usually leave by now, but they were *so close* to gold and Alex needs a distraction. "Why are you here? You never said."

Noah doesn't answer, but he turns back, and despite the beanie pulled low over his ears and the scarf looped around his neck, his cheeks are still rosy from the chill. He looks warm, soft, and entirely too upset for someone who just won gold.

"Hey, I'm the one who lost; you could at least indulge me out of sympathy."

Anderson exhales sharply and another long moment passes where he seems to fall back on his usual play—icing Alex out until he leaves—before he grimaces and says, "Too loud. Too much t—" He pulls his bottom lip between his teeth and his shoulders jump in an aborted sort of shrug. "I don't know. It's a lot. I needed a minute."

Alex doesn't know what to make of the admission, let alone how to respond, but it doesn't matter. He doesn't have time to stumble through asking for a clarification before one of Anderson's teammates bursts through the rooftop door and saves Alex from prying with a loud shout.

"Finally! Thor said you might be up here."

He's as pumped as Alex expected Anderson to be, barely even dimming when he notices Alex.

"Hey, Valencia," Connor says. At least Alex thinks his name is Connor. It might be Cole. Definitely a C.

"Hey." Alex moves to leave. "Congratulations on the win."

"Thanks." Maybe-Connor slings an arm around Anderson's shoulders, unperturbed by the way he tenses under the weight. "Come on, man. The boys are asking for you."

Something twists in Alex's chest, and he wants to ask—needs to ask. Alex has never seen Anderson flinch away from a hit; has watched him celly with his teammates, *just* saw Thorn sweep him off his feet. But here, outside the rink, a casual touch has set him on edge and Alex can't help but wonder if *touching* is what Noah stopped himself from saying.

Once again, Connor doesn't give him the chance. He practically drags Anderson inside, and Alex has the inexplicable urge to fling Connor's arm off Anderson's stiff shoulders and snap at him for not realizing how uncomfortable he's making his friend. But no matter his efforts, he and Anderson aren't friends and Connor is his teammate—if one of them is misreading Anderson, it's probably not Connor.

Alex's fingers really are cold, but he shoves his hands in his pockets and stays put, unwilling to get stuck in the elevator with them, and tries not to dwell on what Anderson meant and why today, of all days, he gave Alex an inch.

# Chapter Three

NOAH WOULD LOVE to spend the five months between World Juniors and the Combine free of Alex, but it's impossible to avoid talking about the tournament, and with every mention of World Juniors comes a new memory of Alex—the heat of him by Noah's side, his assessing gaze in the empty rink, the infuriating way he smiled at Noah after losing, how he seemed so genuinely curious about why Noah wasn't off celebrating. Thankfully, winning gold earns Noah a reprieve from his dad's unrelenting comparisons to Alex, and the reporters' questions roll right off his shoulders when he's not caught up in needing to be *far* better than Alex to impress his own dad.

Paul Anderson can only go so long without criticizing Noah though, and when they get shut out twice in a row in the second week of February, he doubles down. When he's pushing too hard, insisting Noah's game must be flawless since he's so much smaller than Alex, a spiteful anger twists through Noah, and he wishes he'd go second.

Noah wants to be the best more than he wants to piss his dad off, but sometimes, it's so hard to separate hockey from his father's unrelenting criticism. Hockey is both the rush of calm he gets when he steps on the ice *and* the knots of anxiety tightening in his stomach as his dad shakes off his mom's warning hand and moves to the other room to pick Noah's game apart on FaceTime. Noah loves hockey, but it's so much easier in those moments to hate the game than it is to hate his dad and resent his mom for never successfully stopping him.

They don't drop a game after their back-to-back shutouts; Noah finishes the regular season with his longest point streak yet, and he's once again unable to imagine doing anything other than flying down the ice until his body won't let him anymore.

He's so damn happy to finish his last season in the Dub with a playoff run that getting asked about Alex for the first time in months doesn't even ruin his mood. His face, sweaty and flushed after a win, still floods his mind when a reporter brings up Alex's impressive start to the USHL playoffs, but Noah's so pleased with his own performance that his smile doesn't even drop when the reporter asks, "Are you worried about the growing speculation that this tear might be enough for some teams to take him over you in the draft?"

"It's no secret Alex is good," Noah starts, getting a laugh from the scrum, "but that doesn't worry me. It motivates me." He huffs out a laugh. "Maybe more than anything else does."

"What do you mean?" the same reporter asks, the quirk of his eyebrow suggesting he wasn't expecting this much honesty.

"I'd hate to feed into the rivalry or imply I'm losing sleep over being better than Alex Valencia," Noah says, which isn't true, but these guys don't need details on all the sleepless nights his dad's obsession has caused. "But honestly, he's so talented and if I can match him, if I can be better than him, then I'm good too." Noah swipes at the sweaty curls plastered against his forehead. "I don't know how things will go in June; Alex could easily go first. And if he does, I'll need to push myself harder in the league to prove myself. But for right now, I'm focused on winning the championship and then winning the Memorial Cup. Once we've done that, I'll think more about the draft."

Giving the press a sound bite about Alex always gets back to his dad and Noah knows he shouldn't have been so honest. But Noah was happy, muscles burning from a long game, head buzzing with post-win adrenaline, and he wasn't thinking about his dad, or the way he'd insist Noah can't say Alex is better and expect to be drafted first because no team wants a guy who lacks confidence.

When Alex follows him on Instagram after and DMs him a clip of Noah's interview paired with, *I'm so happy I could help shape you into Canada's next golden boy* 😏, Noah can no longer dwell on the sick pleasure his father must derive from being an overbearing asshole. He's too preoccupied with how Alex will be his undoing if the focus on their alleged rivalry doesn't fade into a distant memory once the draft is over.

Noah knows better than to put faith in luck letting him escape Alex and the way he has become a soul-crushing reminder of his dad's criticism. The draft lottery happens, and instead of being separated by miles and miles of land, New Jersey and New York jump spots to land the first and second picks and now, no matter who goes first overall, he and Alex will always be the draft rivals taken by rival teams.

It's a relief when Alex doesn't DM him after the lottery. Noah's a game away from the President's Cup Final and he doesn't have time to figure out Alex's ulterior motives here. Still, he allows himself a moment to wonder if Alex's silence means he's given up on whatever this whole thing was.

Luck really isn't on his side though, and when he swipes into his hotel room at the Combine, he finds Alex splayed out in bed, scrolling through his phone.

It's not too late, but Noah came straight to Buffalo from winning the Memorial Cup. He's tired, a little frayed, a little nervous for the Combine, and the only word he can muster when Alex turns his sleepy, soft expression on him is, "No."

Alex's relaxed expression shifts infinitesimally, too fast for Noah to decipher, and then he smiles, big and bright, like he's won something.

"Anderson!"

"Alex."

Alex nods his head, a strand of hair falling in his eyes, his smile never faltering despite the narrowing of his eyes. "Babe, you're too glum for someone who just won the Memorial Cup."

Noah grinds his teeth and refuses to rise to Alex's bait, or the smug little grin he catches out of the corner of his eye. Instead, he unloads everything for his nightly routine and allows himself to put off unpacking until tomorrow.

"Are you always this quiet?" Alex asks as Noah steps out of the bathroom, steam billowing out behind him.

"I thought you'd be asleep by now," Noah mumbles, glancing in Alex's direction despite his better judgment.

"He speaks!"

Noah climbs into bed, pointedly not looking in Alex's direction. "Sometimes."

"You might not know this about me, but I'm pretty chatty—"

Noah snorts. "I hadn't noticed."

"Yes, well, it's going to be a long week if you're going the silent treatment route."

Noah slides his gaze over. Alex is still smiling, always smiling, and Noah loses the will to ignore him. "Not having anything to say isn't the same as giving you the silent treatment."

"I don't get you," Alex says after a beat.

"There's nothing to get." Noah burrows into his blanket and stares at the ceiling. "Not everyone's got a motor mouth and no filter."

"Hey! I have a filter."

Noah turns on his side to face Alex. "Do you?"

Alex mirrors Noah, blanket pulled up to his chin, eyes glinting in the dim light. "I haven't even brought up being division rivals *once* since you got here. That's me filtering."

"Doesn't really count when you just did, now does it?"

Alex smiles. "Probably not. But I had to prove a point. *And* I haven't asked if you're pissed about it, so in the grand scheme of things, it very much counts as having a filter."

"Sure," Noah says, eyes dropping as he finally gets comfortable.

"Come to breakfast with me in the morning," Alex says, startling Noah out of his half sleep.

"What?"

"Me and Husky are going to breakfast before the interviews start. You should come."

Alex has never given Noah a reason to think he's being anything but kind, but Noah doesn't trust his earnestness, doesn't believe such a bright and energetic person would ever dispense so much time on trying to be Noah's friend when he's quiet, contained, uptight. Even if Noah wasn't suspicious, getting close to Alex would still be an awful idea. For the sake of Noah's sanity, he can never be friends with the living reminder of all things Noah can't have if he wants a long and successful career. "Thanks, but I'm pretty sure me and Thor have similar plans."

Alex blinks slowly; his smile doesn't dim. "Your loss."

*

"SAW VALENCIA LEAVING your room," Julien says when Noah opens the door in the morning. "You two rooming together? Or is he still trying to win you over?"

Noah follows Julien down the hall. "Both."

"You know, if I didn't know he was dating an absolute rocket, I might assume he's into you."

Noah chokes. "What?"

Julien pushes the elevator call button. "I'm totally chill with it. I'm down with whoever wants to fly their rainbow flag. But come on, you've never thought that might be his deal?"

Noah's brain might be short circuiting. "Uh, no. I can honestly say that's *never* crossed my mind."

Julien shakes his head as he steps on the elevator. "Should've known better than to expect your oblivious ass to catch onto anything. But really, I don't get him. No offense, but you're a dick—why does he even bother?"

"Wow. Who's being a dick now?"

"It's not being a dick if I'm stating a *fact*! Anyone who's spent five minutes with you knows you're a prickly little bitch 90 percent of the time."

"I'm *not* prickly."

Julien looks unimpressed. "I've known you since we were what— twelve? And I've seen you smile twice."

Noah shoves Julien's shoulder and smirks when he thumps

against the side wall. "Fuck off. I've smiled *at least* five times in your presence."

"You're absolutely rounding up there, bud."

"What exactly do I have to smile about when you're such an ass?" Noah asks, the frenetic whir of his thoughts quieting as the conversation devolves. This is easy; this is familiar.

"I will literally fight you if you don't smile when you go number one," Julien says, face split into a wide, open smile as they step out of the elevator.

"Alex could easily go first."

Julien drops his voice. "I know your dad likes to shove that shit down your throat to wind you up, make you work harder, but come on. We all know how it's going to go: you, then him."

"Maybe."

"Just me and you, Noah," Julien says, which isn't entirely true since they're walking through the hotel lobby at breakfast time with people scattered all around. "No need to give me the media sound bite. I won't call you cocky for saying you're the cream of this year's crop."

Noah spots JT and Max at the entrance and calls out for them before responding. "Let's see how the Combine goes. Might even let you take a picture of me smiling if it goes the way you say. You know, for posterity's sake."

Julien barks out a laugh. "You're going to regret this deal when I cross-post it on every one of my socials."

Noah rolls his eyes, but it's finally sinking in that Julien would be chill with a hockey player coming out and he ends up grinning even as Julien says, "Jay! Brownie! Is Noah a prickly bitch?"

JT answers without hesitation. "A straight up cactus."

"I'd say he's a porcupine. Soft on the downstroke, but yeah," Max says with an apologetic smile. "Definitely prickly."

Noah huffs, Julien smirks, and the conversation turns into a verbal highlight reel of their favorite examples of Noah being a moody asshole until Noah flushes all the way down his neck and across his collarbones. Unlike his dad, his friends recount them as amusing anecdotes to laugh *with* Noah about, not flaws deserving derision. He isn't laughing, but he's close to it, and that's enough to distract Noah from the unnerving possibility Alex has *flirted* with him.

*

### *NHL Combine: Valencia bests Anderson in fitness testing*

*The last time Alex Valencia and Noah Anderson went head-to-head, Anderson came out on top after setting up Julien Thorn's golden goal at the 2022 IIHF World Junior Championship.*

*On Saturday, the Combine's fitness testing served as a rematch of sorts and Valencia outscored Anderson in every category. As the near unanimous consensus for first overall, Anderson's results likely wouldn't have affected his chances of going to Jersey, but given his smaller stature being the one thing he doesn't have on Valencia, the results were far closer where it matters most.*

*

BY THE END of the week, Noah has a catalog of information he never wanted about Alex. His hair is a mess when he wakes up, but it's good as new once he swipes his giant hand through it. He's an expanse of smooth tan skin with a constellation of small moles across his left ribs. He thinks nature documentaries are the perfect background noise, has a massive sweet-tooth, and the only time he doesn't talk a mile a minute is when he first wakes up and his voice is deep and scratchy.

And the most devastating part of rooming with him is that, despite his best efforts, Noah doesn't find Alex nearly as off-putting as he did when he got to Buffalo. Then Alex outperforms him in every single category of the fitness test on Saturday and reality crashes over him.

His dad's voice is sharp and grating over the phone when he says, for the millionth time, "You needed to outperform him this week to secure your spot, but you couldn't even do better in *one* category. Are you committed to being the best or not?"

Noah grits his teeth. "I am. I'm trying."

"Not good enough."

"I'm still one of the best, Dad. New Jersey's interested. The interview went well."

"Noah."

His dad says his name with such scorn and Noah can't stand hearing how short he falls anymore.

"There was an article I read about the interview process," he says, rushed and desperate, "and how it's basically the most important part. How the tests rarely change their interest because teams know who they want, and the interview will confirm if they're a fit."

"You've never been good at post-games. I doubt you're better at selling yourself to a team than Alex Valencia—"

"No one's as good at talking Valencia up as you, Dad."

Before his dad can go in on Noah, the door opens behind him. Noah tenses, heat creeping up his neck. "Look, I gotta go. My roommate's back."

"We'll finish this later."

But his dad can't get to Noah if he screens his calls until the trip is over. Noah hopes, once he signs his contract, he'll have the nerve to cut his dad out of his life, but until then avoidance works.

There's a hard press to Alex's mouth when Noah turns around. He's standing ramrod straight, eyes blazing.

"Uh." Noah has no idea what he's done to piss Alex off. "What's gotten into you?"

"Was that your dad?"

"Yes." Noah tries to inject every bit of *I don't want to talk about this* into his tone as possible.

He either fails or Alex doesn't care.

"Do you always sound—"

"Don't." Noah gets a pleasant thrill from how fast Alex clicks his mouth shut at the sharpness of his voice. "Whatever you overheard, forget it. My family drama is none of your business, and I won't air it out with someone I don't know. Or trust."

Alex clenches his jaw, staring at him for a long moment as a complicated expression clouds his face. Noah can't stand the silence, and relief washes through him when Alex grins again. "I didn't even know you could string so many words together at once, Anderson. You've been holding out on me."

# Chapter Four

ALEX NEVER NEEDED to hear Anderson's miserable voice while talking to his dad or how small he sounds while saying *Alex's* name. He wishes he could forget the barely there sigh he let out when Alex walked into the room, and the way he sounded relieved to hang up despite how tense his shoulders were.

Before this week, Alex had spent maybe three whole hours with Anderson off the ice, and he thought—or hoped—Ben was wrong. He wanted to believe Anderson was no more standoffish with Alex than anyone else, but now he sees how wrong he was. Now, he knows there's a reason Anderson is so hostile toward Alex in particular.

Which is bullshit, actually. Alex knows expectations are different when a guy has family in the game. He's seen firsthand how hard Nate and Beaver push themselves to live up to their fathers' names and how Kaden measures himself against his brothers. He can't even imagine what his dad could say about Anderson to make Alex sound so small, but he knows the constant comparisons are exhausting.

People have attached Alex's name to Anderson's for years. He's been told more times than not that going first overall could be the biggest NHL draft upset ever. And since World Juniors, Alex hasn't gone a single scrum without a reporter trying to get him to say Anderson doesn't deserve his hype.

So, Alex gets it. He *does*.

He knows how easily he could resent Anderson for the "he's no Noah Anderson" caveat every acknowledgement of Alex's talents comes with. But Alex knows it's not Anderson's fault he's the better hockey player; it's not his fault that any other year Alex would've been the clear number one. So why can't Anderson see the same? Why is he taking out whatever it is his dad's doing on Alex when all Alex has ever done is try to bridge the gap built between them by no choice of their own?

"You're glaring," Ben says as they make their way through the airport. "Can I assume you're finally getting on board with the rivalry?"

"What are you talking about?"

"I don't know what's been on your mind the entire flight, but you might as well be trying to bore a hole into Anderson's head. So, chill maybe?"

Alex glances over; Ben's wearing an amused, self-satisfied grin.

"It doesn't even make sense."

"What?"

"The rivalry! It's not real. We all know he's going first. I should be the bitter one. *I* should be the one icing him out all the time."

Ben shrugs. "Would hate to stroke your ego, babe, but you really think he's a shoo-in?"

"He's fucking fast, bro."

"I mean, you're no turtle."

"And he's more accurate."

"But you're bigger and have a harder shot."

Alex huffs. "Tell me you're not trying to convince me I'm going first."

"God no," Ben laughs. "He's got it in the bag. But you've gotten a lot closer in the last year. I can see why he might see you as competition."

Alex grumbles, "I hate it."

Ben slings his arm around Alex's shoulders and pulls him to his side, slowing their pace. "Yeah, but you hate when anyone doesn't like you."

Alex shoves him off. "Not true."

"Yes, you do. And usually, I enjoy watching you make a fool of yourself, but I really think it's in everyone's best interest if you leave this one be."

"What do you mean?"

Ben purses his lips.

"Oh no, you've gotta tell me now."

Ben rolls his eyes. "I mean, look at you two! I know not laughing at your shitty jokes offends you on a personal level, but there's more preventing a friendship than you two being all anyone can talk about heading into the draft."

Alex doesn't respond; not sure what the hell Ben is talking about or why he's got this suspicious look in his eyes.

"What?" Alex absolutely doesn't snap.

"Why do you care so much if he likes you or not? By now, you'd be well into spite-hating Noah if it were anyone else."

"I've never done that."

"Uh, your billet cat?"

"That doesn't count."

"What's his name? The student council president?"

"Shawn McDermont."

"See! You're sneering! You hate him on *principle,* and he never blanked you as much as Noah has."

"Anderson's never straight up ignored me."

"You're just making excuses now. What's the deal? Why's Anderson so much different than everyone else?"

Alex grits his teeth. They're several paces behind everyone else, but he still drops his voice. "I overheard him talking to his dad yesterday."

"Okay, and?"

"And I only caught the end, but he said, 'no one's as good at talking Valencia up as you' and I think—whatever his dad's saying—it's not my fault." He blows out a loud breath, frustration buzzing under his skin. "I've worked really hard not to resent him for being compared to him since the moment it was clear I could make it to the show, and I'm fucking pissed he can't do the same for me. It's not fair."

"Alex..."

When Alex glances over, the assessing sort of expression he's met with has his hackles rising. "What?"

"You've been trying to get him to warm up to you way longer than yesterday, and I still don't get why."

"Because it's annoying. I know it's not actually about me, but I—"

"Want him to like you?"

"Yes—"

"But not just because he *doesn't* like you?"

"Obviously," Alex grumbles. "You know it's always been more than that."

"Yeah, but you're not explaining in what way. And don't say it's about the draft rivalry—"

"It is!"

"Bud, you wanted him to like you the very first time you met, and that was way before you were a solid second."

"People were definitely talking about us facing each other for the first time though." Alex shrugs. "I wanted to meet and get along with someone my name was being linked to—that's not weird."

Ben makes a soft, contemplative noise. "And you kept going back after your shitty first meeting—why?"

"It wasn't *shitty*. He was awkward. It wasn't obvious until the next time that he—"

"Didn't like you—"

"—took people pitting us against each other too seriously. And then I wanted him to loosen the fuck up and stop seeing me as the enemy."

"And how'd that work out for you?"

"I thought we made progress this week. But then—he knows I overheard him and if that's why he's been extra cold—okay, whatever. But it's still fucked up that he's letting someone else's opinion affect what he thinks of me. If he's going to hate me, he might as well hate me because of me. Not fucking hockey."

Ben narrows his eyes. "And what're you going to do to make him hate you?"

"There's no way he'll hate me once he gets to know me. I'm going to make him like me, duh."

Ben groans. "You're impossible. Like, even if you didn't have everything else working against you, Noah Anderson, of all people, would hate your sunny disposition."

Alex wrinkles his nose. "Maybe my sunny disposition is exactly what he needs. No one can be that uptight forever."

"He's done a good enough job of it until now. But you do you, babe, and I'll do my due diligence and provide all relevant chirp material to the group chat as you continue failing the same herculean task you've been on for years now."

"Fine. And when I succeed, what do I get?"

Ben mulls it over for a moment. "You won't succeed. He's going to hate you *for you* by the end of the draft."

Alex scoffs. "When I succeed, because I will succeed, what are you going to do to make up for doubting my charm?"

"I'm not doubting your charm; I'm accepting the fact that some personality types don't gel."

"Well, I'm not."

"Yeah, because you're stubborn as shit and can't accept that people might think less than positively about you."

Alex tips his head to the side. "Because I'm a delight, Benjamin."

Ben snorts. He doesn't speak again until they catch up with the rest of the group at baggage claim. He gets this shit-eating grin when he notices Anderson scowling, then whispers, "If you successfully befriend the ice king himself, you can have the tiebreaker this summer."

*

THE THING ABOUT trying to befriend someone is Alex rarely needs to. He's always made friends quick and easy. But Anderson's different. Anderson is committed to freezing Alex out because of a rivalry neither of them ever played into—which is *rude*. So, yeah, it's a bad idea to put Noah on the spot in the middle of a joint interview, but Alex is flustered and when the reporter asks, Alex answers without thinking about being filmed.

"I'm actually looking forward to the prospect of being in the same metro area as him."

"Really?" Catherine McDonald asks, bright-green eyes widening almost imperceptibly, mouth curling at the corner. "Looking forward to a little friendly rivalry, then?"

Alex's gaze darts to Noah. His stomach twists as he takes in the sight of Noah flushed red—this definitely isn't the way to win him over. Whoops.

"I do love a little competition. Husky and I—Ben Huskins—we've already got plans for loser-buys whenever we face off against each other this season. Back at the NTDP, we'd do things like that a lot. Pair off and see who got the most goals during practice, see who won the most battles, random stuff to keep each other on our toes, push ourselves with the sweet taste of making your buddy buy you lunch."

Catherine turns to Anderson with a broad smile and laughter in her eyes. "How's that sound, Noah—you up for a friendly little wager?"

Anderson glances at Alex and his mouth twitches in some approximation of a smile. "As long as it's on the diet plan, I don't see why it'd be a problem."

They make it through the rest of the interview without Alex's mouth getting the best of him, but the damage is already done. Before regrouping with the others, Anderson turns to him with steely eyes colder than Alex has ever seen. "What was it you said about a filter?"

He stalks off before Alex can think of a response and Alex knows he's well and truly fucked up this time.

"Okay, maybe you were right," Alex says while they're watching warmups.

"What'd you even do?" Ben's gaze slides to Julien and Anderson down the row. "Noah looks like he's about to crack his jaw."

Alex sucks his teeth. "I didn't mean to do anything! I was talking about how we used to do a loser-buys thing back in Plymouth because who doesn't love friendly competition, you know, and then—"

"Oh God, tell me you didn't."

"I didn't! But Catherine McDonald definitely did."

"While recording?"

Alex knocks his head against the glass, whining, "Yes."

Ben laughs. "There goes his reason to hate you outside of hockey. He's never going to speak to you again after you put him on the spot like that."

Alex grimaces. Ben's probably right, but Alex can't leave it like this. He has to apologize.

"Anderson," he says, coming up behind him and Julien. "Can I talk to you for a minute?"

He doesn't turn around, but Julien does.

"Walk with me, Valencia," Julien says, heading up the stairs.

Anderson's shoulders are tense and he's flushing scarlet, jaw clenched harder the longer Alex stands there. He follows Julien, ducking out of the way as fans file in.

Julien still hasn't spoken by the time the stairs end, and Alex loses his patience. "Why am I walking with you when I want to talk to Anderson?"

Julien hits Alex with a withering glare that makes Anderson's look like a kitten pouting. "Are you actually trying to be Noah's friend?"

"What the fu—" He spots a small child within earshot and stops himself, levels his voice. "What else would I be doing?"

Julien's expression hardens. "Most people don't try this hard with him."

"I'm not most people."

"Yes, but I don't really see what your angle is. Because, okay, maybe with the two of you on rival teams, you'll run into each other more often, but you've been at this for *years*. I don't get it."

"There's nothing to get."

"You're sure this isn't some kind of *challenge*? You're not interested in his friendship because he won't give it to you as easily as everyone else, are you?"

"I—"

Julien pinches the bridge of his nose. "Jesus, Valencia. You can't be serious! You know that's fucked, right?"

"It's not *just* that."

Julien arches a brow. "Then what is it?"

"It's—" Alex has no way of explaining to Julien why being in the same room with Anderson makes his skin tingle, why it puts him on high alert. He has no way of explaining the spark of...curiosity he felt the first time they met and how it's left him wanting to lessen the gap between them as much as he can. The closest he can say is... "I dunno, man, he just gets under my skin."

Julien's voice is sharp but not entirely unkind when he asks, "How's that different from you seeing him as a challenge?"

"Jesus, Thorn, I'm not—" Anger crackles in his veins. He takes a deep breath, calming his voice. "What do you think I'm going to do here? Wait until he thinks of me as a friend and then fuck him over to prove a point and feed my ego?"

Julien considers him for a moment, then gives him a small, amused smile. "Bud, I have no idea what the fuck you're going for here. But if you're committed to making him not hate you—"

"I don't think he actually hates me."

Julien snorts. "He sure as shit dislikes you more than his baseline distaste for interacting with people. But yeah, sure, he probably doesn't hate you, hate you."

"That's something to work with!"

"If you say so. But you two are polar opposites—"

"Are we though?" Julien looks at him judgmentally and Alex rolls his eyes. "Whatever. High-strung people need low-strung people to even them out. We're a perfect match."

Julien considers him for a moment, placid as he says, "Unless you make him more high-strung."

Alex waves dismissively. "That won't happen."

"You're very confident and I *love* a shit show, so if you're going all in, you might as well know he likes chess."

"How's that—"

"Hey." Julien's smile is small and sly. "I didn't have to throw you a bone, bud. Figure out what to do with the information yourself."

# Chapter Five

AFTER HIS WALK with Julien, Alex slinks back to Ben without a glance in Noah's direction.

"What did you say to him?" Noah mumbles.

"Told him you like chess."

"What? No, I don't."

Julien tips his head back in laughter. "I know."

"Why would you—"

"Because it's funnier this way."

"For who?"

"For me, for you, for everyone who gets to witness him trying to use chess as common ground."

"That's messed up, Thor."

"Whatever. He thinks of you as a challenge. Might as well make him work for it."

Noah narrows his eyes. "What do you mean?"

"I mean, look at him."

Noah does.

The rest of the boys surround Alex in a half circle, their eyes bright with laughter as he talks with his hands. Alex always looks good, but he never looks as good as this—glowing from being paid attention to by a captivated audience, basking in the way he transfixes them with his laugh, his shine, his magnetism. It makes Noah's stomach twist, hot and uncomfortable, every time he witnesses it.

"What, you think he's *offended* that I'm not enamored with him?"

"Yeah, dude. He didn't deny it when I called him on it."

Noah huffs. "I knew he had ulterior motives."

Julien elbows his side. "Unfortunately for you, or maybe fortunately for you, since he's really not bad, he seems pretty legit about wanting to be your friend. Even if it's a challenge, or started as one, it's pretty obvious he likes you."

Noah purses his lips.

"It is," Julien insists. "Don't give me that look, Anderson. What'd Coach K used to say when we chirped Pogo for crying at romcoms?"

"People contain multitudes."

"Exactly. Multitudes! Valencia has multitudes!"

*

THE SIX OF them are being interviewed after the first period when the reporter turns to ask Alex and Ben if they're slipping into a little rivalry over the series. Noah is on Alex's right, closest to the reporter, Ben on his left, and Noah doesn't look. He tries so hard not to look, but he still sees Alex sling his arm across Ben's shoulders, voice brimming with laughter. "Oh, Husky's a Boston boy, but we're in Dallas so we're rooting for my team tonight. Aren't we, boys?"

Noah can feel Alex's eyes on him, and he can't resist looking over. Alex is watching him expectantly, and Noah can't resist disagreeing. "I dunno. I'm with Ben on this one. Boston's been good tonight."

With one arm still slung around Ben, Alex throws the other in the air. "This is blatant original six elitism!"

Those are the last six words Alex says to Noah for the rest of the trip. Which is good. Noah thinks a week of rooming together must have been enough—Alex finally got his fill and decided Noah isn't worth the time or effort. It's a relief, really, to have Alex out of his hair and off his mind for two blissful weeks before the draft.

But...Julien said Alex might actually want to spend time with Noah and Noah knows it's ridiculous to care, but he's still a little confused. If Noah is more than a problem Alex can't solve, why hasn't he made another attempt to get Noah's attention?

Alex has always confused Noah though, and it probably shouldn't surprise him when Alex DMs him the Friday after the Cup game like they didn't leave each other on an actual sour note.

### *Alex Valencia*

*June 10 4:13PM*

If I beat you at chess you have to follow
me back

*Why would I do that?*

Because you can't turn down a challenge

*And you can?*

Nope! It's not in my nature

*We'll never be friends*

Are you challenging me here?

*And if I am?*

Then game on baby
I'm gonna be the best damn friend you've
ever had

*Not a chance*

Another week passes and Noah's house is so tense with the draft approaching it's almost a relief to get a DM from Alex telling him to download Chess with Friends.

*

**Alex Valencia**

*June 17 2:30PM*

For someone who loves chess you really
suck at it

*That's the first game of chess I've*
*ever played*

JULIEN LIED TO ME???

*Right to your face*

Wow. That's too bad. Deal's a deal

though and I won

*What's the point? You've got*
*maybe four photos on your grid*

All the hot selfies me and Liv take for our
stories duh

Noah clicks through to watch Alex's story and the first photo is of Alex and a beautiful Black girl lying back on a pink floral bedspread, Alex's head pillowed on his arm, hers on his chest. She has full lips, black roots, and gray hair parted in two thick braids. Next is a video of Liv pressing a kiss to Alex's cheek, gleefully laughing as she stains his cheek with the deep burgundy of her lipstick. She's so beautiful Noah should probably be a little jealous Alex landed a girl so far out of his league when Noah can't even—when Noah knows nothing at all about dating. But all he can focus on is how incandescent Alex is, elated in a way Noah has never seen.

"Uh," Millie says, after a moment of Noah's thumb hovering over the follow button on Alex's page. "Are you having an aneurysm?"

Noah scowls. "Shut up."

"You look like you're dying," she says, her derision elevated by the need to look down at him lying on the bed.

Noah thrusts his phone at her. "Is this girl hot?"

Millie takes his phone, eyebrows knitting together. "Yeah, she's a mega babe. But—"

"So, why am I not attracted to her?"

Millie's eyebrows shoot up. "Noah, you're—"

"Maybe I'm not!"

Millie sets both their phones down, drags him up, and positions them to where they're sitting face to face, knees touching. "Are you attracted to her?"

"She's gorgeous."

"That's not the same and you know it."

"I want it to be the same."

"You'll be miserable if you keep trying to force it."

"I'm miserable now!" Noah is hot all over, face flushed, heart racing. "Maybe I just need to try—I haven't even—how do I know if I've never even kissed a girl?"

"You can't *force* it."

"It's not forcing it if I don't know!"

"But you do know. You *do*."

Noah stands up and paces the room. "But I don't want to, Millie!"

Noah's door opening cuts Millie's response off and there his dad is, wearing the same look he gets when the league's Pride nights come up. Noah's entire world tilts. He might throw up. Did he overhear them?

"Hi, Amelia." His dad's eyes soften; he's always liked Millie. "I didn't know you were here."

"Gotta get time in with my boy before he leaves me for the states," Millie says with a put-upon sigh. "Gonna get all rich and famous and forget about little ol' me."

"Never," Noah says, his voice rough in his throat.

She smiles, gentle and kind, but Noah's ears are still roaring, neck burning as he turns back to his dad. "Did you need something, Dad?"

His dad's gaze darts to Millie, then to Noah. He purses his lips, hand twitching on the doorknob. Noah wonders if he's thinking better of saying anything in front of Millie. He usually bites his tongue in front of guests unless Noah's done something painfully disappointing. But if he overheard, it would be the most disappointing thing of all.

"Remember when we were talking about Taylor Ford a while back?"

Noah swallows. He used to have a little hope; used to think maybe Paul Anderson—Stanley Cup winning defenseman and beloved Winnipeg broadcaster—was just too submerged in the culture. He thought his dad might not actually care if hockey players loved other men; hoped years in locker rooms only desensitized him to slurs flung around in razor-edged chirps.

Noah remembers his dad's face perfectly though. Remembers how FaceTime glitched, pausing on his dad's mouth twisted in unchecked fury as he ranted about how *soft* the league was getting for fining *and* suspending Hank Duberman for calling Ford a homophobic slur. He remembers lying in bed crying at his billet family's home as the last remnants of hope his dad would ever accept him dissipated.

"Yeah, I remember."

Noah's voice is so strained his dad should notice. He doesn't.

He never does.

"I was right about the league going so hard on Duberman because the league's poster boy is a—"

Noah cuts in before his dad can spew his hate. "You still think he's gay?"

His dad's smile is sharp and mean. "Oh, he is. The NHL's got a whole spread of exclusive photos on their site. Shit's about to hit the fan, bud."

Millie is so much more composed than Noah while asking, "What do you mean?"

God, he might actually pass out with how fast the blood rushes to his cheeks, his neck, his chest.

"Lotta naked guys in a locker room and if that's what you're into—it's only natural to look. Everyone knows there's a guy in the room who might enjoy what he sees, who might sneak a peek, but we all prefer not knowing." He turns to Noah. "Right?"

Noah grunts. It's as good as a yes for his dad.

"Good of him to wait until the summer he retired, but he's been the face of the league for years. Who knows what this'll spark? There's been whispers about Ford for a while now, but you can't be staring at your teammates in the locker room if you want to stay in the closet. If guys start coming out—" He shrugs. "I'm not sure how many locker room dynamics will survive."

"I—" Noah's voice sticks; he clears his throat. "I don't know if the league's ready for a guy to be out while playing."

"Dunno if the league will ever be, honestly. Say it's not a problem for every locker room, it's going to be in some, and if all the rainbow shit during warmups pisses people off, imagine what it'll do for business when there's actually one of them on the ice."

His dad turns and leaves, unaffected by their conversation and the way he's left Noah coming out of his skin.

"Noah," Millie says. "Do you want to see the article? I've got it pulled up."

"No." He turns to his closet, skin buzzing. "I need to go for a run. I'm sorry."

"It's fine. I'll be here when you get back."

He glances her way. She's settled back against his headboard, phone in her hand and a worry line between her brows.

"You don't have to wait around."

"We've been lying around all day. And I'll be doing the same after driving home. Might as well wait for you while I do it, don't you think?"

"I won't want to talk about it when I get back."

"Don't expect you to."

"I won't read the article either."

"Again, not expecting you to."

Millie's still pink with anger, and white-hot fury courses through Noah. Why *isn't* he attracted to her?

Millie is Noah's person.

His parents love her. She makes him laugh, never cares when he retreats in on himself, and doesn't mind his bitchiness because she's a little bitchy too. Millie's perfect, beautiful, and kind. She's the one person he can let his guard down with entirely and half an hour ago, Noah would've said not being in love with Millie is the worst thing he'll ever deal with, but there's an ember of hope reigniting in the pit of his stomach and letting it grow would be monumentally worse.

# Chapter Six

### *Do or Die*

Fri, Jun 17, 2:50PM

*Holy shit!!!!!! Holy SHIT!!!!!*
*HOLY FUCKING SHIT!!!!*
*DID Y'ALL SEE ABOUT*
*FORD????*
*HOLY SHIT*

**Beaver**
YES and I have some questions

**Ben**
Share with the class Beav

**Mitch**
Is it how Ford landed a beauty like O'Dell

**Beaver**
YES IT IS

UN FUCKING BELIEVABLE

        *Maybe Ford does it for men*

**Yatesy**
He looks like he wants to suck your soul

out

**Kaden**
Maybe O'Dell's into that

I'm into the whole death glare thing

Remember Katie? She looked like she'd

eat me alive and it was fucking hot

**Yatesy**
But Katie IS hot

        *You saying Ford's not hot yatesy*

**Yatesy**
I have eyes

**Parse**
And you're an expert now?

        *Asked Sierra: Ford's "a total*
        *hottie what're y'all on?"*

**Ben**
I guess that solves it

**Beaver**
Gonna take a girl's word for it Yatesy?

**Yatesy**
No

**Beaver**
Yeah no offense but your sister has

terrible taste 😬 Damien's a five at best

*Won't argue with you there*

*This is pretty wild. Keeping that*

*kind of secret for YEARS sounds*

*exhausting*

**Brett**
Can't believe they did it before O'Dell

retired too, couldn't be me

**Mitch**
I'd rather take a skate to the face than

face that heat

**Brett**
That's a little dramatic

**Beaver**
Is it? At least the MLB has other retired

gay players. We've got none

**Kaden**
I mean we HAVE them. We just don't

know about them

**Mitch**
Statistically one of us is probably into

men

*Prob had a few other teammates*

*who are too*

**Yatesy**
Look boys this is a safe space, secrets

shared are secrets kept, but I will judge

you for thirsting over guys who look like

Ford

**Mitch**
You trying to tell us something here

Yatesy?

**Yatesy**
Nah I just know a beauty when I see a

beauty

THOUGH if we're talking secrets, last

semester I traded handies with one of the

boys to see if I was into it

*Shit college really changes you*

*huh*

**Beaver**
Were you?

Into it?

**Johnny**
One of the boys...as in a TEAMMATE?

**Brett**
BRO you can't leave us hanging like this

Were you into it or not?

**Yatesy**
It wasn't terrible but I'm not sure I'd do it

again

Could still meet a total smoke show one

day that has me gagging for it though

**Parse**
Maybe your boy was just bad at the job

**Johnny**
Ok but WAS IT A TEAMMATE??

**Yatesy**
Does it matter?

**Johnny**
Not in the grand scheme of touching

dicks but if he's into it and you're not it

could go sideways in the room real fast

**Ben**
Yeahhhh fucking with a teammate

doesn't seem like a stellar move

**Yatesy**
I'll let you know if it becomes a problem

*Anyone else got a big revelation*

*to share?*

**Ben**
What about you Alex? How's operation

woo Anderson going?

**Beaver**
Wait wooing?

*He followed me on Instagram*

**Parse**
An insta follow doesn't even mean you're

acquaintances bud

*Fuck off we're making progress*

**Johnny**
What kinda wooing are we talking about

here?

**Yatesy**
Did you finally realize you've got a thing

for Noah?

*EXCUSE ME*

**Kaden**
Oooh I've never considered that before

but you are kinda intense about him

**Mitch**
That wasn't a no

*I don't want him to HATE ME*

*that doesn't mean I want to date*

*him*

**Brett**
Not wanting to date him doesn't mean

you're not into him either

> *What the fuck!!!! You think I'm*
> *hot for ANDERSON????*

**Yatesy**
Why're you surprised? He's straight up
PRETTY

**Beaver**
Yatesy with a point

He's a Bambi eyed dreamboat

**Kaden**
Real angelic motherfucker tbh

**Parse**
He def got his mom's supermodel looks

but hockey isn't the only thing he and

ford have in common. Does resting

murder face do it for you?

> *I prefer people to be happy to see*
> *me*

**Mitch**
And Anderson's never happy to see you

> *Rude*

**Ben**
Didn't you hear? They've got standing

dinner plans for every matchup from

now on

They're basically besties

**Mitch**
PLEASE livestream the first time he has

to buy you dinner

**Nate**
Like he even had a choice with Catherine

McDonald asking

I'd do almost anything she asked

*Nate dropping in to be horny*

*Shocking*

**Nate**
Y'all know who I am and what I'm about

But for real IS your thing for Noah a gay

thing? Because yatesy's right, he's pretty

as fuck

*Pretty sure I'd know if it was a*

*gay thing*

**Nate**
Would you? Maybe yatesy can give you a

handie and help clear it up for you

**Yatesy**
Sorry bro but I'm not touching your dick

Gotta find another buddy for that

*Wow I'm a little offended you*

*wouldn't let me experiment with*

*you tbh*

**Mitch**
You'd do it for a guy you've known less

than a year but not YOUR BOY??? That's

kinda fucked up yatesy

**Kaden**
He's right yatesy

We're supposed to be bros for life

**Yatesy**
Offer your own hands up then

**Johnny**
Maybe Alex isn't the only one who's got a

crush

**Nate**
Ok if I must

Don't lump me in with him

I'm not the one saying he's pretty

**Yatesy**
Should've seen that one coming

Nate oh my god

**Johnny**
NATE

**Nate**
Oh come on what's a handjob between

bros anyway??

But seriously. If you're saying he isn't

hot, you're lying

*He's obviously good looking*

*Still don't want to date him*

*Or fuck him*

*Or anything else*

**Kaden**
Good thing you've got a season worth of

practice dates to really test that theory

then

**Beaver**
You really think Noah will last the entire

season?

**Parse**
Guess it depends on if he's buying or not

*Y'all are so fucking annoying*

*He doesn't even dislike me*

*We play chess sometimes*

**Mitch**
Wow an insta follow AND online chess?

What's next, friendship bracelets?

**Brett**
I give it until the first time he has to buy

you dinner for him to blow you off

**Yatesy**
You get a guy who hates you on principle

of being his competition to buy you

dinner after a loss and I MIGHT let you

experiment with me if the need ever

arises

**Mitch**
Talk about motivation

> *Thanks for the vote of confidence*
> *assholes*
> *Fucking WATCH ME be his*
> *friend and get him to dinner*
> *after every game*

# Chapter Seven

NOAH GETS AS far as finding out Taylor Ford and the Blue Jays' first baseman Jason O'Dell have been *married* since the All-Star Break before he throws his phone across the room. He refuses to look at the wedding photos they gave NHL.com first access to. He won't watch the press conference held by the MLB, and, in an impressive feat of self-preservation, he manages to not read any of the comments on the news. Of course, it doesn't stop various teammates from blowing up his phone. Julien, as Noah expected, has the best reaction. He's happy for Ford and hopeful for what this might lead to in the league. Connor is of the mind sexuality doesn't matter but "did they really have to call a press conference about it?", which is annoying but not *too* bad. Taylor is crass but unbothered, and Seth, who Noah resolutely ignores, has the same opinion as Noah's dad.

By the time he's scrolled through all his messages, Noah is bursting with emotions he refuses to process. Except for confusion. He can't stop thinking about *why* they picked the middle of June—barely two weeks into Ford's retirement and not even the halfway point of the Jays' season. There's something at the edge of his brain, nagging and insistent, saying the timing is no coincidence. There's something important about June, but Noah can't put his finger on it until the Monday before the draft when Alex slides into his DMs to instigate another game of chess.

*

**Alex Valencia**

June 20 7:15PM

Winner gets to choose the loser's outfit
for pride

*Um WHAT??*

BRO you really haven't checked your
email today??

*No?*

My bad for assuming you'd be on top of
your shit
Anyway Toronto's pride is draft weekend
and Taylor fucking Ford wants us all to
walk with him in the parade

*You can't be serious*

Check your email if you don't believe me

> It's from him with the NHL's media
>
> coordinator CCd on it

Then it hits him, why he thought the timing was important—June is Pride month. They must have chosen June on purpose. But even if he realized the importance initially, he wouldn't have expected Taylor Ford—four-time Stanley Cup winner and one of the League's most awarded players—to invite him to attend a Pride event with him. In his hometown. To make a point about what hockey *could* be.

How is Noah even supposed to answer this? He can't deny a guy he's looked up to for so long, but how can he possibly *go?* How will he stand next to someone who's braver than Noah imagines he'll ever be and pretend he's not closeted and scared? There's no way Noah can make it through Pride without dying.

Besides, his dad would never let him go. But...it's Taylor Ford. People love him. Canada loves him. *The League* loves him. God, even a couple of Philadelphia's fans love him. Fuck...Noah loves him. How can he blow off a personal invite from his favorite hockey player? How can he pass up the opportunity to be surrounded by so many people who'd be willing to embrace him for exactly who he is if he ever came out?

His dad wouldn't lock him in the hotel in Toronto to prevent him from going to an event being filmed for an NHL feature. He couldn't be *that* against hockey players liking men, could he?

Probably not.

But Noah doesn't mention it.

Not the night his mother arches her immaculate blonde brow at him over dinner because Noah can't stop picking at his cuticles, nor on Tuesday afternoon when his dad nags him about what his itinerary is for the weekend. Not even on Wednesday when Alex DMs him as he's boarding the flight to Toronto telling him to stop by room 532 when he gets in because he has things to show him for the parade and he tenses up so badly Millie has to push him into his seat.

Halfway through the flight, Millie knocks her shoulder against his. "What'd Alex say this time?"

Noah glances across the aisle, and regardless of Millie being too quiet for him to overhear, seeing his dad wearing headphones soothes his growing nausea.

"Uh...Ford?"

Millie furrows her brow. "He's talking to you about Ford?"

"No. I mean, yes, technically. But..."

He scrubs a hand over his face. He hasn't talked about Taylor Ford out loud since the day the news broke. Not even to Millie. Especially Millie. Can't even think his name without getting a painful flare of *hope* so easily extinguished by the onslaught of reality. There's a reason Ford didn't come out until he retired; Noah's familiar with the risks. He knows he can't explore his sexuality as a *rookie* without risking everything he's worked for. Unfortunately, knowing doesn't make it any easier.

He swipes his phone open; clicks through to Alex's message; scrolls up to the one about Ford; avoids Millie's eyes as he thrusts the phone in her hand.

The silence is thick as she reads. "Ah," she breathes out. Another beat passes, her voice carefully neutral as she asks, "What're you going to do?"

"I want to go," Noah admits, because fuck it, he *does*.

Out of the corner of his eye he sees her place her hand palm up on the armrest between them, an offer for tacit support he doesn't need to refuse this time. "Then you should."

He twines their fingers together. Her hand is smaller, warmer, softer than his own and the touch makes him feel safe. His vision blurs from staring at the backseat pocket too hard. He blinks and slides his attention back to Millie, squeezes her hand. "I want to but—"

"It's for the NHL is reason enough." Her voice is firm. "No one will question it. Not with Ford inviting you. He asks you to jump, everyone asks how high."

"Maybe..." He closes his eyes, inhales through his nose, out through his mouth. "I shouldn't have agreed to Alex's ridiculous wager. I can't—my dad won't—"

Millie tightens her grip on Noah's hand; her expression is stern when he glances over. He's never understood how she can sound so fierce and resolute while whispering, but she always has.

"Noah, losing a bet and looking ridiculous is a time-honored tradition. No one, especially someone like your father, is going to think anything you wear to P—" She stops herself, purses her lips, starts over. "Okay, not true. People will probably have shit to say about the venue and what you're wearing because sports bros are actually the weakest link in humanity, but no one's going to assume you're admitting to something by going to an event the NHL's most loved player invited you and a bunch of other prospects to."

Millie's right. He's seen multiple guys from the NHL at different Prides; has seen them dressed in rainbow tutus and holding rainbow flags. He knows no one, or at least no one important enough to get back to Noah, has ever started shit about *those guys* being queer. But what if this is the time they do? What if someone looks at him and *knows* he's gay? What if Taylor Ford recognizes it in Noah's eyes?

He tries not to worry about it the rest of the flight, pushes the possibility of being discovered into the deepest box in the furthest corner of his mind and starts listing the rest of the plans for the week.

Batting practice with the Blue Jays. Media day. Suiting up. Cameras following him. Busing over. The draft. Getting picked. Finally knowing if he's lived up to his dad's expectations. Photographs. More media.

But the plans round out with Pride and Noah's box bursts open, thrusting the worry right back at him. By the time they're settled into their hotel room, Noah is an absolute mess. This is going to be a long few days.

# Chapter Eight

**_Noah Anderson_**

June 22 5:39PM

Dude are you here yet

_Are you always this impatient?_

It's been hours

_I was on a PLANE_

Whatever
Come to my room before batting
practice. I got a sick little chessboard just
to see your face when I crush you

_I'm not coming to your room to_

_play chess_

Play you for it

*No*

You gotta get your shit

*No*

We played for it
Come get your shit asshole

*

Anderson doesn't come get his shit. Alex didn't expect him to, but on the way to Rogers Centre for batting practice, he wonders if there's more to it than Anderson being difficult. He's paler than usual and won't sit still. His face is closed off, jaw clenched. If these are Anderson's nerves about batting practice with some Blue Jays, Alex doesn't know if he's going to survive the draft when seeing him like this leaves Alex restless in his own seat.

Whatever's set Noah on edge doesn't seem to pass after he takes a couple of swings. He doesn't relax when he posts up by the dugout either, eyes steely and jaw tight as he watches everyone else. When Alex joins him, their elbows brush and Anderson tenses, jaw clenching even tighter, and Alex remembers their rooftop meeting in Edmonton. Alex shifts to the side, mindful they're no longer touching, and when Anderson's jaw loosens, Alex thinks he guessed right. He just wishes he knew *why* Anderson's so against contact off the ice.

"You're surlier than usual, Anderson."

Noah makes a noncommittal noise but doesn't respond otherwise. He doesn't talk to Alex the rest of the night, either. Only mumbles thanks to the batting coach working with them, barely managing a hello when Jason O'Dell and Kirk Stanford come strolling out as they're leaving. With the way he steels himself when he shakes hands with O'Dell, Alex assumes he might be the reason Anderson's been so damn nervous all day. Which is understandable—Alex doesn't even care about the Jays and he's a little intimidated.

But Anderson's nerves don't settle on the way back to the hotel and unease rushes through Alex like he's not anxious enough for the weekend. He's off kilter the rest of the night and when he wakes up in a cold sweat at two in the morning, unable to fall back asleep, he wants to scream. He tosses and turns for an hour before the possibility of being well rested for media day slips through his fingers and he grabs his phone.

### *Noah Anderson*

June 23 3:07AM

*Are you awake??*

No

*Funny*
*Why're you up*

Could ask you the same thing

*I caught your nerves and now I*
*can't sleep*
*Your turn*

What're you nervous about?

*That I'm not nervous enough????*

That makes no sense

*Thanks, I didn't realize*
*You never answered tho*
*Why're you up??*

Same as you
Tomorrow's going to be a lot

*Nothing we haven't done before*

Never for the draft

*True enough*
*Chess? Might calm us down*

Or amp you up more when you lose

*Uh no you're the sore loser here*
*Anyway loser tells winner their*
*dream draft team*

Why would I agree to that when I already
know you'd pick Dallas?
Texas forever or whatever

*Aww you remembered* 😊 😊
*Fine loser tells winner which*
*they'd want: Jersey or New York*
*and you can't bullshit me with "I*

*want whoever wants me"*

Good thing I'm winning this one then

Anderson does, in fact, win this time, and in the dark of his hotel with nothing but the faint glow of his phone, Alex admits something he's never told anyone else—not Sierra, not Liv, not the boys, and definitely not his parents.

*I want New York*

Really? Jersey too boring for you?

*Nah Brett's in New York and I*
*won't need to find a roomie*
*And not to sound like a dick but I*
*don't vibe with the amount of*
*pressure going first overall*
*comes with and I'm glad it's*
*going to be you*

You're serious

*Cross my heart*
*These chess games are sacred*

*

IN THE MORNING, Alex wakes up to an unread DM from Noah, time-stamped well past the point Alex gave up on their conversation continuing and fell asleep, and when he reads, *I want first but I've definitely thought the same thing before* it feels like something precious.

But whatever compelled Anderson to share unprompted information doesn't extend past the wee hours of morning. Nothing about Anderson's outward demeanor toward Alex changes; they're not magically friends once breakfast rolls around. They don't talk; Anderson barely even glances his way most of the time.

But during lunch, Alex pulls out the tiny magnetic chess set he bought, hoping to see how grumpy Anderson gets about losing at something other than hockey, and asks Ben to play with him. Anderson holds his gaze for a moment, a small twitch at the corner of his mouth, eyes wider than usual, and Alex thinks he's a little surprised he wasn't just fucking with him.

The reaction sends a jolt of warmth through Alex, and he can't tamp down on the satisfaction—he's definitely making progress on this whole friendship thing.

DR
TO

# Chapter Nine

EVERYTHING LEADING UP to the draft passes in a blur. Noah wakes up too early, far too jittery to fall back asleep. He slinks down to the hotel gym and runs on the treadmill until his legs ache and he no longer feels like he'll crawl out of his skin if someone so much as shakes his hand.

He takes a shower so hot he's pink for half an hour at least; is so successful at being welcoming and friendly while the cameras are around, his dad doesn't even nitpick. He gets dressed; lets his mom smooth out his collar, adjust his tie, wrap him up in a hug so tight he forgets, momentarily, where they are. He practices his breathing on the bus ride to the arena and staves off a full-blown panic attack.

Noah signs autographs on the way in, cheeks burning when a young teen says his sister thinks he's hot. He rejoins his family, paces, tries to stay focused as Julien's nerves manifest in rapid fire chatter about one mundane topic after another. He gives more interviews, takes his seat, holds Millie's hand as time ticks slowly by, thankful when she squeezes back, and the bite of her nails keeps him from floating away as they wait.

New Jersey calls his name first and everything goes silent for one surreal moment. Millie pushes him out of his seat and the sound rushes back in. His head clears. *I did it.*

Noah hugs Millie first and when she whispers, "I knew you'd do it," he believes every single word. He's so ecstatic this part is over and done with, the usual resentment doesn't cross his mind when his dad parrots the same words.

The excitement of achieving a lifetime dream wraps around him like a shield, reinforcing and smoothing out all the chipped-away barriers between his confidence and the massive artillery of self-doubt born from years of not being good enough for his father.

"Anderson!" Alex shouts as he joins Noah in the lounge set up for them. Once they call the third, pictures will begin in full, but for now, they're given a quiet reprieve from the nonstop hubbub of the entire week.

"Alex." Noah tries, but he can't contain the smile pulling at his lips. *He did it. It's over.* "I'm right here. You don't have to yell."

"I think going one and two in the *NHL Entry Draft* deserves a little shouting. Don't you, babe?"

Noah purses his lips, heart stuttering. "Think you're loud enough for the two of us, bud."

Alex flops down on the couch next to him. "Dude, we're not all reserved like you. This is me keeping my cool for the cameras. There's a 90 percent chance I'll lose it and tackle Husky when he gets back here though."

Carolina takes Ben Huskins third, higher than projected, and Alex really does tackle him.

Ben goes down hard, lands with an *oof* and a choked-out laugh. Alex cradles Ben's head in his hand, preventing him from cracking his skull, and Ben wraps him in a hug before pushing him off with another loud laugh.

They lie next to each other on the floor, Alex slapping at Ben's arm while Ben stares at the ceiling with awe in his eyes, face splitting into a wide, all-encompassing grin as Alex crows, "Second and third, Husky! Second! And! Third!"

There's a camera on them, but neither seems embarrassed to be caught giggling hysterically while lying on the floor in their brand-new jerseys.

It's such a ridiculous sight; Noah can't help but laugh. "Does the NTDP train you guys in barns? What is this?"

Their gazes snap to Noah. Ben's eyes shine with mirth and his mouth curves in a sharp, teasing grin. "Didn't realize you even knew how to chirp, Anderson."

"I save it for special occasions," Noah deadpans.

"Aw, did you hear that?" Ben stands and pulls Alex with him. "He thinks we're special."

Alex's grin is remarkable. "Jot the date down, baby. This is a day to remember."

*

HE KNOCKS ON Alex's door midafternoon on Sunday and is surprised when it opens after one knock.

"Holy shit, Anderson," Alex says. "Way to be punctual. We're supposed to be ready in—" He looks at his watch, an annoyed pinch between his brows. "Twenty minutes!"

"Don't worry, Noah," Julien calls—another surprise—from somewhere inside the room. "He's freaking out about spending the day with Ford. Certified fanboy shit going on in here."

"Fuck off." Alex steps aside to let Noah in.

"Didn't know we were having a party," Noah says.

"We'd be outside enjoying the sun if you were on time," Ben says from where he's lounging against the headboard of the bed closest to the window.

He's wearing bright-green shorts, a rainbow tie-dyed tank top, and bright, glittery rainbow stickers on each cheek. Leon and Emil are wearing bright-orange and yellow shorts, respectively, and similarly tie-dyed shirts. Julien is leaning against the wall by the window in an offensively bright pair of blue shorts and a white Hockey Canada shirt he must have tie-dyed himself.

Noah glances at what Alex is wearing—same as Ben except bright-purple shorts—and understands. "Let me guess, I'm red."

Alex's face lights up. "To match your blush."

Julien snorts, unbothered, as Noah turns his glare on him. "Man's got a point."

Alex swoops up a pile of clothes and tosses it to Noah, then points him to the bathroom. "Hurry up."

"Patience is a virtue," Noah grumbles while going. He's unsurprised his shirt is the same as Ben and Alex's tank tops, and uncomfortably warm about the clothes Alex bought him fitting so well.

When he gets out, Alex is wearing a headband with glittery antenna hearts that bob every time he moves. His grin is sharp and smug when he shoves a cap into Noah's hand.

It's white with "love" embroidered in shimmery black and has a glittery rainbow brim and when Noah pulls it on, Alex huffs.

"No deal," Alex says. "Gotta wear it backward." Noah doesn't move, and Alex crosses his arms. "Deal's a deal. I won fair and square."

Noah rolls his eyes and twists the cap around. "Better?"

"Yes," Alex says, turning to Julien. "Thanks for the assist, bro."

Julien arches a brow and Alex laughs. "You lied about him being into chess—turns out Anderson *sucks* and now here we all are."

Julien looks at Noah curiously and shrugs at Alex. "I think we look pretty good, to be honest. Coordinating was actually a nice touch, Valencia."

"Wait." Noah looks around as everyone moves toward the door. "You guys planned this and didn't tell me about it?"

Alex turns Noah around and shoves him at the door. "Coulda been in the group chat helping us brainstorm, but you like to play hard to get."

Someone behind him snorts and when he looks over his shoulder Julien's covering his mouth with his hand, coughing. He only laughs harder when he catches Noah glaring.

"Sorry, sorry." He doesn't sound sorry at all. "But look at your arms! You'll burn so bad."

"Sun's out, snowy guns out," Emil says with a straight face, making Noah fidget as he sweeps his eyes over Noah's arms and across his shoulders as Noah joins him in the hallway.

Leon produces an aerosol bottle out of nowhere and tosses it to Noah. "Use liberally."

Noah wants to protest, but he knows he needs it, knows he'll probably still be pink by the time they're done with the parade.

They meet up with Ford and Jason O'Dell and Noah enjoys himself while his dad's on a flight back home, none the wiser about the feature the NHL is doing or Noah's participation in it. He'll have to deal with the fallout later, but it'll be over the phone, and he and Millie have a week together in Toronto then it's off to New Jersey for Development Camp and Noah won't have to see his father; he'll be able to breathe.

Ford's gaze sweeps over the six of them and Noah's heart flutters at Ford's easy grin and sincerity as he says, "Digging the getup, boys. Really glad you guys wanted to join me."

Noah tries not to stare as Ford and O'Dell interact. He tries not to watch Ford squeeze O'Dell's shoulders on camera or track O'Dell, leaning into him with this gentle, affectionate smile; and when the interviewer turns to Ben and Alex while the camera is still on them, Noah tries so hard to ignore the way O'Dell tips his head up for a soft kiss from Ford.

Noah tries his best, but he can't get his mind around a hockey player being *married to another man*. He can't even see them in his periphery without the dying ember of hope reigniting; can't watch as Ford and O'Dell meet up with members of their own teams, can't take in the way they clap their backs as they embrace, comfortable with each of them, and pretend this knowledge changes nothing.

He can't watch as Alex and Ben ramble on about how they know there's so much work to be done, but how they want to be positive forces in the room, guys their teammates can trust enough to share this info with even if they don't share it with the world. He can't watch his *draft class peers* speak so positively about people like Noah and not think— *one day*.

"This is the cutest shit I've ever seen," Millie says when she and Jenny catch up with them after the parade.

Her cheeks are flushed pink, eyes gleaming while taking in their group.

"Jesus, Millie." Noah laughs as she flings herself at him. "Are you day-drunk?"

"We're celebrating," Jenny says, waving a pink flask in the air.

"Yeah?" Julien asks from Noah's right.

"Yeah." Jenny's smile is sharp, eyes piercing as she gives Julien a once-over. "We're one step closer to dragging sports into the twenty-first century."

Noah bites down on his smile, but Julien laughs, throws his head back unbidden. "Fair enough."

"Also love," Millie says. "Gotta celebrate the love."

"Of course." Noah slings his arm around Millie's shoulders and pulls her against his side. "Can't forget the love."

"Anderson," Alex says as he slaps at Noah's shoulder.

Noah begrudgingly turns his attention to the left. "Yes, Alex?"

"Wanna introduce us to the one person who can get an actual smile out of you or not?"

"What would you know about my smile?"

Ben tilts his head, considering. "Pretty sure it's in the eyes. Brings the murder vibe down about two whole notches. Really brings out the warmth in the ice king."

"Ice king!" Julien crows. "Oh, I'm definitely stealing that."

"Thor!"

Millie shoves out from under him before he can form a proper thought. She reaches her hand out and shakes Alex's then Ben's—Noah has no idea where Emil and Leon ran off to. "I'm Amelia, but you can call me Millie. And actually..." Her gaze darts to Noah, the mischievous glint in her eyes the only warning he gets before she's brushing her fingers across his cheekbone. "It's in the cheeks."

Julien nods. "You've got a point there, Mils. The pinker he is, the happier he is."

"Dunno," Jenny says, sweeping her gaze across Noah's face. "He's turning red now and still looks like he might murder you guys."

"Duh," Millie says with an eye roll. "First there's gotta be a smile, and *then* it's in the cheeks. But only *if* he's smiling. Or, you know, doing that thing where he's scowling, but his mouth is twitching at the sides because he *wants* to smile. That's when you look to the cheeks."

"Millie!" Noah hisses, turning even redder.

She swats at his stomach. "It doesn't take a genius to figure it out."

"Anderson," Alex says, knocking his hip against Noah's as they make their way down the street.

Instead of answering, Noah watches the loose line of Ben's shoulder as Millie loops her arm through his and starts pulling him along.

Alex elbows Noah. Noah glares. "Yes, Alex?"

"I'm onto you."

There's a wicked grin on Alex's face and Noah's heart stutters against his ribs. "Oh yeah? What're you onto?"

"You *like* me."

Noah's pulse doubles, every one of his fears flooding through him at once.

"I really don't," Noah says, eyes flitting around, unable to look at Alex or the way his gaze sweeps across his cheeks and fuck, he's going to have to kill Millie.

"Yeah, you do." Alex sounds so smug. "And you can't stand it."

"If I liked you—which I don't—why would I hate it?"

"I overheard enough of that phone call."

"And that's enough to know anything about me?" Noah grits out.

"Nah, not really."

That gets Noah's attention. Which might be exactly what Alex wanted, judging by the smug smile Noah gets when he glances over.

"But something keeps you from telling me to fuck off and sooner or later, you gotta accept it. Pretending isn't good for your health, babe."

The words are a bucket of ice water right through his veins. Alex doesn't know; he can't *know*. But Noah's never been nice to Alex either, nothing more than curtly polite—if that—and he could see right through Noah's veneer. There's only so many times Noah can hurriedly avert his gaze before Alex realizes Noah thinks his face is nice. Unacceptable. Absolutely not going to happen. He'll have to ignore Alex entirely now. It's the only way to nip this in the bud.

# Chapter Ten

LAST YEAR, AFTER the rest of the boys got drafted, they met back up in Michigan for one last hurrah before they went off to join new teams, and the two years they spent living out of each other's pocket at the dev program became just another part of their journey to the show. This year, they go down to Alex's family's beach house for a week in the middle of July to catch up and recharge before training ramps up for their upcoming seasons.

Alex loves these guys. He's never more at ease than in the moments they're all together, but as the sun sets on Saturday, the inevitability of leaving the beach and his boys sets in and Alex grows melancholy.

"I'm going to miss you assholes," he says as they sit in and around the pool one last time.

"Oh, no." There's a laugh in Johnny's voice. "Baby's in his feelings again."

Alex flips him off. "I take it back. I'll miss everyone *but* Johnathan."

Johnny snorts. "You'll miss me most."

Brett flicks water at him from the edge of the pool. "And me, none at all."

"Don't remind me," Alex says, despite the warmth bubbling in his heart over already having a friend in the room.

Brett flicks the paper umbrella from his drink at Alex, grinning. "Oh, fuck off! I'm going to be the best roommate you've ever had, Valencia."

"Dunno, Stevenson." Alex's smile grows at Brett's eye roll. "Husky's always been a good one."

"And don't forget," Ben adds with this sly little smile, "Anderson was his roommate at the Combine. Not sure you can live up to those standards."

Water sloshes loudly as Mitch stops floating, hands on his hips in the middle of the pool as he stares at Alex incredulously. "You roomed with Anderson and didn't tell the group chat? Bro. *Bro.*"

"Do we mean nothing to you?" Kaden asks.

"Yeah, I only invite the most meaningless guys in my life out here," Alex says.

Kaden's sprawled out on the chair next to Alex, but his kick doesn't come close to connecting with Alex's leg. He huffs. "Still."

Beaver tips his head to the side. There's a curious furrow to his brow. "You spent a week rooming with him and another doing draft media together and you still don't have his number? Bud..."

"Wow," Alex says. "Y'all really have no faith in me."

"It's not a knock against you, dude," Kaden says. "Anderson's just not like us."

Parse snorts and he and Beaver say in union, "No one's like us."

They clink their beers together with huge grins and Brett tips his cup toward theirs and says, "True. But Kade's got a point. Even with his friends, he's still reserved." He grimaces when he looks at Alex. "Has he given you anything to work with since the draft?"

Ben narrows his eyes before Alex can answer. "Have you heard from him at all since the draft?"

Alex sighs. "No, but that's not—"

"Dude," Mitch cuts him off. "Are you being ghosted?"

"I'm not being *ghosted*!"

"Are you sure?" Mitch asks. "Unless you haven't contacted him, it sounds like you are."

He wants to believe his own words because it's *not* unusual for Alex to go weeks between DM-ing Noah, but every time he has, Noah has messaged him back. Except Alex reached out during Development Camp to congratulate him on signing and Noah ignored him. Alex thought maybe Noah wouldn't give Alex his time if there wasn't the buffer of a game between them, but Noah ignored his next invitation for chess too.

Alex shrugs, the heat of summer suddenly suffocating. "Maybe I am, I don't know. It's only been a week since I messaged him last. Might just be busy."

"Man, I think Yatesy's right," Mitch says. "I think this is some sort of crush."

"Not this again," Alex grumbles.

There's mischief in Yatesy's eyes now. "I dunno, babe. If Mitchy agrees with me, I think that means I'm right."

"But I'm not into men."

Yatesy shrugs. "Would've said the same thing a year ago too."

"Wait," Johnny says. "I thought you said you weren't into it?"

"I wasn't," Yatesy says.

"Holy shit, Yatesy!" Mitch says with a laugh. "So, you *did* find someone who had you gagging for it?"

"Jesus," Yatesy breathes out.

Mitch is unbothered. "Those were your words. Like, verbatim."

"So did you?" Johnny asks, talking over the mocking *verbatim* Nate throws at Mitch. "Yatesy, please tell me it's not another teammate."

"You're really against fucking around with a teammate, huh?"

Yatesy's voice is more curious than anything, but Johnny still laughs uncomfortably. "Straight up gave me hives thinking about it the last time. The stress of keeping the secret and knowing how weird things could be if it ended has to outweigh anything else, right?"

"You got hives thinking about Yatesy getting broken up with?" Parse asks.

"Only technically."

"Bro," Kaden says. "That's *so* grossly soft."

"A real marshmallow over here," Beaver says, slinging his arm around Johnny's shoulder.

Johnny pushes him under the water, but he's smiling. "See if I ever worry about you."

"It wasn't a teammate," Yatesy adds. "But I've been doing some self-reflection since Ford came out and I—"

Yatesy's face is flat, his ears pink, but his nonchalance can't fool them. They're standing on the precipice of something important.

"Set up a faceless Grindr to see what was out there, I guess. And..." He nods, gaze shifting. "Yeah."

Parse is the first out of the pool to hug him; then it's just a press of bodies, most of them not even touching Yatesy, all of them in different stages of soaked as they pile between two pool chairs in a show of support.

Yatesy grumbles about being crushed, but he still laughs as he says, "Will you guys get off me! A guy's gotta breathe to be bi."

A ripple of laughter courses through their hug and somewhere between them all, Parse asks, "Is that what you're calling yourself?"

There's a long pause before Yatesy breathes out, "Tentatively. Now get *off* me."

When they pull apart, Yatesy's looking at him expectantly and ice runs through Alex's veins. "I'm curious to know what he's like when he's not being—when he's not on guard all the time, but I don't *like* him."

Yatesy watches him for a long moment, then nods. "All right, but if you ever think—"

"I'd talk to you, of course."

Yatesy presses his mouth in a thin line, gaze briefly flicking to Mitch, and if either of them don't believe Alex, they don't call him on it.

"Maybe this is your version of getting in the competition's head," Parse snorts.

"Psych 'em out with kindness," Beaver says.

"Chirping with compliments," Nate says. "My favorite."

It sets them all off laughing but leaves an uncomfortable knot in Alex's stomach. He's not trying to psych Anderson out by being his friend any more than he's trying to be his friend just because Anderson has been so stubborn about it. Alex wants to see him with his walls down; he wants to see him lighten up and laugh; he wants to *know* him. Alex wants to share the stress of saving a struggling franchise with someone who understands the weight of those expectations.

Alex wants to be Anderson's friend, but a month of silence is as good as any fuck-off he could give Alex, and after they leave South Padre,

Alex decides not to contact him anymore.

He thought they left the draft on a tentative footing of friendship, but apparently all he needed to stop begrudgingly accepting Alex's repeated olive branches was for Alex to goad Noah into admitting he might actually *like* him.

He probably should've foreseen Noah being a spiteful little shit, but whatever. Alex doesn't let it bother him. He tried. If the preseason comes along and someone asks about their loser-buys dinners, that's not Alex's problem—Anderson can deal with explaining why they aren't, if he's so determined to hate Alex.

Then Anderson likes one of his photo dumps on Instagram in the middle of August and Alex's heart does a stupid fucking somersault. It's probably a coincidence, but Anderson has never interacted with Alex outside of their DMs, and Alex takes it as a sign to give it another shot, anyway.

# Chapter Eleven

NOT LETTING ALEX bulldoze his way into Noah's life has been the plan since Alex's mouth curled around *pretending,* his voice tight instead of playful on *babe.* He carefully ignores each of Alex's attempts to start up a conversation after the draft because they're not friends and they're never going to be.

Noah doesn't even *like* Alex. He doesn't enjoy being compared to him, or looking at him, or the way there's something about his face, his smile, the way he carries himself with an ease Noah has never possessed, that makes it impossible for Noah to see him in the same clinical way he views every other hockey player he's ever met. He doesn't like being attracted to someone so easygoing and energetic; who's as confident in his movements off the ice as he is on it; who flings himself over his friends like the touch of skin is a language of its own and he's speaking to them in his native tongue.

Noah and Alex aren't compatible—not even as friends—and Noah knows better than to let himself get attached to someone who will see that soon enough. He should be happy when Alex stops messaging him—it's what he wanted, really. But Noah can't deny disappointment curls hot through his stomach as he sees a new photo of Alex smiling on Instagram. He's not sure what he expects to happen when he likes the post, but he's unmistakably relieved when he wakes up the next morning to a new message from Alex, regardless.

### *Alex Valencia*

August 11 10:19PM

Ok Anderson one last game
I win: you admit you enjoyed my
company at the draft and give me a legit
shot to charm the hell out of you
You win: you use your actual words and
tell me to fuck off and I'll take the L even
though I KNOW you like me

*

August 12 9:32AM

*And if I tell you to fuck off right
now?*

But you won't

*That's not an answer*

Then do it. Type the words out and block
me right now

And if Catherine McDonald has
followups about our dinners I'll tell her I
called it off because you're a grade A dick

> *As if you'd ever call me a dick to*
> *the press*

There's only one way to find out
But I'm pretty sure you don't want that

> *And I'm pretty sure the same*
> *outcome is possible if I win*

Then play the game and let's get this
show on the road

> *Fine. Let's play*

*

NO MATTER WHAT Millie thinks, Noah doesn't lose on purpose, but once she's long gone, Noah can admit he's a little relieved Alex hasn't given up on this ridiculous mission of his. Whatever. He can privately enjoy a little attention from someone as bright and charismatic as Alex Valencia without it being some sort of indictment of Noah's ability to play it straight. They're never going to be *actual* friends. Noah doesn't have to worry about giving himself away because soon he'll need to focus on the season, and a little attention from a guy he doesn't care about won't mean anything to him at all.

*

### Alex Valencia

August 26 10:35AM

Hey! You never told me I was good
company wtf

*It's been two weeks*

And? Deal's a deal!!

*It's embarrassing you just*<br>*realized*

I was too busy gloating the first day

Thorn really fucked you over here bro
You SUCK at chess

*You've only won ONE MORE*<br>*than me*<br>*And what about the other 13?*<br>*What's your excuse for not*<br>*cashing in then?*

Too busy trying to get you to show me
your PERSONALITY

*Dunno what you're talking about*

Shut the fuck UP
I asked you what your favorite color was
and you said Canadian red

*Because you refused to believe I
don't have one! Not liking my
answer is a personal problem*

You treat everything like a media sound
bite
But no worries! I'll get the real stuff outta
you eventually. There's no way you're as
boring as everyone thinks

*Thanks
I guess you're not as insufferable
as I thought you'd be*

Aww you enjoy my company
I'm touched 😊 honored even

*If that's what helps you sleep at
night*

You'd probably look like you enjoy life
20% more if you stopped lying to
yourself

*Is this your idea of wooing?
Because I gotta say, I didn't
expect to be insulted so much*

Gotta give you the real me for this to
work

Besides it's not an insult if it's a real
CONCERN! You're too young to take life
so seriously

> *Hate to break it to you but this*
> *will never work. We have*
> *nothing in common and our*
> *personalities are too different*
> *But I'm kinda getting a kick out*
> *of how terrible you are at this so*
> *I guess you can carry on for now*

We have hockey in common
And chess

> *What better foundation for a*
> *friendship*

It's the first step baby!
We gotta build the whole house then
you'll see

*

WITH ANOTHER GAME and another wager, Alex finally wins Noah's number, and the first thing he sends outside of their Instagram thread is a gloating selfie. Noah's eyes catch on the smug curve of his mouth, then the bright, delighted glint in his eyes. He can almost hear the teasing lilt of laughter in Alex's voice when he reads the accompanying text.

*Ha! I love the sweet taste of victory in*

*the* morning.

Noah sends back *it's noon* and ignores the warmth bubbling in his chest.

Millie has other ideas. She kicks his ankle and cocks an eyebrow. "Alex again?"

"Yes." Noah knows there's no point in lying.

"Been texting him a lot?"

"Not really."

Millie's expression turns doubtful.

"I haven't. This is the first time he's texted me, actually."

Millie rolls her eyes, but her mouth twitches at the corner. "Tell me you didn't *just* give him your number."

"This is his game; I'm just playing by his rules. Why should I make it easy for him?"

Millie's smile grows. "Playing hard to get, eh?"

Noah snorts. "It's what he wants."

"And who are you to deny Alex what he wants, right?"

Noah flushes despite his best effort. "That's not what I meant."

"Oh, I know. You meant he thinks you're a *challenge,* a game to win, a plaything to keep his summer entertaining."

Noah's face burns hotter. "Okay, maybe not a *plaything.*"

Millie raises an eyebrow, smile turning sly. "Interesting reaction there."

"Shut up. Stop making this a thing."

"I'm not making it a thing—that's all you two! He's enjoying the game, and you enjoy being won."

"I'm not a prize, Millie."

"No, but he *is* winning you over. And you like it."

"I'm not sure I'd go that far."

"Hon, if you didn't want his attention, you'd have iced him out months ago."

"That's what he keeps saying."

"It doesn't take a genius to put two and two together."

Noah swats at Millie's arm. "Shut up."

Millie rolls her eyes. "The world won't end if you admit you like him."

"It might. Imagine if my dad found out."

"Fuck your dad!"

Noah blinks, eyes widening at the hardness of her voice. "Seriously, Noah. You're moving out to play in the National fucking Hockey League. Who cares what your homophobic piece of shit dad thinks about your friends?"

A chill goes up Noah's spine despite no one else being home. "He's not—"

"He is! And I won't pretend otherwise when he's not even in the country—let alone the same house as us."

"Fine," Noah grits out. "But it doesn't matter. Leaving home doesn't mean I'll never see him again."

"What're you going to do, then? Not be friends with people you clearly like because your dad hates them? Because your dad can't stop comparing the two of you? How's that fair to you?"

"It's not, but it's just another sacrifice for hockey. Seriously, not getting to be friends with Alex isn't as fucked up as having to be in the closet. At least with Alex, it's not what I actually *want*. It's not real. It's a game to pass the time until the season starts."

"You gotta stop lying to yourself. It's not good for you."

Noah rolls his eyes, but his cheeks burn as he remembers. "You sound just like him."

"More proof you're fighting a good thing. I'm your best friend! If he's even a tenth as cool as me, you'll love him."

"Millie, come on! We're draft rivals going to rival teams. There's no way this could last."

"Why not? He went on TV and told Catherine McDonald he wants to buy you dinner! You'll have set times to see each other."

"That's a competition, not friendship."

"Right, because friends aren't competitive?" Millie snaps. "Do you and Julien not push each other to be better? Can you only be friends with people who can't keep up with you?"

"Millie, stop! He's going to get bored with this—with me."

"And if he doesn't?"

"He will."

Millie's eyes are blazing; she's getting pissed. "And if he *doesn't?*"

"He will," Noah repeats, undeterred. "He's too much for me."

"What's that got to do with him getting bored?"

"It has everything to do with it. I've seen him with his friends, Mil. They're constantly touching and always up for a good time. You know I'm not like that. You *know* I can't stand anything touching me when I'm on edge. How the hell am I gonna be friends with the most affectionate person I've ever met when he puts me on edge by existing? I won't be able to—you know I won't."

"Not with that attitude! But if you gave him a chance and got to know him, you might not see him as some twisted paragon of what your father wants you to be! Maybe a little friendly competition is all you need to see him as a *person* instead of a stand-in for everything you think you shouldn't want."

"He's not a stand-in."

Millie glares, brows pinched together.

"Okay, he's *maybe* a bit of a stand-in. But it wasn't supposed to be a problem! He was supposed to be on the other side of the continent. I never thought I'd—"

"Have to deal with the complex your dad has given you about him? Yeah, I know. But here we are."

Noah drops his head back against his headboard. "Here we are."

Millie gives him a soft pat on the knee and Noah groans. This isn't how he wanted to spend the last weeks of his summer.

# Chapter Twelve

**Anderson**

Sun, Aug 28, 3:31PM

*Tell me you're in Jersey already*

Fly in tomorrow

*Cool*
*Rooming with someone on the*
*team?*

No

*Really?*

Why would I lie?

*Because you're an evasive little*

*shit*

Well yes. But also really

*So you won't offend anyone if*
*you go somewhere else on your*
*first day in*

No?

*Come to lunch with me and Brett*
*tomorrow then*

No

*Andersoooooooooooooonnnnn*
*Come on you gotta eat*

My parents will be here for the week. I
can't.

*See what I mean about evasive?*
*You could've led with that*

I would've said no regardless

*Food's on me if you come out*
*with us before training camp*

I'm not coming into New York for you

*Ouch*
*Like it's SO far*

Far enough

*We'll meet you then*

You'd buy AND meet me?

*I'm not gonna half ass winning*
*you over bro*

I'll think about it

*Not sure I believe you*

Fair, I probably won't

*You're the worst*
*But it's fine you'll owe me soon*
*enough*
*September 21 mark your*
*calendar*

Pretty cocky for someone who hasn't
even skated with the team yet

*Gotta believe it to achieve it*

# Chapter Thirteen

NOAH IS READY for his parents to leave twelve hours into their stay and by the time their last morning in his one-bedroom apartment rolls around, they've flayed Noah bare. His dad claps him on the shoulder as he's looking at a text from Alex and Noah flinches so badly his dad laughs.

"Don't worry, kid," he says, a genuine smile softening his face. "I saw nothing."

Noah pockets his phone, happy to let his dad assume he's worried about him catching something private until his smile sharpens. "So, who's your girl?"

"What?"

His dad motions to Noah's pocket. "You've been smiling at your phone all week."

"No, I haven't."

"Fine, you've been frowning less when texting whoever you've been texting. Did you meet someone?"

Heat creeps up Noah's neck. "Oh, no, I haven't been texting any-one new."

His dad narrows his eyes. "You never get that look when you're talking to Millie."

The flush spreads as his frustration grows. "There was no look."

Even if he *had* a look—which he doesn't—he wouldn't have one while texting Alex.

His dad throws his hand up, mockingly placating. "All right. Keep your secrets. That's fine."

"I—"

His dad steamrolls Noah's response. "If you want my advice, you shouldn't be looking for something serious at this age, let alone with someone at home. Long distance is a bitch, and the world is your oyster right now."

"My oyster," Noah mouths.

"You're not the smoothest, but I'm sure you'll have enough girls falling all over you to have a good time."

"Dad!"

"Paul," his mom hisses.

His dad shrugs. "What? You expect him to save himself for mar-riage?"

"Oh my God! Can we not talk about this? Let's never talk about this. Ever."

"Yes Paul, let's not," his mom says, looking at her phone. "Besides, we're going to be late if you keep going on about how our *child* should sleep around."

His dad's voice is steely when he shoots back, "He's almost nine-teen, Simone!"

"Enough! I don't want to talk about this."

"All right," his mom says.

His dad still looks like he wants to say something, but for once, when his mom curls her hand around his dad's shoulder, the tips of her red nails biting into his crisp white shirt, he doesn't go any further. Brunch is as awkward as it usually is, but when they leave after, Noah's scraped over and raw from the weight of the week.

Everything—from the way the waistband of his shorts settles against his hips to the stretch of skin against his palms—is wrong. He's crawling out of his skin; his eyes sting and his chest is tight, body vibrating with an intense, angry current, and he can't stand it.

He strips down and lies under the ceiling fan in nothing but his underwear, hoping the chill will settle him a little.

It doesn't.

He takes a shower. Or really, he sits on the cold wet tile with his knees to his chest, head resting on his folded arms until the heat of the water burns the pressure from his skin and warms the tile beneath him.

He texts Millie. She doesn't text back fast enough. He considers texting Julien, but then another message comes in from Alex and his heart skitters as he realizes he texted him by mistake. Because of fucking course he did. That's the type of day he's having.

**_Alex Valencia_**

Sun, Sep 4, 10:35 AM

Your parents are leaving today right?

2:39PM

*Wish you were here instead* 

I knew you liked me 😊

Ugh that obviously wasn't for<br>you

Good thing I can't read

Good thing that makes no sense

It's a selective thing

🙄

Well I know it wasn't for your parents

Could've been for them<br>You don't know

Maybe your mom
But I kinda doubt you were too
concerned with soaking up time with her
when you had SO much for me to annoy
you

Are you trying to annoy me<br>now? Because it's working

Lbr I don't have to try, I just do

And you do it so well

*

ALEX ONLY ASKS Noah to lunch once more; Noah's already at the rink when he does. He expects Alex to suggest they grab dinner instead, but he doesn't. Noah hates that it's equally disappointing as it is relieving. He hates it even more when it's tipped further toward disappointing the afternoon before they face each other for the first time in the preseason when Alex texts him.

> We leave straight for MTL after :( no
> dinner for me I guess.

Noah doesn't respond but at the first faceoff they take together, Alex smiles at him, huge and radiant, and arches an eyebrow. "What about vending machine snacks in the hallway?"

Noah wins the faceoff. At their next, the Renegades are down by two, but Alex is still smiling, eyes glinting. "Okay, maybe I'll be meeting you with vending machine snacks." Noah can't tell if he's joking, but it doesn't matter when he loses the faceoff—he can't let Alex distract him in a game.

The Renegades lose and when Noah steps out of the locker room later, he finds Alex standing against the opposite wall, feet crossed at the ankles, juggling snacks.

"You were serious," Noah says.

Alex's attention snaps to Noah and the snacks drop to the ground.

"I'm still learning." Alex dips down to pick them up. He takes two steps, then he's in front of Noah, pointedly looking between Noah's hands resting on his hips until Noah reaches out for what Alex has.

Noah wrinkles his nose as Alex drops a bag of M&Ms and a chocolate protein bar that has definitely seen better days in his hand.

"It's preseason, so."

"So, I get subpar snacks for a challenge you set up?"

Alex grins, eyes dancing. "Pretty much, yeah."

Noah hands the candy back. "I don't like these."

Alex narrows his eyes. "Do you actually not? Or are you still trying to keep me from learning a single fact about you?"

"I'm keeping your year-old protein bar, aren't I?"

"It's been in my bag a month—max. And how do you not like M&Ms? They're a classic."

"The candy coating leaves a weird taste on the back of my tongue."

"Oh my God, you have actual preferences."

Alex's smile is warm, warm, warm, his eyes so bright Noah has to avert his gaze. "Most people do."

He can't look back, too afraid the warmth of Alex's eyes will further sear itself into his brain, making it even more difficult to view him in the same disinterested way he does all other hockey players.

"Yeah, but most people share them a little more freely than you."

"Maybe I just don't share them with you."

"Hmm. My money's on you not sharing much with anyone," Alex says, so sincerely Noah's gaze darts up.

Alex has this sad pull to his mouth, not quite a frown, but nowhere near the smile Noah's apparently grown used to; it makes Noah's hackles rise, his teeth grind, his skin prickle. Alex doesn't know a single thing about Noah, but he knows enough, and Noah hates him for it.

He spots a reporter walking down the hall before he can let his irritation get the best of him. He tips the protein bar toward Alex and says through gritted teeth, "Thanks for dinner. Have a safe flight."

Alex frowns, but it smooths out into bland indifference almost instantly. "No problem. That's my emergency snack; I really treated you tonight."

"Feeling super spoiled."

Alex starts down the hallway backward, his winning smile back in place. "Keep that in mind when you're buying me dinner this weekend. I expect the same consideration."

*

NOAH WAKES UP fifteen minutes before his alarm goes off to three missed calls and a text from his mom.

> I'm at the coffee shop around the block.
> Call me when you're up.

His heartbeat skyrockets the moment he registers his mom means she's *here*—in Hoboken.

"What happened?" he asks the moment she picks up the phone. "Is something wrong? How long have you been here?"

"I got in late last night, but I know you get up around this time anyway, so I wanted to wait until you were well rested."

"Why do I need to be well rested? What's wrong?"

"Nothing's wrong, but I have something to tell you and I didn't want to do it over the phone."

"So, you flew all the way out to New Jersey? That sounds like something's wrong. Is Dad here too?"

"No, just me. I'll explain everything when I get to your place. I'll be there in a couple minutes, okay? But please try to stop panicking. Everyone's fine, no one's hurt."

The thing is, Noah doesn't know how to stop panicking. He tries, of course he tries. He spends the six minutes between his mom hanging up and knocking at his door breathing in and out.

In and out.

In.

And.

Out.

It doesn't help. His chest is still tight, palms still clammy, head still spinning as he tries to figure out why his mother is here, without his dad, barely two weeks after they left.

When he lets his mom in, she's as put together as ever, smiling brighter than he's ever seen, and Noah doesn't understand. He's been up for maybe fifteen minutes, has practice in less than two hours, and his mom's sitting in his living room looking like she's seen sunshine for the first time in years. He has no idea what's going on, but the floor is slipping out from under him.

"Do you want to get dressed or do you want to get right into it?"

Noah pulled on a pair of shorts before opening the door, but the panic boiling in his chest since he read her text creeps up his neck, across his shoulders, making the idea of a shirt stifling.

He sits on the opposite end of the couch facing his mom, right leg folded on the seat in front of him, lefthand fingers drumming on the other. "Let's just get right to it."

His mom angles her body toward Noah and rips the rug out from under his feet without a trace of regret.

"Your father and I are getting divorced, and I wanted you to hear it from me before the news broke."

"Before the news broke," Noah parrots.

"There's only so much we can keep to ourselves as public figures. Filing for a divorce won't be one of them."

Noah doesn't know how he feels or what he thinks. The news is surprising, for sure, but he can't say he's disappointed or even that he doesn't understand why it's happening. Mostly, he's just shocked because he never expected this—never thought it was a possibility.

"How long?"

Her smile falters, but it's still so much more beautiful than the plastic one he's grown so accustomed to. She's happy to be leaving his dad and Noah wants to be happy for her, wants to tell her he understands needing to flee, doesn't blame her for wanting to leave, but his head is empty save for angry static. He can't wrap his head around this.

"We separated quite a while ago."

"How long?"

His mom's smile finally drops. "Since you left for the Dub."

"That was—Mom! That was three years ago."

Indignation replaces panic, and the prickling of his skin intensifies. His mom reaches out for him, but he leaps up before she can make contact. The elastic bands of his clothes feel too tight, and he needs his mom to leave. He needs to be anywhere but here, with his mom telling him everything he's known since he was fifteen was a lie. He needs to shower until the heat of the water washes away the tightness of his skin and he can handle the touch of fabric again.

"Is that why you've been traveling so much more?"

"Yes, Noah, honey, listen—"

"Why didn't you tell me? You should have told me."

"Your father thought it would be best to keep it from you until the draft. He wanted to make sure you kept focused. And I wanted—" Her eyes slip closed and the happiness she's radiated since stepping into his apartment dims. "We should have told you. I wanted to tell you. But your dad would have fought like hell for primary custody, and I didn't want you to be alone in the house when you were home. I wanted to be around to reel him in sometimes, diffuse him as best as I could. He's always so hard on you."

Noah doesn't mean to, but the laugh bursts through him, hot and hysterical. Tears prickle at his eyes, but he can't tell if they're from sadness or relief or some strange combination of the two. "So, Dad thought—" He heaves in a huge breath, trying to regain his composure. "He thought it'd be better to spring this news on me right before my first season in the NHL starts. How's that better timing?"

"If your dad had his way, we wouldn't be getting a divorce."

He runs a hand through his hair, fingers brushing out the curls. He tries to smile, tries to joke, but it all comes out flat. "No offense, Mom, but your timing sucks."

"When would have been a good time?"

He throws his hands in the air, lets out a humorless laugh. "Never, three years ago, not the morning of an exhibition game, next year, I don't know."

"I'm sorry."

Noah deflates, slumping back into his seat. He covers his face with his hands and groans. "It's fine. You don't have to apologize."

"This needs to be done, but that doesn't mean I'm not sorry. I'm sorry it's taken me this long to tell you, for letting your dad be so hard on you, and for allowing our home to become a place you weren't comfortable being yourself."

Noah turns his head, heart rate doubling again. "What do you mean?"

"Honey, you can tell me anything you want. I'll love you no matter what."

There's red-hot panic painting its way across his face and Noah's throat tightens. His tongue is sandpaper in his mouth. "I don't know what you're talking about. I'm not—there's nothing I'm keeping from you." His mom's expression is painfully sympathetic, and Noah prickles. "What do you think I'm not telling you?"

She purses her lips, picks at her perfect pale-pink manicure. When she looks at him again, it's like a check to the boards.

"Do you remember when you were fourteen, and we went to Paris for Fashion Week?"

"Of course," Noah grits out.

"Your dad wasn't there, and we were next to—"

"I remember."

His mom sighs. "I saw the way you looked at him."

"So? He's famous!"

"Yes, but so was his girlfriend. She was even more famous than him at the time, and you weren't looking at her the same way. I've tried to project acceptance, tried to combat all the toxic shit hockey—and your father—has planted in your head about who you—"

"Mom, stop," Noah whines. "There's nothing. I'm not—I don't—"

This can't be happening. He swallows hard. Takes a breath. Swallows again. Clenches his jaw so tight it hurts.

Noah can do this.

He can tell his mom the truth.

"Whatever you thought you saw," Noah says, an eerie calm washing over him. "That was years ago, and I'm not like that. There's nothing out of the ordinary here. There's nothing for you to know."

Or no, he can't actually.

He's a liar, just like his parents.

His mom sighs and her mouth turns down. She shakes her head and all the happiness she came into the apartment with dissipates. She looks like a rain cloud and Noah hates it, but not as much as what she says next. "Noah, it's been years since you've shared anything meaning-ful with me. I know nothing about your life outside hockey, and I used to think it was some combination of spending most of the year apart and general teen withdrawal—I remember how much I hated telling my mom things at your age—but I think I was wrong. You haven't allowed yourself anything outside of hockey in so long, I don't think you know yourself either."

# Chapter Fourteen

ALEX HADN'T NOTICED, but someone got a picture of him and Noah talking after the game. The boys spam the group chat with the photo until Alex responds, then Kaden sends it another five times with hearts edited around Alex's head. Sierra texts it to their sibling group chat followed by *bromance alert?* while Dani asks, *who's more obsessed with Noah: hockey media or Alex?* followed by a string of cry-laughing emojis when Alex tells her to shut up.

His friendship with Anderson is still touch-and-go, so it's no surprise when Noah doesn't respond to Alex asking if Noah saw the tweet. But he doesn't get a response on Friday, either, or on Saturday when he asks what he's going to buy Alex for dinner. And yeah, Anderson's a little spotty at replying, but Alex can usually count on him to rise to the bait.

At their first face-off, Alex says Anderson better buy him something nice tonight, and the only sign he heard him is the clench of his jaw. He tries again when they're battling for a puck behind the Hellions' net in the second, and Anderson ignores him again. Alex doesn't try after that. He knows how intense Anderson can get, but he still meets him outside the visiting team's room.

The anger radiating from Anderson's piercing blue eyes takes Alex aback. He knows he needs to tread carefully here, conscious of Anderson's mood and the way their last meeting ended up all over Twitter when he decides against mentioning their dinner arrangement at all.

Anderson doesn't stop walking when Alex says hi and Alex is losing his patience. He falls in stride beside him, voice low as he asks, "What's up with you?"

Anderson tenses. "I'm just not in the mood tonight."

"I can tell, but you're excessively pissed." He doesn't know why it seems so pressing, but the need to comfort and soothe Anderson's rage thrums under his skin. Alex knows it's risky, knows it might piss him off further, but he has to try. "It's only an exhibition game."

Anderson stops abruptly, fury coming off him in waves, the angry flush to his cheeks obvious and yep, he played his cards wrong.

"Not everything's about hockey!"

"Yeah, I know. But hockey's all you ever want to tell me about." Then it dawns on him. He steps closer and drops his voice. "Is your dad giving you—"

"Shut up," Anderson says through gritted teeth. "That's not— you're not supposed to know about that."

Alex must've been right. "But I do. Am I not allowed to worry about why you look like you're about to need jaw reconstruction?"

"No. You don't know me enough to worry about me at all, actually."

"Not for lack of trying on my part." For a second Anderson's face softens, but it shutters closed the next and Alex doesn't push. "Fine, but feel free to stop ignoring me if you change your mind and wanna talk about it."

Alex turns to leave and starts heading back down the hall to his own locker room but stops when Anderson calls out for him.

"Changed your mind already?"

Anderson rolls his eyes, but his mouth twitches at the corner and Alex's heart does a strange sort of somersault. He digs something out of his pocket and tosses it at Alex. "Deal's a deal, right?"

Alex curls his fingers around a bag of peanut M&Ms and laughs. "Thought the candy coating was bad. Babe, are you giving me shitty snacks on purpose?"

Anderson shrugs. "You called them a classic, and the peanuts cut the taste so they're bearable."

"Another Anderson fact!"

"I'm a fount of them," he says, the corner of his mouth pulling upward again.

*

### *Anderson*

Mon, Sep 26, 10:39PM

WHY would you tell that reporter it's up
to ME if we follow through on your
dinner bets??

> *Hello to you too Anderson! It's*
> *been so long. How have you*
> *been?*

It's been two days since I saw you

*But so much longer since you*
*texted me back and lbr you tried*
*to ignore me on Saturday too*
*What's going on with you?*

Why does anything have to be going on?

*Because we were getting along*
*and now you're icing me out*
*again*

I don't owe you an explanation and I'm
not interested in playing this game
anymore
This is me finally telling you to fuck off

*

TRUE TO HIS word, Alex fucks off. Not that he actually wants to. He wants to push and needle Anderson until he tells him what's eating away at him. Wants to make sure Anderson understands this was never really a game at all—and even if it was, it stopped being one a long time ago. But he doesn't. He throws himself into getting ready for the season; spends his free time with Brett getting to know the other guys on the team; texts his sisters; FaceTimes Liv; ignores the agitated thrum beneath his skin as best he can.

He does a miserable job. The growing irritation is nearing unbearable as opening night approaches. But Alex doesn't break. Not even the night before his first game, when Beaver texts *your boy all right?* to the group chat with a link to an article about Simone DuPont and Paul Anderson filing for divorce. Alex is certain this has to be, in part, why Anderson has been in such a foul mood. The itch to reach out grows, but the thought of disregarding the clearest sign Anderson's ever given him on what he wants makes Alex's stomach twist. Alex won't walk back on what he said no matter how much he wants to.

Worrying about Anderson mixes terribly with the frantic NHL debut nerves boiling through him and by the time their pregame nap comes along, Alex is going off the walls. It's so bad, Brett steers him into his room and shoves him onto his bed, glaring until Alex stops grumbling about being fine to sleep in his own room. Brett yanks the blanket out from under him and throws it over Alex's head. He's laughing as he climbs into the bed, and the knot in Alex's chest loosens.

Brett ruffles Alex's hair after they're both settled under the blanket. "Tonight's going to be memorable to you in a way it won't be for anyone else. Don't worry about what others will remember about it." Brett smacks Alex's hip. "Just take it one shift at a time, play your game, get those pucks in deep. You'll be fine."

Brett can barely get through it without laughing, and Alex doesn't fare much better. The nerves are still there, but they're lighter now, more like the jolt Alex gets right before the first drop of a roller coaster and less like waiting for a teammate to get up after a brutal hit. He's eighteen, and he's playing the game he loves in the National fucking Hockey League—there's nothing better than this.

He scores his first goal—a one timer assisted by Brett—three minutes into the game. The joy bursts through him, settles into his chest for the rest of the game, and when they win, it explodes, zapping through him like lightning. Back in the locker room, he takes the standard first goal photo for the team's socials while Brett stands behind the photographer, chirping him for his goofy grin. The group chat is buzzing when he checks his phone, the boys doing the absolute most with emojis, and Alex feels good, happy, pleased.

A text from Anderson pops up before Alex can respond and, with two words, the flickering flame of happiness his goal ignited dies. His heart beats rapidly as the agitation under his skin slams back into place, this time fueled by confusion and indignation. Alex vows not to respond, but back home, his phone burns a hole in his pocket. He can't help it. He's too curious.

By sheer force of will, Alex holds out until he's turning in for bed, not wanting to give Anderson the satisfaction of a response any sooner.

***Anderson***

Thu, Oct 6, 7:16PM

Nice goal

11:52PM

*It was*
*But you don't get to say that*
*anymore*

Why not?

*You told me to fuck off and I only*
*accept compliments from my*
*friends*

That's a lie and you know it

*You got me there*
*But you don't get to come at me*
*acting like we're friends when*
*you told me to fuck off for being*
*concerned about you! I think I*
*deserve some sort of explanation*
*before I let you waltz back in*
*here demanding I woo you*

I have never once demanded you woo
me!

*Is this what you call an*
*explanation?*

No, obviously not.

*Then go on, I'm waiting with*
*bated breath here*

*

ANDERSON STARTS AND stops so many times Alex almost falls asleep. He thinks it's Anderson balking again, doesn't expect to get any explanation at all, and almost drops his phone on his face when the text finally comes through. He didn't expect so much honesty.

My parents are getting a divorce. It's not
an excuse to lash out but it was definitely
the primary factor in me being a bitch to

you
And I'm sorry

> I saw and yeah, that's a pretty
> legit reason for being extra
> abrasive

You saw?

> Beav asked if you were okay
> I would've texted but you know

Thanks I guess

> Fuck off is a pretty clear
> boundary man
> Water under the bridge now tho

Are you serious?

> Uh yeah. What kinda friend
> would I be if handling your
> parents' divorce poorly was a
> deal breaker? Besides you
> obviously love me since you
> texted me so I'm way more
> willing to cut you some slack

Let's not get ahead of ourselves here

> Bold of you to still be a bitch the
> night you apologize

Would hate for you to get the wrong
impression

*I bet you're a secret softie under*
*all that bitchiness*
*Just gotta figure out what makes*
*you tick*

Hockey duh

*You're hilarious*
*But seriously, how are you?*

Not good, obviously. They apparently
separated years ago and if I didn't care
enough to realize how fucked up their
relationship was do I even deserve to be
upset about it?

Alex doesn't even think about it. He calls Noah, not really aware
of what he's done until Noah's answering the phone with a small, confused "hello."

"Hey."

Noah blows out a breath. He sounds defeated. "What do you want,
Alex?"

"To check on you. To tell you, it's okay to be upset even if your
parents should get a divorce."

"Can't really say I blame my mom."

"Doesn't mean it doesn't suck."

"Yeah, but it's whatever." Noah sighs. The sound wrenches

through Alex, a fierce protective instinct rearing up in response.

"Doesn't really sound like it's whatever."

"Yeah, well, it should be whatever. This is good for me, considering—"

"Considering what?" Alex prompts after Noah goes silent for a long beat.

"I dunno, I've just been planning on not going home if I don't have to, and without my mom there, I mean, we don't really have the best relationship either, but she's always tried and without her there—I guess I don't really have much of a reason to go home. But I don't know; he's still my dad."

"Only technically," Alex says before he can think better of it.

"Ah yes, I'm sure the media will love to hear all about how I'm no longer going home to visit my recently divorced, Stanley Cup winning, adored Winnipeg defenseman turned broadcaster, charity man of a father because he's only *technically* my dad."

There's an undercurrent of laughter in Noah's bratty little tone, which is all the encouragement Alex needs to stop filtering himself. "Look, can I call your dad a dick?"

Noah laughs, stark and loud in Alex's ears after how quiet he's been.

"Oh, yeah, definitely going to call him a dick," Alex says, grinning as Noah's laughter turns into a quiet fit of giggles.

"Don't think him being a dick makes him any less of my dad."

He's quiet and forlorn again, and Alex hates how much Paul Anderson affects Noah even when he's not around.

"Look, Anderson, I don't know shit about having a dad in the game who's won big and has opinions people care about, but I've heard what you sound like when you're on the phone with him—"

"Don't—"

"No, you need to hear this, man. You sound small, and you sound small now, and dads aren't supposed to make their kids sound like kicked puppies no matter who they are. And yeah, he's your dad, you share his DNA, but if he's a dick, and all signs point to yes, then you don't have to give him your time. That's basic life 101 shit here."

"Don't think most people would agree with you," Noah says after another long stretch of silence.

"They're not reading the right life manuals then."

"Maybe not. But I don't really have a choice. They're already writing shit about how this could impact my debut."

"What the hell? Fuck them."

Noah snorts. "You know how it goes. And you know it'll be even worse if they get a whiff of me and my dad having a fallout. I can't just cut him off."

"Ugh." Alex hates how resigned to all this Noah sounds; hates how easily he's accepted putting optics over his own comfort. "Can't you stay with your mom?"

"She's thinking about moving back to New York."

"Wait, your mom's American?"

"No, but she lived there when she was modeling."

"Oh, huh, I thought she was French."

"I mean, she's French Canadian."

"Ah, well, either way, I was going to say you just got more interesting, but I guess not."

"Seems like I'm interesting enough for you to know my mom's some sort of French."

Warmth unfurls in Alex's chest at the sound of Noah's teasing, any trace of his earlier discomfort swept away. "Husky's sister, Addie, was born in Canada. She likes to make sure we all know how inferior she thinks the NTDP is. The second year we were in Plymouth—"

Alex laughs as he remembers, barely pulling it together enough to tell the story. "She saved all our numbers from Husky's phone over the winter break or something, and then, during one of our games, added us all to a group chat and spammed it with trivia and stats about Canada's U18 team. After the game, we each had over a hundred new messages. You should've seen Ben's face."

"Oh God, she didn't."

"She did! She's always doing shit to get on Ben's nerves."

"How'd my mom come up though?"

"Oh right! Like half of us were taking French and Addie texted us *if you ever need a tutor, I hear someone's fluent* with a screenshot of some interview your mom did. Does she still email you in French?"

Noah huffs, but he sounds a little fond when he says, "Yeah. My grandma does the same thing. They started when I left for the Dub—said they wanted to make sure I didn't get rusty."

"And did it work?"

"It helped my spelling."

"Oh yeah? Gotta tell Dani—she can't spell for shit in Spanish. Or English, so actually, that might not help."

Noah laughs, soft and breathy, and never circles back to what he's going to do about going home. Alex doesn't bring it up, unwilling to force the small, sad little tone back into Noah's voice after he let his guard down in front of Alex.

Then he remembers with a burst of glee. "You watched my game tonight!"

"I d—"

"You did! That text was from the beginning of the game!"

"Whatever," Noah mumbles, probably through a clenched jaw, and Alex is over the moon.

"I knew it! You definitely like me; you wanna be my friiiiiiend."

"Whatever," Noah repeats, but this time Alex hears the laugh in it. "I'm hanging up on you now. Can't let you get a big head about it."

"Yeah, yeah. Goodnight, Anderson. Good luck on Saturday. If you score faster than me, I'll buy you a treat."

"I try not to do sweets—"

"During the season," Alex finishes. "Yeah, yeah, I know. But fuck the diet plan. If you get your first goal faster than me, I'm definitely buying you dessert."

Noah huffs, but it's more amused than anything. "How's that an incentive when you're buying me dinner next Saturday, anyway?"

"Who's got a big head now?"

"Gotta believe it to achieve it, right?"

"Right." Alex is so glad Noah can't see his grin. "Guess I'll have to watch on Saturday to see if I'm buying dessert regardless of dinner then."

# Chapter Fifteen

***Alex Valencia***

Sat, Oct 8, 7:11PM

NINETEEN FUCKING SECONDS HOLY
SHIT
Breaking records in your first damn
game
Fucking unbelievable Anderson
What a sick goal

*

"NOAH, YOU'VE STARTED the season hot," a reporter says as the scrum is rounding to a close. "You had two goals and two assists in your first game, even setting a record for fastest debut goal, and you've put up at least one point every game since."

Noah nods as the man speaks, wondering if he's going to be the one to finally ask about the Hellions losing to the Renegades in his and Alex's first official matchup. He was expecting it to be the first question, but small mercies still exist or whatever.

"As expected, you and Alex Valencia—" *Yup, there it is.* Noah knew someone would bring it up. "—are both putting up fantastic numbers for your respective teams. Have you been keeping track of how close you are in points? Do you still see him as a motivation when it comes time to push yourself harder?"

"Right now, my primary focus is helping the team win," Noah says. "I don't want to get caught up in what I'm accomplishing individually. I want to be a team player. Nothing I do individually matters if I'm not contributing enough for us to win. With that said, Alex and I have a little bet on who can make it to ten points in the least number of games so I'm aware of where we both are, but I'm not checking his stats before I go to bed at night or stressing myself out over it." *Not anymore, not when I don't have my dad breathing down my neck about the draft anymore.* "It's just a fun thing we're doing as we focus on impacting our respective teams."

"Leading up to the draft," another reporter cuts in, "you and Alex made a deal in an interview to buy dinner for whoever won when your teams face each other. Is that something you two are actually going to do this season? Is that what your bet for ten points is going to be?"

"Uh, I'm not sure what we're doing there, actually. There's no set plan, but during preseason there wasn't much time to go out, so we exchanged snacks after the games, but yeah, we're supposed to meet up after this. I'm sure Alex is going to gloat a little about it, but I'm confident in our team and I'm sure the next time we see each other, he'll end up buying."

Talking to Alex is so much easier when Noah can't see his face. It's ridiculous, really, how easily Noah's been able to stop viewing Alex through the eyes of his father's expectations, but how hard it still is to be near him without tensing up as his mind slips and starts slotting him into all the places a future boyfriend could go.

So, yeah, Noah's having a hard time looking at Alex, and yeah, Alex is doing most of the talking, but Noah's never the talkative one, and it trips him up when Alex blows out a quick breath and drops his fork with a loud clatter. He's not expecting to look up to see Alex frowning—he never frowns.

"What's wrong?"

Alex's nostrils flare. "You tell me, man."

"Other than the obvious post-loss annoyance, nothing." But Noah's pretty sure Alex isn't upset about Noah being quiet. Noah's always quiet.

Alex leans back in his booth, arms crossed defensively against his chest. "You know that's not what I meant."

"Then what do you mean?"

"I mean"—Alex rolls his eyes dramatically—"what is your problem with me, specifically?"

Noah glances away, heart rattling against his ribs. He doesn't want to talk about this, but he wants to get rid of Alex's kicked-puppy expression even more. "Nothing. I don't have a problem with you. I'm here, aren't I?"

"Yeah, but, you're—you won't even look at me. We're cool when we text, and then in person you're like this." He throws his hand out, gesturing at Noah's stiff posture; it only makes Noah more tense. Alex deflates. "I don't get you, man. You're a completely different person when we're in the same room and I got it last time, and I get this whole thing must be tough on you, so is that what this is? Did something else happen with your parents?"

"No, nothing happened."

"Then what about my face makes you so uncomfortable you can't even look at me? Because the difference between you on the phone and you in person is really giving me whiplash. What the fuck is up with you?"

"Nothing, there's nothing up. This is just how I am! I'm not like you. I told you we'd never work out as friends because we're not compatible."

"No, shut up! That's not it. We get along. We're friends."

"Yeah," Noah says, because what's the point of denying it?

Alex's smile is radiant. "Then what is it? My face too good for you to look at head on?"

"It's a fine face." Noah's proud of himself for keeping it together; his stomach barely even somersaults. It's only, like, rolling. He's doing great.

"Don't lie. You totally think I'm hot." Alex rests a hand over his heart. "I'm touched."

Noah's heart stutters, his stomach plummets and twists up, and any semblance of control he had over his emotion bleeds away.

Alex's eyes narrow a little and Noah's face burns. "I don't."

"It's cool. You're not the first friend to tell me I'm hot."

"Alex, stop."

He hates the way Alex looks at him, eyes sharp and judgmental. Noah's heart drops; he thought Alex was different.

"I'm not into you," Noah says through gritted teeth, gaze darting around the room for signs anyone's paying attention to them.

Alex snorts. "Oh, I know, you've made it pretty clear I'm too much for you. But see, I would've never guessed your thing about touching—"

Noah's attention snaps back to Alex. He flinches at Alex's visible anger. His throat is too tight, his voice cracks. "My what?"

"How you hold yourself, how you don't like to be touched sometimes, how you freeze up even when it's your own teammates celebrating with you."

"You've noticed that?" No one but Millie has ever noticed before, and Julien's the only other person he's ever been able to tell about it.

"Yeah, and I thought it might be an overstimulation thing—we play a pretty physical sport, you know—but then I noticed it over the draft weekend too. We weren't playing then though, so I thought maybe you're an anxious person who has sensory issues when you're overwhelmed—my mom's like that sometimes. But I didn't think you're comfortable with Millie touching you because she's a *girl*. I didn't think you'd be so homophobic your own friends can't touch you outside a celly, Anderson."

Noah chokes on his own spit. "You think I'm—"

"Paired with the way you're reacting to a little teasing about thinking I'm hot—yeah, I do. What, do you think someone's going to think you're into men if you let a guy touch you for more than a split second? Do you think someone might hear me chirping you and think you're actually into me?"

Noah doesn't know what his face is doing, but it's unbearable how quickly Alex softens. "Oh."

"Whatever you're thinking, you're wrong. I *am* an anxious person." He stands up, pulls out his wallet, and throws what he has at Alex. "That should cover us both. If not, I'll Venmo you the rest."

"Anderson, stop."

Alex pulls back midway through grabbing for Noah's wrist. His noticing and adjusting his behavior might be touching if it weren't for the crisis he's currently having and all.

Noah pulls his jacket on and starts walking out; he can hear Alex shuffling around, but he doesn't wait to see what he'll do. He needs to leave.

Alex is hot on his heels and catches up to him at the door. "Jesus, Anderson, will you wait up?"

"Leave me alone."

"I swear I won't tell anyone."

Noah glances over. "You don't know what you're talking about."

"Noah."

His name from Alex's mouth throws him off; he almost trips over his own feet. Alex keeps talking. "I'm not judging you, man. You don't have to panic with me. Liv's bi, my aunt's a lesbian, I know other guys in hockey who are—"

Noah stops at the corner; pulls his phone out to call for a ride. "Will you shut up!"

"I'm trying to—"

Noah looks up and he can tell Alex is being sincere, but he can't do this. "You need to stop talking."

"I want to—"

"Alex, don't make me beg. I can't talk to you about this. I *won't* talk to you about this."

Alex opens his mouth; snaps it shut. He bites his lip and Noah can practically see the gears turning in his mind; can see him trying to figure out what he can say. Noah doesn't expect him to drop it, but Alex is full of surprises, isn't he?

"Yeah, all right. Whatever you want."

They stand there in silence for a moment, then Alex asks, "Are you gonna let me share this car with you, or do I need to call my own?"

Noah looks over; Alex is watching him like he's a spooked animal ready to attack at any moment. Noah sighs, "Yeah, of course."

Alex gives him a ghost of his usual smile.

"Wouldn't want your carbon footprint on my conscience after all."

Alex's face splits in a grin. His eyes light up as he tips his head back and laughs. Noah's chest squeezes; the panic thrumming under his skin seems so much stronger than before. Alex is so beautiful, and Noah has no idea how he can hang out with him now that he knows Noah's attracted to him. There's no other option if he doesn't want to die of embarrassment, really. He can never see Alex again. For real this time.

*

IT'S LATE, BUT he calls Millie the moment he shuts the door to his apartment, anyway. He's contemplating whether he should leave a message when she answers.

"Noah, you're up late," she says, her voice loud over the music in the background.

His throat is tight. "Yeah."

Millie's voice goes serious. "Are you okay? You sound panicked."

"Uh, Alex knows I'm gay," he says in a rush, heart racing.

"What? Wait, let me just find somewhere—" There's some shuffling and Millie apologizing to someone, then the din muffles. "—quiet. I can hear you now. What did you say?"

"Alex knows...about me."

"What do you mean? Did he say something? Or are you assuming?"

"We went to dinner."

"Wait, *what?*"

"We played tonight, and I lost."

"Oh, no, I know. I checked the score, duh. But I didn't think you'd actually follow through with buying dinner for him. Noah, that's great! You two are becoming legit friends here."

"Yeah, but now I can never speak to him again."

"Noah."

"What else am I supposed to do? I can't talk to him! Can't give him any more reason to think I'm gay."

"So, you *are* assuming, then?"

"No, Millie, I'm not assuming." He presses his fingers hard against his forehead, rubbing back and forth. "He called me out on not being the same in person as I am when we're texting—and then he, you know, made a joke about how maybe I have trouble looking him in the eye because I think he's too hot."

"Ah."

"Yeah!" Noah is hysterical. How could he let this *happen?* "Then everything spiraled out of control. He said he noticed I don't like to be touched—"

"Really?"

Noah huffs. "Yeah, I was shocked too. My parents—I mean, I guess they're not a stellar litmus test, but even they don't notice. No one notices other than you."

"He pays a lot of attention to you."

Noah snorts. "So much so he thinks I'm one huge, uncomfortable homophobe!"

"No!"

"Yes, Millie! Yes!"

"And when you said you weren't, I assume he came to some

conclusions with the whole neon-red face situation you have every time it comes up."

"Yeah," Noah sighs.

"What did you say?"

"Nothing. I left."

"What do you mean you *left?*"

"I mean, he took me to some diner, and I freaked out when he figured it out, and I got up and left. But don't worry, the universe is against me, and he followed. And God, he's so fucking nice about it, Mils."

"Yeah?"

"Yeah." Noah's throat is dry and scratchy. His eyes prickle. He might actually cry about this and shit—maybe his dad's right. Maybe he is too fucking soft for this game. "He tells me he's not judging me. His girlfriend's bi, and his aunt's a lesbian, and—" His chest hurts, each beat of his heart a strike against his ribs. "He said he knows other guys in hockey, who're—who like other guys, I guess."

"Sounds like a good person to have on your side. I know you didn't mean to, but what're you worried about? Do you think he'll tell someone?"

"No, I don't think he will." Noah isn't sure why he believes it, but he does.

"Then I think maybe you should let yourself have another friend you can talk to about this. What's the point of ignoring him if he already knows? What's the benefit of never talking to someone you trust not to betray you? Someone who obviously cares about you."

"I don't know, but not feeling all the shit I feel when I look at him seems pretty beneficial right now."

"Oh, are we acknowledging your crush on him now?"

"I don't have a crush on him—"

Millie laughs, but it's muffled, like she's trying to hide it. "It's just us. You don't have to hide this from me. It's okay if you have feelings for him."

"I don't have feelings for him. I don't! He just makes me want—" Noah sighs, because that's the crux of it all, isn't it? "He makes me want things I can't have."

"Do you hear yourself? You're describing having *feelings*."

"But I don't want things with him."

"Are you sure?"

"No! I mean, yes, I'm sure I don't want things with him. I just want—"

He can't stop thinking about how much Alex has noticed, how mindful he's been while in Noah's space, and how he's adjusted his behaviors for him. How soft his face was when he realized; how firm he was when he said Noah didn't owe his dad anything.

He thinks about Alex and his chest aches. He thinks about Alex and wonders what it would be like to be wanted by someone who notices that much. Noah looks at Alex and wants someone as thoughtful and perceptive to care about him. He looks at Alex and wonders what it would be like for love to be easy, wonders what it'd be like to be in a relationship as outwardly fun and caring as the one Alex has with Liv.

"It doesn't matter what I want, Mils, I can't have any of it, anyway."

"You *can* have the things you want."

"That's not true. You know I can't pursue anything right now. What's the point of building up a fantasy when I know it can never be a reality?"

"I hate your father," Millie says after a beat of silence.

"What does—"

"He's responsible for this! For how you see yourself! Yeah, hockey's rotten to its core, has maggots festering in it and making things unbearable from top to bottom, but he's made you hate everything about yourself he thinks is too soft. He's a hateful piece of shit and he's made your life hell, but you can't stop wanting his approval even though it's hurting you. So don't tell me your dad making you feel worthless more times than not and his complete inability to show even a sliver of support for queer men in the NHL isn't the driving force behind your stubborn commitment to never wanting another man."

"I—" Dammit. He really is going to cry tonight. This is too much. His brain is heavy with the truth of her words, and he can't stand how right she is.

"What do I do about Alex?" Noah asks, because everything else is too much for him to handle.

Millie sighs but lets him shirk the other conversation. "What do you want to do?"

Noah huffs. "If I knew, I wouldn't be asking."

"Let me rephrase: do you want to keep hanging out with Alex?"

"Yeah, but—"

"But nothing! For once in your life, please listen to your heart and don't worry about all the variables—not what could go wrong or who might get upset. Just do what makes you happy. You deserve to be happy."

"I'll think about it."

# Chapter Sixteen

**Anderson**

Sun, Oct 16, 10:00 AM

*What are the odds of you telling me to fuck off again if I bring up last night*

11:27 AM

Pretty sure this counts as bringing it up

*So are you going to tell me to fuck off or what*

Haven't decided yet

*You know I won't tell anyone right?*

*Even if Liv wouldn't murder me*
*with her bare hands for pulling*
*shit like that I still wouldn't*

Had a feeling you wouldn't

*Then what're you basing the*
*decision on?*

12:32 PM

You weren't supposed to know
No one involved with hockey was ever
supposed to know

*So you're uncomfortable because*
*I play hockey too*

No I'm uncomfortable because I didn't
want you to know and now you do and I
don't want you to be weird about it

*Ok so idk how I'd react if you*
*knew something this big about*
*me without me wanting you to*
*but I can assure you I won't be*
*weird around you. I know I was*
*chirping you about not looking at*
*me because I'm too hot but I*
*want to make it clear I'm not a*
*dick who assumes all guys*

*attracted to dudes will hit on me*

Good to know

*And even if you DO think I'm hot*
*I know it doesn't mean you*
*wanna smash or whatever*

I am begging you to never say smash in
that context ever again
And stop fishing for compliments. I'm
not saying you're hot

*I wasn't fishing!*

You totally were

*Whatever*
*I know I'm hot. I don't need your*
*validation*

Cocky

*It's not cocky if it's TRUE*
*But seriously. This has to be*
*weighing on you and I know I*
*wasn't even top hundred people*
*you'd choose to tell but I want*
*you to be comfortable around me*
*and I promise this won't change*
*how I treat you*

But idk if that's possible

You weren't wrong about me being

anxious and you knowing isn't exactly

helping

*

### *Do or Die*

Sun, Oct 16, 9:02 PM

**Nate**
So how'd last night go?

*Good*

**Mitch**
Yeah? He even paid after losing?

*Yes*

*It's almost like I was right and*

*we are friends*

**Beaver**
Huh

Did not see that coming

**Nate**
Good for you man

**Ben**
Was it everything you wanted it to be?

Was it worth all the work?

**Brett**
Must've been, he hasn't stopped smiling

since he got home

*Shut the fuck up that's not even*

*true*

**Brett**
Fine you haven't stopped smiling in

SPIRIT

Your vibe was way better than when he

blew you off in the preseason

**Parse**
Not sure that's the bar we want him to

clear

**Mitch**
Gonna collect on your handjob from

yatesy then?

*I hate you*

**Yatesy**
Since you DID get the job done I guess

I'll offer a hand if you need to experiment

**Kaden**
Watch out bud you might give johnny

hives again

**Parse**
Johnny if you're reading this please take

a Benadryl

> *SHUT UP*
> *I still don't need you to jerk me*
> *off to know I'm not into dudes*
> *I'm never going to need that*
> *actually*

**Nate**
I guess I'll take one for the team then

> *OR YOU NATHAN*

**Yatesy**
Alright but the offer still stands
I'm not gonna chicken out

> *Like I'd care if you did. I'm not*
> *worried about you losing gay*
> *chicken here lol*
> *As for you BENJAMIN I expect*
> *you to bitch out on what YOU*
> *PROMISED before the draft*

**Johnny**
For the love of god please tell me husky
didn't offer to have sex with you too

**Ben**
Obviously not

> *Worse, he gave me the tiebreaker*
> *for the summer*

**Johnny**
BEN WHAT THE FUCK

**Beaver**
Can you do that??????

:)))))))))))))))))))

**Ben**
I DIDN'T THINK HE'D SUCCEED

**Mitch**
Noooooooooooooooo
What the fuck are we gonna do if Nate
and Kaden lobby for skydiving again
AND YOU CAN'T STOP US FROM
GOING??????

*Sucks to suck boys*
*Shouldn't have doubted me*

# Chapter Seventeen

**_Alex Valencia_**
Tue, Oct 18, 11:51PM

> *Take it you're going to want*
> *dessert for getting to ten in*
> *seven?*

Throwing in the towel already? You could
get a point next game

> *Might, might not*

Didn't think you were superstitious

> *I'm not, just know I played like*
> *shit tonight*

Still came through with a secondary
assist tho
But I don't think you really want me to
pep talk you, do you?

*Not particularly*

In that case I still owe you for scoring
first. You wanna meet up and swap
desserts on your next day off?

*Seems like it cancels out that way*

Not if you're getting two desserts for
winning both bets
Not if I choose three scoops of ice cream
when you go for a kiddie size

*We are definitely not going to*
*meet up for ice cream during the*
*season*

What if it's VEGAN ice cream?

*I might allow it*

THAT'S THE SPIRIT BABY

Thu, Oct 20, 12:30 PM

Did you mention the ten points thing in a
post game or something?

*Uh yeah after our game when a*
*reporter asked about you. Why?*

Didn't expect to be asked about it after
morning skate is all
But hey the guy pointed out we'll TIE at
ten in seven if you get one tonight so I
guess you're gonna have to get two if you
want that dessert

*Pretty sure you're the one who*
*decided dessert was the payout*
*here*

What would you pick instead?

*I wouldn't be doing this in the*
*first place if not for you*

🙂

What's your idea of an in season treat
then?

*Honey in my coffee*

HONEY IN YOUR COFFEE???
You're fucking with me

*I'm not*

You're about to tell me it's in black coffee
aren't you

*ICED black coffee*

That doesn't make it better

*It's good*

I truly doubt that bud
But I'll file gross coffee preferences away
with doesn't like candy coating as the two
facts outside of hockey I know about you

*Three you mean*

Yeah but I wasn't mentioning that when
you're uncomfortable with me even
knowing lol I'm not that much of an
asshole

*You're not an asshole at all*
*Which makes you so much more*
*annoying*

Awww you think I'm charming

*Not quite what I said*

But the sentiment was there underneath

10:52 PM

You're practically begging for dessert
with the night you had

*I will let you buy me ONE scoop*
*of vegan ice cream if I must*

A scoop of vegan ice cream is not a
TREAT worthy of 12pts in 7 games OR
for setting a record for fastest goal scored
by a rookie

*Remind me whose reward this is*
*supposed to be?*

Yours, which is why I found a place with
a bunch of different honey lattes and shit
for us to try

*I thought you said that's gross*

I'm certain putting honey in iced black
coffee is disgusting, but these are
professionals and I'm willing to give it a
shot

*Do you always undermine your*
*own thoughtfulness by following*
*it up with an insult?*

Only with people I like duh

*

### *Alex Valencia*
Sun, Oct 30, 11:17PM

*So did I stop being challenging
enough to entertain you or what*

Uhhhh?????

*You've been ignoring me and I
want to know if it's because you
finally proved your point and
never actually cared to be my
friend at all*

Pick up my call asshole

*No. Guys are already giving me
shit about being on my phone at
the party. Kev will steal it right
out of my hand if I CALL
someone*

Are you drunk? Is that why you aren't
making sense?

*I had one drink
And I'm making perfect sense
actually*

Last time I checked you haven't
responded to me in days so idk how I'm
ignoring you

*Because I realized you've only
been texting me back*

So you started ignoring me instead of just
asking what was up?

*I thought you'd eventually text
me since you never back down
from a challenge*

You're not a challenge, you're my friend.
And you said you didn't know if you'd be
comfortable around me now that I know
and I wanted to give you the space to
figure it out

*That's stupid*

Fuck you man I was trying to be
respectful

*Maybe those first two days. But
then I texted you about the ten
points. I said you could buy me
ice cream! You told me about the
coffee place. In what world did
any of that make it seem like I
hadn't figured it out?*

Maybe the world where the only reason I
even found this out is because you

weren't comfortable sitting at a fucking
diner with me. So maybe cut me some
slack for thinking you'd set a date to meet
up for this when you were sure you
wouldn't clam up again.

> *When you put it like that I sound*
> *like an asshole*
> *So thanks for that*

Then don't be one next time

> *Uh, fine*
> *And I'm sorry*

I'll make a note that you get pissy when I
don't text you first and act accordingly

> *I hate you*

You miiiiiiiiiissed me

> *I did not*

Keep telling yourself that babe
Go enjoy your party before you get your
phone confiscated
Text me tomorrow if you feel up for
coffee

# Chapter Eighteen

ALEX EXPECTED NOAH to follow through on getting coffee—if not because he was comfortable, then at least because he's stubborn as shit and wanted to prove a point. He's not even that surprised they have a good time. Noah's quiet but he doesn't avoid eye contact with Alex, and he gives Alex such a sweet smile when he takes the first sip of his drink that Alex's chest goes all warm and fluttery and it's *nice*. Alex does most of the talking, but Alex does most of the talking in a lot of situations. He doesn't mind.

What does surprise him is the way Noah asks if he wants to come over to watch the lunar eclipse with him as they're saying goodbye. He rambles on about how Derek wouldn't even watch the sunrise for a girl, so he refuses to get up for pretty sky shit he can see on Noah's Instagram at a reasonable hour, while Kevin promised to FaceTime him to keep him company but doesn't want to get dressed and take a rideshare over that early.

Noah goes a little pink when Alex says he'll watch it either way but it's nicer to have someone there with him so he doesn't feel like such a nerd, and Alex can't even pretend to be offended he's a last resort when Noah's watching him with this soft, barely there smile, willingly revealing a little piece of himself.

Alex rides the high of Noah wanting to spend time with him outside of what Alex plans all week and despite the game going late, he's wired by the time he gets to Noah's. He has to call three times from the lobby before Noah buzzes him in and means to give him shit for falling asleep on Alex, but when Noah lets him in, the chirp dies behind his teeth. Noah's eyes are heavy lidded, and his curls are flattened on one side. He's wearing a Hellions Hockey hoodie and thick wool socks. His black shorts *barely* fall mid-thigh though, and Alex has never seen him so relaxed before.

As Alex takes his shoes off, his attention snags on a yellowing bruise marring the pale, pale skin of Noah's thigh, and his fingers ache, blood fizzing with the need to touch. He wants to press into the bruise and watch the skin turn white under the pressure so badly he can feel it in his teeth.

"Are you hungry?"

Alex doesn't look away from the bruise fast enough and Noah pulls a face, brushing his fingertips against the part showing below the hem of his shorts. Noah pushes down, the skin turning white just as Alex imagined and Alex has the inexplicable urge to knock his hand away, to cover the bruise with his own hand.

"Kev got me pretty good at practice last week."

Alex drops his bag by the door; slips his coat off; hangs it on the hook next to Noah's. He lines his shoes up on the rack Noah has his own on and tries to shake the feeling creeping under his skin. He's never reacted this way to a bruise before.

"So, are you hungry?" Noah asks. "Derek and Kev dragged me out for sushi to make up for, as Derek said, 'not geeking out over an orange moon' with me and I got extra for lunch tomorrow. You can have some though."

"Did you buy me dinner?"

"No, I bought myself lunch and I'm offering it to you because I'm *polite*," Noah says, but he's flushing a pale pink.

"You totally bought me dinner."

"If you say so…"

"I do, yeah," Alex says, following Noah the few steps he needs to see the rest of his apartment.

The kitchen is to the right and Noah busies himself in there as Alex takes stock of the place. The living space is about the same size as his and Brett's place, but the walls are bare, the bar top separating his living room from his kitchen a stark white marble, his appliances sleek silver, and everything feels so much bigger, so much colder, so much lonelier.

"Oh man, we gotta get you some decorations," Alex says, turning to take the container Noah holds out for him.

"I don't need decorations." Noah frowns, then hands Alex a glass of water.

"I didn't ask if you needed decorations."

"If I wanted decorations, don't you think I'd have some by now?" Noah asks, pulling a large, fluffy white comforter off the couch and wrapping it around his shoulders before curling up on one side of the couch, leaving Alex with more than enough space to spread out.

"You might not need decorations, but you can't convince me you don't want at least a little something to liven this place up. Maybe get a splash of Canadian red in here."

Noah makes a small harrumph of a noise and Alex snorts, almost choking on his first bite.

"Blood moon red it is, then."

Noah bites his lip, but his eyes are bright with a suppressed smile as he tips his head to the side and leans further into the couch. "You can go meet up with my mom and her art guy when she comes down here next month—pick the stuff out yourself if it's so important to you."

"I will absolutely spend the day with your supermodel mom picking out weird art for your apartment."

Noah wrinkles his nose. "Oh God, you think my mom is hot, don't you?"

"She's literally a supermodel, man, duh."

"Gross."

"You should be pleased," Alex says. "You got her looks."

Noah blows out a dismissive breath, but pink creeps over his cheekbones.

"Oh, don't pretend you don't know you're pretty as hell."

Noah's really blushing now, dark red smattering his cheeks. "Shut up."

"Just calling it like it is."

Noah makes a frustrated sound in the back of his throat, and Alex doesn't push it. Noah's so quiet while Alex finishes his food, he thinks he's fallen asleep again, but when Alex gets back from throwing his trash away, Noah blinks at him with a question in his bleary eyes.

Alex stretches his legs out on the couch, pleased when Noah doesn't tense up. "What's that look?"

"A little surprised you're here," he mutters.

"Why?"

Noah gives him a flat look and Alex raises one eyebrow, curious but willing to wait him out.

"Because we barely know each other," he says, somehow quieter than before.

"We know each other plenty," Alex says.

Noah sighs, the blanket cocoon shifting around him as he sits up a little. He doesn't mumble this time. "A lot of guys aren't comfortable finding out their friend is gay—" Alex blinks and Noah's eyes narrow. He sounds defensive when he asks, "What's that face for?"

"Nothing bad," Alex assures. "But you never actually came out to me, so I didn't know if you were interested in girls or not."

"Oh," Noah says, sinking back into the couch a little. "I guess thanks for not assuming?"

Alex laughs, and he catches Noah's grin before he shifts to hide it behind his blanket.

"You're welcome. But hey," Alex says, "I told you one of my boys likes guys—"

"What?"

"At the diner, when I said my aunt and Liv—"

"No, you said you knew guys in *hockey*."

Alex frowns. "Is that why you're surprised I showed up? Because I'm not actually comfortable around guys who like guys?"

Noah rolls his eyes. "No, you already showed up for coffee—you obviously don't give a shit. I'm just surprised in general. Like, it could've gone a lot worse. You know your reaction to me, and your friend, isn't always a guarantee, but especially not athletes."

"Yeah, I know."

Noah shrugs. "Maybe surprised wasn't the right word. I'm just glad you're not an asshole."

Alex smirks. "What was that? Can you use your best enunciation while I record you repeating that for the boys? They'll love to hear it."

Noah groans. "I knew, I *knew,* the moment that left my mouth you were going to be an asshole about it."

"But you like me, anyway," Alex says.

Noah makes a quiet, dismissive noise and Alex lets him have it this time—no need to push when he's already gotten more than Noah ever really gives.

"Hey." He nudges Noah again. "Don't pass out on me before you tell me where I'm sleeping. Do you have a spare room or am I crashing out here?"

"Out here, yeah," Noah says, making no move to get up. "The couch pulls out. And pillows and sheets are in the bathroom closet."

"Gonna move so I can sleep or—" Alex's mouth twitches, but he manages not to laugh at how hard Noah's trying to stay awake. "Don't make me carry you to bed, Anderson."

Noah huffs but disentangles himself from his blanket cocoon enough to stand. "Do you need anything?"

"Nah, just show me where your bathroom is... Oh wait, do you have a toothbrush?"

"You didn't bring a toothbrush?"

"I came here straight from the rink because you were being a big, impatient baby!"

"I was not!"

"You absolutely were! But it's chill—I'm pretty great, and you wanted to see me. I get it."

"I'm going to bed." Noah rolls his eyes, the fading pink flaring on his cheeks again. In the hallway, he points to a door on the left. "There're extra toothbrushes in the top right drawer by the sink. I've got an alarm set for half an hour before the cool part starts."

"Are there not cool parts?"

Noah wrinkles his brow. "I mean, the sun is constantly moving, but sunrise and sunset are what people wanna watch because it's pretty. Do you *want* to watch the full hour it takes for the moon to turn red?"

Alex raises his eyebrow. "Would you if I weren't here?"

"No. I set the alarm early enough so we could catch the last part of it. Since it's still pretty cool to see it transform."

"Then I'm good—this is your show."

Noah's mouth quirks with a ghost of a smile. "Okay." With his handle on the door, he pauses. "Goodnight, Alex. Sleep well."

The gentle smile Noah gives him makes Alex's heart go all warm and fluttery. His throat feels weird when he says, "You too."

It must be the chill in the air.

# Chapter Nineteen

IN THE MORNING, Noah wakes up to find Alex shirtless in his kitchen making eggs. He turns as Noah approaches and levels him with one of his megawatt smiles, and Noah doesn't know why he thought this was a good idea. He's tired and Alex is soft with sleep, looking at him like there's no place he'd rather be, and Noah can't stop himself from wanting in time. Noah aches when he gets a flash of Alex smiling at him first thing in the morning, face smushed into the opposite pillow. He wants it so badly it's hard to counter Millie's singsong voice in the back of his mind saying, *you have a crush.*

Alex drags his blankets onto the balcony and promises to start the laundry himself when Noah wrinkles his nose about them being outside. It is nice though, and Alex lights up when Noah tells him so, genuine and pleased, without a trace of smugness. This early, with this little sleep, the smile hits Noah hard, and his carefully maintained air of indifference slips when he can't contain his own. Alex is quiet in the mornings, but the silence between them is comfortable and when Kevin calls one minute before the time Noah told him the moon would be at its maximum eclipse, Alex perks up.

He takes the phone and affects his voice, giving his best impression of a planetary guide as he tells Kevin all the brand-new facts he looked up about the lunar eclipse. They get along the same way Alex seems to get along with everyone, so it's no shock when Kevin says, "Hey, we should go to breakfast after this."

Noah doesn't hate the idea but— "I wanted to watch the sunrise too."

Alex's eyebrows fly up and Kevin huffs out a quiet laugh. "Seems like you forgot to tell your guest there, Red."

"He can go back to sleep if he must," Noah says.

"I'm also still right here," Alex mumbles.

"Oh, don't worry. I'm passing out as soon as I hang up. I meant *after* Derek wakes up. We'll come to you—go to that place with the crepes Derek won't shut up about. Isn't it on the same street as Tiki's bakery with the croissants you like? We could stop and get you one."

Alex's eyes widen and he turns to Noah with a huge grin. "Is this your loophole for no sweets during the season? You love breakfast food because half of it's just morning dessert, don't you?"

Noah's neck heats and he frowns. "I will *occasionally* have an almond croissant if it's put in front of me, but it's not *dessert*."

"It is sweet though," Kev says with a sly grin. "He's got you there."

"I'm hanging up on you now," Noah says. "Go back to sleep—see if we wait for you for breakfast."

"You will," Kevin says. "You'll need someone to show all those sick moon pics to."

Noah grumbles and when the call ends, Alex slumps back in his chair, head tilted to look at the moon. "You good with me coming to breakfast?"

Noah purses his lips, disappointment curling through his stomach. "Uh, yeah? Unless you don't want to—"

Alex turns to Noah with a mischievous grin. "Oh no, just checking. This little interaction was not enough—I'm pumped to see what you're like in front of your teammates for real."

"The exact same I am with you."

"Mm-hm. You told me honey in your coffee was your idea of a treat when you like breakfast pastries! You're holding out on me—gotta see what other hidden depths you have."

Noah rolls his eyes. "You're so annoying. Tiki brings in croissants for everyone when we fly out on a road trip. It's part of his routine or whatever—he's apparently been doing it since juniors—"

Alex's eyes shine in the moonlight and there's a soft, amused grin tucked in the corner of his mouth. "Did you give him as hard of a time as you gave me about sweets during the season? Or am I just special?"

"More like you're not a goalie."

Alex's smile spreads and laughter bubbles out of him. "Of course, it's a goalie who's got a feeding teammates routine."

"Tiki's a big team guy—kisses the blade of everyone's stick for luck before we go out for warmups," Noah says.

"Really? That's sweet."

"Oh, yeah, real sweet. Then he smacks our helmets and says, 'keep the puck outta my fucking net, baby.'"

Alex barks out a laugh, claps his hand over his mouth as his shoulders shake, and his eyes crinkle with the force of it all. He takes several deep breaths, the laughter still obvious in his voice when he says, "Holy shit, what I would do to see the face you made when that happened."

Noah shoves at his shoulder, blushing as he remembers. "I take it back. I'm uninviting you from breakfast."

Alex smirks. "Can't, Kevin invited me."

"A lapse in judgment."

"Mm-hm, for sure." Alex nods emphatically. "So, what's that say about you letting me sleep on your couch?"

"Pullout bed."

Alex rolls his eyes. "Couch, pullout bed, whatever. You still invited me to sleep in your house—"

Noah can't hide his smile when Alex cuts himself off and corrects, "*Apartment.*"

But Alex is grinning as he says, "You're such a bitch sometimes—I love it."

Noah doesn't have a response, but Alex doesn't seem to mind lapsing into silence. He pulls his phone out and starts snapping photos for his story. Once done, he demands Noah abandon his blanket long enough for them to take a selfie. Alex holds himself carefully, making sure they don't touch as he tries to angle the phone right to get both them and the moon.

Noah blows out a frustrated breath, grumbling, "Will you come here?"

Alex's arm drops and he looks at Noah with furrowed brows.

The minute of chill is worth it to see the way Alex's face transforms in shock as Noah leans into Alex's side and pulls at the front of his shirt before he can think better of it, so Alex is leaning down next to Noah, finally close enough to duck their heads together. "Still not the best lighting, but at least now we're both centered in the frame."

Alex's posture loosens, and he swings an arm around Noah's shoulder, pulling Noah flush against his side. Alex seems unfazed, maybe even pleased, by Noah pushing him around if the way his smile has grown is anything to go by.

But Alex doesn't give Noah enough time to examine his own response, neither the pleasant warmth seeping through his body nor the flash of panic he gets from liking it, before he's pulling away and saying, "Not my fault you're pint-sized."

"I'm a perfectly average size."

"I have at least half a foot on you."

"It's at most five inches," Noah says, settling back in with his blanket. "Besides, you're just a giant."

"Gonna stick with you being pint-sized. It's better that way."

"Better for who?"

"Me, because it flusters you."

"God, you're such a dick."

"But you love me, anyway."

Noah can't help the noise he makes. "Don't get ahead of yourself—I tolerate you."

"Didn't we already go over this?" Alex asks with a smug grin and a raised eyebrow. "I could've sworn we already went over how inviting me here means you do more than tolerate me."

Noah twists his wrist through the air, unable to completely contain his quiet huff. "And it'll never happen again."

"And I totally believe you," Alex says.

When he glances over, Noah expects to see a sarcastic smile. Instead, Alex is looking at him with a soft little grin, and Noah doesn't know what to do with it or how to react, especially when he looks back out at the sky and says, "But seriously, thanks for having me over. This has been nice. Real pretty too."

It frustrates Noah how easily Alex can switch between teasing and genuine, and how it tugs at something deep in his heart every time Alex makes it clear he enjoys spending time with Noah. It's annoying that he even wants to hear it, and alarming how nervous he makes Noah.

Alex makes Noah's heart skip and his stomach swoop; makes him want until he's angry with it, but Noah likes being around him so much and as much as he tries to push it away, Noah knows it can only mean one thing.

It becomes harder to ignore the way his feelings for Alex are shifting when they start their next road trip off with an overtime loss he's not even on the ice for after taking a puck to the face. His face is sore and all he wants is to go to sleep, but he has a text from Alex waiting for him after getting stitched up and suddenly he's a little more awake and a lot warmer knowing Alex was watching him play.

### *Alex Valencia*
Mon, Nov 14, 10:03PM

How many stitches did you need for that
and are you on concussion protocol??
If you don't answer I'll assume you are

11:00PM

*Don't you have better things to
do than mother hen me*

Travel day tomorrow, I can sleep on the
plane
I take it you're not on protocol then

*Obviously not if I'm using
screens*

You could break the rules

*Don't like you enough to strain*
*my brain*

Rude

And here I was concerned about your
pretty little face being fucked up

*Depends on whether or not you*
*consider five stitches fucked up*

The phone rings almost immediately with a request to FaceTime, and Noah really should have expected that. He thinks about not answering, but there's a Chel tournament going on in Kev's room and Derek won't be back for a while and he really has no excuse not to.

"Even with a travel day, you should be asleep," Noah greets.

"Now who's mother-henning?" Alex asks, eyes soft and sleepy from where he's propped up against his headboard shirtless.

"What do you want?" He doesn't sound nearly as annoyed as he intended to be.

"Wanted to see the damage," Alex says with a small smile. "Not as bad as I expected after all that blood."

He must be more tired and banged up than he thought, because what he's thinking slips out before he can filter himself. "Take it I'm still pretty then."

The corner of Alex's mouth twitches. "Absolutely."

Noah rolls his eyes, but he knows he's blushing; heat burning through his cheeks and up his neck, the warmth of it all settling in his gut. "You can't keep calling me pretty, Alex."

Alex's mouth is a flat line for a moment, his eyes narrowing in a way Noah hates. "Why not?"

"Because—" *I like it. You don't mean it the way I want you to. I'm not supposed to be.* "It's not true."

"Are you fishing for compliments here?" Alex asks, his voice softer now. "Because I'm game for dishing them out, but you should know you can just ask me to hype you up without putting yourself down."

Noah's glad he's only got the bedside lamp on because his face is flaming now. "No, I'm not—" he huffs, all the warmth gone now that he's having to explain this. "I don't want you to hype me up; I'm saying I'm not *pretty* because guys aren't supposed to be pretty."

Alex snorts. "Uh, who said?"

"Don't be obtuse."

Alex's frown deepens. "Is this about your dad?" Noah says no too fast, and Alex sees right through him. "God, Anderson, your dad is the worst."

"My dad's not the only one who thinks like that, and you know it."

"Yeah, but he's the one who drilled it into your head so hard you can't even see plenty of people don't."

"Do you know what my dad said to me when he saw the pictures of us at Pride?"

Alex's face clouds with anger, his voice hard as he says, "Something terrible, I'm sure."

"He told me I couldn't get away with that shit." Noah's throat tightens as he remembers the tone of his father's voice, how lucky he was to not have to see his face as he'd ripped into him about it. "He made sure I knew I wasn't like *you*, or Thor, or any of the other guys, because I look like my mom—"

"Your mom is beautiful. That's not a bad thing."

"He means I already look *effeminate,*" Noah says, the word sharp on his tongue. "And since I'm already so fucking soft and prim, people will assume—" He swallows, tongue heavy, eyes stinging. "My dad made it perfectly clear a long time ago what he'd think of me being who I am."

Noah can still remember everything about the moment. The spatter of water coming from his mom's shower, the muffled voices of a couple talking about a wine tasting in the hallway, the contrast of the purple suit jacket his mother put him in lying against the white sheets, the slight itch of the lace collar of his shirt. He remembers how excited he'd been when his dad asked if he liked the fashion show, how his neck prickled under his dad's gaze when he spoke about meeting Sebastian Notting-ham, how the bubbly glee he had after spending the day with his mom twisted and soured at the cutting way his dad looked him over. He remembers how casually his dad said, "Better watch it, Noah. Guys might think you like them if you fawn over them looking like you do."

He remembers shrinking in on himself as his dad spoke, skin prickling beneath his dad's hardened eyes, so different from his casual tone, and how disappointed his mom was when Noah spent the rest of Fashion Week with his dad instead of going to another show with her as planned. Noah remembers going home so much more aware of the warm curl of curiosity he got looking at other guys.

"I'm really sorry, Anderson. No one should say that shit to you, but especially not your own fucking father."

"Yeah, well, it is what it is."

"But it shouldn't be. You shouldn't need to—"

Alex cuts himself off with a grimace and Noah's heartbeat spikes. "What?"

"Nothing."

"It doesn't *look* like it's nothing.

Alex frowns and he sounds a little annoyed when he says, "Come on, forget it. I wasn't thinking, and it's not my business to tell you what you need."

A frustrated growl rips through him. "I got hit in the face with a puck, got five stitches, couldn't play in the overtime *I* got us to, and *my face hurts*. Tell me what I want to know."

Alex looks a little dazed. "Of course, you're demanding when you're in a shitty mood."

"Stop deflecting."

"It's *nothing*. Why would you even care what I think?"

"Because you're my friend," Noah says, quietly pleased by Alex's surprised little blink. "Millie tells me I need to lighten up all the time."

"Yeah, well," Alex says, with a small grin. "She's right. You need to lighten up, try not to worry so much about being a generational—"

Noah snorts and Alex rolls his eyes. "Thought you were above fishing for compliments?"

"I am. It's far too early to be putting that label on me."

Alex purses his lips. "Yeah, all right. If that's how you wanna play it. Fine."

"It is. Now, what were you going to say?"

"Remember I tried to keep this to myself when you get upset."

"I won't."

Alex looks skeptical, heaving a huge breath. "I was going to say you shouldn't need to stop seeing yourself through your father's eyes."

The words fall heavy between them.

"This is why I wanted to keep it to myself!" Alex says, expression twisting into a mix of guilt and irritation.

"It's fine. You're not wrong."

"Yeah, but you already know that. I shouldn't be reminding you about it when you're telling me how much of a dick your dad is. And I know it probably sounds like an empty platitude, but I'm sorry you have to deal with this, and I wish it wasn't so hard for you."

"Yeah, well," Noah says, making an aborted shrugging motion he's unsure Alex can see other than the way it shifts the screen a little. "My dad could be the most supportive ally in the world, and this still wouldn't be easy."

"I know, and that sucks too! I hate all of this. It shouldn't still *be* like this."

"Obviously not," Noah says, amused by Alex's indignation. "But what the hell can we do about it?"

"I'll fight all the homophobes in the league. Absolutely rock their shit any time I hear it on the ice until you're comfortable coming out."

"Oh my God." Noah smiles despite himself. "Please don't."

"Why not? It's what they deserve."

"Maybe so, but you're way too good to be a goon."

"I can be both! I have layers." Alex's smile widens. "Besides, you're one of my boys now. I'd throw down for you anytime, anywhere. I'd do anything for you, babe."

Alex's sentiment makes Noah warm all over, the endearment making his cheeks burn bright and his heart do a flip. Of all the terrible, ridiculous hockey players to give him butterflies, Noah had to pick this one. Alex is a problem for Noah, something out of control, unknowable in a way Noah hates, but what's he going to do? He can't turn back to a time where Alex wasn't in his life. Not now, not when he's started to expect Alex's insufferable but endearing presence.

"I'll keep that in mind when you complain about my snack choices next time."

The way Alex claps his hand to his mouth, eyes crinkling as he tries to suppress his laugh, really drives home the point—Noah likes the one person he insisted he couldn't even be friends with.

# Chapter Twenty

THE HELLIONS DROP all four games on the road trip and the plane ride home is tense and quiet. They left Minnesota straight after the game and by the time Noah's back in his apartment, it's so late it's going on early. There's an afternoon skate tomorrow, and he really needs to catch some sleep if he expects to be at least semi-functional, but his mind is buzzing, and his skin feels stretched too tight.

He's desperate for the quiet calm he gets from playing chess with no obligation to text in between—but it's way too late to ask Alex to play and playing on his own does nothing to improve his state of mind. He tosses his phone aside and tries to sleep, but it becomes quickly obvious he won't be able to fall asleep without combating the rabid frenzy of his mind first. So, when Noah gets the urge to soak in lavender-scented water and relax, he ignores his father's sneering voice telling him boys don't like *spa shit* and fills the tub with the hottest water he can stand.

The heat stings then soothes the phantom stretch of his skin and while he doesn't think the lavender is as relaxing as Millie swears by, his mind slows as his fingers wrinkle. He dunks his head underwater and holds his breath until his lungs burn and when he comes up for air, his brain is blessedly quiet. He stays in the bath until the water cools, and when he falls into bed, he's out within minutes.

### *Alex Valencia*
Tue, Nov 22, 2:25PM

What do Canadians do on Thanksgiving

9:45PM

*Ignoring you*

Ouch
Not my fault Canadians celebrate on the
wrong day

*Oh I don't care about*
*thanksgiving*
*You were a bitch to me in my*
*dream so I'm ignoring you until*
*further notice but I didn't want to*
*leave you on read*

Think that kinda fucks up the whole
ignoring me thing

*Had to tell you I was ignoring*
*you so you knew it was different*
*than when I usually leave you on*

*read*

Maybe be a better texter so I'll know
you're actually ignoring me next time

*And give you what you want?*
*Absolutely not*

Since you've obviously given up on
ignoring me what did dream me do to
put real me in the dog house

*You disparaged my choices of*
*"living a little"*

What was your idea of living a little

*I'm not telling you*

Noooo you have to tell me
You know it'll drive me nuts

*I know :)*

YOU DID THIS ON PURPOSE

*Obviously*

You are the worst person I've ever met

*No I'm not*

Top five at least

But really what ARE you doing for
thanksgiving

*The Blackwoods are hosting a*
*thing for all the guys who don't*
*have their own American*
*thanksgiving plans*
*And then my mom thought this*
*was a perfect time to fly in for*
*her move lol*

I thought she wasn't here until December

*Deal closed early I guess*

When are we going art hunting

*..........*
*I'm not actually sending you in*
*my place*

Yeah but I'm down for going WITH you

*And why would I want that?*

Because you don't know shit about art

*Neither do you!*

Yeah but which one of us is more likely to
sweet talk the art guy into showing you
something cool instead of boring stuff

they think will be a good investment

*Not sure our definitions of cool*
*are the same*

Another reason you shouldn't go alone
You'll end up with bland art for your
bland apartment

*Back to insulting me I see*

YOUR APARTMENT IS IN GRAYSCALE
BUD
YOU DON'T GET TO PRETEND THAT'S
NOT BLAND

*So many feelings*

Think about it Anderson! You know it'll
be fun

*Our definitions of fun are*
*definitely different*

Only because you haven't TRIED my
definition of fun

*IF you're not on a roadie when*
*we go I'll text you*
*But that's all I'm giving you*

I knew you wanted me to go

           *That's not what I said*

You talk a lot of shit but I see right
through you
You love my company

           *Love is such a strong word*
           *But you do have a certain appeal*

That's practically a declaration of love
coming from you

*

WHILE DISCUSSING WHAT kind of art he might want, Noah makes the mistake of mentioning Alex, and his mom latches on like a limpet. He refuses to ask Alex about his practice schedule, but he's certain his mom checks the Renegades' game schedule before deciding on a day to meet with Sam. The Wednesday she chooses has only a morning skate for both of them—a fact his mom and Alex are far too pleased with. But what Noah imagined as a day full of his mom and her art guy dragging them around the city while steering them toward tasteful options and limited time for Alex to actually talk to her ends up involving a lot more input from Noah and far more strange looks from his mom than expected.

Sam Laurent, his mom's art *advisor,* is nothing like the stuffy man Noah expected either. He's tall and ridiculously handsome and he shows up to Noah's apartment with a tablet and an overeager attitude, asking Noah a million and one questions about what he likes, listening to Noah stutter through his answers with a heavy, rapt attention that only makes

Noah more flustered.

Alex talks as much as Noah expected, but he keeps giving these strange, steely looks to Sam when he ducks his head that Noah can't parse but have his mom smiling in an amused way. Then Sam swipes over to a set of landscapes featuring the moon and Alex's whole demeanor shifts.

"Can I see that?" Alex asks, taking the tablet from Sam and scooting in closer to Noah so he can lay the tablet across their thighs. "You gotta get something from this guy."

"I thought my apartment was *bland,* and I needed *more color.*"

Alex points to the lunar eclipse in the top right corner. "This one has red in it." To a moon caught over the ocean at sunset. "This one's multi-colored, bro." Another, of a full moon surrounded by swirls of bright green in an inky sky. "Oh hey, this is your jam."

"My jam?"

"Yes, it's like—what was it Derek called astronomy?"

Noah can't contain the quiet huff of laughter. "Pretty sky shit."

"Right! This is like *the* pretty sky shit. I bet even Derek would skip some sleep to see the Northern Lights." He clicks on the photo to enlarge it and hands the tablet back to Sam. "Is this something he can get, or is this one you're only gauging his interest in?"

"This is a limited print and could be acquired."

Alex knocks his knee against Noah's. "Get that one."

"No."

"But you like it."

"No, *you* like it."

Alex rolls his eyes, smile never faltering, "You do too. You're just being difficult."

His mom gives Noah the same amused look she's been directing at Alex. "I like these as well."

Alex looks so smug Noah facewashes him. "You're not supposed to agree with him, Mom."

Alex's eyes glint mischievously. "I seem to remember you saying I could pick your decorations out. A sweet photo of something I *know* you're dying to see one day is way better than what I'd cross-stitch you."

"You cross-stitch?"

"I haven't actually yet."

"Then why would you think to cross-stitch me something?"

"Oh right, Beaver's trying to get us all into it. His ex got him into it and now he thinks it's a good way to de-hockey for an hour. He bullied us into giving it a go for this year's secret Santa."

"And you haven't tried yet? Christmas is so soon!"

Before Alex can answer, Noah's mom cuts in, voice bubbly with laughter. "Have we lost you two? Do we need to call it a day? Let you think about whether you want any of these photos?"

"Please," Noah says, then turns to Sam. "I hope this wasn't too terrible an inconvenience. But I can't let him win on principle, you know?"

Sam gives him a small smile as he locks his tablet. "I'll have to take your word for it. But if you're interested in astronomy and this style of photography, there's a gallery opening that Simone and I are going to you might be interested in. Corrine Finch's photos will be there if you'd like to see them in person before deciding, but everything there will have a celestial theme, so you might find another artist you like if that is something you actually like."

"Oh, uh, I do."

"When is it?" Alex asks, shooting Noah a grin when he makes a noise of protest. "Oh, come on, it'll be fun. I'm sure you can convince Kev to get out of bed for this when it's not in the middle of the night. And

Brett will definitely be down."

"It's in January," his mom says, glancing between him and Alex with a knowing smile that sets Noah's teeth on edge. "And I know I'm biased, but I do think it'll be fun."

"January 12," Sam says. "That's the actual date."

"We should at least check our schedules," Alex says.

His mom looks so happy, and Alex's eyes are bright with excitement, and Noah can't find a reason to say no. "Only if it works with both our schedules because I'm not going alone."

He doesn't know where that answer comes from and the amusement his mom seems to get from it is annoying, but the twinge of anxiety he's been too obvious about how much he's enjoyed the day with Alex is soothed away by Alex's incandescent smile.

His mom gives them one more of those soft, amused smiles before seeing Sam out and despite all the space she's left in her wake, Alex doesn't make room between them when he grabs his phone off the coffee table. He just plants himself right along Noah's side, no space between them from shoulder to knee, and Noah doesn't hate it. It's actually kind of nice after how careful Alex was to not get too close to Noah last time.

His mom comes back a moment later and when she clears her throat Noah feels caught out, his cheeks burning as he looks away from Alex. Luckily, Alex doesn't notice, but Noah does his best not to look at him unless they're talking the rest of the day. He thinks he does a pretty good job of not being weird, but when Alex leaves to meet up with Brett and a couple of teammates for dinner, his mom gives him yet another knowing look and with sudden, pressing urgency, Noah must know. "Do you think Alex knows I like him?"

His mom looks surprised, and she asks carefully, "What do you mean?"

"Let's skip the part where you pretend to be surprised that I'm gay."

"I *am* surprised you're telling me. The last time I tried bringing it up didn't go well."

"Yeah, well...you're only the third person who knows, so."

"Thank you for telling me. I'm glad you felt comfortable doing so."

Noah rolls his eyes, mumbling, "Yeah, well, I kinda have an ulterior motive."

His mom arches a brow. "Oh?"

"I need to know if you think I'm obvious enough for him to see too. Like, you weren't exactly subtle about noticing I'm into him or whatever."

"Or whatever," she repeats, her mouth twitching at each corner.

"Yes, 'or whatever,'" Noah says, bringing his knees to his chest and curling his arms around his shins. "Sums up all these terrible feelings pretty well, actually."

"Why are they terrible?"

"Mom, come on."

"If you're worried he'll notice *your* feelings, I'd think it'd be obvious he's pretty"—her voice turns flat—"into you or whatever."

"Don't be ridiculous."

"No? You don't think so?" She sounds amused. "What reason would Alex have to be glaring at Sam the entire time he was here then?"

"He wasn't *glaring*—" Noah starts but stops when his mom gives him an unimpressed look. "Okay, so he was being weird, but he'd tell me if he likes guys."

"You think so?"

"I mean, I would hope so since I told him."

His mom looks shocked. "You did?"

Noah snorts. "Not intentionally, but yes. He's very perceptive."

She arches an eyebrow. "Is he now?"

"*Yes*, annoyingly so. Which is why I'm asking."

She looks thoughtful for a moment. "I'd say I'm pretty perceptive myself and what I'm seeing is telling a much different story than what you're seeing."

"Mom, please just tell me if I have to stop hanging out with him. I can't be around him if I'm broadcasting my feelings all over the place. I don't want him to know."

She considers him for a moment, works her jaw in the same way Noah does when he's trying to choose his words carefully, then sighs. "To me, he is much more obvious than you. He was frustrated about Sam making you nervous but ecstatic when you said you'd only go to the gallery if he went too. But if you're *sure* he'd tell you he was into guys, then I don't think you have anything to worry about. I'm obviously off my game, right?"

"Way off. He's got a girlfriend."

"Really?" Another emotion Noah can't interpret flickers across her face before her expression smooths out. "In that case, I'm pretty confident Alex isn't picking up on anything at all."

He's not entirely convinced, but the idea of Alex learning how he feels is mortifying, so he tries to internalize what his mother says. He and Alex don't get a lot of time to hang out in person, but when they do, Noah doesn't want to ruin what little they have being paranoid about Alex finding out how fast he makes Noah's heart race every time he calls him pretty, how much Alex makes him want, how much time he thinks about where things could go if they weren't public figures. Noah doesn't want to mess up this friendship and the easy acceptance Alex has given him by being obvious. So, he lets his mom's assessment soothe his racing brain, and for once, at least for now, refuses to worry about the what-ifs rattling around his head.

# Chapter Twenty-One

**Anderson**

Sat, Dec 3, 8:45 AM

> *You couldn't let me have the first*
> *hat trick in peace??? You had to*
> *one up me with FOUR GOALS*
> *ON THE SAME NIGHT*
> *Fucking infuriating*

10:20AM

How was I supposed to know you got a
hatty if I was in the middle of my own
game?

> *You obviously have a sixth sense*

Time zones worked in your favor though
You still got there first

You gotta buy me dessert next<br>week

And what do I get for the four goals

Whatever you want

*

THE HELLIONS WIN their next matchup and this time around, Alex doesn't have to seek Noah out. He meets Alex outside the Renegades' locker room with damp hair and a huge grin Alex doesn't get to see often.

"Holy shit, Anderson," Brett calls out from next to Alex. "Have you gotten faster?"

The tips of Noah's cheeks turn pink as he laughs. "No, but maybe you should start checking your skates for lead."

"Screw you," Brett says, but he's grinning, and Noah looks pleased with himself.

Watching their easy back-and-forth tugs at Alex's heart. The golden warmth of something *right* blooms through his chest.

They end up ordering in from a place around the corner from Noah's and after, Noah surprises him with a pint of his favorite ice cream.

When Alex says so, Noah's cheeks go pink, and Alex's heart flutters when he mumbles, "I know, I texted Brett."

As Alex expected, Noah won't split it with him, but after watching Alex lick his spoon clean with a pained expression as he stands to put it away, he lets Alex coax him into taking a bite.

He insists on getting a new spoon, because of course he does, and Alex follows him to the kitchen, not trusting Noah to indulge in one bite of dessert. His eyes catch on the smear of chocolate on Noah's bottom lip before he licks it away.

An indescribable ache for *something* threatens to crack Alex open, and Noah narrows his eyes when he turns around from the freezer. "What is with you tonight?"

"What do you mean?"

"You're smiling more than usual, which, frankly, should be impossible."

"I'm in a good mood."

Noah's eyes only narrow further. "I don't understand. I mean, you played well tonight but—"

"You don't have to sugarcoat it, babe," Alex laughs. "Y'all crushed us tonight."

"And you're still vibrating."

"Not everything's about hockey. You know that."

Noah rolls his eyes. "Yes, obviously. But you're not even a little down. I expected you to be—" He makes this aborted little motion with his shoulder, not quite a shrug, and heads back to the living room. "Dimmer than usual."

"Dimmer?"

Noah picks the remote up off his coffee table and settles in on the right side of the couch, back against the armrest, legs spread all the way out. "Yes, dimmer, more subdued, not the bright radiant ball of sunshine you force me to endure every other day."

"I think it's cute you still pretend to not like me," Alex says, patting Noah's leg until he makes room for him to sit.

"I think it's impressive you think I do anything but tolerate you," Noah says, punctuated by a quick kick to Alex's thigh.

Noah makes a soft, displeased little sound when Alex catches his ankle and the same warm, pleased thing heats his veins when Noah crosses his ankles over Alex's lap instead of shaking out of his grip.

"You never answered," Noah says after a moment. "Why are you in such a good mood?"

"You got me peanut butter ice cream."

Noah's face scrunches in curiosity, and Alex aches with the need to press his thumb to the slight furrow between his brows. Without thinking, he rubs his thumb over Noah's ankle bone and the warm, fluttery ache of Noah letting Alex touch him burns hot in his veins when he still doesn't move.

"You're this amped because I got you ice cream?"

"No, you got me my *favorite,* and had to text Brett to figure it out. Which explains why you were so comfortable chirping him; he's probably incessantly texting you now, huh?"

"Not nearly as much as you."

"Yeah, well…" He shrugs. "He's gonna add you to a group chat one of these days and you'll learn the hard way that we've got nothing on Nate. Wait until you wake up to twenty unread messages about who he's fallen in love with for the night, and then you'll realize how good you have it."

"Why would Brett add me to a group chat?"

Alex's cheeks burn a little, but laughter masks the embarrassment in his voice. "He says you're moving in on his and the boys' territory, so instead of a turf war, he'll just fold you into the group instead."

Noah's eyes widen as he chokes out, "What?"

"He's probably *mostly* joking, but there's enough chance he's not, so don't say I didn't warn you when it happens."

"That's insane; you know that, right?"

"Yeah, well, that's Brett for you."

Noah uncrosses his ankles and digs his heel into Alex's thigh. "Kinda embarrassing you like me so much your boys are jealous."

"Nah," Alex says, easy despite his heart suddenly rabbiting against his ribs. "I think you're pretty great. That's not embarrassing."

Noah ducks his head. "You're all right, I guess."

Alex runs his thumb over the knob of Noah's ankle again, the novelty of Noah letting him touch still just as intense. "High praise coming from you."

Noah rolls his eyes, but the corners of his mouth twitch even as he presses his lips together, and Alex doesn't need Noah to tell him upfront how he feels—the reluctant smile and the bright shine of his eyes says enough.

*

ALEX ENDS UP crashing at Noah's place and in the morning, he rifles through Noah's closet for a shirt that might fit only to get distracted by Noah's hat collection. There's an unbearable warmth taking root in his heart when he tosses the hat to Noah in the kitchen. "You actually kept it."

Noah's eyes widen as he catches it and his cheeks go pink even as he says, "This is a pretty generic Hockey Canada hat."

"Sure, but that's still my hatty hat."

Noah rolls his eyes, but the corners of his mouth tip up. "It's at least the same design."

"That it is." Alex's fingers itch to trace the pink across Noah's cheekbones, to point out that he's given himself up already, that Alex knows the truth whether Noah admits it or not. But then Noah pulls the hat on backward, and getting him to admit Alex is right doesn't seem as pressing with the satisfaction of Noah wearing the hat fizzing through him.

They walk to the same place they'd gone to with Derek and Kevin for breakfast after the eclipse and Alex can't stop smiling, not even when their waitress does a double take and grins. "I figured you two hating each other was a contrived story or whatever, but I'm gonna be honest; I didn't expect the NHL's shiny new rivalry to be brunch buds."

"This is an NHL mandated brunch," Noah deadpans. "We actually can't stand each other."

Her eyes light up and her mouth curls in a beautiful smile. "You're funnier than people make you seem."

Noah's cheeks turn pink, and Alex hides his smile behind his menu, nudging his foot under the table when he doesn't reply.

Noah blinks, looking lost when his gaze snaps to Alex, but then he turns back to the waitress, pastes on some approximation of a smile, and says, "I have my moments."

Her smile softens and her gaze lingers on Noah for a moment before she shifts back into server mode. When she leaves with their drink orders, Alex huffs out a laugh. "Bro, she's into you."

Noah snorts. "Unfortunate for her."

It is, but Noah fields her subtle flirting better than Alex expected, and it makes his teeth itch. He can't stop thinking about it, actually. He wants to know how differently Noah would respond to a guy flirting with him; if he'd blush as easily as he does when Alex compliments him; wonders what Noah's smile would do—if he'd bite down on it like he so often does with Alex or let the guy see how much he's into it.

On their way back to Noah's, Alex catches Noah checking out a tall man with broad shoulders and blond hair, and the desire to see Noah loved up and happy overwhelms him.

"Is that your type?"

Noah's gaze snaps to Alex and he stumbles a little. "What?"

"The blond guy at the crosswalk who looks like he stepped out of a magazine. Is that what you're into?"

Noah's face flushes. "Alex, we're in *public.*"

No one is nearby and the sound of cars passing is as good of a cover as any, but shame still curls through him. "Sorry."

Noah clenches his jaw. He's silent the entire way back but in the elevator's privacy, he turns to Alex with a steely expression. "Why do you even care?"

"I dunno. Curiosity, I guess. You never talk about it."

"For a reason."

"You could though...if you wanted to."

"You've said that before but—"

"But what? We're still not there yet?" Alex asks, chest tight while he waits for the answer.

But the elevator opens, and Noah exits without a word. He turns on Alex the moment the door clicks behind them, trapping him in place with the stubborn look in his eyes.

"We're never going to be there."

Noah's response is a kick to the gut. "Oh."

"I don't mean it in a bad way, I just mean—ugh." Noah's shoulders slump and he turns to the living room, flinging himself face first into the couch, barely comprehensible as he mumbles, "It'd be weird. I'd feel weird."

Alex has the sudden urge to run his fingers through Noah's hair.

He wants to pull where his curls are growing out around his neck and make him look at him; make him understand he would listen to whatever he has to say. He doesn't, of course. Instead, he curls his fingers into the armrest of Noah's oversized armchair until the need subsides and he can find his voice. "Why?"

Noah turns his head to glare at Alex. "What would you even say?" He affects his voice, deep and overly chipper. "Oh, Noah, he's so hot. Good choice."

"Wow, bud, you need to work on your impressions. When do I ever call you Noah?"

Noah rolls his eyes, but he doesn't turn away, doesn't hide his face in the cushions again. "Shut up, that's not the point."

"Then what is?"

"You're not into men."

"And?"

"And? What do you mean *and*? That's all there is to it. You don't actually want to hear about who I think is hot."

"I mean, I asked, didn't I? You think I would if I wasn't interested?"

"But why?"

"The same reason I let Sierra and Dani cry to me about their asshole boyfriends? The same reason I listen to any of the other guys talk about who they're seeing. I'm invested in your happiness, bro."

Noah's eyes narrow, his face clouding. "I just don't see the point. What're you going to do with the information? Send me guys on Instagram to follow? Set me up? Show me all the possibilities I'm missing out on?"

Noah sounds mean and Alex knows he's trying his luck, can see the way he's closing off, but... "I could..." Noah's eyes widen. "Set you up, I mean, not, like, taunt you with hot guys."

Noah rolls over, every line of his body rigid, and speaks to the ceiling. "No, you couldn't."

"Sure, I could. I know people. Liv definitely knows people." Noah cuts his gaze to Alex, and he recoils a little. "Or not...forget I said anything. No setups for you. I got it."

The space between them is taut with tension, the energy uncomfortable, and Alex can't stand it. "Have you ever thought—like, would you want me to introduce you to my friend?"

"I said I didn't want you to set me up, Alex."

"Ugh, no. I don't want to set y'all up. I meant you could talk to him about this shit. Y'all could lean on each other for support, understand each other in a way I obviously don't, communicate through bitchiness as you're both known to do."

Noah laughs and when he turns to Alex again, his face is softer and more open. "Thanks, but no. I don't actually *want* to talk about any of this. Like, ever. Not even to your bitchy bro who might understand."

Alex rolls his eyes, a mix of fondness and frustration twisting through him. "You can't bottle your feelings up all the time."

"You don't have to worry about me, Alex."

Noah's bright pink across his cheekbones, and Alex is about to say he does anyway when Noah grins, playful as he says, "Besides, I've got a Calder race to win—I don't have time to think about boys."

# Chapter Twenty-Two

"NOAH, BABY!" NATE calls out as soon as he spots Noah making his way toward their table.

Noah's cheeks turn pink, and Alex grinds his teeth as Noah lets Nate wrap him up in a hug and laughs into his shoulder as Nate practically lifts him off the floor in his excitement.

"Nice to meet you too, Nate." Noah pats his shoulder before dropping into the seat by Alex. "Didn't expect such a loud welcome."

Noah is loose and happy, unbothered by the brutal loss Jersey suffered against Anaheim, looking at Nate with bright, bright eyes and a tiny grin. Alex has spent the last week since he saw Noah ignoring the impulse to text him every second, and it's embarrassing how much he wants Noah to stop looking at Nate and pay attention to him instead.

Brett catches his eye as their food is being dropped off, then Alex's phone buzzes on the table. Brett's name lights up the screen and he stares pointedly until Alex picks his phone up.

Loosen your jaw, Nate's not your
competition.

Brett laughs and Alex glares back as embarrassment burns through him. He takes a deep breath and holds it as he rolls his shoulders. He should be happy Noah's comfortable enough with one of his friends that he's not tensing up at all, that the last few months in the league have opened Noah up to tactile affection outside the rink. Alex blows the breath out and does his best to unclench his jaw and stop being weird about Noah and Nate.

Nate dives into a story about losing his footing on his way off the ice and faceplanting right in front of Lisa, Anaheim's rinkside reporter, and Noah has to slap his hand over his mouth to stop his burst of laughter. Alex can't think of anything better than the sight of Noah laughing and the knot in his chest loosens, the desperate clawing need for Noah's attention settling as he says in his flattest, most disinterested tone, "I thought Alex was the most embarrassing person I know, guess I gotta readjust my list."

Nate's eyes light up and a wide, delighted grin spreads over his face. "I can't wait until we get you out to meet the rest of the guys. You're gonna fit right in, bud." He glances at Alex. "You think your mom's gonna let us crash at the beach house again this summer?"

"Uh." Alex's brain takes a moment to adjust to the rapid change of subject. "We'll need to check the schedule and make sure Sierra's not trying to have the girls out the same week, but yeah, I don't see why not."

Nate nods. "Cool. Noah, you should come."

Noah blinks in surprise, a little pinch of confusion forming between his brows. "What? No. Why would you—I don't even know most of you."

Nate's scheming smile mirrors Brett's and Alex knows Noah's just played right into their plan. He's not even surprised when Brett gets his phone out and says, "Seems like the perfect reason to finally add you to the group chat, huh?"

Alex folds his arms over his chest and grins when Noah turns a flustered pink and looks at him like he can stop this.

"I told you they were mostly joking. Not that there was no chance he'd do it."

Brett rolls his eyes, a sly grin on his mouth as he thumbs across his phone. "Like I'd joke about getting another source of material for roasting you."

Their phones start buzzing and Noah looks horrified when notification after notification keeps popping up. "I'm going to mute this immediately."

"No, you won't," Nate says with unwavering confidence.

Noah lets out an incredulous laugh. "How would you know? This is the first time you've met me!"

"Bud, if you're friends with Alex, you'll love us all." Noah opens his mouth to protest, and Nate adds, "*And* no one does summer like us. You don't wanna miss out on this just because you refused to contribute to the group chat and Mitch got his feelings hurt and banned you from coming."

"What—he doesn't even *know me.*" Noah sighs, but it sounds resigned and when he glances at Alex, there's a small smile tucked in the corner of his mouth. "Do all of you make a habit out of deciding someone's your friend with no input from the other person?"

"Only you, baby," Brett says.

A faint blush rises on Noah's cheeks and down his throat, but his voice is full of laughter when he says, "Can't imagine what I did to deserve such special treatment. I'm truly honored."

Alex presses his knee to Noah's under the table and when Noah presses back, Alex's stomach swoops. Noah doesn't even last all of dinner before he sets off a furious argument in the chat when he tells everyone Nate implied Mitch has the final say on who comes to group events. Alex's chest aches with how *good* it feels to have him slotting in so seamlessly with his favorite people.

*

THE WEATHER IS bad before the game, the snow coming down so hard Alex feels the bite of it lingering on his cheeks as he and Brett walk into the locker room.

"Dunno if you'll be able to grab dinner after," Brett says, already pulling his suit jacket off and unbuttoning his collar. "Heard it's only getting worse."

He expects Brett to be right, but he doesn't expect Coach Webb's soft but scathing indictment of their sloppy third period to be interrupted by the announcement that the blizzard conditions arrived faster than forecasted and they should stay put until the snow lets up. Which is understandable, a real logical safety precaution Alex is more than glad to follow—in theory. In reality, the teams don't have the option to brave the weather and Brett gets bored about fifteen minutes after he exits the showers, and his restless energy gets under Alex's skin.

"Hey, Joey!"

"What?" Joey calls back, not even glancing up from his phone.

"You think we can go back out on the ice?"

Joey looks up with a slow blink, his lips an unimpressed line.

"Why the hell do you wanna get back on the ice?"

"Brett's three seconds away from going feral."

Brett huffs but doesn't disagree. "Yeah, can we?"

"Why are you asking me?"

"Because Ax and Ketch ditched us for the WAG suite and you're the only A in here," Alex says.

"Ask Webber," Joey says. "Or play some fucking sewer ball like everyone else."

"If we wanted to kick things for fun, do you think we'd be in the NHL?" Brett asks. He claps Alex on the shoulder, a determined glint in his eyes. "Let's go sweet-talk the Zamboni driver."

The most strenuous part of the plan is finding the Zamboni driver but, in the end, they don't even have to sweet-talk Trent. There's a concert the next night and they'll have to resurface the whole thing after, anyway, so him and Brett messing around to get some energy out isn't any added hassle.

Ten minutes later, he and Brett are stepping out on the ice and Alex sees Brett relax as he skates backward, a huge grin on his face. "Wanna race?"

"Do *you* want to race?"

"I want to go to sleep. But we're stuck here, so...we might as well entertain these people."

Alex looks around. There's got to be more than half the audience still in the stands and he can feel their attention shift as they realize he and Brett are out on the ice.

He shrugs. "If you're fine with embarrassing yourself in front of all these people."

Brett laughs, a big burst of sound, as he drops his stick and takes off down the ice. "Screw you, bro. I'm definitely winning."

He doesn't then he does and by the time they've sprinted down the ice for the third time, Alex has settled.

"I see you ditched the lead in your skates tonight, Brett!"

Alex whips around at center ice so fast he nearly loses his balance. Noah's skating out with Derek and Kevin by his side, Reggie and Bowie stepping on the ice behind them, and Alex should call out to his teammates but all he can focus on is the pink flush of Noah's skin and how soft he looks in his team issued hoodie.

"Hey," Alex says. "Fancy seeing you here."

Noah rolls his eyes, but his mouth quirks up at the sides. "Someone stood me up for dinner and I had nothing better to do."

"How dare they!"

"Wait," Bowie says as he comes to a stop by them. "You two actually buy each other dinner after our games?"

"Uh, yeah," Alex says. "Why wouldn't we?"

"I don't know, but I thought you were fucking with us."

"Honestly," Reggie chips in. "I didn't think Anderson would actually have the patience to stomach your shit."

Alex scoffs. "Bro, Anderson loves me."

"Eh, I wouldn't go that far," Noah says.

Derek tsks. "You wouldn't go that far for anyone."

Kevin makes a low, thoughtful noise. "Maybe Tiki. But for the moon, Alex is definitely still in the lead."

Something ugly twists in the pit of his stomach, but Alex focuses on the rush of victory crashing through his veins instead. "I knew I was your favorite."

"As determined by *you*."

"And Kev too."

Noah rolls his eyes and Kevin shrugs, unbothered by the small scowl Noah has turned on him. "I call it like I see it, Red. But hey—" He shoves the bucket at his feet forward a little with his stick, revealing a bunch of pucks inside. "We didn't come out here to watch you two bicker. You wanna do drills with us or not?"

"Let's do something more exciting," Brett says.

Kevin looks skeptical. "Like *what*? I don't exactly think competitive bag skating is fun like you two apparently do."

"Nah, four-on-four."

Derek raises an eyebrow. "There's seven of us."

"And one of you is a goalie," Kevin adds, amused.

Reggie scoffs. "Fucking rude, bro. It's like you don't even know you're standing in front of the only goalie to score a goal in the last ten years. And I've done it *twice*."

Kevin actually looks a little impressed. "Well, in that case, let's go get ourselves another guy and see what you've got, baby."

"That's right," Reggie mumbles, posture straightening at the challenge.

"That's the spirit, boys," Brett says, the sharpness of his grin sending a zip of adrenaline through Alex as the thrill of competition sets in again.

*

**SNOWED IN SHINNY: Renegades and Hellions come together to entertain fans stuck at the Garden**

*With blizzard conditions setting in far sooner than expected and the mayor advising New Yorkers to stay put as the storm raged on, thousands of people were stuck at the Garden after the Renegades' December 21 game against the New Jersey Hellions. But the night wasn't a complete disaster according to fans at the game, especially for Artie Daniels and his six-year-old twin boys.*

*"There were a lot of guys out in the stands talking to kids and signing autographs and when Axelson came by and signed Sam and Tanner's jerseys, I'm thinking to myself 'this is better than anything we could get them for Christmas—nothing can top this,'" Daniels said when asked about not leaving Madison Square Garden until the early hours this morning.*

*"But then about an hour after the game ended, [Alex] Valencia and [the Hellions' Noah] Anderson are standing out at center ice chatting with a bunch of their other teammates and next thing we know, they're playing a little pickup game out there. At this point, the twins' eyes are popping out of their heads, you know. Those two are already so much fun to watch, really talented guys, but witnessing them messing around and having a blast outside of the game is something me and my kids will never forget, and it ended up being a really special night despite the circumstances."*

*

## Anderson

Sun, Dec 25, 12:45 PM

My mom says Merry Christmas

And what do you say

I'm just the messenger here

Merry Christmas to you too ya
fucking grinch

My dad's here
Not feeling festive atm

Shit I thought you were with
your mom

I am but he showed up at my place last
night

Gross

Probably should've seen this coming
With me ignoring him and everything

Maybe he should take a fucking
hint

Oh he knows
He just doesn't care
There's an image to uphold and all that

Why don't you come to mine then

It's Christmas

Which is why I'm offering

Alex come on

                                        *I'm being serious*
                                *It's Christmas and you don't*
                                *deserve to be around him*

I can't kick him out of my apartment
though
And I don't want to bail on my mom
either

                                        *She can come too*

And force my dad to go back to his hotel
alone on Christmas?
I'm sure that'll fly with Paul

                        *Anderson I straight up don't care*
                            *what the fuck your dad thinks*
                        *Tell him you had plans and bring*
                                    *your mom along*

But I don't want to be rude

                        *Showing up at someone's place*
                        *with no notice is rude, keeping*
                                    *your plans isn't*

We didn't have plans though

                                *But he doesn't know that*

Okay but he's not wrong about the image.
I don't really want to find out what the
reaction will be if people realize we're not
talking

*Take a Christmas photo and*
*throw it on your story and THEN*
*say you had plans and you gotta*
*go*

Isn't YOUR family in town

*Yeah, and?*

I don't want to intrude

*Seriously Anderson get your ass*
*over here*
*The more the merrier*

Let me talk to my mom

*HELL YEAH*

I didn't say yes

*Yeah you did*
*Lmk when you leave*

*

"SO, UH..." ALEX scratches the back of his neck as he looks up from his
phone, inexplicably nervous. "I hope y'all don't mind, but I invited a

friend over."

"This is your home," his mom says, gaze flicking up from the cookie dough she's rolling out in the kitchen. "You don't have to ask—you can invite whoever you want."

"Is it one of your teammates?" his dad asks, sneaking an undecorated cookie from the counter, mouth twitching in a small smile when Mom doesn't notice.

"Oh, no," Alex says, fidgeting in his seat, "it's Noah Anderson."

"Noah Anderson?" Sierra asks, twisting on her barstool to face him head on, eyes narrowed and the horrendous cookie she's decorating all but forgotten. "Like, your rival?"

"They're not rivals," Dani says from the breakfast table, phone in one hand, sticky gumdrop midway to the gingerbread in the other. "They're doing dinner dates after games."

"How do you know that?" Alex asks.

The look she gives him is cutting. "I have Twitter, Alex."

"Okay...and?"

Dani sets her phone aside, finally places her gumdrop on the gingerbread house, and gives Alex her full attention. "*And* when y'all were stuck at MSG during the blizzard, someone's thread about the game y'all were playing went viral and people are seriously into y'all's friendship."

"But that doesn't explain how you know we get dinner."

Dani rolls her eyes. "Yeah, but Addy and I text each other the most ridiculous things we see being said about you and Ben, so I'm always reading the replies—" She wrinkles her nose. "Which I don't recommend—and someone was giving the masses a whole timeline of y'all's relationship."

"A timeline," Alex repeats.

Dani smiles, shrugs one shoulder. "Like I said, people are obsessed with you two and apparently that guy is y'all's number one fan."

"Huh." Alex doesn't really know what to do with that information, but his chest is warm for reasons he doesn't want to untangle.

He turns back to his parents. "His mom's coming too."

Sierra drops her cookie. The tip of its hat crumbles as she whips back around to face Alex. "Simone DuPont is coming here?"

"Uh, yeah," Alex says. "That's his mom."

"Oh my God, Alex!" Sierra practically shrieks.

"What?"

"You didn't think hosting one of the most famous models in the world was information we needed before coming over?"

"She doesn't model anymore," Alex says.

"That's *not* the point and you know it!"

"Then what is?"

"The point is, I would've done my hair if I knew I was meeting someone famous today!"

"Your hair looks fine," Alex says.

"He's right, Sierra," Mom says, setting the rolling pin aside. She turns to lean back against the counter and surveys Sierra's appearance. "You look beautiful."

"And festive," Dad adds, cookie still in hand as he motions to her hair. "The tinsel scrunchie really bring the whole look together."

"Dad," Sierra whines. "Stop."

"Sierra, you look fine," Dani says, adding another gumdrop to her gingerbread monstrosity. "Besides, she was married to a hockey player and her son's one too. She's bound to have seen some truly horrendous clothes over the years." She glances at Alex, her smile sharp. "Just look at Alex."

"Hey! I also look fine."

Dani sweeps her gaze over him. "You've looked better."

"*I* look festive!"

Dani shakes her head. "It's not even your best Christmas sweater. If you're going tacky, you gotta go all in. Where's the one with you and your boys' faces on the reindeers?"

"You think *that's* my best one?"

"It's the funniest one for sure."

"Yeah, where's that one?" Sierra asks. "You wear that eyesore, and the one I'm wearing looks fine."

"Yours is seasonally appropriate already! Besides, I'm not changing so you can feel better about yourself."

"So, you agree—it's ugly?"

"Yeah, it's literally supposed to be!"

She narrows her eyes and drums her fingers on the countertop, her haughty expression turning into a smug little grin. "Looks like I'm not the only one worried about good first impressions."

"I've already met her."

"Wait, really?" Sierra asks, genuine shock written across her face.

"Yeah." Alex sits up a little straighter and brings his knees to his chest. "A few weeks ago, Anderson had me over to keep him company while her art guy tried to sell us some stuff."

"Weird."

"Okay, he wasn't actually trying to sell us art, but Anderson doesn't know the importance of decorations and—" Alex stops short. Sierra's giving him a funny look. "What?"

"Nothing," Sierra says, already turning around to get back to icing her cookies.

"No, obviously not nothing."

"It's nothing!" She turns back to him and crosses her arms, eyes blazing like she's gearing up for a fight. "I just think it's a little weird you and Noah Anderson get along, let alone enough to be chilling with each other's parents."

Alex's hackles rise. "Why?"

"He's kind of got a reputation."

"Yeah, and it's all wrong," Alex says through a clenched jaw.

"What kind of reputation?" Dad asks. "He seems quiet and well mannered."

"For sure. It's nothing too terrible," Sierra says, grimacing as she glances between their parents. "But he's not like Alex."

Mom purses her lips. "What do you mean?"

Dani snorts. "She means people think he's an awkward bitch with no personality."

"Daniela Rose!" Dad hisses.

Dani throws her hands up in surrender. "I didn't say it's what I think." Dad gives her a flat look and Dani bats her eyes like she always does to get out of trouble. "It doesn't count as swearing if it's a direct quote!"

Alex's temper boils under his skin and heat creeps up his neck. "He's got a personality."

Dani cocks an eyebrow, but before she says anything, his mom cuts in with an amused voice, "Does that mean he *is* a bitch?"

She startles a laugh out of Alex, amusement spiking through his anger. "I mean, a little, yeah."

His dad heaves a sigh, pinching the bridge of his nose. "Can we please stop calling this kid a bitch?"

"Pretty sure Alex means it super affectionately," Sierra says, mouth curling up on one side like she's caught Alex red-handed.

Alex narrows his eyes. "Now what?"

Sierra glances at Dani and when Alex follows, Dani is staring at Alex with a similar grin, but her wide eyes cut through the smugness Sierra radiates.

"What?" Alex snaps.

"You like him, don't you?"

"What? Of course I do, Dani! You think I'd invite him over on Christmas if I didn't?"

Sierra groans. "No, you *like* him. You've got a crush on him."

"No, I don't," Alex says, annoyance flaring.

"Sierra," his mom says, warning. "You know he and Liv are—"

"Not actually dating," Dani interjects.

His mom rolls her eyes, the same as always, ever persistent in her belief the two of them will end up married one day. Then her face goes serious as she looks at Sierra. "Still. Don't tease your brother. It's cruel to use sexuality as a joke."

"Wow." Sierra rears back. "I would literally never."

"Well, you're wrong," Alex says. "I'm not into him or any other guy. I'm still just as straight as ever."

Sierra narrows her eyes, but doesn't push, and no one else speaks for a long moment. When his dad does, he sounds gently cautious. "It would be okay if you weren't though."

"Obviously."

"But if you were unsure—" his mom starts.

"But I'm *not*. I'm not."

"Okay," Dad says after a beat. "That's okay too."

Alex huffs out a laugh, smiling despite himself. "Glad we got that all cleared up."

The room is tense. Neither of his sisters look particularly convinced, while his parents are communicating across the kitchen entirely through micro expressions and coming to God knows what conclusion. Alex doesn't understand why everyone thinks his feelings for Noah are anything different than his feelings for his other friends.

They've always been good at moving past awkward moments, but the heaviness lingers for longer than usual and Alex is about to retreat into his room when his mom taps the rolling pin against the countertop. "Well, I hope none of you think having a supermodel over will stop us from playing charades. Me and Dani have a title to defend."

"Absolutely not," Sierra whines. "If I can't change out of this outfit, I draw the line at playing charades with anyone outside of this room. Y'all are embarrassingly competitive. And you—" She jabs her finger through the air at Alex. "Are embarrassingly bad at charades and I can't believe I'm still stuck with you."

"Wow," Alex says, laughter bubbling out of him, the last remnants of tension disappearing from the room. "I think you've misremembered your own talents here."

Sierra cocks an eyebrow. "Oh, you're confident in yours, then?"

Nothing good ever comes from the look in Sierra's eyes and Alex knows there's a challenge waiting on the other end of her tone, but he always ends up taking the bait and Sierra knows it. She's counting on him not being able to back down, and part of Alex knows not giving her the satisfaction of playing right into her hand would infuriate her and give him a win, regardless. But Alex is who he is, and Sierra knows he won't be able to let this be. She knows he'll walk right into her trap, no matter what, and this time is no different.

"Yeah," Alex says. "I think I'm pretty good, actually."

"So, I guess you won't mind putting it to a test?"

"Not at all," Alex says, wondering where exactly Sierra is taking this.

"If we lose, again, which we will, I get to ask you a question and you can't lie to me."

Alex is hot all over. "No deal. There's no way to keep you from sabotaging us."

Sierra beams at him, eyes glinting like she's already won. "Mm, thought you might say that."

"Then you should've come up with a better plan. Now you get nothing."

"I have a backup," Sierra says, her smile sharp. "I'll join mom and Dani; you can team up with Noah and his mom. They're a wild card—we don't know their skillset—it could go either way."

Dani snorts. "It could not! Me and Mom have this on lock. Guarantee it."

"And if you don't, what do I get?" Alex asks.

"First dibs on the beach house this summer. You get to block out whatever week you want—no negotiations needed."

"Sierra, you know all I need to win is the proper motivation," Alex says, the thrill of competition already tingling beneath his skin. "And you just gave it to me."

# Chapter Twenty-Three

NOAH PAUSES WITH his fist an inch from the door, grimacing as he glances at his mom. "Maybe we should go?"

His mom's gaze snaps to him. "Go as in leave?" Noah nods and she pinches her eyebrows together. "Why would we do that?"

Noah pulls at the hem of his sweater. "We're intruding. We should just go back to your place."

Her expression softens. "Oh, honey, his family's going to love you."

"That's not—" She cocks an eyebrow and Noah sighs. "I get nervous and then don't make a good impression and I—"

"Want them to like you?"

Noah huffs, looking at his shoes. "Yeah, obviously. But I'm used to that—Mom, please, I know I rub a lot of people the wrong way. You don't have to pretend otherwise."

She purses her lips. "Fine, then what is it?"

He shrugs, tracing his finger over the edge of the box of cookies they brought, resisting the impulse to undo the bow of ribbon his mother had tied it up with. "Alex will be weird if they don't, and I don't want it to ruin Christmas for him or whatever."

"Did you tell him we were coming?"

"I texted him from the lobby," Noah says with a sinking realization.

She hums. "We obviously can't bail if we already said we'd come, but even if we could—" She raises her fist to knock. "Don't you think not showing up would ruin his Christmas more?"

She knocks before he can answer and the door swings open almost immediately, which seems to please his mom.

Alex's smile is radiant, and Noah tries not to fidget as Alex looks him over.

"Anderson, look at you! A red sweater? I thought you were allergic to anything other than shades of blue and gray."

"I wear red all the time," Noah says, smoothing out the front of the outrageously soft knit sweater his mom bought so he could coordinate appropriately with the green sweaterdress she's wearing.

"No, you wear black with *splashes* of red on team issued clothes. I haven't even seen you wear one of the red hoodies the other guys have!" Alex reaches out to pluck at the sleeve of his sweater. "This is so much color. And so soft—" He looks at Simone, smiling softly. "Merry Christmas, Ms. D., you made him wear this, didn't you?"

"Merry Christmas, hon. Thank you for having us over. And *made* is such a strong word, Alex. I bought it and gently suggested it would be nice for him to wear."

Noah snorts and Alex's eyes shine with laughter as he moves back to let them in. He doesn't get more than a couple of steps inside before

Alex catches his wrist to stop him from following his mom.

Noah closes his eyes. His heartbeat skips and when he doesn't look back, Alex tugs at his arm until he turns to face him.

"Thank you for coming over," Alex says, the weight of his gaze heavy and intense.

Noah tries to smile, but it feels sticky at the edges, heat creeping back over his cheeks, up his neck. "Thanks for inviting us. I don't think my dad bought it, but—" He shrugs. "He left without a fight, so...I appreciate it."

"I'm glad you're here," Alex says, his fingers tightening around Noah's wrist momentarily.

Noah's pulse skyrockets; he can feel it in his ears. His gaze dips to Alex's fingers curled around the cuff of his sweater.

His heart sinks when Alex drops his sleeve. He lifts the box of cookies up, skin vibrating. "I brought my grandma's maple brown sugar cookies. The icing turned out pretty bad, but I think—"

"Did you bake cookies for me?"

"No, I made cookies for your family and my mom brought wine. You know, host gifts or whatever."

Alex laughs, his eyes bright and shining as he waves his hand dismissively. "Whatever. You totally made me cookies. Come on—" He nods down the hall.

As Alex shuffles him forward, fingers intent on Noah's shoulders, he catches his mom's eye and his face flushes at the unspoken *I told you so* written all over her face.

"Also," Alex says as they turn the corner toward his living room. "I hope you two are good at charades, because I've got a lot riding on the game we're about to play."

Noah glances toward his mom; her eyes glint, and Noah groans.

"You don't know what you've set yourself up for, here, Alex. She's a monster about party games."

"Perfect," Alex says. "We're gonna need that kind of energy if we want to take down my mom and Dani."

*

ALEX PRESSES THE tips of his fingers against the middle of Noah's back as he introduces him to his family. The touch sears right through his sweater, distracting him to the point the intense assessing looks both Alex's sisters give him, and the pointed way they turn to Alex after, barely even crack him open with nerves. But then Alex pulls his hand away and the frenzy he was working himself into before comes crashing back down. Noah tries not to vibrate out of his skin when Alex's parents pull him into a conversation about the season, tries to stop the rabbiting beat of his heart, tries not to fidget with the collar of his sweater even though the longer the conversation goes, the itchier the fabric becomes. But it's hard when he wants their approval in a way he's never cared about anyone else's opinion—except his dad's, which Noah knows is entirely different from this.

When he gets a loud, vibrant laugh from Lucas Valencia after he tells the story of Derek getting locked out of their Dallas hotel room in just a towel, Noah's nerves settle some, leaving room for excitement to build as their game of charades begins.

Noah's mom is as over-the-top as he remembers her being, but she fits right in with Alex's family and Noah can't help but get caught up in it all. The ever-present thrum of unease is forgotten somewhere between Alex's ear-piercing argument with Sierra over whether he cheated by saying no instead of shaking his head when Noah was wrong and Alex throwing a pillow at Dani when he fails and she taunts, "Better prepare your answer, Sierra's coming for you."

It's hard to worry about being too much or too off-putting when Alex is sitting beside him swatting at Sierra's arm every time she guesses correctly, when Dani is heckling Noah the same as she does Alex, when Jasmine Valencia is telling his mom she wants her on her and Dani's team next time—as if this could happen again. It's hard to get caught up in his own insecurities when Alex's family is every bit as welcoming and enthusiastic about Noah and his mom being there as Alex himself.

They're tied in the last round, and Lucas, who kept score with a gentle chirp here and a snort of laughter there, gets up, tells Noah and his mom he's the only one who gets to act out the tiebreakers. He's already pressed hip to thigh with Alex on the couch, no room to wiggle, but he still manages to crowd further into Noah's space as Lucas draws from the bowl. Alex's palm is hot against Noah's neck, breath tickling across his ear when he whispers, "If you get this right, I'll take you to that new brunch place you've been wanting to try."

Noah swallows, the sound clicking in his ears, and despite Alex's proximity, he sounds unaffected, playful but a little loud, as he asks, "Are you trying to bribe me into winning your bet against your sisters?"

Alex squeezes Noah's neck and lets go, laughing as he falls back into his spot, no longer invading Noah's space. "Yeah, I am. Are you gonna lose just so I will?"

"I might."

"Liar," Alex says, eyes glinting with a challenge.

"Don't worry," Dani says. "You're gonna lose even if you try."

"So, you'll still get the satisfaction of Alex losing," Sierra adds. "Might soften the blow of losing yourself."

But Noah gets it right on the first try, and Alex crushes him against the armrest with the force of his hug, punching a huff of laughter out of Noah and a groan from Sierra.

"You just won us first dibs on the beach house!" Alex says, so close his lip drags against the shell of his ear in the commotion.

"Yay?" Noah says, flushing deeper when he notices Sierra watching them over Alex's shoulder.

She looks a little smug, but Noah doesn't have time to parse out why, because Alex leans back just to shove at Noah's shoulder, pressing down when Noah tries to sit up.

"Yes, yay," Alex says, exasperated. "Now we don't have to worry about Sierra calling dibs for the Fourth. We just have to make sure our schedules line up and we're good to go."

Alex sits back, a pleased grin dimpling his cheek, and without Alex holding him in place, Noah's mind is clear enough for understanding to dawn on him. He sits up, gaze flickering back to Sierra, whose expression has only grown more intense, and she beats him to saying anything. "You're inviting Noah to your boys' trip?"

"Yeah, he's still being stubborn but"—Alex looks to Noah's mom—"I'm counting on you to make sure his schedule is free."

His mom laughs. "Alex, you should know by now Noah never tells me his schedule." She gives Noah a significant look before turning back to Alex. "But don't worry, I'm sure Noah will make it work for you."

Noah flushes, blood rushing in his ears. He mutters, "Oh my God," under his breath as his mom makes her way to the kitchen, casually asking Alex's parents if they'd like some of the wine she brought like this isn't the worst conversation Noah has ever been a part of.

Lucas gives Noah a reassuring smile over his shoulder as he follows Jasmine and Simone, and Noah isn't sure what for until the three of them are chattering away in the kitchen. Dani waits a beat, then plops down on the coffee table to stare at Alex for a long, drawn-out moment, while Sierra makes room for herself on the couch, a pleased but curious smile blooming across her face when Alex makes no room between himself and Noah.

Noah's heartbeat kicks up like he's about to be caught, like any moment he'll blurt out they need to stop before Alex thinks better of letting his boys goad Noah into spending the week with them. Alex must notice because he knocks their knees together and shoots him a reassuring smile. "Will you two quit being weird? You're freaking Anderson out."

Noah makes a strangled noise in the back of his throat and Alex beams at him when he mumbles, "Don't drag me into your family drama."

"Sailed straight past that when you got an invite to Christmas," Sierra says.

And okay, fair, but Noah's ears still burn.

Dani looks back to their parents, who don't seem to be listening, but probably are, and drops her voice, sort of, to say, "I'm sorry, but can we get back to the truly astronomical news of you inviting him to your NTDP boys' trip? He's not even NTDP adjacent!"

"Yeah," Sierra says, still looking at Noah. "He's *Canadian.*"

Noah snorts, but Alex bristles, muscles working in his jaw. "And?"

"He doesn't know anyone but you and Ben," Sierra says, finally dragging her gaze away from Noah and looking at Alex.

"And Brett," Dani says.

"Uh," Noah says. Alex's tension makes him nervous, makes him want to direct the attention away from him. "Nate actually invited me."

"Oh my God," Dani says, face lighting up with delight, the hush she'd been using forgotten. "Nate as in *Nathan Hoffman?*"

"Yes?" Noah answers as Alex asks, "Why're you saying his name like that?"

"Well one, he's a fucking smoke show—"

"Jesus, Dani," Sierra laughs.

"What? It's the truth," she says, unabashed. "Anyway, he's obviously the coolest of all y'all, so—" She shrugs when she looks at Noah. "You're obviously nothing like people say you are if he likes you."

"Or, Nate just likes stick-in-the-mud assholes," Noah deadpans.

Despite the furious flush of his cheeks undercutting his delivery, Alex's sisters both laugh, the sound slicing through the strange tension building around them. Dani's laugh is loud and bursting, much the same as Alex's, and Sierra's is quieter, doesn't fill the space the same, but her eyes twinkle with it and Noah has to bite down a smile when Alex looks at him like he's accomplished something great.

# Chapter Twenty-Four

### *Do or Die + Noah*

Sun, Dec 25, 10:45 PM

**Sean Yates**
Remember how I said my dad sent me an

NDA to keep on my phone after I came

out?

**Brett Stevenson**
...yatesy wrong chat

**Mitch Lawrence**
Watch what you say Anderson

**Kaden Devine**
We play in a couple days and I won't

hesitate to fuck you up if you say the

wrong thing here bro

**Sean Yates**
Yikes maybe we did need a more distinct

chat name 😬 ok so Noah I'm bi

Don't be a dick about it because it'd

really hurt Alex's feelings if he couldn't

be your friend anymore and that'd bring

the mood down for everyone

**Alex Valencia**
You can trust him yatesy

*Seriously, you can*

*But I'll sign your NDA if you*

*want*

**Nate Hoffman**
hell yeah 🙌 I knew I liked you bambi

**Nate named the conversation "the one with bambi** **"**

Sun, Dec 25, 10:59 PM

**Aidan Beaverton**
Vibe check passed

*Nicknames already?*

*Do I even want to KNOW why*

*you're calling me bambi*

**Johnny Russo**
Aww he'd even sign your hookup NDA,

maybe Alex IS a good judge of character

**Alex Valencia**
Thanks I guess??

You're really not gonna give him shit

about BAMBI??

**Mitch Lawrence**
Good bc I'd hate to deprive hockey of the

next great one but 🐀 do or die baby

**Ben Huskins**
What'd I say about murder threats in the

group chat

**Sean Yates**
Non dicklosure agreement actually

And the eyes duh

**Mitch Lawrence**
Maybe I meant I'd break his knees you

don't know

**Nate Hoffman**
'Do or get a career ending injury' doesn't

really have a ring to it Mitchy

*I know better than to complain*

*about a nickname*

*Julien STILL calls me ice king*

*thanks to Ben*

**Ben Huskins**
Whoops 😊

You can thank beav for this one though

**Mitch Lawrence**
Death for not loving the boys it is then

Deal with it husky

**Aidan Beaverton**
I was so right for bambi eyed dreamboat

You're welcome Noah

*Could be worse*

**Aidan Beaverton**
Okay now that we've established no one

needs alibis can we get back on topic

What about the nda?

**Sean Yates**
Oh right I think my dad's part of some

gay hockey whisper network?????????

He said the NDA is always the safest bet

while staying in the closet but if I hated

it, I could always go for other hockey

players (or athletes) since mutually

assured destruction is a pretty good

substitute for trust

And I kinda laughed it off but he got all

serious like "I know this is a tough spot

for you to be in, Sean, but Ford wasn't

the only one in the league, and he isn't

the only one at our agency, and I know

ways to get my clients, and my son, in

touch with the support systems they

need"

**Shane Parson**
Bro that's wild. If you end up hooking up
with Tate Bradley please do whatever you
have to do to convince him to let you tell
me

**Aidan Beaverton**
Guess it does kinda make sense for the
agent with the most nhl clients to have
experience with closeted athletes

**Sean Yates**
Why? Are YOU going to want to hook up
with him

**Shane Parson**
I might fucking consider it for him

*

WHEN THEIR FAMILIES left, Noah told his mom he'd be back at hers later. But before the movie even started, and without Noah having to ask, Alex dumped his huge, fluffy comforter on Noah's lap, and not even halfway through *The Santa Clause,* Noah was warm and sleepy and re-gretting the inevitability of removing himself from his blanket cocoon on Alex's couch.

Now though, his heart jackrabbits against his ribs as he looks be-tween his phone and Alex in rapid succession. The air has been tense since Noah picked his phone up, but even if Alex isn't saying anything, the space between them has turned thick and expectant as Sean's last messages go unaddressed. He won't let Noah avoid this forever.

"I guess—" His throat is tight, mouth dry. He licks his lips, tries to swallow down the scratch of his voice. "So, Sean's the friend you were telling me about?"

"Yup."

"That's cool. Nice of his dad—" He has to clear his voice again. "It's good of his dad to be supportive like that."

Alex looks far too pleased. "It's good for you too."

"How so?"

"Proves you don't have to bottle yourself up just so you can play hockey. There are guys out there doing what you think is impossible."

"Yeah, that's good to know but—"

He can already feel the little piece of hope he can never quite get rid of flaring up. Noah frowns. "I still don't want you to set me up."

"Rude," Alex says. "But fine. Yatesy's dad is your agent, right?"

"Uh, yeah."

"So, he could help you."

"Set me up?"

A series of emotions flit across Alex's face, none sticking long enough for Noah to interpret, but he ends up smiling, amused and a little sly, so Noah doesn't think too much of it.

"I meant get you an NDA or set you up with your own gay mentor or whatever, but I think you're onto something here, babe. You're hot, the next face of hockey, and good company when you want to be. I'm sure any guy in the league would be happy to take you out."

All Noah can do is blink, stomach hot with Alex's assessment, cheeks burning in embarrassment. He throws the blanket off, too hot. "I don't know about all that."

Alex rolls his eyes. "Bud, straight guys think you're pretty. You're gonna clean up once you put yourself out there."

"I don't think other guys calling me a pretty boy is the compliment you think it is."

Alex furrows his brow. "Who's calling you a pretty boy?"

Noah shrugs. "Guys on the ice, people in Instagram comments. It's not usually followed by anything nice."

"Who? Which guys on the ice?"

Alex looks furious and Noah doesn't mean to laugh but— "I already told you; you can't be a goon."

Alex makes a dismissive sound and waves his hand in the air abruptly. "There are other ways to fuck guys up."

"Alex," Noah says, amused.

"No, I'm serious. I'm not on your team, Anderson. I don't hear the shit that gets said to you outside of our games. And I know it's not coming from our guys." Noah purses his lips and Alex raises his eyebrow. "Is it?"

"Not that I've heard, but—sometimes people aren't who you think they are."

Alex huffs, arms crossed over his chest. "I'm not saying every guy in my locker room doesn't have shit to unlearn from the environment we've grown up in, but Ax made it pretty fucking clear when we watched that presentation about creating a welcoming locker room culture for *everyone* that he'd gleefully use us for slapshot practice if we ever said shit like that."

Noah's laugh bursts through him. "He what? He's got the hardest shot in the league—"

Alex grins. "Exactly. It's a good deterrent. And I know it's not—" His smile drops. "If you're hearing it on the ice, then there aren't enough captains running their teams the right way, but I know Ax isn't the only one. Nate and Kaden's captains might not be threatening their team-mates with slapshots but from what the guys said, they're serious about it too."

"Okay, yeah, the league's making progress. But—"

"Look, I'm not saying it's perfect, and I still want to know who's saying it so I can at least accidentally high stick them in the mouth about it next time I see them, but I'll circle back to that because we're getting off track. This is about you being a total fucking catch I know guys will want to take out."

"I really appreciate your conviction here, but I told you I don't want anyone in hockey to know about this."

"Even if they're into guys too?"

"I know mutually assured destruction is a pretty good incentive but I'm not ready for people to know yet, Alex. You, Millie, and my mom are the only ones who know, I'm not doing any NDAs or letting anyone set me up when I can't even come out to Julien!"

"You haven't told Thorn?"

Noah glares. "No. I told you it was only ever supposed to be Millie. You and my mom are the ones who fucked it up for me."

"My bad," Alex says, unrepentant and smiling. "But look how it brought us together!"

"That's one way to look at it."

"It's the only way," Alex says and after a quiet moment, he cautiously adds, "You know him better than me, but I think Julien would be cool about it."

"Yeah, probably. I've been thinking about telling him when we play Detroit again. But even if I do—"

"Still no setups, I know. I just want you to have people you can talk to. And if you won't take a gay Yoda—"

Noah groans. "Never say that again."

Alex rolls his eyes, grinning still. "A gay *mentor* from your super connected agent with a bi son—"

"Oh my god, shut up," Noah says through laughter. "I'll tell Julien eventually, but I don't wanna talk to him about boys any more than I want to talk to *you* about boys."

"Yeah, I know. But you gotta tell Julien before you'll consider telling Yatesy, and that's the real person I want you to connect with. He could use someone to talk to who actually *gets this* just as much as you."

Noah's chest aches, his heart fluttery. Affection warms him all over as he realizes Alex wants Noah to be there for Sean as much as Sean is there for him. He's worried about them *both*.

"Once I tell Julien, I'll consider telling Sean, okay?"

"Really?"

"Yeah, I mean, I don't know how much good I'll do him but"—he shrugs, the tips of his ears burning—"it might be nice to have someone who knows first-hand what I'm going through."

Alex smiles, big and bright and honest. "That's all I want, bud."

*

JULIEN TEXTS HIM a couple of days later to set up dinner after their game the next night and the fiercely protective way Alex's friends reacted to Sean accidentally coming out to him flashes in his mind. He can't be sure, but he remembers Julien's reaction to Ford and thinks he might find the same thing in Julien as Sean has found in all his friends.

He runs through a million different scenarios before meeting Julien outside the visitors' locker room and any lingering apprehension is pushed aside when he sees Kaden hanging all over him. Noah's mind stutters to a stop; he forgot one of Alex's boys played for Detroit and didn't prepare to meet another one of them, doesn't know what he'll do if Kaden ends up greeting him the way Nate did—loud and affectionate like Noah's more than a friend of a friend.

Julien spots him first and Kaden makes a displeased noise as Julien disentangles from his clinging grip, but he perks up when he sees Noah. He has a split lip and a nasty bruise blooming on his cheek, and when he smiles at Noah, he hisses, bringing his hand up to his mouth.

"Fuck." He pulls his hand away, but there's no blood and it only makes him smile harder, fist pumping. "Nice."

Julien looks back, rolling his eyes. "I swear, Kade, if you bust a stitch...."

"You'll get to say I told you so, which I know you love to do," Kaden says, winking at Noah behind Julien's back.

Noah snorts, because he's not wrong, and Julien shakes his head, amused when he asks, "Wanna tell me why all these Americans are obsessed with you?"

"My exceptional personality."

"That's definitely it," Julien says with a wide grin.

"One hundo percent," Kaden says. "Bambi's our favorite Canadian."

Noah can't help the heat creeping across his cheekbones, and Julien doesn't miss it, gaze flicking between him and Kaden with raised eyebrows. He doesn't question it, just tells Kaden, "You're gonna be late if you don't call a ride soon."

Kaden waves his hand. "Alex and Brett won't mind." He tips his head, a small smile curving his lips as he looks Noah over. "Don't wanna risk offending Alex if he finds out I didn't jump on the chance to meet his boy in person."

"You literally shook my hand at World Juniors," Noah says, but his cheeks still burn brighter.

Kaden rolls his eyes. "So not the same, bud. Then you were the man, the myth, the legend—"

Julien almost chokes on a laugh. "Jesus, Kade."

Kaden shrugs. "Call it how I see it, baby. But *now*—" He turns back to Noah. "Now you're one of the boys and it'd be criminal if I didn't come say hi."

Julien raises an eyebrow, amused curiosity breaking across his face. "One of the boys, huh?"

"Jury's still out on if he considers himself one," Kaden says. "But yeah. That's why I'm here, positive reinforcement."

"Very selfless," Noah manages, despite his whole body burning, blood thrumming with embarrassment.

Kaden's smile turns impish. "If I'm also here to put my name in the running for Bambi's actual favorite, that's between the three of us, yeah?"

"Trying to usurp your own?" Julien asks. "Ruthless."

"Can't let Nate have all the fun, can we?"

Kaden's response startles a laugh out of Noah, easing the growing tension in his body.

Julien looks between the two of them, curiosity bleeding into confusion. "Nate?"

"Nathan Hoffman," Noah answers, before his gaze darts back to Kaden. "Even if Nate was my favorite, which he decided on his own with no input from me, I think it'd take more than a hi to overthrow him."

"Baby steps," Kaden says, eyes bright, smile wide. He claps Julien on the back. "But really, I *will* be late if I don't get outta here." He walks backward, shooting Noah finger guns as he says, "It was a pleasure,

Bambi. I'll be your fave in no time."

Julien's eyes are sharp as he glances between the two of them. He opens and closes his mouth in quick succession before saying, "Let Alex know he might want to step his own game up if he wants to win the title."

Kaden laughs. "I'll let him know your expert opinion, Thor. But between you and me, Tex ain't even in the running."

To Noah's utter horror, Kaden winks at Noah before pushing through the locker room doors, making him flush hot. When he glances at Julien, he finds what he expects—one eyebrow raised and a smirk across his lips. But Julien doesn't say anything, not until they're back at Noah's place, stretched out on the couch after dinner. Noah should have known better than to expect Julien to keep his questions to himself, but it still takes him by surprise, somehow, when Julien asks, "So. You and Alex are pretty close now, huh?"

"We hang out," Noah says, but the heat creeping across his face contradicts any casualness his flat voice might earn him from someone else.

"Yeah, I'm aware," Julien says, pulling one leg up on the couch as he turns to face Noah. "How's Kaden factor in?"

"Brett added me to a group chat," Noah mumbles. "Apparently, Alex isn't the only one who sees someone and decides—that's my friend."

Julien rolls his eyes. "Admit it, you and Alex are besties now."

"I wouldn't say that."

"Can't get by on a technicality here, bud. I know you wouldn't say the word bestie." He nudges Noah's thigh with his foot, a smile blooming across his face. "It's fine. You don't have to say it, but I think it's cool— it's good you're making friends."

"Don't be weird," Noah says, mouth twitching in a suppressed smile.

"I'll be as weird as I want when the prickliest pear I've ever known has shed his thorns for a bunch of obnoxious Americans he would never have given the time of day to before I told Alex he needed to work for your friendship."

"Oh God," Noah groans. "You're taking credit for this."

"Obviously," Julien says, but then his face goes serious. "You two are close though, right? I'm not gonna have to kick Kaden's ass because Alex and all his friends think winning your friendship is some kind of game, am I?"

Julien's genuine concern makes Noah's throat itch. "No, I think we're good on that front."

"Good."

Noah furrows his brow. "I mean, I don't really think Nate and Kaden are serious about wanting to be my favorite or anything. They're just incapable of not one-upping each other."

"So, what you're saying is you and Alex *are* besties and now all his friends are trying to be your favorite, so he isn't?"

Noah's burning. "I didn't say that."

"Nah, but your cheeks sure did."

"Whatever," Noah grumbles. "We're friends. It doesn't mean he's my favorite."

"Mm, maybe not, but you're definitely his."

"I wouldn't go that far."

"Of course you wouldn't. But I've seen Kade chirp before. Kinda seems like giving Alex shit about being into you is something he's done before."

"He's straight," Noah says, heart hammering.

"Maybe, maybe not." Julien shrugs. "But it sure seems like I was right. Being into you explains why he was so determined to break through your ice-cold shell a lot more than anyone being capable of caring *that* much about someone not liking them."

Noah's brain screeches to a halt. He can't comprehend this. "You think—what are you saying? You think Alex is gay?"

"I don't know, but I definitely get the vibe he's into you. Could be anywhere on the rainbow, right?"

"You genuinely think Alex is into me?"

"Yeah, man, I think it's pretty obvious."

"He has a girlfriend."

"Does he? I think they broke up."

"Why? She was just here for his birthday—over her Thanksgiving break."

Julien shrugs. "Yeah, I saw. But maybe they're not exclusive? I follow her on Instagram—what? Don't look at me like that! You had a super romantic moon date with Alex, and I got curious if they were still together. She posts the same kind of photos with this girl as she does with Alex and *her* birthday was last week and there was a picture of them kissing in the photo dump she did. Like, it definitely seems like they're dating too."

"None of that means he's interested in me."

"No, but I still think he is. Like, a super-hot maybe-ex-girlfriend doesn't mean he's perfectly straight. It's not like we're in the most welcoming environment to discover your sexuality, are we?"

"No, we're not," Noah says, gaze dropping to his lap, picking at the inseam of his sweats. If he doesn't tell Julien now, when will he? It's now or never. "I, uh, actually needed to—" He smooths out the fabric bunched up over his knees, gaze flicking there and back from Julien. But it's enough time to catch the serious set to Julien's mouth, the alertness of his eyes, the way he's straightened his back. He looks like he's watching game day tape—focused and ready to listen.

Noah takes a deep breath, tries again. "I wanted to tell you something, actually."

"Yeah?"

"Yeah," Noah sighs, shoulders so tight they might snap. "I'm gay."

He can't look away from his knees, too afraid to see what Julien's face is doing.

"Cool."

Noah jerks his head up, chest tight. "What?"

"I appreciate you telling me."

Noah doesn't know what to say. He didn't expect Julien to hate him, not actually, but he wasn't expecting it to be this simple. Julien tugs at Noah's sleeve and gives him a soft, reassuring smile before tugging him in for a hug. He practically pulls Noah into his lap with how tight he has his arm around his back, but Noah doesn't really mind when Julien has him tucked up against the crook of his neck, cradling the back of his head in his big, warm hand. Noah sinks into it, happy to let Julien take some of the weight he's been carrying for so long.

*

### *Julien Thorn*

Sat, Dec 31, 12:01AM

Happy birthday you prickly bitch

*One minute late you're slacking*

You're welcome dickhead
I even checked your schedule to make

sure I wasn't early

*Aww you planned for me*
*How sweet*

Wait shouldn't you be asleep

*You're such a mother hen*
*sometimes*
*Sucks you woke me up*

No I didn't you're just being an asshole

*Obviously*

You and lover boy doing anything today?

*Thought you said you checked*
*my schedule*

Could have a phone date

*You know we're not dating*

Yeah but you're both into each other

*No we're not*

You so are

*Kinda fucked up to assume I'm*
*into a guy just because you know*
*I'm gay*

Buddy you're in a group chat with his
friends are you telling me you're NOT
into him

*I had no say in that*

Yeah but you haven't removed yourself
from it either and I expect a thank you
dinner when you two finally get together

*Even if that happened why the*
*hell would you get rewarded for*
*it?*

I got this ball rolling duh
You'd still be dead set on hating him
without me

*I never HATED him*

Wish you could see the face I'm making

*I didn't!*
*Hate is so much stronger than*
*disliking him a lot*

Lmaaaaaaao that's one way of putting it
But seriously, you should go for it
I really think he's into you

*Did you forget about his*
*girlfriend?*

The girlfriend I'm pretty sure he doesn't
have?

*I've seen them kiss???*

On the CHEEK! And she's kissed other
people!!!!

*Okay even if he's single there's
still no "going for it"*

Why not? You're basically dating now

*Oh my god shut up*

No, I'm actually being serious now,
Noah.
It's no secret you two are friends who
make time to hang out and I'm not
dismissing your concerns but this isn't
some random guy you started taking to
dinner all the time, this is Alex, who you
already hang out with more than most of
your teammates and no one thinks
anything of it

*It'd be different if we were
actually dating*

How? I think you're so used to denying
yourself what makes you happy you can't
see your available options

*It's still a secret we'd have to keep*
*There's still a risk of getting*
*caught*

Yeah but not as big
It'd be like if we fell in love and started
hanging out AND hooking up after games
No one would know what you're doing
behind doors

*First, I'd never date you*

Right back at ya

*And second, what are you*
*suggesting I do here? Go up to*
*him and be like "oh hey Julien*
*thinks you've got a big gay thing*
*for me, wanna date?"*

Maybe not with those exact words

*Not at all Julien*
*I'm not ruining what I have*
*because you're misinterpreting*
*this*

Okay first, does he know?
That you're gay, not that you're in love
with him

*I'm not in LOVE with him*

Whatever
Does he know

*Yes*

Then test it

*What the hell does that mean*

Fucking flirt with him man!!
Make your intentions as obvious as you
can without saying it
See what he does

*Jfc Julien my MOM could tell I'm
into him
I really don't think I can be any
more obvious*

There's no way you've been FLIRTING

*Obviously not*

Then your intentions could be clearer

*There's no way he hasn't noticed
how flustered I get around him.
He's probably just being polite
and ignoring the obvious.*

Buddy you get flustered by everything

*Okay fair, but there's no way he's*

*straight up oblivious. He has to know.*
*Besides flirting with a straight guy, even one as chill as Alex, is just asking for trouble*

UGH
You're so difficult

*I'm not the one concocting ridiculous plans!*

I'm trying to get you your MAN

*I hate you*

FINE! At least try to make him jealous then!

*I'm going to bed*

Seriously! Start blowing him off for your teammates and see how he takes it

*Go bother your other friends!*

I'm going to give you so much shit when I end up being right

*GOODNIGHT*

You'll literally never hear the end of it

# Chapter Twenty-Five

ALEX IS DRUNK.

It's New Year's Eve and Alex is drunk.

They just blew out Vegas; they're in some sleek penthouse celebrating and Alex is drunk. His head's fuzzy, body loose, and there's a girl—Erin, he thinks—who keeps brushing her mouth against his ear when she talks. She's beautiful and her dress is soft against his palm and when she kisses him, she tastes like birthday cake vodka and champagne. Alex's stomach twists. His arms fall away from her hips.

"Is everything all right?"

He steps back and her eyebrows pinch together. "Yeah, I just need to make a call."

"Right now?"

"Yeah, right now," Alex says, fishing out his phone and pressing call when he gets to the number in his recent calls list.

"Oh, you mean *right* now," she says, but it's distant. He's already heading for the door.

"Alex, baby!" Beaver yells when the phone stops ringing and Alex's heart stutters. He drops his phone.

"Why are you answering Anderson's phone?"

"What? Ah," Beaver says, before yelling, "Parse! We finally got one of Alex's drunk dials."

Rustling and loud voices layer on top of each other before Beaver switches to FaceTime. When it goes through, he and Parse are pressed close to fit in the frame better.

"Where the hell are you?" Beaver asks.

"Are you in the hallway of a hotel?" Parse asks.

"I dropped my phone," Alex says.

"And then you didn't get up?" Beaver asks.

"Is Anderson with you?" Alex asks, head swimming.

"Why would Anderson be in Boston?" Beaver asks.

"Because you answered his phone?"

"Bud," Parse says, slowly. "How drunk are you?"

"Where's Brett?" Beaver says.

"Inside. Taking body shots, the last I saw."

"I'm texting him." Parse again. "You need some fucking water."

"I need to call Anderson. He's not with you?"

"No," Beaver says slowly. "You dialed the wrong number."

"Oh. I have to go."

"I don't know if that's a good idea," Beaver says.

"No, it's his birthday, and I forgot. I have to call him."

"Alex, don't you dare hang up this phone," Parse barks. "You are too drunk to be calling Noah right now."

But he's not.

He tries again.

Noah sounds upset when he finally answers.

"Happy birthday, babe."

There's a long pause. "Alex, what the fuck?"

"I'm sorry I forgot, but I remembered just in time."

"Alex, it's almost three in the morning! You forgetting my birthday isn't what I'm upset about here."

"Oh. I missed it entirely."

"It's not a big deal."

"It is a big deal." Alex is pouting, he knows this, but— "I wouldn't have even remembered if that girl didn't taste like birthday cake vodka. I'm the worst friend."

"Who? Liv?"

"No, Erin, I think. Demmer loves that shit; she must've had some before she kissed me. And then I remembered and had to leave."

Another long pause. "Alex, did you—" Noah stops. He makes a noise Alex is too drunk to interpret and when he speaks, he sounds like he did when they were strangers. "Did you remember it was my birthday while cheating on your girlfriend because of *cake-flavored vodka?*"

"Yes. Wait, cheating? Who am I cheating on?"

"Your girlfriend? Liv?"

"Liv's not my girlfriend."

"What?" Noah sounds strangled. "I—you've—I saw you kiss her on Instagram!"

"Yeah, and?"

"And I assumed you two were dating! You had her over for Thanksgiving. You've been talking about seeing her when you play in Dallas!"

"Yeah, because she's my best friend."

"You're not—" He clears his throat. "You've never—"

Alex laughs. "You sound like my mom. She thinks we're going to get married one day. But just because we fool around sometimes doesn't mean we're in love."

Another long pause.

"Anderson?" He looks at his phone. Still connected. "Are you still there?"

"Yes, I'm still here," Noah grumbles.

"You stopped talking."

Noah laughs. "Are you pouting?"

"Yes," Alex answers. His brain is molasses, thoughts slow and sticky, and once the idea pops into his mind, he can't unthink it. "You've never fooled around with a friend?"

"What?"

"Are you choking?"

"No, I'm not choking," Noah says, but he sounds strangled again, voice tight and thin.

"So, have you?"

"Alex, I'm *gay*."

"I know but—" Alex sits up straighter. "You hear things about juniors."

"I told you Millie was the only one who knew before you. And I *just* told Julien. So, unless you think I hooked up with Millie before I came out to her, who the hell do you think I've been sleeping with?"

Noah sounds strange. Alex doesn't like it. "But that means you're a—shit, you've never even kissed anyone? Not even Millie?"

Noah laughs, but it's kind of shrill and deranged. "Why would I do that?"

"I dunno, to practice? That's what me and Liv did—so we wouldn't fuck it up when we wanted to impress someone." Noah makes another strangled noise and Alex sighs, slumping further down the wall. "Are you judging me?"

"I'm not! That's just not something I would've even considered; let alone something I've done."

"You could."

"I thought you weren't trying to set me up with Sean."

Something hot twists in Alex's stomach and his mind races. "I'm not. What the fuck? I meant me."

"You what?"

Alex perks up a little as he imagines it. "Yeah, like, let me be your Liv."

"Alex." Noah sounds upset again. Alex doesn't understand. "How much have you had to drink?"

"A lot, but don't change the subject. I'm trying to do you a favor."

"I don't think you know what you're saying," Noah says, after another long pause.

Or maybe it's not long at all. Alex's brain is soup, every blink like lead. He wishes Noah was here. "What's a little spit-swapping between best buds?"

"You're *straight.*" Noah sounds pained now. "You are going to be so embarrassed if you remember this in the morning."

"No, I won't."

Noah sighs. He sounds so tired. "I don't want or need your pity kisses."

"It's not a pity kiss if I want to." Another pause. So many pauses. "Are you falling asleep on me?"

"No! Just give me a minute! It's three in the morning and I'm trying to *think.*"

"About kissing me?" Alex asks, something buoyant shifting in him, his brain on high alert.

"No."

His heart does a weird, uncomfortable swoop. "Rude, I'm a good kisser."

"I'm sure you are."

"Then what's the problem? Why won't you kiss me?"

"Because you're drunk, and you don't mean any of this."

"Yes, I do. I know you like to be the best and that practice makes perfect. I know you give everything 100 percent. So why wouldn't you—"

The door opens next to him, and Reggie nearly falls over as he and Brett rush out into the hallway.

"There you are!" Brett says.

"Come back to the party!" Reggie says, too loud for this quiet hall. "You're going to miss the ball drop!"

"Didn't we already, with the time zones?" Alex asks.

Reggie rolls his eyes. "Ketch found a disco ball, Ax said we could drop it at midnight. Come on."

Brett elbows Reggie. "We're supposed to be stopping him from embarrassing himself."

"Why would I embarrass myself?"

Noah snorts.

Brett grimaces. "Oh Jesus, you're on the phone. Please, tell me I got here in time and you're not actually talking to Noah right now."

"Noah?" Reggie asks. "Who's—"

"Hey, give that back—" Alex says, reaching for his phone.

Brett is standing though, and Alex's body is so heavy. Getting up is so much effort.

"Dammit," Brett hisses. "It is you. What did he say? That's it? Are you sure? Okay, yeah, fine. I'm just making sure." Brett looks stressed, his laugh a little strained. "Yeah, he's notorious for drunk dials—had to make sure he didn't embarrass himself."

Reggie holds his hand out for Alex. He giggles when Alex ends up pulling him down. Brett rolls his eyes, and the exasperated way he says both of their names, is the last thing Alex remembers before falling asleep.

In the morning, the night comes to him in flashes. The champagne toast they did out of bottles when Ax yelled he was going to be a dad. Reggie snorting beer out of his nose. Joey's hand on Reggie's cheek telling him to keep up before knocking back a shot. Brett in the corner with Casey licking salt off his neck while Casey's girlfriend, Amber, laughed into his other shoulder. The sickly-sweet taste of birthday cake vodka on his tongue. Calling Noah on his birthday. The swell of hope and plummet of disappointment when Noah said... Casey diving to catch the disco ball Ketch dropped... Trying to get Noah to understand what he meant... Reggie holding the disco ball up over people's heads like mistletoe... Brett snatching his phone away before he could finish his thought...

"Oh God," Alex says the moment Noah's face appears on his screen. "Did I offer to kiss you last night?"

"You look like shit," Noah says instead of answering.

"You don't look much better," Alex says, noting the huge purple bags under his eyes. "Did you have a good time last night?"

"I would've had a better time if you didn't wake me up at three in the morning."

"I definitely hung up before three."

"You know how time zones work, right?"

"Yes, but Brett took my phone before midnight my time. Which means it wasn't three your time. So, ha!"

Noah rolls his eyes. "The difference is negligible."

"So, did I? Offer to kiss you."

"Yeah," Noah says, not really looking at Alex.

"Oh, well, uh—"

Noah cuts him off. "Are you really not dating Liv?"

"Wait, what? Did you think I was?"

"Yeah! You literally talk about her like she's your girlfriend!"

"No, we're just—"

"Yes, I know all about how you sleep with her when you're bored—"

"Hey!" Blood rushes in Alex's ears. "I don't judge you for your choices! Don't judge me for mine."

"Uh, what part of telling me you could be my Liv—"

"I could be your *what?*"

"—told me all about how you two practiced kissing with each other; offered to let me practice on you." Noah's face twists in a way Alex hates. "What about making me feel like shit because I can't do what you do is you not judging me?"

"I didn't mean—"

Noah's face shutters off. "I know you didn't mean it."

"No! I mean, I probably wouldn't have had the idea sober, but drunk-me had a good point. Practice *does* make perfect."

Noah flushes, but he doesn't seem embarrassed or flustered. His eyes are sharp and his curious gaze makes Alex prickle. "If you meant what you said, then what the hell didn't you mean?"

"I mean, I didn't mean to make you feel bad about yourself. I never want to make you feel like shit. But if—" Alex's palms are clammy and his head spins. This hangover is killing him. "Like, I mean, obviously we won't sleep together—"

"Obviously."

"But if you ever wanted to practice or take the pressure out of it or whatever, the offer def still stands. Like what's a—"

"Little swapped spit between a couple of bros," Noah finishes, rolling his eyes.

"Exactly! And it's not like there's any chance it will complicate things."

"Oh, for sure, how could a kiss complicate anything between us? What could go wrong there?"

"Nothing could! You're not into me; I'm not into you. It's a perfect scenario."

"I don't think you know what a perfect scenario is."

"I can't believe you don't want to practice kissing on me," Alex says, despondent suddenly. "You're the worst."

"*I'm* the worst? Do you hear yourself?" Noah asks, mouth twitching in the way it does when he tries not to laugh. "You're a straight guy upset your gay friend doesn't want a pity kiss."

"It's not a pity kiss if I want to!" Noah raises an eyebrow and Alex's heartbeat hammers against his ribs. "If I want to help a friend out. That's good friendship!"

"Alex." Noah's voice is steady despite the red of his face. "I'm not kissing anyone who doesn't want to kiss me for regular reasons."

"Okay," Alex says, throat tight.

Noah gives him what Alex is sure must be a significant look, but his brain is thick and sticky again. He can't process anything other than Noah's blue, blue eyes boring into Alex's soul.

"And since that doesn't apply to you," Noah says after an excruciating moment of staring, a moment Alex knows he's supposed to understand but doesn't.

Alex swallows. He needs some water. Some ibuprofen too. "Right. At least let me find you someone who wants to." He clears his throat. "For regular reasons."

Noah tips his head back until his skull clunks against the hotel headboard. "What did I say about setting me up?"

"That you'd consider it after you told Thorn," Alex says, gaze catching on the line of Noah's throat, the mole he has to the left of center at the base of his throat, right at the start of his collarbones.

When Noah looks up, his gaze isn't as intense; he no longer looks like he's trying to bore a silent message into Alex's mushy, achy brain. He looks amused, actually. "That is *not* what I said."

"Not in so many words."

The façade breaks and the twitch of Noah's mouth blooms into a smile. "Not in any words! Julien's already meddling in my nonexistent love life—I don't need to add you to the mix either."

"Wait, Thorn's trying to set you up?"

Noah groans. "Something like that."

"Then you really have to let me try!"

"Why? So, you can turn it into some challenge too?"

"You gotta admit, I'd be better at it."

"I don't have to admit anything."

"It's okay. I know the truth. I'd find you a much better guy than Thorn."

"Saying it doesn't make it true."

"There's really only one way to find out."

Noah laughs, quiet but indignant. "Are you trying to goad me into letting you set me up?"

"This is a product of your own making, bud."

"Oh yeah, how so?"

"This wouldn't be happening if you'd hook up with guys in the league." Noah makes an indecipherable face and Alex pushes forward before he interrupts. "*And* you gave me the idea!"

"I was making fun of you!"

"You know I'm incapable of embarrassment," Alex says, feeling lighter somehow. "And that I love to prove you wrong."

Noah lets out a quiet laugh. "You love to *annoy* me, more like."

"Same thing. Now, does Thorn have to buy me dinner when I find you a guy you'll actually go out with, or do you?"

"That won't happen."

"If you're so confident, you shouldn't have a problem wagering a dinner."

Noah blows out a breath, more amused than annoyed when he says, "You find me a guy I'll go out with before the season's over and I'll buy you and the guy dinner too."

# Chapter Twenty-Six

**Julien Thorn**
Sun, Jan 1, 8:45PM

*Turns out you were right about
Alex not having a girlfriend*

HELL YEAH HELL YEAH HELL
FUCKING YEAH

*I already regret sharing this
information with you*

Yeah but now that I have it, what're we
gonna do about it

*There's nothing to do about it*

...you're so fucking annoying

Flirt! With! Him!
SEE. WHAT. HAPPENS.

*You know I can't do that*

You don't want to know that I'm right

*No, I don't. What good would*
*that do? It's not like I can DO*
*anything about it. It's too much*
*of a risk and if you're wrong it'll*
*be weird.*

YOU ARE INFURIATING
At this rate I'm going to rage blackout
and crosscheck your teeth out the next
game

*Seems a tad dramatic*

Okay, let's forget about Alex. Are you
going to be this stubborn about every guy
you're interested in? You can't put your
personal life on hold for the next 20
years bud (and I stg if you say it might
not be that long I AM going to fight you
next game)

*You don't fight*
*And I can try*

I understand why you want to do that, I

really, really do, but you're a huge softie
underneath your prickly cactus exterior
and I've known you far too long for you
to ever convince me you don't want to be
loved up
You'll be miserable if you try to do this
until you retire
Read 11:04PM

# Chapter Twenty-Seven

THE ROSTER FOR the All-Star Game gets announced the morning after his conversation with Noah. Nate sends a screenshot to the group chat of the announcement with Alex's name circled and a giant heart drawn around Noah's. The heart spills over onto Blackwood's name, and even though his hangover is long gone, Alex's stomach twists uncomfortably.

On Tuesday, Alex wakes up from a dream he can't remember past Noah kneeling on the ice, leaning into Blackwood as they laugh during the skills competition. He's hot and flushed, restless in a way he can only assume is because of the late night of travel, but even after sleeping another hour in the comfort of his own bed, his mind won't settle. Images of Noah and Blackwood keep flashing in his mind, and he doesn't know why an innocuous dream about the All-Star Game has stuck with him so much until he's out to lunch with the guys in Detroit. Reggie's complaining about his sister's douchebag new boyfriend and her terrible type in men when it hits Alex why the dream has stuck with him—Blackwood could be Noah's type and Alex doesn't even know. How is he supposed to set him up if he doesn't even know what he's looking for in a guy?

*

***Anderson***

Fri, Jan 6, 12:05PM

*Are you interested in Blackwood?*

MY CAPTAIN?? What the fuck

*Are you?*

He's married??? AND ALMOST TWICE
MY AGE???

*Ok so what's your upper age*<br>*limit? Is Tikkanen too old too?*

TIKI????? Are you just throwing darts at
my team's roster?

*No I'm using what little I have to*<br>*go on and the process of*<br>*elimination*

Which is WHAT? When have I shown
any interest in either of those guys to
you?

*You haven't really but*<br>*blackwood's blond and*<br>*handsome as hell just like that*

*guy I saw you check out and Kev*
*was saying you love Tiki so I'm*
*taking a chance to see what I'm*
*working with*

What did I do to deserve someone as
insufferable as you in my life?

*You can pretend you hate this all*
*you want but YOU said you'd buy*
*me dinner if I found you someone*
*before the end of the season and*
*you know I love when your cheap*
*ass has to shell out money*

Fine if you wanna spend all your free
time figuring out what type of guy I'm
never going to give the time of day to for
a dinner you're never going to get, then
be my guest but don't blame me when
your game suffers because you're
distracted

*Joke's on you baby. Watch me*
*find you a guy too hard to resist*
*AND never slip from calder*
*contention*

You do that.

*I expect dinner AND dessert*

*when I do asshole*

*

**J. Thorn**
Fri, Jan 6, 12:37PM

*In your expert opinion what's
Anderson's type*

Why are you asking?

*Heard you're meddling in his
love life and figured we could
team up*

Surprised you're not trying to prove
you'll be better at it than me

*Oh no, I was definitely going to
do exactly that but then
Anderson said I wouldn't be able
to set him up before the end of the
season without my game
suffering and now I've REALLY
gotta prove him wrong*

Who says I don't want to see that happen
too?

😣😣😣

Lmaooo

But seriously I'm not sure I can actually
help you out here. I'm pretty sure we
both have the same info about what
Noah's into

*You have to know more than he
MIGHT like tall blonds*

Why do you think he likes tall blonds?

*Because I saw him check one out*

If that's what you're going off, then I
guess he might like tall guys of any hair
color lol

*Part of me thinks you're fucking
with me but part of me knows
he's the most evasive and
secretive person I've ever met so I
guess you wouldn't know either*

Tbh I think you'd have a better time
picking up on it than me

*You're one of his best friends*

Yeah but you see him more than me and
I don't know if you know this but Noah is
NOT afraid to leave someone on read
when he doesn't want to talk about

something anymore lol

UGH<br>He's IMPOSSIBLE

Buddy he's been impossible since the day
you met idk what you expected here

I don't know A LITTLE less<br>difficulty

Lbr you either figure out he's into
someone and set them up or you give up
because there's no way in hell Noah's
going to let a stranger know he's gay

OR I could set him up with<br>someone he knows is into dudes<br>but isn't a stranger

Sounds like you have someone in mind

We have one mutual friend who<br>likes dudes but idk if he's<br>Anderson's type

Oh I can't WAIT to see how this goes

Thanks asshole

I expect a full recap

*

### *Anderson*

Fri, Jan 6, 1:25PM

I thought you didn't want to set me up
with Sean

> *I don't but then Julien made a*
> *very solid point. You're never*
> *going to go for a stranger so I*
> *obviously gotta start with*
> *someone you already know,*
> *there's dinner on the line*

I'm not going to go out with someone
just because he's the one other queer
guy I know

> *Then go out with him because*
> *he's hot and you'll have a good*
> *time*

You have no idea of knowing that

> *I mean, you have a good time*
> *with me and Yatesy's a lot chiller*
> *than I am, so yeah I think it's a*

*pretty safe bet you'd at least*
*enjoy one dinner with him*

Wait, you think I'd have a good time with
Sean because I have a good time WITH
YOU???

*Obviously*
*We'd make hockey's hottest*
*couple if I liked guys but you and*
*yatesy could crack the top five*
*for sure*

*

NOAH DOESN'T RESPOND right away, and Alex tucks his phone in his pocket and forgets about it as they head back to the hotel. Casey gives him shit for finally tuning back in until Reggie socks him in the arm and scoffs, "Bro, you were way worse before Amber made an honest man out of you."

It sets them off arguing but doesn't get Alex off the hook entirely; Brett slows his pace and waits until they fall a few more steps behind Reggie and Casey to say, "Been in an interesting mood today."

"What?"

Brett gives him an amused but judgmental look. "What were you and Noah talking about that annoyed you so much?"

"How do you know I was texting Anderson—were you reading over my shoulder?"

Brett frowns. "I don't need to snoop to know what you look like when you're talking to him. You've got a Noah face, man. But you don't usually look this irritated when you are, so…what's up?"

Alex rolls his eyes. "Nothing, he's just being stubborn."

Brett gives him a sideways glance but drops it and Alex puts it out of his mind as Kaden pulls up in front of the hotel moments after Alex and Brett have arrived. They spend the afternoon in Plymouth catching up with Kaden's parents and it feels good to be back in the familiar warmth of the Devines' kitchen, being doted on by Kaden's mom the same way they were in the dev program when she was everyone's second mom, even the ones who were billeting with a different family. When they leave for Ann Arbor for the Michigan game, Alex feels as settled as he did after his family's visit and by the end of the game, he's buzzing from watching good hockey and excited to see the guys for the first time in months. The lingering exhilaration of watching his friends win a game that has absolutely no bearing on his team's standings only lasts until the six of them are back in Kaden's apartment and Alex finally remembers to check his phone. He frowns when he reads Noah's response.

*Maybe so but idk if I could betray hockey Canada like that*

Brett asks, "Noah being stubborn again?"

Alex pockets his phone as his mind prickles with…something. "No, just being an ass about USA hockey."

"Rude," Mitch says, giving Alex a long, discerning look before raising an eyebrow. "You look a lot more bothered than some national rivalry chirping though. What'd he say?"

Alex rolls his eyes. "Thorn and I are kinda trying to set him up, and he's turning his nose up at all my suggestions."

"Wait," Kaden starts cautiously. "Why are you trying to set Noah up?"

"Because Beav's right about needing things outside of hockey. And because he said I couldn't, so now I have to."

Kaden grimaces, but Mitch responds first. "You can't be serious. There's no way you're trying to set him up."

"Why not? I'd do the same for any of you if you were all hockey all the time."

Mitch scoffs. "Because you don't want to date any of us."

Alex's stomach drops and heat flares up his neck. He has to work to not clench his jaw. "I'm not interested in him like that!"

"Alex, come on."

Johnny doesn't say it unkindly, and his face is soft with sympathy, but it makes Alex prickle, regardless. "Come on, what?"

"Holy shit! How are we still doing this?" Mitch asks, cheeks flushing as his temper flares. "It's been years. You've gotta realize by now that what you feel for him is not what you feel for literally anyone else, except maybe Liv!"

"What are you talking about? World Juniors was a year ago and we haven't even been actual friends that whole time!"

Mitch looks at him with a mulish set to his jaw, his eyes blazing, but Alex's gaze slides to Johnny when he clears his throat. He's not pissed like Mitch is, but he still looks irritated and Alex's stomach twists. "Why are you looking at me like that?"

Johnny bites his lip, thoughtful for a moment, before finally sighing. "Because World Juniors isn't even where this started. Because from where I'm sitting—" His gaze flits around the room. "From our perspective, it's pretty clear in hindsight that your crush on him was the real motivation for getting him to like you."

Alex flinches. "You think I've been interested in Anderson since, what, I was fifteen?"

Johnny shrugs. "In some way, yeah."

Alex looks around the room, stung. "All of you think that?"

They nod and murmur in agreement while Brett asks, "Do you really think you'd give anyone else a second chance after you spent weeks excited to meet them and they couldn't even manage a smile when you finally did? Let alone a third or a fourth one if you didn't like them already?"

Alex's hands are sweaty and hot and he rubs them down his jeans as the nervous energy fizzing through him ramps up. "Yeah, if it was because of the same rivalry. I think I would."

"I can give you that," Kaden says. "But before that tournament, only the most tuned-in prospect reporters were talking about you two as each other's competition. There was no rivalry, and you were still super worked up about meeting him." He lets out a quiet, reluctant laugh. "I've never seen you that flustered over anyone other than actual NHL players."

The first time he saw Noah floods his memory—a video of an impressive trick shot. He remembers watching it over and over as he tried to replicate it; remembers the first time he'd let the video run all the way through instead of starting it over right after the puck hit the net; remembers the exaggerated cheers of a girl in the background and the sweet smile it drew from a blushing Noah. He remembers the way his heartbeat kicked up in anticipation the next time he started the video; remembers the inexplicable desire to see it in person; remembers looking at other videos Noah posted and being disappointed he rarely smiled.

"Shit. Okay, maybe I had a little hockey crush on him."

Brett groans and Mitch snaps, "Are you kidding me, Alex? Look me in the eye and tell me you'd be saying the same shit if one of us was in the same spot as you!"

Alex slouches back in his chair. He doesn't know what to say and his throat is tight even after several swallows. "Not if I didn't know you were into guys. No."

Mitch's nostrils flare, but he shuts his mouth with a snap when Johnny puts a hand on his knee. He purses his lips but lets Johnny cut in. "If this were you and Natalie Graham or hell, even Yatesy and Noah, would you still be saying everything you've done, all the effort you've put into charming Noah was about being friends?"

"But it's not those things. It's me and Anderson, and I'm not interested in men."

Mitch rolls his eyes and roughly scrubs his hands across his face. "What are you trying to do here? Why do you really want to set Noah up? Are you trying to out of sight, out of mind your crush? Because I hate to break it to you, man, but this is way beyond being hot for good hockey, and if you're getting irritated thinking about him being in a relationship what the hell do you think is going to happen when he is in one and you don't get to see him as much and you finally realize you've got big gay feelings for him?"

"I'm not trying to push him off on someone else and I'm not attracted to men!"

"Maybe you're just attracted to Noah," Johnny says.

Nausea rises in Alex's throat. "What about Anderson gives you the idea he'd ever be an option for me in the first place? Why are y'all so damn set on me being interested in someone I can't even have?"

The quiet that follows is tense, only broken when Mitch sighs. "It's not just about Noah. It's about self-acceptance and shit."

"There's nothing to accept," Alex says. "I don't like men."

Kaden rubs a hand over the back of his neck. "Have you talked to

Yatesy about any of this? Because he literally said the same thing."

"No, because I don't need to."

Brett asks, "Is this what you were texting about at lunch?"

"Yeah."

"So, you weren't irritated he's stubborn. You were jealous."

"No, that's not—"

Brett blows out a sharp breath, cheeks flushing with anger. "Jesus Christ, Alex, you had him and his mom over for Christmas! You go all lovesick and swoony when he pays attention to you, you get irritated when he's paying attention to someone else, and if we're being real— you're practically his boyfriend already!"

Alex blanches. "What the—no, I'm not. I like to spend time with him because we're friends."

"Buddy, you and your best friend have been sleeping together off and on since you were seventeen," Mitch says matter-of-factly. "You are not defending yourself the way you think you are."

Kaden's face lights up. He snaps his fingers and points at Mitch with a huge grin. "That's an excellent point!" He turns back to Alex, earnest as he says, "Maybe you're not in love with him, but you definitely want more from him than what you've got. Maybe you want him to be your other Liv."

"My other Liv," Alex says, tongue heavy in his mouth, throat dry.

Kaden's mouth thins out. "I mean, it feels kinda fucked up to just refer to you two as friends with bennies, you know? But, like, I know you're not dating her but still hook up when you want. Maybe that's what you want with Noah."

Alex doesn't know what to say, but his neck and cheeks are burning, and his stomach twists uncomfortably. "I think I'd know if I wanted to fuck Anderson."

Images of Noah pulling back from a kiss with a slick red mouth and a pleased smile pop into Alex's mind unbidden and his stomach drops as Noah's reasons for not letting Alex be his first kiss replay in his mind. Alex leans his elbows on his knees and presses the heels of his hands to his eyes until white stars spark through his vision. He groans. "Fuck, am I into dudes?"

The boys are silent for a long moment, then Mitch says, "At least one."

When Alex sits back, he finds Mitch watching him with a devious look in his eyes that has his stomach clenching in anticipation. "Oh God, what are you plotting?"

Mitch's responding grin is devilish. "Wanna find out if it's two?"

Alex doesn't understand until Johnny smacks Mitch's leg and laughs, exasperated and a little hysterical. "You are not about to offer to help Alex figure out his sexuality right now!"

Mitch shrugs, unrepentant. "I mean, someone's gotta step up when Yatesy isn't around."

"And since Nate's not around either...Mitch should do," Kaden says, the tension in the room snapping when he laughs.

Mitch scowls. "Are you saying Yatesy and Nate are hotter than me?"

Kaden's smile spreads. His eyes bright are with mischief. "Baby, I'd never." He tilts his head toward Alex. "I actually think you're pretty close to Alex's type."

Mitch preens and Alex laughs, the absurdity of it all settling his nerves. "Y'all are so fucking annoying. If I had a type in men, I wouldn't be so fucking confused. I'd just know."

"Maybe. But you have a general type," Brett says, looking Mitch over. "And Mitch and Noah fit the bill pretty perfectly."

"What? How?"

"Small and a little bitchy," Kaden says.

"Mitchy's too bitchy for it to be exact though," Johnny says, lit up with laughter.

"And not as short as Noah either," Mitch says. "But I've been told I have a nice mouth so—" He shrugs, one eyebrow raised challengingly. "I'm sure you'll know one way or another when we're done if you're not into men."

His gut response is to say no, but then he thinks about offering to kiss Noah, and the twist in his gut when he turned Alex down, and how he's no longer sure he doesn't meet the criteria of interested in him. "All right, gimme your best."

Mitch takes two steps, but Johnny grabs his wrist before he gets to Alex, exasperated and amused as he says, "If shit gets weird between you two after this, I'll never stop saying I told you so."

Mitch grins. "Noted."

"But it won't," Alex says. "I am not even slightly confused about my feelings for Mitch."

"Same," Mitch says as he stands. His expression turns serious as he puts his hands on his hips and stares at Alex. "But if you're not repulsed by this, you've gotta talk to Yatesy or Liv or—God, even your aunt would do! But you have to talk to someone about all your mixed-up feelings because obviously talking to a bunch of straight guys is not cutting it. Deal?"

"Yeah, all right."

Mitch moves across the room and doesn't let Alex stand to meet him. Instead, he straddles Alex's lap, grin turning smug when Alex's hands go to his waist on instinct.

"Oh Jesus," Brett says. "Just going all in, huh?"

"Gotta give it 110 percent," Mitch says, looking over his shoulder and shifting his weight in a way that makes Alex's grip tighten.

Mitch's smile is sharp and knowing when he looks back, but before he can say anything about the flush burning across Alex's cheeks, Kaden clears his throat. "I feel like one of us here should mention, just for the record, that you don't need to kiss a guy to know you're into guys."

"Yeah, and if we're pointing out why this is a dumbass idea," Johnny says. "I'd like to say kissing a friend might skew the results. Like, there's a good chance he'll think it's too weird kissing you to realize it's hot."

Mitch glances over his shoulder. "Yeah, but Alex has slept with his best friend and it's not weird for them."

Mitch turns back to him and slides his hand up Alex's neck until his thumb rests at the hinge of his jaw. "I'm sure you'll know if you like this or not."

"Can't really argue with that logic. Can you, Johnny?" Brett asks.

"No, I guess not," Johnny says. "But having an audience still might."

Someone scoffs and the ensuing bickering about who's seen who kiss and ignoring the show are all secondary as Alex's attention narrows in on Mitch's fingers sliding further into his hair. He raises an eyebrow, head tilted in question, and Alex's throat constricts when Mitch pulls at his hair. All he can do is nod.

Kissing Mitch is...tense at first. The boys are watching and the second, more insistent, press of his mouth startles Alex. He jerks back and Mitch's fingers tighten in his hair, keeping him close. His breath is warm against Alex's lips as he says, "Oh no, if we're experimenting, we gotta do this right."

Mitch slots their mouths together again, and Alex relaxes into it this time. Mitch's lips are soft, and he tastes like cherry Chapstick. The solid weight of Mitch in his lap makes his skin buzz in a way he doesn't hate, and when he tugs at Alex's hair to position him where he wants before slipping his tongue in Alex's mouth, the scratch of his nails at the base of his neck and the warm wet slide of their lips are as nice as it has been with any girl Alex has ever kissed.

When Mitch pulls away, Alex doesn't chase after him or whine, but his blood is thrumming and the unmistakable heat of desire burns through him.

Mitch looks him over, no trace of his prior teasing smugness in the gentle curve of his smile. They've known each other so long Mitch has to know, but he still asks, "What's the verdict?"

Alex swallows hard. "I'll talk to Liv."

*

HE CALLS LIV the next morning, voice unsteady as he starts, "Do you think—" He exhales sharply, picks at a loose strand on the hotel bedspread, twists it around the tip of his finger until it pales and tries again. "You know me better than anyone. Do I give off any sort of gay vibe?"

She lets out a quiet huff, surprise or concern; he'd have to see her face to know which one for sure. When she answers, Alex can tell it's a bit of both. "Are we finally talking about Noah?"

"Yeah, I think—" He blows out a sharp breath. "Fuck, I have no idea, Liv. But I kissed Mitch last night—"

"Wait, what? Why?"

"To see if I'm into the idea of kissing more than one guy—"

"And you decided to test that on Mitch?"

"No, it was Mitch's idea. He said if it didn't repulse me, I needed to talk to someone other than a bunch of straight guys because they weren't cutting it for figuring out my mixed-up feelings."

Liv hums. "Pretty solid advice, honestly. So I take it kissing Mitch wasn't repulsive, then?"

"No, but I like kissing and Mitch knows what he's doing. So I don't really know if that says much."

"Maybe not. It is just a kiss. But you're too stubborn to call if you really didn't think it meant something. You'd kiss him again just like you'd kiss me, wouldn't you?"

Alex lets out a ragged breath. "Yeah. I would. But I—"

"Don't want to kiss Mitch, or me, or anyone who isn't Noah," Liv says all too gently.

Alex can't stand how true it sounds, how it immediately conjures up an image of Noah in his lap instead of Mitch, his body hot and firm above him as they make out on the couch, Noah's body flushed pink from his cheeks to his navel, laid out in Alex's bed and chest heaving as he recovers from—

Alex's stomach roils and his heartbeat skyrockets. "This makes no sense. I can't even—I can't imagine going any further with him. I've never even thought of anything other than kissing him and that's just—" He blows out a breath. "Liv, come on, you know as much as anyone that I like sex and don't need to have romantic feelings for someone to want it either. I'm not even sure I actually want to kiss Anderson. Like, why have I never thought about him like that before?"

"Denial's a hell of a thing, babe."

"That's what I'm saying! Why would I be in denial about this? I know it's okay to like guys."

"Alex, I've known you since you were four. I know exactly what it looks like when you like someone, and you've been into Noah Anderson for a long fucking time without being able to admit it. I think it's pretty reasonable it's going to take you more than, like, twenty-four hours to adjust to wanting him."

Alex's stomach churns uncomfortably. "That makes me sound repressed. That I've been into men this entire time and only realized it because the guys think I'm in love with Anderson and wouldn't shut up about it."

"Well, first, bisexuality exists, and it's not a fifty-fifty split."

"I know that!"

"Exactly, so you should understand there's a chance Noah's the first guy who did it for you. But even if that's not what happened, even if it took getting knocked on your ass by feelings for a guy you so desperately wanted to like you that your dumbass hockey bros could see you were in love—"

"Okay, calm down," Alex laughs, a little choked. "I'm not in love."

"Sure, whatever. You really, really, really fucking like him. Better?"

"A little, continue."

"Thanks for the permission, asshat." Alex can hear the smile in her voice and the roiling unease in his stomach settles just the tiniest bit. "What I'm trying to say is, it's fucking hard out here, Alex. Not everyone has a quick and easy journey and even though you grew up in a really accepting home and you and your boys have no qualms about showing that you love each other with physical affection and borderline flirting—"

"I think it's fair to just say flirting—which is why I'm saying I should have known if I liked guys. Like I'm obviously not uncomfortable being that way with guys, so how could I be so ashamed of being attracted to men I couldn't even admit it to my best friends? I know better than to think it's shameful to be queer, Liv. You know I do."

"That's the point I'm trying to make here!" Liv takes a deep breath and sighs. "Look, hockey culture sucks so bad. Don't pretend it doesn't. You know what people were saying about Taylor Ford after he came out and you know why he waited until he retired to do so, and if all of that made it to where you could never face your attraction to men head on, that's okay. You're not a bad person for subconsciously avoiding something you knew would be hard and you're no less queer because Noah's the first guy you've ever felt this way about and not being able to picture having sex with a guy the day after you accept you like him doesn't mean you're ashamed of wanting him. So please don't beat yourself up about this."

"I can try," Alex grumbles.

"That's all I can really ask."

"Okay," Alex says, trying to inject levity into his voice. "Enough about me. Tell me about Hilary. Has your mom warmed up to her yet or is she still holding her to impossible standards because she's subconsciously rooting for us to get married?"

Liv's laugh is warm and loud, the perfect balm for his fried nerves. "Oh, she's absolutely still wistfully dreaming about the wedding she envisioned for us at my quinceañera. But Dad loves her—wants me to invite her to the lake this summer."

"Oh wow, it's that serious?"

"Yeah, I think so."

She sounds so happy Alex's chest aches. "If you've gone and found true love, I think it's about time I meet her."

Liv snorts. "Shut up. No one's said anything about love yet."

Alex laughs, the stress of their conversation finally abating. "Now you know what it feels like, asshole."

"Yeah, yeah, I guess I deserve that."

"But seriously, I wanna meet her. I think we're in Dallas next month, if you wanna bring her to the game."

"As long as you promise not to embarrass me."

"No chance, babe. I've been waiting so long for you to be serious about someone so I can unleash all these stories I've been saving."

"Hope you're ready to get a taste of your own medicine when your parents invite someone down to the island."

"I would expect nothing less of you."

# Chapter Twenty-Eight

**_Julien Thorn_**
Sun, Jan 8, 11:00AM

> _Let's say I told Alex it would
> never work out between me and
> his friend because I'd never
> betray hockey Canada like that
> and then he left me on read all of
> yesterday, what should I do?_

Noah what the hell

> _I was JOKING! I didn't think he'd
> take it personally!!_

Right because the usa hockey player
who's totally into you was definitely not

going to be upset you turned him down
by default

> *How can you still think that*
> *when he's trying to SET ME*
> *UP???*

Is he actually? Or is this just another bit
of competitive flirting that ends with you
on a date with him?

> *Those are NOT dates and since*
> *when is making bets flirting?*

Since Alex started doing it to get you to
LIKE HIM. And whatever you want to
call those dinners, you two always end up
alone together. Is this one of those times
or not?

> *Yeah, but there's no way Alex*
> *wants to find a guy I'll take on an*
> *actual date because he thinks the*
> *dinner he'll get after is one too*

I'm not saying he thinks of them that
way either, but I'm pretty sure he's
been betting you into paying attention
and spending time with him since the
draft and you've been going along with
it the entire time. This doesn't feel very

different to me. He wants your
attention and this is a surefire way to
get it

*But he WON'T win. The only*
*reason I agreed is because we*
*both know he won't. None of this*
*makes sense if he's into me like*
*you think*

But if you never say yes, he still has a
guaranteed dinner to look forward to

*Why wouldn't he just say he's*
*interested*

Why haven't YOU

*Because HE'S straight*

Are you saying if you knew he was into
guys you'd think he was into you?

*No but I might see where you're*
*coming from*

Come on why else would he be this upset
about you blanket turning down
Americans?

*You know Kaden, you know how*
*weird they are about each other*

You think he's ignoring you because you
won't date HIS FRIEND?????

> *It's more likely than him being*
> *interested in ME*

You are so goddamn stubborn about this.
Tell him you might make an exception
for the right American but his friend isn't
the one and see what happens

> *What good will THAT do?*

It'll at least prove he hasn't been ignoring
you because you won't go out with his
friend for a bogus reason

> *That still doesn't mean he wants*
> *to date me*

No, but it at least lets him know he's got
a chance if he IS

> *I don't know if that's a good idea*
> *when he DOESN'T have a chance*

Buddy you can tell yourself that all you
want but I think you gave him a deadline
because part of you really hopes he'll
figure it out
Read: 12:03PM

1:38PM

I KNEW IT! I know you won't do
anything to help him figure it out but tell
him you were being an ass about
Americans. Let him know he has a
chance without revealing your feelings
just in case he doesn't return them.

> *And if you're right and this gets*
> *his hopes up about me changing*
> *my mind on dating?*

Again, I think you've already changed
your mind about all this. At least a little

> *Only because Alex makes me*
> *stupid*

More like he makes you COMFORTABLE
and it's getting harder for you to insist
I'm wrong when I said you two could
start dating right now and as long as
you're not making out on the street no
one will assume you're anything other
than friends on different teams.

> *It might be harder but it's not*
> *impossible and I'm still not sure*
> *I'll ever be able to take that risk*

And you don't have to know right now
but if you want to keep the option on the
table you need to do SOMETHING and
make sure Alex isn't currently ghosting
you

*He's not ghosting me*

Is THAT a risk you wanna take?

*UGH FINE*

*

**Alex Valencia**
Sun, Jan 8, 2:30PM

*Idk if you're trying to give me
space again or something but I
hate it just as much now as I did
the last time you didn't text me
for days so stop it asshole*
*Read 2:35PM*

4:15PM

Since you asked so nicely

*Nice to hear from you again*

While I'm glad to know you missed me
enough to do something about it this

time, I haven't been texting anyone back
so it wasn't about giving you space or
anything.

> *So you weren't giving me the*
> *silent treatment because I said I*
> *wouldn't date an American*
> *hockey player?*

No but you ARE wrong for that

> *I might change my mind if you*
> *find me my Lyla Beck*

Wow not even 48hours without your
favorite American and you already saw
the error of your ways

> *Figured if it's good enough for*
> *Naomi Park then it's good*
> *enough for me*

Are you saying Yatesy isn't your Beck?

> *Yeah*

Why must you make my life so difficult?

> *You could always give up*

And lose out on gloating? Not a chance
But speaking of Yatesy, have you told

him yet?

                                                    *No. Why?*

Just curious

                              *I know I said I'd consider it but it*
                              *feels weird to tell him out of the*
                              *blue when I've never even hung*
                              *out with him in person*

Want me to bring him to the art show?

                              *I don't want to tell him in person*
                                                    *either!*

I know that dipshit
But if hanging out in person will help you
see him as a real person you can trust
then it seems worth a shot

                              *I can't tell you not to bring him to*
                                                    *an open event*

Would it kill you to just tell me what you
want me to do for once in your life?

                              *Obviously not if I'm still texting*
                              *you after telling you to text me*
                                                    *back*

Maybe ghosts can text I don't know

*Guess you'll have to wait to find*
*out at the gallery*

I look forward to it

# Chapter Twenty-Nine

ALEX WORKS HIMSELF into a frenzy on his way to the gallery, runs through a million different scenarios of how he'll give himself away and make Noah uncomfortable now that he's aware of his *not bros* feelings for Noah, but seeing Noah for the first time since kissing Mitch and talking to Liv doesn't feel any different from before.

He spots Noah in the back corner of the gallery talking to an elderly couple, and the tense line of Noah's shoulders makes his stomach twist, the same as always. And the smile Noah gives him when he sidles up next to him sends the same warmth fluttering through his chest. And Alex is just as thrilled to see the mischievous glint in Noah's eyes right before he turns back to the couple to say, "You said you liked the Renegades?"

"Yes, but," she says, patting the arm of the man standing next to her. "We secretly root for you when you play them."

Noah's gaze slides to Alex, the smug smile erasing the lingering tension in his face. "Did you hear that, Alex? Even lifelong Renegades fans like me more than you."

The laugh bursts out of him and the couple seems to notice Alex for the first time, turning to him with wide eyes; the man's mouth drops open in surprise as the woman gawks at him.

"Oof, gonna have to work a little harder the next time we play." Alex smiles and holds his hand out. "Hi, I'm Alex Valencia. It's nice to meet you."

The man responds first, shaking Alex's hand as he says, "Jim McEntire. I'd tell you Cat was lying but—" He shrugs, unapologetic.

Alex laughs, and so does Cat, her smile warm and kind as she takes Alex's hand. "It's nothing personal, dear."

"None taken. He's certainly got a way about him," Alex says, gaze flicking to the side. He's unsurprised at the pink creeping across Noah's cheeks and how pleased he is to have caused it. "But once you get past his charm, it's quite easy to hope he loses."

Noah rolls his eyes, his put-upon annoyance cut down by the smile curling at the corner of his mouth, and victorious delight bursts through Alex. It's a familiar sensation, one he's been chasing since the first time he worked a reluctant smile out of Noah, and it brings reality crashing down on him at dizzying speed. The boys have been right all along. Alex has *liked* Noah Anderson since he was fifteen fucking years old and never even realized it.

By the time the McEntires wander off with a promise to root for them *both* at their next game, Noah's expression has calmed and though his grin isn't as bright as Alex likes it, his shoulders are looser as he glances around the room.

There's a hint of relief under Noah's curiosity, and Alex huffs. "No, he had *team obligations* in the morning and didn't want to do the commute. He's really fucking with my plans here."

Noah raises an eyebrow. "Which are?"

"Expanding your support system, duh."

Noah's smile slips away. "Were you this concerned about Sean's support system?"

"No, but he had all of us and his family. And you have what, four people?"

Noah's nostrils flare, his eyes flash, and Alex throws his hands up. "Okay, dropping that." He cups his hand around Noah's elbow and drags him away from the corner. "Come on, let's go pick you something to brighten up that gray abyss you call an apartment. Where're your mom and Sam? I saw a painting at the front that I think might make Sam's eye twitch if we say it's the one you want."

"Good, let's get that one and go."

His clipped tone startles Alex and when he glances over, Noah looks pissed.

"So, your tense shoulders weren't just about having to talk to those fans, huh?"

"No."

Alex arches a brow, mouth thinning. "Wanna be honest?"

"Not really."

"You don't wanna be here?"

Noah clenches his jaw. "Not particularly."

Alex switches tracks and leads them back toward coat-check. "Let's go then."

"I can't just—"

He stops when Alex puts his hand at the center of his back and nudges him forward. "Go get your coat. I'll find Sam and your mom and make some excuses."

"Alex, I can't let you—"

"You're not *letting* me do anything. You can bail with me or not, but I'm making my excuses and leaving with or without you."

Noah sighs out, resistance slipping away. "Fine. Give me your fucking ticket."

Alex grins. "I'll meet you outside."

Noah snatches the ticket out of Alex's hand before he can hand it over, but Alex still catches the tiny smile quirking the corner of his mouth as he turns and walks away.

He knows bailing is the right decision, but he still feels a little guilty when he finds Sam and Simone in front of the photos Sam initially showed them.

Simone's mouth thins as she sees Alex and before he can say anything, she smiles, small and a little sad, and holds up her hand to stop him. "You don't have to make any excuses."

Alex blinks, hesitating for a moment as nerves prickle along his neck. "He's upset."

"Yes," she says. "I know."

"Is it...it's not about art, is it?"

Sam laughs nervously beside her while Simone smiles, genuine and amused. "No, but I'm sure he'll tell you all about it if you ask."

Alex snorts. "Ms. D., I'm sure you know this, but your son is the most tight-lipped person I've ever met. He won't tell me anything just because I ask."

"I think you underestimate yourself."

There's an odd spark in her eyes that Alex doesn't know what to make of, and he's not sure what to say. Thankfully, Simone doesn't seem to expect a response and Alex is relieved when she motions toward the door with a warm smile and tells him to go enjoy his night.

Noah's nose is already pink by the time Alex steps outside and he turns down every one of Alex's suggestions of what to do now that their night is free until, finally, he grumbles, "I just want to go home." Disappointment twists through him, but washes away almost as quickly as it came when Noah asks, "Are you bailing on me?"

"Absolutely not," Alex says. "I'll go home with you any day, baby. You just have to ask."

The way the flush of Noah's cheeks deepens sends a jolt of satisfaction through Alex and for a moment, he thinks...*maybe*.

*

ALEX KNOWS IT'S bad when Noah goes straight for the freezer. He tosses Alex a pint of ice cream, then goes back for one of the frozen protein bars he thinks of as a *cheat snack*.

Alex does not ask. Instead, he grabs a spoon and waits Noah out on the couch. It doesn't take as long as Alex expected before Noah flops down on the opposite end of the couch, arms crossed tight against his chest and frowning.

Alex eats three spoonfuls of ice cream before Noah speaks.

"Do you think I'm ashamed of myself?"

"What? Where is that coming from?"

"My mother."

Alex rears back a little. "What? Your mom thinks you're ashamed of yourself?"

"She thinks—" Noah purses his lips and tilts his head back until he's looking at the ceiling. "We had a...disagreement."

"About?"

Noah scrubs his hands over his face and groans.

"We don't have to talk about it."

Noah drops his hands, frowning as he meets Alex's eyes. "I brought it up."

Alex huffs. "Doesn't seem like you want to."

"I never want to talk about this shit."

Alex hasn't heard Noah like this in so long and he forgot about the rush of outrage he gets knowing there are things out of Alex's control that make Noah sound so beaten down and defeated.

While Alex replaces the lid of his ice cream and sets it aside, Noah sits up. He crosses his legs in front of him and taps his fingers rapidly against his thigh. Alex mirrors him, fingers and all, and Noah's mouth lifts at the corner before he presses his lips together to smooth out the smile.

Alex cocks an eyebrow. "Do you want me to pester it out of you, or do you want to hear about Liv's new girlfriend?"

Surprise flickers across Noah's face. "Liv has a girlfriend?"

"Yeah, why do you look so shocked? Didn't you know she's bi? I thought I told you."

"You did."

"Then why the surprise?"

"I dunno, I figured..." He knits his eyebrows together and purses his lips. "You two might not be into commitment or whatever."

Alex lets out an incredulous laugh. "You think I'm not dating Liv because we have *commitment issues?*"

"It's crossed my mind."

Alex's pulse jumps. "You think about me dating?"

Noah frowns and pink creeps across his cheekbones. "It's hard not to when you're always talking about me *not* dating."

Alex scoffs. "You exaggerate. I've talked about setting you up three times."

"Did you forget how to count?"

"Did you? The last time we talked about it, *you* brought it up."

"Because I thought—" Noah snaps his mouth shut. His shoulders tense as he averts his gaze. "Never mind. I'm sorry I brought it up."

"For what it's worth," Alex says tentatively, unsure how to course correct. "We don't have commitment issues. Much to our mothers' dismay, we just don't want to date each other."

Noah looks back at him, eyebrows jumping. "Your moms want you two to date?"

Alex laughs. "So bad. Like, *so bad.* Apparently, it's taking Liv's mom a minute to warm up to Hilary. But she charmed her dad from the jump so..."

It doesn't ease the tension in the room, but Noah's posture isn't rigid, and that's a start.

"Good to know moms having opinions about their children's love lives is universal."

"Ah. That's what you and your mom were fighting about?"

"Disagreeing."

Alex tries not to smile. "Right. Disagreeing. Your love life was the point of contention?"

Noah sighs. "There's a model she wants me to meet."

Alex's stomach churns. "Your mom is trying to set you up?"

Noah smiles, tight at the corners. "Seems you've got more competition now. She might be even more insistent on this than you."

Jealousy claws hot at his chest. "Are you going to meet him?"

Noah rolls his eyes. "No, that's what the disagreement was about."

Alex furrows his brow, trying to knit the pieces together, hesitant as he asks, "And that's why you asked if I think you're ashamed of yourself?"

"My mom thinks I'm punishing myself because of all my...daddy issues or whatever." Alex blinks, unable to suppress the little huff of laughter, and Noah's mouth lifts in a tiny grin. "My words, not hers."

"I don't know if that's more or less shocking, to be honest."

"What, I don't look like someone who says daddy issues?"

"No, not at all," Alex laughs and when Noah falls quiet, he takes another chance. "What makes her think you're punishing yourself?"

Noah blows out a sharp breath through his nose. "She, like everyone else, doesn't think I should *repress* myself my entire career and the only reason I'm so insistent on all this is because I don't want to be anything or do anything my dad's made it clear he hates."

"Okay," Alex says, still treading carefully. "Is...that why—" Noah glares and Alex tries again. "Like, obviously you have legitimate concerns but...I mean, so does Yatesy, so do the guys his dad could put you in touch with, but you don't want—" He sighs, rubs his palm along the underside of his jaw. "Would you have come out to more than just Millie sooner if your dad wasn't like he is?"

"I don't know. There'd still be hockey to worry about, even if my dad were supportive. Like, it'd still be hard. I don't think I'd be particularly jazzed about being gay while playing under any circumstances, but I don't think I'm punishing myself just because I think dating is an unnecessary risk."

"Okay."

Noah gives him a scathing look. "You don't have to placate me. I know you agree with her."

"No. I don't. I think you're being hard on yourself."

"Like that's any different."

"It is," Alex insists, neck heating as he remembers his talk with Liv. "You throw yourself into everything 100 percent, of course you'd do the same with this. But I don't think knowing the realities of our sport and not wanting to jeopardize your career means you're ashamed. You just have different priorities."

"Maybe," Noah mumbles, looking away. "Or maybe I am a self-hating closet case."

Alex's stomach lurches. He hates seeing Noah like this—wilted and worrying his lip between his teeth, his eyebrows drawn tight and eyes downcast. Alex can't resist anymore; he kicks his legs out and nudges at Noah's calves until his mouth twists in irritation.

"There you go," Alex says. "Stop beating yourself up and be annoyed with me instead."

Noah doesn't laugh, but the line of his mouth softens. "I'm always annoyed with you."

"Liar. I am *so* close to dethroning Thorn as your second favorite person."

Noah does laugh then. "What? Since when is Julien my second favorite person?"

"Who else would it be?"

After a moment of consideration, Noah deadpans, "Toronto Millie."

Alex grins. "Yeah? Does Julien know he doesn't even stack up to your best friend in a different city?"

"Everyone knows they don't stack up to Millie."

"She has set a pretty high bar to clear."

Noah's face softens and his smile is sweet, despite the way he says, "Don't tell her; it'll go to her head."

"Well, now I gotta. She'll be at the All-Star Game, right?"

"Yeah, she'd come regardless, but someone's gotta keep the peace between my parents with all those cameras around."

"Your dad's coming?"

Noah snorts. "After Christmas? No way he'd pass up a chance to see me in a place I can't escape him."

Anger rises hot in his throat. "That sucks. He can't just let you have your weekend?"

"Your parents are coming, aren't they?"

"Yeah, but—"

"The divorce was supposed to be *amicable*. Maybe it'd be different if this wasn't my first All-Star Game but right now, it'll be a whole thing if one of them is there without the other and I'd prefer a weekend with my dad over Jenkins asking me again if my point production is down because my parents split."

"Production," Alex scoffs. "God, that guy's such an ass. You haven't gone more than two games without a point. You're playing out of your mind and on pace for a historic rookie season. He was baiting you."

Noah's eyes widen, his cheeks flush bright, and Alex's stomach turns over when he grins. "You're checking my game logs?"

"Like you stopped tracking my stats after ten either."

"No," Noah says, expression unreadable. "But I always check the box scores and league stats before going to sleep. You'd have to do more than look at the rookie leaders to know how long I've gone without a point."

Alex's face goes hot, stomach twisting. "Gotta keep up with the competition, you know?"

"Oh, for sure," Noah says, smile so wide and bright Alex's embarrassment doesn't really linger, pushed away by the warm satisfaction of saying something to make Noah so pink and pleased.

Heat pools in his gut and sparks up his spine as the image of where else Noah might look flushed and happy pops into his mind unbidden.

He has to look away, blood thrumming as it hits him just how much he wants Noah, how much he wants to touch him, to see how flushed he gets from the exertion of sex, to hear the sounds he'd make and how he'd look after.

His stomach drops and for the first time since accepting his feelings, Alex worries he really *will* give himself away, that what he wants will only be more obvious as time passes, that he'll fuck this up by wanting something Noah might want just the same but refuses to let himself have.

# Chapter Thirty

***the one with bambi***

Sun, Jan 15, 12:25PM

**Beaver**
Ok boys settle a debate for us: is it gay to

kiss your homie?

**Parse**
You didn't ask it right jackass

He means under what circumstances is it

NOT gay to kiss your homie

**Beaver**
I didn't ask it wrong! THAT was the

debate

**Yatesy**
Is this how you two are telling us you've

explored each other's bodies?

**Johnny**
Do I even want to know how this debate

started?

**Kaden**
The answer is obviously no it's not

automatically gay

**Nate**
Or if a girl tells you to

**Mitch**
Or if you're helping your boy embrace his

sexuality

**Anderson**
That's very specific Mitch

**Beaver**
Or winning gold at the Olympics

**Mitch**
Someone's gotta pinch hit when Yatesy's

not around

**Brett**
Anything for the cup

**Ben**
Wait Johnny, does not fucking around

with teammates extend to not kissing

after the cup?

*What girl asked you to kiss*
*another guy???*

**Nate**
She didn't directly ask me but her bio

said she was only interested in guys

who'd kiss another guy and since I didn't

OPPOSE the idea I swiped right

**Parse**
Ofc you did

And yeah johnny, would a cup kiss give

you hives?

**Yatesy**
And what if I was around? Still gonna

offer your services then?

**Kaden**
Don't encourage him, he's already riding

the high of being someone's first gay kiss

a little too hard

**Mitch**
Bet you wish you could go back in time

and ask me instead of a guy who gives

such shitty handjobs you still weren't

sure

**Kaden**
Don't get too cocky Mitchy

You didn't exactly kiss anyone into 100%

certainty

**Johnny**
I would make an exception for the cup

and gold medals

*Talk about GROWTH*

**Beaver**
Mitch has a point there

A handjob def should've been more

clarifying than one kiss

**Parse**
Yeah your boy def let you down yatesy

**Yatesy**
I told you it wasn't bad! And it obviously

made me THINK ABOUT IT

**Anderson**
Hives?

*Johnny's allergic to messing*

*around with team and maybe*

*fucking up the locker room*

*~vibes~*

**Mitch**
And former teammates! Because he's A

BABY

**Kaden**
And because he wants to hold it over

y'all's heads if it ever gets weird because

he's a bitch under that angel face

**Nate**
What about you Bambi? You seem more

like a Johnny than a Mitch

**Brett**
You'd certainly know since you're two

sides of the same coin

**Anderson**
I'm not interested in kissing friends or

teammates
Not even for the cup

**Yatesy**
IT'S THE CUP
No one's THAT straight bambi

**Johnny**
I dunno about that bud I think some

people might think we're all a little gay

for having this conversation

**Beaver**
Yuuuuuup that's why we were having the

debate in the first place because the golf

guys are super boring and uptight

**Parse**
SO uptight

**Anderson**
It has nothing to do with being straight

because I'm gay. I just don't think I

would

**Nate**
HOLY SHIT BAMBI!! NO LEAD UP? NO
WARNING? JUST COMING OUT IN
THE MIDDLE OF THE DAY???

**Parse**
Pretty sure the lead-up was yatesy saying

he was too straight

**Yatesy**
Whoops sorry about that but WELCOME

TO THE TEAM

**Ben**
Thanks for telling us

**Mitch**
Wait Alex have you been trying to set him

up with a GIRL? No wonder he's been

stubborn about it

**Anderson**
Alex has known for a while

Found out pretty much the same as you

guys when he accused me of being a

homophobe because I wouldn't agree

he's hot

**Brett**
YOU WHAT???

**Kaden**
Yikes that's way worse than you yatesy

*It was a fair assumption with
how freaked out you were by a
chirp*

**Anderson**
ONLY because none of my teammates

ever spent so much time borderline

flirting with each other as you guys do

and I didn't want to play along just in

case you took it seriously

**Nate**
It's not flirting if it's stating a fact bambi

*SEE*

*

### Do or Die
Sun, Jan 15, 1:11PM

**Yatesy**
Holy SHIT! You've GOT to shoot your

shot here Alex

*What are you TALKING about?
Just because he's gay doesn't
mean he feels anything close to
what I feel for him*

**Mitch**
BUDDY you literally found out he's gay

because he thinks you're hot and didn't

want you to know

> No???? That's not what
> happened at all

**Parse**
Then how did it happen? I can't really see
you jumping right to bigot because he
wouldn't say you're hot

**Mitch**
Nah it sounds like that's exactly what
happened actually

> It was after our first game and
> he was being really standoffish
> and not making eye contact with
> me again like we weren't even
> friendly anymore and I was
> annoyed and being an asshole
> and asked something like "what,
> I'm too hot for you to look at"
> And he obviously got super
> defensive but I thought he was
> being an Aaron about it. Not that
> he was actually CLOSETED

**Ben**
How the hell did you go from thinking he
was the same as the high school bully to
him telling you he was gay?????

*He never actually told me that
night. But I was pissed and he
was offended and when I pushed
him on why else he'd be so
worried someone might think he
was into me he looked
TERRIFIED so that kinda clued
me in and when I tried to talk
about it he bolted and now here
we are.*

**Mitch**
Alex...you literally just detailed what I
said happened

*It wasn't about ME
It was about me being a GUY*

**Beaver**
I'm not so sure about that. I think I'm
with Mitchy on this one

**Johnny**
Definitely sounds like you hit the nail on
the head and he panicked

**Brett**
WHEN has Noah ever passed up an
opportunity to disagree with you? If he
didn't think you were hot at all don't you
think he would've been an asshole right
back?

**Yatesy**
Obviously he could be different but imo it

seems more likely he was that defensive

because YOU were sitting right there in

front of him accidentally stumbling onto

the truth about his feelings FOR YOU. So

again I'm saying 🔫shoot 🔫your 🔫shot

**Nate**
Holy shit Alex I thought you were better

at reading people than this. I can't

believe you've been trying to set bambi

up with someone else when he's been

into you this whole time

*You can't know that for sure*

**Parse**
Bro you denied your feelings for him this

long but still charmed your way past all

his walls and into being good friends and

now you're just giving up?

*I'm not giving up but I need to*
*think about this. He's been pretty*
*adamant about not wanting to*
*date and I don't want to fuck this*
*up by asking for something he*
*doesn't want or asking too early*
*when he's not ready to say yes*

**Kaden**
OOOH I get it now. When you said you
and Julien were trying to show him the
importance of having things outside of
hockey, I thought you meant he thinks of
dating as a distraction but that's not what
you meant is it? He's decided hockey is
more important than something that
could out him

*Yeah. He doesn't want anyone in*
*or around hockey to know. So*
*much that I'm legit surprised he*
*dropped it on y'all like this when*
*he's been refusing to tell Yatesy*
*even after he found out it was*
*him I was trying to get him to tell*

**Beaver**
Okay that's fair but you're not anyone.
You're his friend and someone he trusts
and all that'll really change in your
relationship is what the two of you do in
private. From anyone else's perspective
it's going to look the same as it has all
season

**Yatesy**
Definitely relate to worrying about that
but I think Beav's right on this one. You
two literally have dinner dates after every

game and no one thinks anything of it
outside of the novelty of two rivals being
such good friends.

**Brett**
SEE! Like I said before you two might as
well be dating already and that's going to
make not getting outed so much easier

> *Look I really appreciate what*
> *y'all are doing but under NO*
> *CIRCUMSTANCES can you say*
> *that to him.*

**Nate**
Noooooo we've spent so long watching
you pine you gotta let us help you get
your man

**Johnny**
Why not? Wouldn't showing him nothing
will visibly change in your relationship
cut down on some of his anxiety about
getting caught?

> *OR he could stop talking to me*
> *entirely.*

**Beaver**
You really think he'd do that?

**Ben**
There's no way

*I hope not but I doubt he'll react
well to finding out anything we
do might make strangers think
we're gay for each other and it's
not a risk I'm willing to take
when I don't even know what my
chances are in the first place*

**Nate**
So what's the play here?

*Idk but not that*

**Mitch**
Hate to break it you here bro but if you're
trying to avoid making a move before
knowing he's into you, you're gonna have
to DO SOMETHING so he knows you're
NOT STRAIGHT

**Yatesy**
Wtf I can't believe I didn't think of that
but Mitch is right. Without knowing
you're interested in guys he won't read
your obvious crush as anything other
than you being a flirt

*How the hell do I do that without
telling him he's the reason I
realized*

**Johnny**
Just do what everyone else does and drop

it in the groupchat that you kissed Mitch

and liked it

**Mitch**
Ooooh YES! You should definitely do that

but not in the groupchat. You won't be

able to tell if he's jealous over text

*I'm not doing that but I'll try to*

*figure something out if y'all*

*PROMISE not to meddle*

# Chapter Thirty-One

NOAH HAS NO way of knowing who Mitch kissed, or if it was even one of the guys in the chat, but he can't stop thinking about it being Alex. About Alex offering to kiss him while he was drunk and then again, the next morning, serious even in his sobriety, or the way his face fell, the offended pinch between his brows when Noah said he didn't want Alex's kiss. He can't stop thinking about how maybe Alex might actually want to kiss Noah for regular reasons, that maybe he was so unsure of himself he went to one of his friends to test if he could be into guys.

Alex and his boys are all so easy with their affection, so willing to do anything for each other, so comfortable in their own sexualities that one kiss wouldn't complicate things. It's easy to imagine him going to one of them and asking for a favor. The only thing keeping Noah from being consumed by white-hot jealousy is that whoever kissed Mitch wasn't *certain* he liked men afterwards. But the problem with that, the thing Noah keeps coming back to is that maybe the uncertainty didn't come from Alex not enjoying a kiss with a man, maybe he was uncertain because he wanted to be kissing someone else, that God forbid, if Noah had ever taken Alex up on his offer, it might have been different, he might have been certain at the end of it.

It's a terrible thing to think, and it settles into his brain unbearably. His heart clenches anytime his attention skims over the thought, skin buzzing with frenetic, restless energy that he can't get rid of, no matter how long he stays after practice or how much more he works out. It makes him reckless. He sits a little closer and looks a little longer after being caught. He takes a little more of what he always wants from Alex, as if doing so will make Alex's feelings any clearer.

It does nothing to answer the question he's typed but never sent, but it does leave him wanting Alex even more and when Alex goes a little quiet every time the boys spam the group chat with questions about who Alex has been trying to set him up with, the little spark of *maybe* he's tried so hard to smother becomes impossible to ignore. He just wants to know, wants Alex to figure him out, wants him to *do* something so he can stop thinking about the possibility.

### *the one with bambi* 😈😊

Sun, Jan 22, 2:35AM

**Nate Hoffman**
Holy shit you will NOT believe this but

an absolute rocket just asked me and Kip

to go home with her

9:15AM

**_Kaden Devine_**
I don't have any trouble believing

someone tried you after striking out with

Kip tbh. Didn't that happen to you like

two weeks ago?

**_Sean Yates_**
Don't worry babe I'd try to pick you up

first if you were both strangers in a bar

**_Mitch Lawrence_**
Ooooh what about you bambs? Nate or

Kipping?

> *Does it look like I'd be hitting on*
>
> *strangers in a bar?*

**_Shane Parson_**
🙂 that's why it's a hypothetical bambi

**_Mitch Lawrence_**
Don't be boring

> *Is everything the same? We just*
>
> *don't know each other?*

**_Mitch Lawrence_**
Sure

> *Then Kipping*

**Aidan Beaverton**

Would it be Nate if you weren't a hockey
player?

*If I'm not a hockey player I*
*wouldn't be interested in a*
*hockey player at all*

**Shane Parson**
Wait does that mean it's Nate if you are
but they aren't?

*I guess yeah*

**Aidan Beaverton**
Okay no that was an easy Nate's hotter
question so I'm gonna need you to
explain what criteria you're working with
here

**Johnny Russo**
Why does it matter if they are or aren't
hockey players?

*It doesn't. It matters that kipping*
*isn't from a hockey family*

**Mitch Lawrence**
ALEX WAKE UP!!! We just found out
everyone you CAN'T set bambi up with

**Shane Parson**
Got any other deal breakers?

**Aidan Beaverton**
Shit me and kade don't make the cut

either

Cold hearted man

**Kaden Devine**
Way harsh bambi

*Oh my god why are you all LIKE*

*THIS*

**Aidan Beaverton**
SORRY WE WANT TO BE INCLUDED

**Ben Huskins**
This is NOT the conversation I thought

I'd be reading when I saw Nate's first text

What's the deal with hockey families?

*Don't particularly want two sets*

*of legacies to live up to. And no, I*

*think that's pretty much it. It'd*

*probably be a problem if he*

*didn't like hockey though*

**Aidan Beaverton**
Ok you know what that's a pretty solid

point there

**Sean Yates**
Likes hockey you say??? What about

PLAYS hockey??? Because I've heard

some stories about the ASG

**Nate Hoffman**
Okay first off ASSHOLES that happened
ONE TIME and that's NOT what this
was! I mean she wanted to bring me and
Kip home TOGETHER. At the same time.
Second are you saying guys hook up with
each other at the ASG?? And THIRD you
only GUESS???? I'm hurt bambi

*What the hell*

**Nate Hoffman**
My thoughts exactly!! Me and you would
be so hot together I can't believe it's I
GUESS

**Mitch Lawrence**
You're right I don't believe that

**Shane Parson**
How'd that go for you??

**Mitch Lawrence**
There is no way you and Kip had a
threesome

**Nate Hoffman**
Yeah bc Kip wasn't into it

But I swear it happened

**Brett Stevenson**
It's too fucking early for all this

**Shane Parson**
More like you guys are late to the party

**Johnny Russo**
Nate would you have been into it if he

was?

**Mitch Lawrence**
It's Nate johnny ofc he would

**Nate Hoffman**
I think I should be offended but you're

right. Always up for a good time and it's

not gay if there's a girl involved so why

not, you know???

*I don't think that's true*

**Ben Huskins**
Are we just skipping yatesy's asg

bombshell??

**Mitch Lawrence**
It is 100% true

**Aidan Beaverton**
Yeah can we circle back to the ASG?? I've

got some questions

**Shane Parson**
So you're saying there's a chance Noah

could hook up with Bradley next

weekend

*I could WHAT???*

**Sean Yates**
I can't believe out all the guys in this

league Tate Bradley is who you'd go gay

for


**Shane Parson**
Are you saying you wouldn't let him pick

you up?


**Sean Yates**
I absolutely would but if I was picking

one guy in the entire league as my gay

exception he wouldn't be it

> *Is everyone in the ntdp insanely*
>
> *chill about sex/being a little gay*
>
> *and that's why Alex thought I*
>
> *was experimenting with*
>
> *teammates in juniors or???*


**Kaden Devine**
I mean you DO hear things about juniors

> *I've never heard ANYTHING*
>
> *about juniors!!!!!*


**Aidan Beaverton**
Who would yours be then?


**Mitch Lawrence**
Brett where the fuck is Alex?? He's

missing out on all the intel

*Intel?? Alex I stg if you send me*
*headshots of guys in the league*
*who don't have hockey families*
*I'm never speaking to you again*

**Alex Valencia**
Ouch it's like you don't even know me

Who even looks good in their headshots?

I'd def send you their instagrams first

*DON'T DO THAT EITHER*

**Sean Yates**
Easy. Erik Lindholm.

**Shane Parson**
That tracks. You've always been a goalie

fucker.

**Brett Stevenson**
Yatesy did your DAD tell you about stuff

that goes down at the ASG? Or have you

been secretly fucking around with

someone in the league

**Sean Yates**
I literally just told you about the girl in

my econ class I'm talking to. Ofc it was

my dad 😫 APPARENTLY his idea of

being supportive is making sure I know

whatever I'm doing there's another

player doing the same and that league

events are the perfect place to meet up
with them lmao
But I also lowkey think he wants me to
date another player because we'd both
have the same to lose

*Really?*

**Sean Yates**
Can't know for sure but he has said that's
the benefit of dating another athlete

*No I meant I would've thought he
wouldn't want you to date
another player because it'd be so
much more complicated*

**Johnny Russo**
Do I need to do another PSA about not
fucking around with teammates

**Mitch Lawrence**
No you've made yourself clear there babe
but think about how much EASIER it'd
be to date a teammate??? Never have to
worry about getting laid on the road
when he's right there with you

*Uhhh what if you break
up????????? What if it's a BAD
breakup???????*

**_Johnny Russo_**
THANK YOU!!!! I knew someone other
than Ben had to agree with me on this

*

NOAH WAS ALREADY struggling with sticking to his plan, but his agent—the best in the game—telling his son there are benefits to dating another guy in the league cracks right through his conviction. He doesn't know how much more of this he can take. How much longer he can ignore his feelings, or the growing signs Alex feels the same, before coming out of his skin. How he can keep forcing himself to make the responsible decision when he's no longer sure it's irresponsible to try. He doesn't know how much longer he can spend with Alex before the desperate ache to be reckless for once wins out.

From the moment he gets out of bed, he's on edge, every shift of fabric as he strips down to shower lighting him up. He doesn't even know if Alex is the one who kissed Mitch, but the only time he's safe from thinking about it is when he's asleep. So of course, the morning he and Alex are having their trip to Vegas documented for an ASG feature, he wakes up hot and flushed, aching for a reality where he gets to kiss Alex the way Mitch might have, to touch him in all the ways he did in his dream.

The water is just the edge of too hot, but it doesn't work the way it usually does; it doesn't burn the thrum out of him like it does when he's panicking, and his skin is too tight. It does nothing to stop his dream from replaying in Noah's mind. Mitch pulling Alex in by the neck, their mouths slotting together perfectly, Alex opening his mouth for Mitch's tongue, the quiet whimper Mitch made when Alex pulled at his hair and changed the angle, kissed him harder, more urgently, taking what he wanted as Mitch clung to Alex.

The dream had shifted, and instead of Alex pulling away from Mitch, it was him instead, cheeks pink and mouth red as if it'd been him the whole time. Alex's mouth on his neck and the scrape of his teeth across the hinge of his jaw and the way it made Noah gasp, the gentle way Alex steered him back onto his bed and how good it felt when Alex dropped his weight and pinned him down. The hopeful look in Alex's eyes as he ran his thumb across Noah's bottom lip, his quiet, pleased laugh as Noah whined from the slightest touch, and the earnest way he'd whispered, "All you have to do is ask—you know I'd give you anything you want."

He turns the water down; no need to be a furious shade of pink, skin raw if the heat isn't helping the way it should. He jerks off, vision blurring as he focuses on the tile in front of him, reciting the roster of last year's Cup winner, then two years ago. He keeps going until he comes. It works to keep any image of Alex out of his mind but barely takes the edge off and Noah has no idea how he's going to survive hours on a plane with his captain, Alex, and two of the NHL's social media team dead set on turning their private flight into a feature on their rivalry-defying friendship, or the subsequent weekend with his father, when he's already coming out of his skin because of a dream he can never have.

Alex tests Noah's ability to not be weird from the moment they see each other. He practically vibrates with excitement as they wait for Erin and Felicity, the NHL's social media people, to board the plane, talks with Woody like he's another one of the guys, not at all intimidated by talking to Austin Blackwood the way Noah had been the first time he met his captain.

When Woody tips his head back on a bark of a laugh after Alex tells him they used to use pictures of Hockey Canada captains for accuracy targets in the dev program, the tips of his ears go pink and he looks pleased in a way that has jealousy searing through him, hot and bitter.

It sets Noah off. He's jittery and his mind races as the frenetic energy he's tried to keep at bay finally wins out. Alex glances over when Noah starts fidgeting but doesn't address it until takeoff, when he flattens his hand on Noah's bouncing knee just long enough for Noah to register the touch and stop moving, just long enough to burn right through him.

Woody's swept up in a conversation with Felicity or Erin, but Alex still drops his voice when he asks, "You good?"

It's stupid how pleased Noah is to have Alex's full attention on him again, and his answer comes out a little more snappish than he intends. "I'm fine."

Alex's mouth thins. "Try that again."

Noah crosses his arms, but Alex just waits him out with an expectant look that makes Noah's skin buzz. He blows out a sharp breath and doesn't even lie. "I'd be better if we could film this thing once we landed. They're probably going to give Woody a tiny mic to shove in our faces, and we won't even have anywhere to escape to."

Alex snorts. "You and Kev's seatmates video really wasn't that bad."

"Wow, checking my stats and watching my media," Noah says, unable to stop his smile from spreading. "You like me so much. It's embarrassing."

Alex rolls his eyes and grins. "Nah, it's not embarrassing. Not even for a second."

Noah really should know better by now than to set Alex up for being earnest, should have expected Alex's honesty in the face of a chirp about their friendship, but the response still knocks him back, makes him so bubbly and warm all over that when Felicity hands Woody a stack of cards but no microphone and starts filming, Noah forgets to be nervous about what his dad will think when he finds out about this feature.

Woody starts the whole thing off by giving the camera a spiel about competition being the foundation of Alex and Noah's friendship and how if they'd known the trick to getting a private flight to their first All-Star Weekend was befriending his draft rival, he and Castillo would've made more of an effort to be more than acquaintances. Noah mostly loses track of the rest of it, his attention focused on nothing but Alex knocking their knees together then leaving them pressed together as he ducks in and whispers, "I've got you; we'll look so good. Everyone's going to love you after they watch this."

Noah isn't so sure about that, but the whole thing is so much less stressful, the answers coming so much easier, with Alex by his side needling him into forgetting they're on camera. Throw in Woody going off track two questions in and adding his own anecdotes from his rookie year to their answers and Noah ends up having a pretty good time.

By the time they land, Noah no longer feels three seconds away from vibrating apart. When Alex bullies him into going out for dinner instead of ordering room service, he has fun there too, and when he falls asleep that night, he dreams Alex took him back to his room. In the morning, Alex meets him before they head down for media and their fingers brush when Alex hands him the second coffee in his hands. Noah lingers on the curve of Alex's lips as he smiles and doesn't look away when Alex catches him.

The dream wasn't like the last one. The only part he really remembers is Alex saying, "I only kissed him because you wouldn't let me kiss you," but it cracks his resolve more than anything else, leaves his blood thrumming with how badly he wants to give in and get what he wants.

He sticks with Woody most of the day, and he knows he should be more careful, but something about being here this weekend and the easy way he sees guys embrace their friends from other teams when they stop to say hello sweeps away the urgency of hiding how much he likes Alex.

In Noah's last interview of the day, Alex joins the group of reporters behind the camera and the heavy weight of his attention as he finishes his answer lights Noah's nerves on fire.

Noah raises an eyebrow when he's done and Alex grins, tipping his head to the side, and alerting Noah to where Felicity is standing next to another cameraman, before he says, "I've got a question for you, bud."

Noah huffs, trying not to smile as the reporters glance between the two of them. "It better be good."

Alex's smile turns smug. "It is." He waits a beat. "Everyone knows you're on pace to beat Taylor Ford's rookie stats and I just wanted to know—do you think you will?"

Noah's pulse jumps. "If you say you're going to match his, do you think the jinx will come for both of us?"

A zip of satisfaction goes up Noah's spine when he gets a laugh out of the reporters, but he feels crazed by the way Alex looks at him, with a wide smile, deep dimples, and a challenge in his eyes when he says, "I guess there's only one way to find out."

Noah is positive his face is doing something obvious, but he can't seem to contain it as the last bits of his resolve crack. A reckless abandon muddies his inhibitions and screams for him to just give Alex what he wants—even if that's Noah himself.

Noah shouldn't even be entertaining the idea, not when he knows the ramifications, not when his dad will be here tomorrow, not when he has rules, but here, in this moment, all Noah wants is to keep Alex looking at him like he's the only one in the room. Here, with the cameras rolling and a dozen different reporters as witness, Noah can't give him everything, but he can give Alex the confidence he's trying to goad out of him to keep that look on his face for a little while longer.

"If we don't, we probably owe Ford dinner for losing, but yeah, I think we both will."

# Chapter Thirty-Two

ALEX HOPED BLACKWOOD'S presence would make Noah more comfortable than he usually is around so many people over the weekend, but even in his ideal version of this weekend, he never imagined Noah like this. He thought for sure Noah's nervous fidgeting from the beginning of their flight, the anxiety Alex could still see in the flit of his eyes when they were at dinner, would linger over the weekend but it doesn't.

Alex doesn't know what happened, but when they meet up Friday morning, Noah seems less cautious, more confident, more *something* Alex can't put his finger on but leaves him off kilter all the same. The only time he's not one step behind, confused by what the shift in Noah's demeanor means, is when he's behind the camera at his media scrum. But even that leaves his head spinning when he successfully goads Noah into being confident, almost cocky, *on camera.*

Alex catches Noah watching him while they're waiting for the room service Noah insisted on this time, but he doesn't look away like

Alex would. There's a slight flush across his cheekbones but he doesn't seem embarrassed. His gaze doesn't waver as the understanding that he'd been intentionally looking settles between them. Alex doesn't know what other way there is to read that, and he wants to know if they're on the same page, but he can't bring himself to ask when the bubbly excitement under his attention quickly gives way to nervous anticipation for what's happening tomorrow.

For the first time since they announced the rosters, it really hits Alex that he's barely nineteen and doing something some guys never do once. Alex knows his talents, knows he's good, knows he's capable of achieving great things, but in no way did he imagine he'd ever be the only representative from his team at the All-Star Weekend his rookie year.

It doesn't take long for the day to catch up to him once they've eaten and as the night wears on, he keeps expecting Noah to get up and leave, but Alex likes that he doesn't. He likes that by the time he realizes how late it is, Noah has sunk so far down the headboard he's practically lying in bed with Alex.

Alex's plan to tell him to just crash here gets derailed when Noah catches him looking and gives him a soft, sleepy smile that makes his chest ache.

His face must do something weird when he thinks about how far they've come because Noah's smile dims and his eyebrows knit together. "You good?"

Alex gives his head a little shake and clears his throat. "Yeah, I was just thinking how crazy it is that we're here right now."

Noah blinks in surprise, his mouth twisting curiously. "Are you nervous?"

"Aren't you?"

"I'm always nervous."

Alex looks away. "Didn't look it today." The sound of Noah's quiet laugh draws his attention back. "You look like you belong here." His stomach flutters, warmth flowing through his veins as he takes in Noah's soft, pleased smile.

"You always look like you belong. And this weekend is no different."

Alex doesn't know what to say to that, but Noah doesn't seem to expect him to, and the quiet moment settles like a weighted blanket, warm and calming, over Alex.

He wakes up hours later, the first light of dawn barely peeking through the edge of the curtains, and he's too sleep-groggy to overthink it when he curls into the warm body next to him and falls back asleep.

He wakes again to the sound of a blaring alarm that is not his own and finally registers who he's sharing a bed with. Noah stirs awake the moment Alex gets up to shut off the sound, grumbling about how they have time for one snooze, and Alex can't even think about what it means that Noah set an alarm, that he *decided* to sleep here last night.

Alex tosses Noah's phone on the bed next to him and flees to the shower to think. It does nothing to quell the desire building hot in his stomach, and neither does the way Noah, still soft with sleep, doesn't even try to disguise the slow drag of the once-over he gives Alex on his way to collect fresh clothes.

They're sharing a locker room later today, but Alex still changes in the bathroom, his heart pounding and his head hazy with how badly he wants to pin Noah down and—

"Morning, sleeping beauty."

The smile Noah gives Alex is nothing like the eye roll Alex expected. It's breathtaking and Alex wants... Shit. Alex wants so much, wants Noah with a desperate, burning ache he's only ever associated with his drive to excel at hockey.

It should be impossible to want someone so badly, for him to feel any stronger about Noah than he did last week, but Noah asks, "Do you want to get breakfast before I have to go play nice with my dad?" with this playful grin Alex has never seen him wear while talking about his dad and the feeling explodes.

It's overwhelming, really, how it sticks to the walls of his heart, crams itself into the open spaces in his mind, seeps through his veins, and across his nerves, consuming him. Alex won't call it love, but he looks at Noah and he knows he'd do anything to keep him like this, playful and happy and looking at Alex like they want the same thing.

But the thing is, Alex doesn't think Noah will give him the chance to try. He fully expects whatever's gotten into Noah, whatever progress he might've made in convincing himself he can have what he wants, will disappear once he's spent time with his dad again. He feels guilty thinking it; but hope has taken root and the idea that Alex is reading too much into Noah's behavior, or Paul Anderson's potential to obliterate the chance Alex might have before Noah can give it to him makes his stomach churn, uncertainty rising like acid anytime his mind hovers over the possibility too long.

But when they meet back up, Noah doesn't look upset. He's fidgeting, but they're about to step on the ice with the league's best players and Alex can't really blame him for that. He's so amped he can't stop talking, and Noah just lets him, unfazed by Alex running his mouth the whole night.

The night passes in an electric haze, every moment knocking Alex back, leaving him giddy, but some are sharper than others, some carry more punch. There's Chris Fortier coming up to him and Noah in the locker room and asking them to sign sticks for his kids, the two of them wide eyed like he and Noah are on their father's level, a nervous tremble to their voices when Alex asks what their names are. There's Tate Bradley tapping Noah's skate and *winking* at him as he says, "This one's for you, rookie," and the shock that plays across Noah's face when Bradley goes up for the Breakaway Challenge and does the same trick shot Alex first watched Noah do. The flash of white-hot jealousy when Bradley comes back for Noah's assessment and Alex can tell how pleased he is by Bradley's attention. Ending the reigning Vezina-winning goalie's save streak and tying first in the accuracy challenge and being able to watch and enjoy Noah compete in fastest skater with no need to *be better* brewing under the surface of his skin. The bright, beaming smile Noah gives Alex when he skates back to him after winning fastest skater and how it cracks Alex open, affection overflowing with nowhere else to go but out, written across his face in the curve of his mouth and the crinkle of his eyes for anyone to see.

When they meet up with their families after, Alex's parents are chatting with Noah's like they're old friends, and his sisters are so enraptured with whatever Millie's saying that they don't even notice Alex and Noah join the group.

Noah's dad is the first to see them, and if Noah's behavior today has been a mindfuck for Alex, it's nothing compared to how disorienting it is for him to witness Paul Anderson give Noah a broad smile before congratulating him like he means it.

Noah turns a little pink, but he doesn't look uncomfortable, just quietly pleased about his dad's praise, and if Alex didn't know better, he wouldn't suspect that someone so seemingly proud of their child could be responsible for cutting him down so much.

It's almost a relief, really, when there's a lull in conversation and Sierra pulls him away by the wrist because at least his sister being annoying is familiar.

"We need to talk about your fucking crush, asshole." Alex rolls his eyes and Sierra's nostrils flare. "Don't you dare deny it."

"Pick a better venue next time. I'm not talking about this here."

Sierra's expression twists in scorn. "Obviously. This is just your courtesy warning that I'm going to make you talk about it tonight whether you like it or not."

Alex snorts, but is stopped from arguing when Tate Bradley calls out for him and Noah, polite and charming as he tells their families he needs to steal them for an hour, then he can't think about Sierra's demand, all he can focus on is keeping up when Bradley drags them into a loud bar full of raucous NHL players, buys them drinks, and herds them into a booth of various guys from the Western Conference. It's so late when he gets back to his hotel room, Alex is sure he's escaped whatever conversation his sister was going to subject him to.

But when he finds Sierra cross-legged at the edge of his bed, Alex isn't *that* shocked. He should have known better than to underestimate Sierra's commitment to butting her head into shit that's none of her business.

"I can't believe Mom gave you my spare key."

She stops channel surfing and throws the remote aside. "But can't you?"

Alex grunts and flops down on the bed. He pushes at Sierra's back. "Get off or I'm not talking."

The bed shifts. "Okay, let's talk."

Alex pillows his head on his crossed arms and looks to Sierra set up in the chair, arms crossed and expectant as she stares Alex down.

"What do you want to talk about?"

"You ready to tell me you're in love with Noah Anderson yet?"

Alex's stomach swoops. "I wouldn't go that far."

Sierra blinks but doesn't comment on how easily Alex gave her the information she wanted. "What are you planning to do about it?"

"I don't know."

Sierra purses her lips. "What do you *want* to do about it?"

"A lot of shit I don't wanna say to you."

"Fair enough. Do you think he feels the same?"

"Sometimes."

"*Sometimes?*"

"Yeah, that's what I said," Alex grumbles. "It's fucking compli-cated, okay?"

"No," Sierra says decisively. "It's challenging because sports suck, but it's not complicated."

Alex scoffs. "Yeah, I'll make sure Noah knows it's only *challenging* when he—"

Alex's throat constricts. He can't say it.

"You think he's going to turn you down?" When Alex refuses to answer, annoyance flashes across her face, but she softens a moment later, and her voice is gentle and sure when she says, "He looks at you like Dad looks at Mom, Alex."

He doesn't even know what to do with that but— "That doesn't matter."

"Alex—"

"Stop, please. I know what I'm talking about. It's not as easy as him feeling the same when hockey comes first. It's about him wanting to *try*. About him thinking it's worth it—that I'm worth it."

Sierra's expression turns stormy. "You are."

Alex lifts one side of his mouth in a smile. "Thanks, but you're not really who matters here."

Her nostrils flare and she blows out a sharp breath. "I had an interesting talk with Millie tonight."

"Oh, yeah?"

"Well," Sierra says, smile sharp. "Dani was being nosy."

Alex sits up. "What did she do?"

"You know her, works everyone's life story out of them without them realizing. Turns out Millie has never been Noah's girlfriend, never even blurred the lines of romance and friendship like you and Liv."

Alex huffs. "I knew all that."

"Mm-hm. You wanna hear what she said when Dani asked if he had one now?"

"That he doesn't."

"Not even close." Sierra pauses for dramatic effect, radiating smugness. "She laughed and said, 'Not unless you count Alex.'"

Alex's chest goes tight and his blood thrums. "I don't know what I'm supposed to do with that."

"You lay it all out on the line and take the fucking chance. What's that Gretzky quote? You miss one hundred—"

"Shut the fuck up," Alex says, smiling despite himself.

"Percent of the shots you don't take," she finishes.

She lets out a squawking sort of laugh as she bats away the pillow Alex throws, and Sierra's conviction doesn't soothe Alex's worries, or bolster his confidence, but she takes the other bed that night and whispers, "Thank you for telling me, I know it wasn't easy," into the dark of the room, and Alex falls asleep feeling lighter than he did when he woke up.

# Chapter Thirty-Three

NOAH NEVER COULD have prepared for the wild delight playing hockey *with* Alex brings him. He's been on the ice when Alex scored several times. He's been on the receiving end of his smug smile when he skates by after a celly, even more. But he's never passed the puck through the opponent's legs to set Alex up for a goal; he's never scored on a no-look pass from Alex or been on the receiving end of Alex's delighted smile in the middle of hockey; never skated back to the bench shoulder to shoulder with Alex as he says, "Holy shit, Anderson, we are so fucking good together."

Being on a team with Alex is electrifying, winning with Alex makes his blood sing, scoring the game-winning goal off Alex's pass in the championship game isn't even close to the most important goal he's ever scored, but when Alex crashes into him after and yells, "Thanks for the money, baby," Noah's sure it will be one he remembers forever.

Noah gets named MVP and in the rinkside interview with Catherine

McDonald after, he isn't thinking about what his dad might say about setting her up for another soundbite about how good Noah thinks Alex is, all he's thinking about is how good they played together and how much fun he had.

"You two looked like you've been playing together for years," she says after Noah mentions how perfectly Alex set him up for the last goal of the game. "I don't think anyone would've guessed this was your first time playing together with how natural you looked."

Noah's cheeks hurt with how hard he's smiling. "Yeah, it was fun to play with him instead of worrying about shutting him down for once. Definitely didn't expect to click so easily, but yeah, we looked pretty good out there, didn't we?"

"You did. Do you think your on-ice chemistry has anything to do with the way you've clicked off ice?"

The words fall out before he second guesses them. "Oh, for sure."

"It's not unusual to have friends across the league, but I don't think anyone really expects two draft rivals who were never teammates before the draft to form a meaningful relationship. But despite being pitted against each other in the lead-up to the draft, and the constant comparisons as your seasons flourish on rival teams, you two seem to have done just that. Would you agree?"

Noah catches Alex's eyes over Catherine's shoulder; he's not even trying to hide his smirk, always so smug when Noah has to talk about him.

He glances back at Catherine McDonald and grins. "I wouldn't."

Her shock hasn't even turned into a question before the laughter spills out of Noah. "Sorry, I'm just messing with him—he's standing right behind you."

Catherine follows Noah's gaze. She lets out a quiet laugh when she sees him, then turns back to Noah with a playful smile. "Just between you and me, then. How would you describe your relationship with Alex?"

"Competitive," Noah says, heart soaring when he glances over and sees Alex watching him with a soft, satisfied smile. "He's a constant thorn in my side, but he's also one of my best friends."

*

NOAH'S BARELY OUT of the shower, not even all the way dressed, when Alex knocks on his door.

"Can't believe you insulted me *while* calling me your best friend," Alex says first thing, as if they didn't already have this conversation, then stutters to a stop. His gaze sweeps across his body and lands on the shirt still in Noah's hand. "I always forget how jacked you are. Jesus, your abs make me sick."

Alex is teasing, probably, but Noah still pulls his shirt on to hide the flush creeping across his face and tamp down on the heat simmering low in his belly.

When he reemerges, Alex has moved to the edge of Noah's hotel bed and is watching Noah with scorching intensity.

Hunger curls through him, the want that's been building since the first time they met boiling over unbearably, and by the way Alex grins at him, it's written all over his face.

Alex licks his lips and Noah is sure this must be the moment he finally forces the issue and makes them talk about the tension and desire growing between them. But Alex goes right back to the conversation they already had.

"Rude of you not to just call me your best friend. Had to make sure the whole world knows I annoy you too."

Irritation sears through him. He doesn't hide it. "Not even close to the whole world, bud."

Alex narrows his eyes. "Look at that. I'm annoying you right now. You gonna tell me what I did or just glare at me?"

"You didn't do anything."

"Don't lie to me."

Noah's temper flares. "You didn't! That's the fucking problem."

Alex's expression sours. "Are you going to tell me what I didn't do so I can fix the problem?"

There's so many things Noah should say, so many questions he wants to ask, so many reasons to kick Alex out before they go somewhere they can't come back from. The one that comes out is, "Are you the one who kissed Mitch?"

Surprise barely flickers across Alex's face before he clenches his jaw and closes himself off.

"I think you are."

Alex is tense, his fingers curled tight in the sheets. "Why?"

"Call it a hunch."

The muscle in Alex's jaw jumps. "Does it matter to you if I did?"

Blood rushes in Noah's ears, heart pounding uncomfortably. "Yeah."

"Why?"

"Because it does!"

Alex watches him for a moment, the look in his eyes one Noah can't quite parse, doesn't really want to either. When he stands, Noah's stomach drops.

"Do you think it should've been you? Did you *want* it to be you?"

Noah is on fire. "Did you?"

"I did. I do." Alex steps closer and curls his fingers around Noah's wrist like Noah might leave if he doesn't. He strokes his thumb along the soft underside of his wrist and Noah catches the sound behind his teeth and goes stock still.

"Alex—"

"Will you finally let me do something about it?"

Noah's eyes fall shut. His stomach twists and his pulse jumps. He swallows and meets Alex's gaze. "You know this is a bad idea."

"I don't care."

"This won't change anything."

Alex's grip tightens around his wrist momentarily. "We both know that's not true."

"It doesn't change what's working against us."

Alex hums and Noah's breath hitches when he moves his hands to Noah's waist and closes the gap between them. "But do you want it?"

"Alex..."

"Noah, please, for once in your fucking life, be selfish and take what you want."

"I—" Noah can't think of a single reason not to. All his carefully considered reasons come up short against the want burning through him. Noah takes a shuddering breath, hooks one arm over Alex's shoulder, and breathes out. "Okay. Kiss me."

Alex grins like he's won something and slots their mouths together. He's slow and tentative, but when Noah makes a frustrated noise low in his throat, fingers tightening at the nape of Alex's neck, his laughter vibrates through Noah as he gets a hand in his hair, grip loose while he mumbles right against Noah's mouth, "Demanding."

He pulls at Noah's hair then, tilts his head back to change the angle, and when their mouths meet again, there's nothing careful about it. Alex's tongue is hot against the seam of Noah's lips and when Noah opens for it, everything goes white hot and hazy. Noah doesn't know what to do with his hands, or what Alex likes, but none of it seems to matter, as Alex sets the pace, works these little sounds out of Noah when he bites at his bottom lip before pressing back in for another searing kiss.

Alex slows it down as he turns them toward the bed, every press of his mouth just as hot as the slick and filthy kisses from before. When the back of Noah's knees hit the edge of the bed, Alex doesn't push him down, just keeps kissing him and Noah wants more, needs more. When Noah leans back and drags Alex in, he follows, boxing him in on the bed before pressing open-mouthed kisses down Noah's neck. The drag of his stubble sends sparks up Noah's spine, the scrape of his teeth along the underside of his jaw makes him shiver.

Alex shifts on top of him, hand hot like a brand as it slips under Noah's shirt. His thumb strokes just above the waistband before he lines their hips up and grinds down. Noah is so hard, and he wants so much, and he can't think past how good it feels to be pinned down by Alex, to chase the friction of another man's body.

The brush of his sweats along sensitive skin doesn't stop Noah from thinking he could come like this, that he will come like this if Alex doesn't stop grinding their hips together, moving their mouths slow and filthy.

Everything slams back to him all at once and he freezes underneath Alex. He hates how hard it is to force himself to say, "Wait."

# Chapter Thirty-Four

NOAH PUSHES HIM off, and Alex's blood runs cold. His stomach roils as he sits up. Noah's flushed and rumpled and Alex fists the sheets as the desire to touch him more, to touch him everywhere, washes away with a wave of nausea.

"Was I moving too fast?"

Noah won't even look at him and icy dread floods his veins.

"No, but—you know we can't go any further." Noah sits up, still refusing to look at Alex. "This was a mistake."

"No, it wasn't."

Noah turns to Alex with a wild, panicked look in his eyes. "We can't pretend this didn't happen—we can't go back to ignoring the obvious now."

"I don't want to do that. I don't want to pretend I don't like you. That I don't want to—"

Alex stops, throat going hot, and Noah laughs, harsh and mean.

"You can't even say what you want! You don't know how to make this work anymore than I do. Why couldn't you leave it alone? Why did you have to ruin—"

"Ruin? I didn't ruin anything!"

"Yes, you did! You make me want everything I've—God, you make this so fucking hard. I was perfectly fine pretending you didn't feel the same, and now I can't."

"Don't," Alex grinds out. "Don't put this all on me like you didn't flirt with me all fucking weekend! Like *you* didn't set this in motion by asking if I was the one who kissed Mitch! Don't act like you don't want this!"

"People want a lot of things, Alex! Wanting something doesn't mean we can *have it*."

"We can try. We can. I want to try, but if you really don't, if you don't think it's worth it, you have to say so. You can't lash out at me and push me away, so you don't have to live with making another decision for the sake of hockey instead of yourself." Noah looks guilty and something ugly and hot twists in his chest about being right. "Say it then. Tell me it's not worth it."

"I don't want to."

Alex's anger fizzles out. "Then let's try."

Noah's mouth twists, eyes wide and imploring. "What happens when you get bored of me or decide you're not really interested in men or that it's easier to pretend you're not when you have girls to fall back on? Then what? What do I do then?"

Bile rises in Alex's throat. He hates how unsure Noah sounds. He swallows hard and tries to keep his voice steady. "That won't happen."

"You can't—"

"Yes, I can!" Alex snaps. "Do you think I kissed Mitch outta the blue? You think the guys haven't hounded me for *months* about my big gay thing for you? Jesus, Anderson, I've spent the last three weeks accepting that I've been a nervous wreck every time I've seen you since we were fifteen fucking years old and I wanted you to *like me* because you made me feel weird and giddy and I just wanted you to look at me, to pay attention to me at all. I've thought about this, and I've thought about you. About what I want to do with you, about how making you happy feels like getting a breakaway. Noah, I *won't* decide I'm not into you."

"Alex," Noah says, quiet and broken. "That was my first kiss—what do you think you're going to get from this?"

"What? Is this seriously about experience?" Alex asks, incredulous. "I've kissed one more guy than you! I don't know what the fuck I'm doing either. We can figure it out together."

Noah is bright red. "Not having experience with another person's dick is *not* the same as being a virgin and you know it! You know what you like, and you know what feels good and you don't have to worry about disappointing me because you're going to be my first for everything! It's not the same. This isn't the same."

Alex deflates. "You underestimate how much I want to impress you all the time, Anderson. And I'm sorry, but there's no way in hell you actually believe a first time can't be disappointing. Neither of us know what we're doing and that's fine. And helping you figure out all the things you like isn't a burden. That's part of the fun! Seeing what makes someone come undone. I *want* to be the one you figure this out with. I want to do this."

"How?" Noah demands. "What's the play here?"

"We're friends; people know we hang out. No one will think anything of it as long as we're not all over each other in public. It's not impossible. You just have to let yourself have it."

"But I don't know if I can. I don't know *how*."

Alex's stomach drops. "You need to decide. I can't just—" He grimaces, throat tight again. "If you don't want this, I don't know how easy it'll be for me to put my feelings aside and go back to how we were. I'll need time to—" He huffs out a humorless laugh. "I'll need time to get over you."

"So, either we do this, and I lose you down the line, or we don't, and I lose you now?"

"No, that's not what I'm saying. But I don't know, and I don't want to promise something I can't give you."

"You can't promise we won't break up or that playing for different teams while in a relationship won't be too hard either. You can't promise that we won't fuck this up."

"And what if I never get over you? Or I do and it still sucks to know you didn't think I was worth it, and it hurts too much to be in the same room with you? Or if it's just weird after everything that's changed, maybe it can never be like before. I don't know. We could mess this up either way."

"One of them doesn't come with the risk of getting caught."

"Noah, come on. You are the most committed person I know. If you decide you don't want to get caught—we won't."

"That's not how any of this shit works, Alex!"

Alex huffs. "And kissing someone and pretending you don't want to isn't how things work either, but that's what you want to do. Seems like we both have some far-fetched ideas, huh?"

Noah's nostrils flare. "You kissed Mitch! You have sex with Liv! You're the same with them as you were before. Why does it have to be different here? Why do I have to be different? Why can't we stay friends?"

"Because I'm stupid about you. Because I want you, because you're the first person I've ever even thought to *be* in a relationship with. I want to do this—date, be exclusive, whatever you want to call it. I want to be with you in all the ways I've never wanted to be with anyone else, and it fucking sucks you think I can turn that off because you're scared."

Noah's face falls. His eyes are bright in the worst way. "And it's really fucking shitty that you love Liv and sleep with her, but you can't even promise me we could be *friends again* because you kissed me one goddamn time!"

"You're not Liv."

"I know," Noah snaps.

"That's a good thing. You mean something different to me." He tamps down the frustration rising in his throat, but the pained noise he makes might be worse. He sighs. "You know she thinks I'm in love with you?"

Noah's eyes widen. "Don't you dare."

His grin comes easier this time. "I wasn't going to say she's right."

Noah looks skeptical. "Then what were you getting at?"

"You know, Liv and I have known each other since, like, pre-k, I think. We've been neighbors and basically inseparable since they moved in next door from Dallas. There was this stupid thing kids did in fifth grade; they'd go off and kiss behind this big ass tree near the swing set and Liv said she didn't want to be unprepared if she ever got dared into it or whatever, so she kissed me after school for practice. Our parents are good friends too, and our moms have always thought we'd get together, and you know, when people think you should do something, it's hard not to think you should do that too."

"Okay," Noah says, apprehensive. "What are you saying?"

"I'm saying Liv and I have tried to love each other the way our parents want us to. We slept together that first time because we were best friends and everyone thought we were and it was a safe way to get our first times out of the way, but it never felt different after that, it didn't change how we felt about each other or the way we acted—"

When Noah makes a judgmental face, Alex huffs. "Okay, I mean, we obviously kept having sex, but it never felt like it needed to be more. It never changed my gut reaction to people saying we were going to end up together. I know what it feels like when someone says I love someone I don't want to date, someone I know I'll never love differently than I already do. When the guys say I'm in love with you, it feels like I could. That if you let yourself do something you want, that if you take a chance and try this with me, that I will."

Noah's shoulders slump. "You make it really hard to put hockey first."

"What I'm hearing is you think you could love me too."

Noah rolls his eyes, but he's smiling, the barest hint of one, but honest and there, and all for Alex. "We're going to have to get your hearing checked one of these days."

"Mm-hm, definitely."

Noah is quiet for so long Alex's mood starts to wilt and uncertainty sets in when Noah finally says, "We both have a lot to lose if people ever find out."

"I know."

"You maybe more than me."

Alex hums. "The pitfalls of not being *the* generational talent."

Noah's face twists in irritation. "I'm being serious."

"So am I. People will bend over backward to keep benefiting from the talents of someone great even when they don't like them, even when they've done terrible things, and right now, you have far greater expectations than I do. People are going to give you more leeway. I know you're being serious when you say it could be worse for me."

Noah shakes his head, frowning. "And you still want to take the risk."

It's not a question, but Alex still says, "I risk a career-ending injury every time I get on the ice and that's still worth it. And I'll keep risking it because I love hockey and I'm good at it. And I know we could be fantastic if we tried. Think about how good it felt to play together? We're already good together and we're going to keep being good together no matter what we're doing."

Noah laughs, sharp and loud in the quiet hotel. "What? Dating isn't *hockey*."

"Don't be stupid. You know we could get hurt out there. But you're not gonna stop playing hockey because you *might* get hurt and it *might* fuck up your career. Have you ever once thought hockey wasn't worth it?"

"No, but—"

"Then why should this be different?"

"You can't possibly compare getting outed to a career-ending injury."

"I can. I mean, I'm no stats nerd but I think if we compare the number of outings in the league to career-ruining injuries, the numbers suggest an injury is far more likely. That's just math."

Noah mouths *that's just math* as he presses the heels of his hands to his eyes and drops his elbows to his knees. He's tense and quiet for a long time and it's a shock when he eventually mumbles, "I need to talk to my agent."

He glances over at Alex with a worried expression, speaking louder, more confidently this time. "I'm not saying no, I really don't want to say no, but I need to know what all of this will entail, what we can do to keep it from getting out, if there are any outcomes between keeping a secret and getting outed that we're not thinking about, if we're compounding the risk by dating someone in the league, someone on another team." He takes a deep, heaving breath and finally holds Alex's gaze. There's still a wild energy behind his eyes, but his face is softer than before, the edge of stubbornness falling away into something sad and apologetic. "I can't give you anything more than that right now."

"Okay."

"You don't have to say it's okay. I know you're disappointed."

"Yeah, well. I know what it means for you to consider this at all."

Noah rests his hand over Alex's. He's quiet for another moment. "If I could worry less, I wouldn't even hesitate. I hope you know that."

"Yeah, I do," Alex says, which is probably the hardest part of all.

It's just not fair that they have to worry about this at all. But they do and he can't begrudge Noah for being taught this part of him is wrong and that hockey is all he's worth. He can't hold it against him, but it doesn't make it hurt any less that they can't just do what they want without a risk assessment.

*

**WEEKEND DREAM TEAM: *Noah Anderson and Alex Valencia dazzle in 3-on-3 despite rivalry***

*Just six months ago, Alex Valencia was almost an afterthought in his own draft, not because of his lack of talent, but because of the long shadow Noah Anderson's generational talent cast. Last night, the league's hottest new stars shone brighter than ever as a two-headed offensive machine.*

*The two rookies combined on 9 of the 17 goals the Metro scored across both games, earning them comparisons to some of the greatest duos in the game and leaving many hungrily imagining how unstoppable their team would be if they had them both.*

*Though their Metro teammates were quick to agree that Anderson and Valencia's chemistry was unreal, the general consensus amongst them when asked how impressive they could be given more than 40 minutes at 3-on-3 was summed up best when Philadelphia's goalie, Rasmus Pettersson, said, with a huge smile in his post-game interview, "If we ever find out, I hope I'm in net behind them."*

# Chapter Thirty-Five

NOAH NEVER THOUGHT he'd be thankful for having to spend extra time with his dad, but he is a little relieved he's not on the same flight back with Alex. Besides, his dad's been almost pleasant this weekend. He hasn't criticized Noah once, not even as a caveat to any of his praise as usual. It's not enough for Noah to think he's turned a new leaf, but it is nice to have lunch without being three seconds away from a panic attack the whole time. But at the end of lunch, when his dad pounces on the lull in conversation to mention, again, how well he and Alex played together, Noah wonders if he's ended up in a twilight zone of some sort.

"Yeah, it was a lot of fun." He looks to his mom for help, but she looks just as confused as he feels and Noah laughs, a nervous huff of a sound. "Who knows, maybe we'll get to do it again next year."

"You rarely find chemistry like that at an All-Star game. You two had lots of people talking. Especially after that feature they did."

There's this gleam in his dad's eyes that makes Noah nervous.

"You watched it?

His dad nods. "Mm-hm. Blackwood as the interviewer was a nice touch. You're not the most personable person, but you came off very likable in what they edited together."

"Uh, thanks?" The backhanded compliment is familiar, but he still feels like he's missed a step. "It went a lot better than I expected."

His dad makes an indistinct sound of approval. "There's a lot of ways the league has changed since I was playing. No matter how you feel about it, marketing players, selling you guys to fans as people to root for, is a huge part of growing the game now."

"Good thing people like him," his mom says, voice crisp and airy.

"People like him when he's talking about Alex Valencia, when he's playing with Alex Valencia, when he is *with* Alex Valencia," his dad says, voice hard as the other shoe drops.

"We've already talked about this," Noah mumbles. "He's my *friend*."

"I know, and people love that," his dad says. There's a weird twist to his mouth Noah can't read. "It hasn't escaped me that there's been a growing interest in your little rivalry friendship, but now that people have seen you two play, everyone's talking about what it'd be like to have the two of you as permanent linemates."

The very idea makes Noah's brain whir. His mom's voice is icy when she asks, "What are you saying, Paul?"

The only sign of annoyance is the thinning of his dad's mouth, there and gone almost as fast. He is perfectly composed when he looks at Noah again. "Jenkins said you two'd be the next Ford and Fortier if you were both on the same team. Dameron called you star-crossed lineys. What I'm saying is they're about to build a franchise around you but Valencia is the type of guy the league loves to sell to the fans. Keep him close, make him part of your brand, and Burgess will bend over backward to get him for you."

"My brand?" Noah says, too loud for where they are. "He's not an endorsement deal, or a piece of equipment the team can give me, Dad! He's my *friend* and the Renegades are going to build their team around him just the same. I'm not—I won't exploit him or our friendship because you think he makes me look better and Jersey could poach him one day."

"You might not want to exploit it, but you've given the league and the fans a story they're eating up. They're going to talk about it whether you like it or not. You might as well benefit from it professionally too."

Noah's heart sinks. People will talk about whatever they want. They talked about him and Alex for years before there was anything real to talk about, and they talk about them even more now. If his dad's right, and Noah thinks he might be, people are only going to be more interested after this game and that's just another thing to add to the list of obstacles keeping them apart. Because how the hell are he and Alex going to get away with dating if people are already paying too much attention to their lives—to who they are to each other.

Not for the first time, Noah aches for the reality where the draft lottery went different—the one where he and Alex were in different divisions, where the rivalry would've faded into something obsolete, and he wouldn't have to worry about people caring about them at all. But he's not sure Alex would've made such an effort with him if they were in different divisions. He doesn't think they would be actual friends if the distance had been greater, and the thought of not having Alex nauseates him.

But Noah might've fucked that up already; he might've pushed Alex right out of his life just by wanting him in it too much. The possibility seeps into his bones like he's already lost him. He's in over his head and doesn't know how to start the conversation with his agent, doesn't know why he can't be like Alex and just *go for* it, and by midweek he's so caught up in his head his teammates notice.

Derek and Kevin only give him until Thursday before they ask him to stay behind after morning skate to drop pucks while they practice faceoffs. Noah knows a ploy when he sees one, but Kev lost every faceoff he took against Buffalo, so it's not like he can say no.

"Does this count as snake bitten?" Derek asks after he's won the tenth in a row.

"If our best faceoff taker can't win a draw, yeah, I think that counts," Noah says.

Kev makes a face. "You swap in."

Noah wins three in a row, but Kev wins the next five and while he no longer looks frustrated, his smile back where it always is, he still wants to face Derek again. He wins the first, loses the second and third, then wins the next seven.

After the eighth win, he quietly breathes out, "Oh, thank God," before turning to Noah and poking him in the chest with the blade of his stick. "Now it's your turn."

"I don't think I really need to practice faceoffs any more than normal."

Derek snorts. "Kev, he's onto us. Red never turns down extra practice."

Noah frowns. "What do I need to say to get out of here and shower?"

"What's got you so bummed?" Kev asks. "Because it can't be hockey."

"And if it *is* hockey," Derek says, "then we need to take you out and find you a girl or something because you're playing out of your mind and shouldn't be stressing *at all.*"

"I'm not bummed, and I'd really rather not see you two play wingman, ever," Noah says, thankful his cheeks are still pink from exertion and the chill of the ice so they don't betray his embarrassment.

"I'm a great wingman," Kev says, affronted.

Derek's face twists in disbelief. "You absolutely are not. But that's not the point. The point is, right now, you're only engaged when we're on the ice. Everywhere else, it takes forever to even get your attention. If you're not bummed, you're definitely preoccupied by something. So, what's the deal here, bud?"

"I—" Noah stops, clears his throat, starts again. "I need to call my agent about something and—"

Kev's eyes go wide. "You don't have some sex tape scandal brewing, do you?"

Noah breathes in wrong, and Derek can barely talk from laughing so hard. "Why is *that* the first place you went?"

Kev shrugs. "Seems more likely than a drug scandal."

"Why does it have to be a scandal at all?" Noah grumbles.

"Unless you're firing the guy, I don't see what else would have you stuck in your head like this."

Derek rolls his eyes. "Yeah, but you never stress about making calls because you love to hear yourself talk."

Kev tilts his head in concession and Noah huffs. "No scandal, no firing. It's just—" Noah can't *think,* he doesn't know how to say anything without outing himself. He's grasping at straws. "Just wanna get his opinion on some shit my dad said over the weekend about *marketing myself* and *creating a brand* and it's...a lot. I don't want to worry about public image. I just want to play hockey, you know?"

Derek grimaces. "Ah, your dad's one of *those* dads."

Noah laughs, bright and genuine. "Former player who's now in sports broadcasting? Buddy, he's one of the worst."

"Well, fuck that," Kev says. "Don't worry about that shit. Your brand is being God's gift to hockey. All the marketing will fall into place around you."

Noah flushes hot from the tips of his ears to his collarbones. "Maybe so, but—" He shrugs, at a loss for words again. "Belanger can't grow the game if all his stars are boring and unlikable, you know?"

"Okay, calm down," Derek says. "You keep making insane shit look easy and people won't care if you're flat as a board or a Grade A asshole. They'll just want to see you play."

Noah wishes that were true, but he knows it only extends to people who are already fans, that to get new ones he needs to be at least a *little* fun, and that to keep the old ones he can't step outside of the mold too much. Being gay will be a problem for some, and for others, they'll need to humanize the guy who plays sweet hockey to keep coming back. He has no idea how he can avoid getting outed if the thing that makes him likable is the one person people can't read too much into his relationship with. Most of all, he doesn't even know if Alex will be okay with Noah benefiting from being friends with him or if one day he'll grow resentful of always being linked to Noah, of making Noah more personable while still being cast as inferior.

On Friday morning he wakes up in a cold sweat, having dreamed Alex got traded to the Hellions and blamed Noah for ripping him away from his team, and calls the only person he wants to talk to when he feels like this.

"Anderson?" Alex garbles.

"Yeah, shit, did I wake you up on your off day?"

There's a beat of silence, then muffled sounds and Alex is back, talking clearly again, "No, I was brushing my teeth. We've got film review because we got our asses handed to us last night."

Noah sucks in a breath. "You did okay though."

Alex snorts, no humor in it. "You know as well as me that doesn't mean shit."

"Yeah, I know but—" Noah huffs. "Gotta take the positives from the negatives and move on because you can't win 'em all, champ."

Alex laughs, loud and unexpected in Noah's ear, then clears his throat. "Jesus, is that what Kirkpatrick calls a pep talk?"

"God no. It's what Tiki tells the backup goalie when he loses—"

"You've gotta be fucking with me. There's no way Tikkanen says that to a two-time Vezina-winning goalie."

"Right? I was *sure* there'd be a problem the first time I heard it, but no, Jelly thinks it's hilarious."

Alex hums. "Gutsy saying it the first time though."

"Yeah..."

Alex sighs. "Don't leave me hanging here; what's up?"

"I wanted to ask—ugh. God, look, I know you're going to think this is stupid, but I need to know—are you okay with how much attention we're getting for being friends?"

Alex's voice is flat. "Is this your way of saying *you* aren't?"

"No! I—fuck. I don't know how to say any of this. But I had lunch with my dad and—"

"It's no surprise your dad has a problem with it, but that doesn't mean I do. And I don't. Like I've been saying, it helps us out if people know we're friends."

"That's not what—he wants me to make you part of my brand! He thinks I'm only likable when I'm with you. He thinks I should take advantage of the benefits I get from being your friend, so I look good because he's got it in his head they wanna build a franchise around me and they'll try to poach you if enough people keep comparing us to Ford and Fortier based on one All-Star Weekend. And I don't want you to *resent me!* I don't want you to—to get fed up when the rivalry bullshit never fucking fades away and we're stuck together our entire careers. I don't want—Alex...how are we going to do this if people never stop talking about us? If you end up hating me because of it?"

"You're likable all on your own, Anderson."

"That's not—" Noah scrubs his hand through his hair, pulling at the ends. "I'm not arguing about that because it's not the point."

"Uh, yeah it is. You're better in media now because *you've* stopped trying to impress your dad and started enjoying hockey again, because you have guys on your team who took the time to get you out of your shell and didn't believe just because you're the next Gretzky you think you're better than anyone, and everyone is more likeable when doing media with their friends instead of alone because it's not as nerve-racking. You don't need me to make yourself likeable!"

Noah's throat feels tight. "You're biased."

"Yeah, but I'm also right. So, you don't need to worry about me thinking you're using me or whatever. *You* hate them linking us to each other way more than I do. Should I be worried you'll resent me because guys like your dad think you're only likeable when you're with me?"

"No, that'd be stupid."

"Exactly."

Noah lets out a ragged breath. "I know you think I'm just a pessimist, but you have to know this is going to be hard. That the increased attention people pay to us, both as individual players *and* rival friends, could just as likely make it harder to get away with this."

"I know it won't be a cakewalk, but we can do it. I want to *try*."

Noah makes a low, embarrassing sound. "I do too, you know I do. But I need to know what this looks like, Alex. I have to know."

"I know you're not trying to hurt me, but this still sucks. I hate that we need a fucking *contingency plan* and can't just be impulsive about what we want! I hate that you're going to have to tell your agent that it's me—"

"What? No. I wouldn't *out* you."

"Uhh, pretty sure you need to tell your agent which player you want help getting away with secretly dating if you want a good plan."

Panic shoots through Noah. "If you don't want me to, I won't. I wouldn't do that. I can get a good enough idea without that."

"Tell your agent it's me, Noah. I don't want you to say yes and then him find out it's me and that change something major, and you tell me to fuck off. I can't *do* that."

"I wouldn't do that. I'm going to get a plan and get my shit together. I want to do this. I want you. I don't half ass anything, Alex, and I haven't really proven it outside of hockey, but I don't bail on commitments. You've gotta know, I'm all in from the jump or not at all. Especially here. Especially with you."

Alex is quiet for a moment and Noah's panic spreads; he really has fucked this all up before he even had it.

Alex huffs, not quite a laugh, not quite humorless, and Noah goes still, as if holding his breath will do anything to change what Alex has to say.

"Tell your agent everything." Alex doesn't sound mad, not even necessarily hurt; he just sounds tired. "Call it my contingency plan."

*

HE TAKES A shower, eats breakfast, paces the entirety of his apartment three times, does some yoga, pulls up the contact for his agent and—

Accepts the call from Tiki, makes plans to meet him at the bakery down the block, eats a whole croissant—

—doesn't call his agent.

Wakes up, eats breakfast, goes to morning skate, gets hassled by Derek and Kev, goes home, lies in the middle of the floor and wonders if it still counts as savasana off his mat, pulls up the contact again and calls his agent.

David answers on the second ring, the same as always.

"Morning, Noah. What do I owe the pleasure of an actual phone call?"

"I call sometimes," Noah mumbles.

"You *reply* to emails more."

Noah laughs, just a quiet puff of air. "Life's easier for you if I have no problems though."

"Sure, but I'd be a terrible agent if I didn't field questions and concerns and offer my expert opinion on how much money is too much money to spend on your ELC."

"Fair enough."

"So, which can I do you for?"

Noah picks at the hem of his shorts, smooths it down. "Uh, I guess a little bit of everything except the money part."

David sounds all business when he asks, "The problem part too?"

"Not—I mean, potentially. But nothing newsworthy yet. Hopefully ever."

"Okay. I know a thing or two about keeping things out of the press, so let me have it. What are we working with here?"

Noah takes a breath and rips the Band-Aid off. "I'm gay."

"Okay," David says with no inflection. "Thank you for telling me."

"Yeah, well...helps that you're Ford's agent too and that...I mean, I'm friends with Sean and know he's..."

"Ah," David breathes. "Regardless, I know it's not always the easiest, that it's taken a lot longer for other clients to share this information. It's good you can trust me no matter the reason. And given the way you communicate, I assume this is something you're only telling me because you're being proactive."

"Wow, should I be worried I'm this predictable?"

"Everyone is. Even the unpredictable are predictable in the way they'll leave you scrambling," David laughs, and the knot unfurls in Noah's stomach. He can do this.

"Okay," Noah laughs nervously. "I *am* trying to be proactive. I've always planned— I mean, I've never wanted anyone even close to hockey to know, but that's...not how things panned out this year. God, this is so stupid—"

"Hey, none of that. Any concerns you have about getting outed, or the relationship you're trying to keep secret, or hell, even questions you have about discreet and trusted escort services, I've heard it all."

For a brief, dizzying moment, Noah imagines Taylor Ford asking David Yates for escort recommendations his rookie year and somehow, that's what makes the words come out. "Well, I know you told Sean getting involved with other players is likely the safest option because of the mutually assured destruction of it all but, uh, it's probably different for long-term involvement, isn't it?"

"Are we talking a guy you have a long-standing casual but mutually beneficial sexual relationship with—" Noah makes a sound and David lets out a quiet, amused huff. "Okay, so I take it you've gone and caught feelings and want my advice on…"

He leaves it open for Noah to fill in. Noah grits his teeth and forces himself to say, "On how bad of an idea it is to date another NHL player."

If David thinks it's a bad idea, he doesn't react, just carries on like this is another day at the job, "All right, teammate or not?"

"Not."

"Okay, are you two friendly or will seeing you together shock people?"

"Like, do people know we're friends or—"

"Is it a guy you met on an app who you've never been teammates with or share a mutual friend with who might turn a few heads if you're seen at dinner together?"

"No, we're friends, but—it already turns heads when we're together."

David breathes out. When he speaks, there's a note of *something* Noah can't interpret in his voice. "Knowing your press and that it's not a teammate, that really only leaves—"

"Alex Valencia, yeah."

"Okay. So, my view on closeted relationships is there's no such thing as a bad idea, only situations that will be more challenging to manage."

Tension bleeds out of his shoulders. "And how challenging would this be?"

"Probably less than you're expecting. The two hardest relationships to manage are the ones with teammates and the ones with no connection at all."

"I thought teammates would be the easiest."

"To keep secret from the public? Absolutely. But keeping it from your teammates may be more difficult when you both share a locker-room and road schedule with the same people. And say you manage to keep that under wraps, or if you were out to your team, if the breakup's bad, one of you could lose the room the same as you could by coming out. So if I were to say one relationship was a bad idea, it'd be the one with a teammate because you really need to go into it knowing if it ends, one of you might get traded for the sake of yourselves or the team."

"Oh." Noah swallows hard. "I guess that makes sense. But trades happen all the time, what if—"

David's laugh comes out as a quiet puff of air. "If one of your GMs gets in a bidding war over the two of you, we will deal with that when it comes. But most likely, if you're ever teammates, it won't be until you can choose the same team as UFAs. GMs don't like to give up cornerstone players when the power is still in their hands."

Noah laughs, a little hysterical. "That's what I told my dad, but he's buying in *hard* on our potential to be the next Ford and Fortier thing Jenkins has been pushing."

"Yeah, that's not going away any time soon. People love a good narrative almost as much as they love imagining how much better their team would be if they had *just this one guy* and you and Alex have both— unreal talent and the most compelling story the league's had since Petrov and Newman went from brutalizing each other every chance they got to best men at each other's weddings."

"Won't all that attention make this harder for us to keep it a secret?"

"As long as you two aren't booking honeymoon suites or having semi-public sex someone might catch on camera, the attention won't change much. Since we don't have to phase you into being public friends, your biggest priorities going forward are being conscious of how you interact around people, and how you talk about each other, and most of all, where you choose to stay the night together outside of your own homes."

"That's it? Just go for it? What happens if we do our best and people still start talking? Or it doesn't get out publicly, but it gets around the league? What do we do then?"

"Alex's agent and I deal with it. We'll need to touch bases sooner rather than later and make sure we're on the same page, but I'd approach one or both of you being bothered about being talked about by connecting you to women in the same situation as you—"

"Like a fake relationship?"

"Doesn't need to be all that. Maybe just a couple dinners people will talk enough about to quiet all the rest of it."

"And if it's more than people talking?"

"We get ahead of the story and gain public sympathy for your privacy being violated, we send you out to do community outreach and show kids there is room for them in this league, we give the league its very own Park and Beck rivals in love talking point, we do what's necessary to make you both so well liked that if anyone tries to mess with your careers, they'll get run out of town for it. I know it seems like you'll lose everything if this got out, but I will not let that happen. We will make it work, however this goes."

Noah breathes through the tightness in his throat, but he still sounds choked up when he says, "Okay. So go for it, then."

"Yeah, if that's what you want to do."

"I—yeah, I do, but"—Noah wipes at his eyes—"I've never kept a secret with this many variables and I'm not sure I can."

David makes a sympathetic sound. "I know why you're apprehensive, and I wish I could eliminate that completely, but all I can do is assure you I know what I'm doing and you're neither the first nor the last players to try out dating."

Noah breathes. In, out. In, out. In...

"Do you want to know what I'd tell Sean in this situation—as a dad, not an agent?"

...Out. "Yeah."

"I'd say to go for it, that when the reward is something that makes you happy, the risk will always be worth it. But I'd also tell him things get real messy real fast when one of you has doubts, so if he has any at all, it's not very fair to get involved with someone who doesn't."

# Chapter Thirty-Six

THEY LOSE AGAIN and there are no personal positives to draw from the game, just two crossbar misses and a botched pass in the last minutes of the game that directly led to the Nashville's game winner. He's in a bad mood and all he wants to do is call Noah and sulk until the mood settles into something quieter, but even if they were in the same time zone, he's not sure he'd pick up the phone. He doesn't sleep well, and he doesn't even get a moment to assess how much of his mood has carried over before Brett's throwing a pillow at his head and saying, "Get up. Nate's having an actual crisis."

**_the one with bambi_** 🎭😊

Sun, Feb 5, 8:21AM

**_Nate_**
Hey assholes wake up

**Anderson**
Isn't it super early for you? Why are you

up?

**Nate**
Haven't slept!

**Mitch**
No way you're just getting in

**Beaver**
Why not??? Do I need to send you that

article about sleep hygiene again?

**Nate**
No, my sleep hygiene is fine. I can't sleep

because Kip hates me now and I don't

know what the fuck to do

**Parse**
Wtf do you mean he hates you???

**Anderson**
What happened?

**Nate**
I'm pretty sure he thinks I want to fuck

him and now he can't even look at me

and got dropped to second because the

chemistry's nonexistent at this point and

Trip pulled me aside after practice a

couple days ago to tell me whatever

happened, Kip and I needed to figure our

shit out because he needs his actual top

line and now trade deadline rumors are
popping up and I'm freaking out

*Johnny*
HE WHAT??

*Brett*
Why would he think that?

*Yatesy*
First, you know better than to believe
every trade rumor. Second, you didn't
even have that threesome so why the hell
does he think you're into him?

*Nate*
Turns out "it's not gay if there's a girl
involved" is NOT universal and he read
waaaay too much into it when I said I'd
follow his lead but was game if he was

*Mitch*
It'd be one thing to assume that if you
paid more attention to him than the girl
but he thinks it because you said it was
up to him?????? what the FUCK

*Nate*
At first I thought he was pissed because
he'd spent the entire night talking to her
and she ended up not wanting either of
us if it wasn't both and it would blow
over but it only got worse after the all-

star break

**Ben**
Ok so you don't know for sure he thinks
you're into him? Could this just be a
terrible misunderstanding and he's going
through something not related to you?

**Kaden**
Is there a chance he's just a prude who's
having trouble processing his rookie's a
huge slut?

**Mitch**
No way he didn't figure that out after the
first month of living with him last season

**Anderson**
Wait you don't still live with him, do you?

**Nate**
No but we used to carpool and now he
always goes in early or stays late so he
doesn't have to be in the car with me and
everything SUCKS

*How are you even thinking about*
*carpooling right now??*

**Parse**
Have you talked to him yet? Or is this
based solely on him avoiding you?

**_Kaden_**
Yeah, is there a chance he's not a huge
homophobe and this is just a terrible
coincidence like ben said?

**_Nate_**
No, before the asg I apologized for
cockblocking but he brushed me off and
said that wasn't why he'd been weird but
wouldn't really elaborate and left before I
could get him to admit what the real
problem was. I was hoping the time off
would help him get the fuck over
whatever got up his ass but nope! It got
WORSE! I finally had the chance to
corner him after last night's game and he
told me I need to be more careful
because something like that can spin out
of control real fast in this league and I
was like????????????? So he tells me that
if I'm into guys that's fine, but I need to
work on not slipping up when I'm drunk
because not everyone will react well.

**_Brett_**
Uhh does he think HE'S reacting
well????

**_Mitch_**
Are you fucking kidding me?? React
well??? In what world is he reacting

well????

**Beaver**
Did you tell him it's not gay if there's a
girl involved?

**Nate**
Yeah, I told him being open to a
threesome while wasted didn't mean I
was into him or any other dudes but then
he asked if my answer would've been
different if I was sober and I guess I
paused too long and before I could
answer he was giving me this spiel about
how it was FINE to like men but now that
he knew MY BEHAVIOR toward him has
been my way of FLIRTING it would be
irresponsible of him as the captain to
encourage my crush by not establishing
clearer boundaries between the two of us.
Then he wouldn't fucking LISTEN when I
said I haven't been flirting with him and
that I AM straight and just kept insisting
we needed to spend time apart.

**Beaver**
Jfc what a fucking ego

*So what, he thinks it's responsible*
*to fuck up the locker room vibes*
*by refusing to believe what you*

*say?*

**Nate**
I don't know. I told him he can believe
whatever he wants but he has to know all
I want is to play good hockey and that I
can't do that if he's avoiding me like the
plague and he said he'd WORK ON
THAT but I don't know how much longer
this can go on before it gets weird in the
room

**Parse**
How could he live with you for an entire
season and not understand that flirting is
your default setting?

**Mitch**
Seriously fuck this guy, you flirt with
everyone. He's not SPECIAL

**Yatesy**
Jfc I can't believe he's trying to repackage
his homophobia as being a responsible
captain.

**Anderson**
Can't you though

**Mitch**
Don't be a dick bambi

**Anderson**
Sorry, I wasn't trying to be. I just mean,
that's the risk, right? Guys saying they're
good with it but still being uncomfortable
around you once they find out?

**Yatesy**
I know but it's fucking pathetic to spin it
around like he's doing Nate a FAVOR
instead of just owning his shit

> *But he didn't find anything out.*
> *He assumed and then decided it*
> *was true even when Nate said it*
> *wasn't.*

**Nate**
I don't really care that he thinks I'm into
men but what the fuck am I supposed to
do here? Trip wants me back on the top
line and it won't happen if Kip can't get
over himself but I don't know how to
convince him I don't want to sleep with
him??????? Like he knows I'm into
women so it's not like picking up will do
much good

**Johnny**
Is there a chance this really isn't
homophobia and he genuinely believes
distance is what you need to get over

him?

***Kaden***
Does that make it any better?

***Nate***
I guess there's a chance, but the results
are still the same, aren't they? My best
friend on the team is still avoiding me
and now I'm being shopped and
everything sucks and I'm worried
everyone on the team is going to think
I'm into them because I've apparently
been FLIRTING WITH EVERYONE
THIS ENTIRE TIME and even if he gets
over it I'm still going to know he didn't
believe me and that I meant so little to
him as a friend and a teammate that he'd
rather me get demoted than talk to me

***Johnny***
I just mean, if there's a chance he isn't
being a homophobic dick about all this
and he's only being a dick about a friend
having a crush would it help if you told
him he's not your type and that you're
into one of us instead?

***Anderson***
How is lying about being into men going
to fix the problem that started because

his captain thinks he's into men?

**Yatesy**
There's still a chance he won't believe
you, but I think johnny's onto something
here. If he thinks you're into someone
else and still avoids you then idk how
you're supposed to think he's okay with
you liking guys.

**Brett**
I don't know if that's a good idea guys.
Should Nate really confirm something
that's not even true to someone who
might be homophobic? What if he tells
people and Nate has to deal with this shit
from more than just him?

**Nate**
Okay who wants to be my fake
unrequited love?

**Mitch**
Me duh 🙃

**Ben**
You're really going to do this?

**Anderson**
Nate, Brett's right. Rumors spread fast
and this could stick with you forever.

**_Nate_**
I haven't decided but I don't think telling
him I'm in love with Mitch is going to
make it much different than him
thinking I'm in love with him. If he's
going to tell people, he's going to tell
them because the truth doesn't fucking
matter. He already thinks I am.

*

ALEX CAN'T SAY he's *surprised* when Noah calls him later, but his stomach drops all the same. Luckily, or unluckily given the way Casey and Joey look at him the rest of the night, he can't answer because they're at team dinner. Theoretically, it gives Alex time to prepare for being turned down, but his heart clenches and annoyance still flares hot through his veins when Noah says, "I think we need to talk about what's happening with Nate."

Brett is in the shower, but Alex still steps out on the balcony, not sure he wants Brett to walk in on this conversation. "Unless you're telling me this shit's made your decision, then I don't see why."

Noah blows out a sharp breath. "Alex, this is *our reality*. This is what could happen if the wrong person even *thought* we had feelings for each other; if we do an awful job hiding we're together."

"I know," Alex grits out, head spinning and stomach churning painfully. "I know people might talk. And we can handle that. You're going to be the best in the game—"

"Nate won the Calder last year! He was leading Anaheim in points when he got knocked down. It only helps so much if people who matter have a problem with it."

"If you've decided you can't do this, Anderson, just say so, because you can't talk me out of it."

Noah makes a frustrated noise. "I'm not trying to! But you're just like Nate; all of you are. What if *you* say something about me by accident? What if you can't keep this secret because you don't even realize how much of yourself you always give away?"

Noah's words hit hard and a sharp cracking pain sticks between his ribs like blocking a shot. "I don't—"

"Alex."

Noah says his name like a quiet plea, and Alex doesn't know what to do. "So, you—that's it then? You don't trust me to keep it a secret, so we can't even try."

"I talked to my agent."

It's not the answer Alex expected, and every possible response is a wisp he can't quite catch, nothing sticking long enough for the words to form in his mouth.

Noah goes on without one. "He gave me a pretty detailed plan and I can see how it works for people, how Ford made it his entire career without getting outed. I believe David Yates can spin a story to keep anything secret and make people love us if something terrible ever happens. I want this so bad, and I think you're worth it—I really do. But I don't want to lie to you and say I'm not worried we can't pull it off. Jesus, I like you so much *my dad,* who thinks I'm too robotic for even old-school hockey men to like, thinks I'm likable when I'm with you. I feel like a walking billboard when I look at you sometimes and I don't want to be the reason something happens to you. I don't want to be the reason guys around the league start suspecting we're together like my dad said they did with Ford. And honestly, I'm not sure you've thought about this enough to have any doubts and I—it would hurt me a lot if it turned out you did."

"I'm not some naïve optimist here. I know we could fuck up and get caught, but is it really possible for either of us to go into this without a little doubt in the back of our minds that it might blow up in our faces? How many people go into a relationship 100 percent sure it's going to last forever, that somewhere down the line it won't just stop working? If we both think it's worth it, why can't we have that?"

"We can have that! We can. I'm not saying you have to be sure we're going to last forever but I would like a little more certainty that you're not just jumping headfirst into something because it *feels good* and the moment it gets too hard or too real you'll decide it's not worth it when you can find happiness with a woman and don't have to go through *any of this*!"

"Is that what this is about? You don't believe me when I say I'm into you? What the hell do you think I'm doing here, Anderson? Do you think I'm trying to sate some curiosity and once I do, I'll bail? Because if that were the case, I would've had sex with Yatesy like he offered if we became friends!"

"What?" Noah asks, quiet and small.

Alex's blood runs cold when he recognizes Noah's tone as the one he overheard at the Combine. "Wait, Anderson, no. No. Whatever you're thinking, it's not—"

"So, you didn't have a sex bet with Sean on the little friendship challenge this started with?"

Noah's voice is icy, and Alex feels sick. "No. *No.* It was not a real bet. It was a chirp because none of them thought you'd give me the time of day and they all thought I was into you—and I obviously was—and wanted me to just accept it already. It was—it only happened because we'd just found out about him experimenting with one of his teammates and the boys were giving him grief for saying he wouldn't be mine. It wasn't serious; I did *not* have a sex bet over you."

"But did he follow through? When it became clear we were friends, did he offer again?"

"Yeah, but—"

"That's what Mitch meant when he said someone had to pinch hit when Sean wasn't around, right? Because if given the chance, you would've gone to him instead."

"No. I never planned to go to Yatesy, and I only kissed Mitch to prove a fucking point that I ended up being completely wrong about, anyway. He kissed me and I wanted it to be you. Please, don't make this into—please. You have to believe me."

"I think I need—"

"Noah, please."

"I don't want to be another person you have sex with because everyone else thinks you've got feelings for me, and you think you *should*. I can't be that."

*Fuck.* "That's not—no. You aren't. I promise. I told you; I told you in Vegas that you're the only person I've ever felt this way about. You're the only person I've ever thought I could care about enough to finally get my mom to believe me when I say I won't end up with Liv. You're not an experiment. You're not something I think I should do. You're someone I want; you're someone this will all be worth it for. I don't know how else to say it, but you make me feel like hockey does. You know that's not casual. You know that's serious."

"I want to believe you—"

"But you don't," Alex mumbles, slumping against the wall and sliding to the ground. "And I don't know how else to make you."

Noah is quiet for so long, Alex has to check he didn't hang up.

When he speaks, it's like they never got derailed. "Call your agent."

"What?"

"Our agents need to be on the same page and if yours thinks this will jeopardize your career, it won't work."

The balcony door slides open and Brett peeks out. His curious expression slips into worry when he meets Alex's eyes.

Alex holds up his hand to keep him from talking, asks Noah, "And if he doesn't—what then?"

"I hope I'll believe you by the time you tell me he's on board."

Alex curls into himself, rests his arm across his knees, and drops his head. It feels hopeless, like he doesn't have a chance, like failure is inevitable. Still, he says, "I'll let you know, then."

When Noah hangs up, Brett sits to where there's no space between them, squeezes his shoulder, and scratches his head. He doesn't ask and for a long while, Alex doesn't answer.

"I think I really fucked it up with Anderson just now."

"Do you want to tell me about it?"

Alex turns so his cheek is on his arm and he can see the pinched concern in Brett's eyes. "We kissed in Vegas."

Brett blinks but doesn't show any other signs of surprise. "Is that why you've been a little moody the last week?"

Alex tries to smile; his face feels too tight. "We ended up arguing about it; ended with him saying he wasn't saying no, but he needed to call his agent first."

Brett hums in acknowledgement but doesn't offer input of his own. Alex carries on. "We talked on Friday and I thought—it didn't feel so hopeless. Then today happened and he—I mean, I get it. I get why he's worried that we'll get outed. And we're arguing again about how he doesn't think I've thought about how hard it's going to be and if it's worth it and all that shit and I realize he thinks I'm going through a phase and I said—*fuck.*"

Brett scratches through his hair again, but otherwise waits him out.

"You remember when Yatesy said he'd give me a handjob when—" Brett grimaces and Alex breathes out, ragged. "Yeah. He called it a *sex bet.*"

"*Shit.*"

"And you know how Liv and I started fooling around because our parents kept saying we'd end up together?"

"Yes," Brett says, slow and hesitant.

"He knows that too. And I guess when I was explaining how the Yatesy thing even came up—God, Brett, I don't think like him, I wouldn't have come to this conclusion *ever*. But he said he doesn't want to be another person I sleep with because I feel like I should, because everyone else thinks I've got feelings for him."

"But that's obviously not true. There's no way he believes that when you look at him like he hung the moon."

Alex snorts. "Well, that's not good either. He thinks it's going to be harder for me to keep a relationship secret because I never realize how much of myself I give away." Brett makes a face and Alex's stomach drops, cold like lead. "You agree with him?"

"I'm not saying you're incapable of this, but he's not wrong. You broadcast your feelings for everyone to see and it might make people talk. And what happens if they only think it's you?"

Alex hadn't thought about that, and Brett must see it in his expression by the way he frowns. "Before I tell you what I think—what're you letting Noah know?"

"He said he won't do anything if my agent thinks it's going to jeopardize my career—but it's fucking stupid, and I don't need *permission* from my agent to date someone."

"Okay, well," Brett starts, voice so cautious Alex's hackles rise before he even says, "I don't think you need permission but if you hadn't even thought about how obvious it is that you're in love with him—shut up, I'm not fighting you on that—then there're probably other things you haven't thought about and your agent is the one who will help you see the big picture."

"But if he's not on board, it won't even matter if Noah believes me. He still won't go for it."

Brett's mouth curls in disdain. "Buddy, if your agent thinks a gay relationship will ruin your career, you'll need to get one who's on board with *any* gay relationship for your own sake, so that's a nonissue."

Alex huffs out a laugh. "I mean, getting a whole new agent is a *little* bit of an issue."

Brett rolls his eyes. "But not for getting your man."

"You're pretty confident he's going to believe me."

"Yeah, because he's hurt right now, but he's not an actual fucking moron."

The conviction in Noah's voice as he said Alex was worth it echoes in his mind; that's more than Alex thought he'd get in Vegas.

Brett wraps his arm around Alex's shoulder, pulls him in, and drops a kiss to his head. "It's going to work out."

Alex settles into the crook of Brett's shoulder, lets him take his weight. "Hopefully."

*

ALEX DOES HIS best not to think about Noah the next day. He goes to morning skate, has lunch with Liv, and meets her girlfriend. He gets a snapshot of Liv's life without him, and when Hilary makes her laugh so hard she almost does a spit take, Alex understands why Liv's voice goes all soft when she talks about her. When Liv has Hilary's complete attention, Alex wonders if everyone passing by can see how much she cares or if he only notices because they've been friends for so long. But the soft curve of Liv's smile reflects the warm, giddy happiness he gets from Noah giving him the attention he wants, and he worries he's as obvious as Liv and that he'll ruin everything just like Noah said.

For days he thinks about people talking, about Noah distancing himself if the rumors only end up being about Alex. He thinks about Nate and how fucked up everything is, thinks about them getting outed, thinks about it ruining them, making Noah hate him. He thinks about every way this could go wrong and not once does he doubt wanting to be with Noah.

He talks to Yatesy about what he did between thinking he was curious and making a Grindr profile. He doesn't watch a lot of porn about it, but he watches some, and he reads a lot of wikiHows. In the middle of it, he sends Noah an invitation to play chess and when he accepts it, when Alex knows Noah's not completely icing him out and that he probably hasn't fucked this up beyond repair, Alex finally lets himself think about what he wants to do with Noah, about how badly he wants to touch him, taste him, lay him out and mark him up and *please him.*

It doesn't feel like he's just curious when he's in the shower, smothering his moans into his arm and coming while he thinks about getting on his knees and blowing Noah. It doesn't feel like anything other than white-hot want when he fingers himself for the first time and his mind keeps flitting between Noah's mouth on him while he works him open and Noah laid out in Alex's bed, squirming and pink when Alex finds his prostate.

He never doubted his attraction to Noah but after a week of letting his mind play out the fantasies he's kept locked away for so long, he's so fucking horny and so fucking sure Noah isn't something he'd give up because being straight is easier.

He's still concerned he might give them up, still putting off calling his agent, still hoping Noah will believe he's serious if he waits the right amount of time when shit hits the fan so hard, Alex doesn't have time to think about his own problems.

# Chapter Thirty-Seven

**the one with bambi** 😈😊

Sat, Feb 18, 3:25PM

**Mitch**
Nate wtf is this shit all over twitter about

a brawl during a team only meeting

**Anderson**
And did you actually get injured during

it? Or was listing you as day to day just a

coincidence

**Beaver**
Was this because of Kip? Did he say

something to you?

**Nate**
It wasn't a brawl. And both I guess. I

would've been day to day no matter what
happened after tape review but I
definitely came out of the team meeting
worse than I went in lol

**Brett**
Did kipping hurt you?

**Nate**
Technically I landed weird

**Yatesy**
And did you land weird because of
something Kipping started?

**Nate**
It started because Jimmy and Newt
called a closed door meeting to figure out
why shit's still weird with me and Kip
and it got out of control.

**Parse**
Do you want to talk about what
happened?

> *I thought getting moved back to*
> *the top line meant it was getting*
> *better?*

**Nate**
I thought so too! A couple days after we
talked I told him I'd have a threesome
with any guy a hot girl told me to if that's

what it took to get laid and that he
needed to get the fuck over himself
because he wasn't special

**Johnny**
THAT'S what you picked?

**Kaden**
And it made things better???

**Ben**
So what went wrong after that?

**Nate**
I guess it depends on what you mean by
better. We still aren't carpooling but he's
not avoiding me in the locker room and I
was back on the top line that night and
we were clicking again and the hockey's
been GOOD. But the guys have obviously
noticed Kip's still not really talking to me
like before and they wanted to force the
issue today

**Yatesy**
And forcing the issue ended with you
hurt worse?

**Nate**
Yeah, well. Newt said we needed to get to
the bottom of our lover's quarrel because
we were bringing the kids down and that
set kip on edge. He tells them not to be

assholes and if it's no longer affecting our game it's not the team's business. But Jimmy says that's bullshit because Kip's clearly icing me out and that's unacceptable from a captain and Kip's livid at this point and when I told Jimmy to drop it fucking Gunnar says "kid it's obviously not fine, you two were obsessed with each other last month and now kip can't even look at you." Then Svech chimes in with "did you two break up or something" and kip fucking loses it then, yelling about how it's not like that and we don't joke about shit like that in our room and Gunnar gets in his face yelling "you said this wouldn't be a problem, you swore you wouldn't get involved with him" and it didn't get further than that because kip tried to punch Gunnar and when I tried to stop him he pushed me off and I caught myself on the stall weird. Overextended something. Again.

**Anderson**
What happened after that?

**Yatesy**
Holy shit did he try to turn it back around on you?? Make it seem like you

were the one who's been coming on to him???

**Beaver**
Wait Gunnar thought KIP was into YOU last year and that's how kip reacted to you saying you'd go home with him and that girl???? Wtf

**Nate**
No, he didn't turn it around on me, didn't mention the threesome at all. He apologized to me and then stormed off and left me there to deal with the team's questions
So I told Gunnar that me and kip have never slept together but we had been sleeping with the same girl without realizing it and kip's been sulking since she chose me over him lol

**Brett**
And they believed that

**Nate**
Eh if they didn't they didn't push it and since the gay of it all hasn't shown up in the gossip yet I'm hoping that means no one's going to spread it around but I guess I just gotta wait and see

**Mitch**
Sounds like kip has more to worry about

than you babe


**Yatesy**
Do YOU think Gunnar's right and he's

been into you this whole time? Because

uh....


**Nate**
I don't see how that could be true


**Parse**
Really? Because from here it sounds a lot

like kip was into the idea and freaked out

because he'd already been called out

about his feelings for you and didn't want

it getting back to the team


**Mitch**
Yeeeeah did anyone else seem

unsurprised when Gunnar said all that?

Like I know they were joking about you

two breaking up but do you think anyone

really would've been cool about that?


**Nate**
Not that I remember but I don't know,

Svech said none of them had a problem if

either of us WERE into guys but as a

general rule getting involved with

teammates was probably a bad idea and I

said I'd keep that in mind if I ever
actually get the hots for a teammate and
then jimmy said that applied to the
WHOLE TEAM and that was that. But
that doesn't mean they think the same as
Gunnar

**Ben**
How do you feel about all this?

**Mitch**
That's a dumbass question and you're not
a dumbass ben

**Ben**
Fuck off I'm trying to check on his
emotional wellbeing asshole

**Nate**
I feel fucking awful but they probably
won't be able to trade me when I have an
injury that won't have a clear recovery
timeline by next week so at least there's
that

*

### Do or Die

Mon, Feb 20, 1:11PM

**Nate**
Given everything that's going on in my
life I've decided enough time has passed

and I'm allowed to meddle in your love
life Alex

*I've got it covered thanks*

**Ben**
Really? Because I caught up with him
after our game last night and he looked
fucking miserable

*You don't know that. He doesn't*
*even believe I have actual*
*feelings for him*

**Mitch**
And they lit you guys UP last night so
he'd have no reason to be upset

**Ben**
Sugarcoat it for me next time jfc
But he's right, he should not have been as
moody as he was

*You know he could be moody*
*about things that have nothing to*
*do with me right? His life doesn't*
*revolve around me.*

**Yatesy**
Touched a fucking nerve there
Are you two fighting?

**Brett**
They're not talking at the moment

because Alex won't do what Noah asked

him to do

Way to oversimplify to make it<br>
my fault asshole

**Beaver**
Why aren't you talking then?

**Johnny**
What did he ask you to do?

**Brett**
You tell them or I do because someone

needs to talk some sense into you before

you procrastinate yourself into losing

your chance

**Mitch**
HAVE YOU MADE PROGRESS ON

BAMBI AND NOT TOLD US?????????

**Nate**
And Brett was COMPLICIT in

withholding it from us???? Ouch

I didn't want to bother you with<br>
my shit when you're going<br>
through your own and it<br>
would've been a dick move to tell<br>
everyone but you

**Brett**
I'm pretty sure he wouldn't have told me
if I didn't overhear the end of his phone
call

**Parse**
Guess you have no reason to keep it from
us if Nate brought it up

> *Other than I don't want to talk*
> *about it ofc*

**Kaden**
Brett's already eliminated that as a
reason and do you really want brett to
oversimplify your shit again?

> *FINE*
> *The highlight version: We kissed*
> *in vegas. We had a fight. He said*
> *he'd say yes if he didn't worry so*
> *much but he needed to call his*
> *agent. Said he wanted to try but*
> *didn't think we'd succeed and*
> *that he wouldn't do anything my*
> *agent thought would fuck with*
> *my career. He thinks I'm going to*
> *decide I'm not into him. I fuck up*
> *and mention Yatesy letting me*
> *experiment on him. He got really*
> *upset because he thinks it was A*

*SEX BET. Nothing I say fixed it.*
*He told me to call my agent and*
*let him know and hopefully he'd*
*believe me by the time I did. And*
*here we are.*

**Yatesy**
Oh god

**Mitch**
Shit

**Ben**
Oh bud

**Nate**
Ok that blows but have you not called

your agent yet?

**Brett**
No he hasn't

**Johnny**
Why the hell not??

**Beaver**
Are you worried your agent won't be chill

about this? Because no matter what you

can't have a homophobe for an agent if

you like dudes and I really fucking hope

Noah understands you'd need to find a

new one

*Beau he doesn't even think I'm*
*into him. It won't matter if I'll*
*need a new agent he won't do*
*anything while I find one either*

**Ben**
So you're just not going to call? Because

he might not be on board and you might

have to wait longer?

*NO. I'm trying to give him*
*enough time so he might actually*
*believe me when I say I'm not*
*going to fuck and run*

**Nate**
How long have you given him at this

point?

*Two weeks*

**Nate**
That's long enough

Call your agent

*Can ONE of you be on my side*
*here ffs*

**Ben**
We are on your side. But Brett's right

man, waiting any longer won't help prove

your point

*The only way to prove my point*
*is him taking a chance on me and*
*I'm kinda worried that doesn't*
*even exist anymore with how*
*things are working out for you*
*Nate*

**Nate**
Fuck off with that. Don't use my shit as
an excuse

*It's not an EXCUSE! I'm actually*
*worried. This is exactly what he's*
*afraid of happening and he*
*already doubts we can keep it a*
*secret.*

**Kaden**
So you don't believe him either, it's not
just him

*I guess so*

**Mitch**
Kinda fucked you want him to take a
chance on his doubts when you don't
want to do the same

*Putting it like that makes me feel*
*like a huge dick thanks*

**Mitch**
Don't worry I don't think you're doing it

on purpose

> *Because that makes it so much*
>
> *better*

**Mitch**
It should tbh but you know what'll

REALLY make you feel better?

> *Calling my agent.*

**Parse**
DING DING DING WE HAVE A

WINNER BOYS

*

**Anderson**
Mon, Feb 20, 11:11PM

> *I talked to my agent.*
> *GENERALLY Jeff advises*
> *against players in the same*
> *league getting involved because*
> *trades happen. But he's worked*
> *with Yatesy's dad on something*
> *like this before and knows all*
> *closeted relationships are a*
> *calculated risk so he's not, like,*

*AGAINST against players dating*
*he just REALLY wants everyone*
*to know they can end up on a*
*team with an ex one day if the*
*romance doesn't last. Let me*
*know what you want to do.*

Either you called your agent at a truly
inappropriate time or you waited until
you thought I'd be asleep so I wouldn't
answer right away

*Whichever pisses you off the least*

When do you fly to Montreal?

*Uhh Wednesday evening*

Practice that morning?

*Just the travel before the back to*
*back*

Wednesday is completely free for us if
you want to come over after my game
tomorrow

*What? This conversation is not*
*going anything like I expected*

How'd you expect it to go?

*Tbh I expected it to take you at*
*least a full day to respond and I*
*thought there'd be a phone call or*
*three between seeing you again*

You caught me at the right moment I
guess. Turns out I miss you

# Chapter Thirty-Eight

NOAH'S HEART LEAPS in his throat when Alex calls. "I guess we are getting a phone call in before seeing each other."

Alex lets out a quiet huff, frustration clear when he says, "Anderson, you can't say shit like that without telling me what we're doing here."

A jolt of adrenaline runs through him. He should've known better than to start this conversation this late; it's going to take him forever to fall asleep at this rate. "I think that's up to you."

"Excuse me? If this was up to me, we would've been together in Vegas! This has always been up to you."

Noah's stomach turns even though it's fair. "I've been thinking, and I want this *so bad,* but—"

Alex makes a strangled noise. "Did you want me to come over so you could turn me down in person? That's—"

"You know I wouldn't do that," Noah snaps.

"Yeah," Alex says quietly. "But when has 'but' ever been a good thing in a situation like this?"

"When I'm trying to tell you how it's your choice! Just be quiet and listen to me for a second."

"Okay."

"I was trying to say that I've thought about this, and I want to try. I want to believe you when you say this isn't an experiment or an obligation or whatever and I know you mean it when you say it, but I still expect you to decide I'm not worth all this trouble and I know that's not fair to you. So, like I said, it's your choice."

"Can I talk now?"

Noah huffs. "Yes. Go ahead."

"Oh good," Alex says. "Got a few questions for you before I tell you my choice."

"Okay."

"Do *you* still think I'm worth all this?"

"Yes."

"And if what's happening to Nate happens to me, are you going to publicly distance yourself from me?"

Noah's stomach plummets. "What?"

"Like you said, I'm just like Nate and you *are* going to be better at hiding this than me and if it comes down to it, where no one ever wonders about you, but they do about me, are we going to pretend we're not friends anymore?"

Noah's chest tightens. "Alex, *no*. I swear."

Alex sounds pleased when he says, "All right. One last question, then. Do you trust me enough to let me show you I want you, to prove to you I'm all in on *you*?"

Noah feels warm but strange—he doesn't really deserve any of this when he can't take Alex at his word. "You shouldn't have to prove any-thing."

"Noah, listen to me. I've spent a very long time trying to prove that how much I wanted you to like me, how much time I wanted to spend with you, wasn't a gay thing and that makes me feel like shit because I should've recognized it, and I shouldn't have been so defensive when the guys pointed it out, and I *really* shouldn't have needed to kiss Mitch to prove to myself I'm attracted to guys. But now I know, and now I have no doubts, and I want to do this. I want to be with you. I know you know how much I care about you because you chirp me for it all the fucking time—so that's not what this is about, and I need you to answer my question. Do you trust me enough to show you I want to put my mouth all over you, that I want to find all your favorite places to be touched, that I haven't stopped thinking about how it felt to have you under me in Vegas? Do you trust me enough to prove that I'm going to keep coming back?"

Noah flushes everywhere, blood rushing in his ears and heat pooling at the base of his spine. His throat is tight and clearing it does nothing; his voice is still affected when he says, "Yeah, I do."

"Then let me show you."

"All right...if you're sure. But I don't know what you'll get for being right when buying each other dinner is pretty standard for dating."

"How embarrassed are you going to be if I say you're all I need?"

"Super embarrassed for you."

Alex laughs, the sound perfect in Noah's ears. "Yeah, that's what I thought. So here's the deal; once I prove I'm the best damn boyfriend you'll ever have, I get to deck you out in USA Hockey gear."

Noah snorts, warm and bubbly all over. "God, that's worse. You're so embarrassing."

"And you like me *so* much for it."

His smug delight should be annoying, but Noah has never really thought it was at all. Especially now. "Yeah, an absurd amount."

*

**Alex Valencia**
Tue, Feb 21, 4:17PM

Score a goal for me tonight and I'll buy
dinner

*Thanks for the jinx*

You're welcome for the MOTIVATION

*How will you know which one's*
*for you?*

THERE'S MY COCKY BITCH
And it's the second one ofc

*Oh ffs I walked myself right into*
*that*

Yup :)

*

NOAH'S ON EDGE when he answers the door for Alex, his body buzzing with a mix of nerves, anticipation, and desire.

"Not gonna lie, thought you might fail for a second there," Alex says first thing, crowding into Noah's space as he drops his backpack on the floor and shuts the door with his foot. "But you outdid yourself with that wraparound in the last minute. Game winner just for me."

Noah rolls his eyes, but he's been on the other end of Alex's teasing grin so many times before and it's never been this flirty or made him this warm. "Sure. It had nothing to do with winning. It was all for you."

"Don't lie." Alex puts his hands on Noah's hips. His thumbs are firm against the bones. "It totally pissed you off when Hendrickson tipped in your slapshot on the last power play."

"Tying the game would never piss me off."

Alex tracks the flush of Noah's cheeks. There's a delighted gleam in his eyes as he lets go of Noah to step around him. "Said nothing about tying it up."

It's a relief when the loss of Alex's hands momentarily freezes Noah, if only for the way it prevents him from seeing Noah blush even brighter. Except Alex radiates smug satisfaction when Noah joins him on the couch, still pink and flushed.

The moment fizzes out and tension grows between them. Noah is suddenly aware of their proximity and how different tonight is than the last time they were alone together. He's allowed to want Alex, allowed to take what Alex gives him without needing to stop and think about it, but allowing himself to ask for anything seems impossible now. His tongue is thick in his mouth, his brain whirring as he looks at Alex watching him with a small grin and an intensity in his eyes that zips through Noah's veins, leaving him hot and flushed for entirely new reasons.

"So, I was thinking—" Alex starts.

"Haven't we done enough of that by now?"

"Only about the serious stuff."

Noah swallows. "I dunno, I might've done enough unserious thinking too."

The heat in Alex's eyes is undeniable. "Oh, yeah? Wanna tell me about it?"

Noah swallows. "You're the one who was thinking."

"I was, but you distracted me."

Noah grins, his nerves quieter now that they're talking. "Better get back on track, then. You know how important focus is."

"God, you're so..." Alex laughs. "I was thinking instead of dinner I could reward you for my goal by letting you choose whatever you want me to do to you—"

Noah shifts in his seat and Alex's grin turns cocky.

"But now..." Alex drops his hand to Noah's thigh. His palm is warm, and when Alex swipes his thumb under the hem of his shorts, Noah can't do anything about the goosebumps, but Alex's grip tightens on his thigh as they spread, and Noah thinks that's probably a good thing. "Since you're being a brat—"

"—something you're stupid into."

Alex flushes, and want sears through Noah as he grins, pleased to know he's right.

"Yes," Alex grumbles. "But if I don't get to kiss you soon, I'm going to—"

"—if you'd finish a sentence, you could—"

Alex's voice is almost a whine. "Anderson, please."

Noah stands and pulls Alex up with him. "What were you going to say?"

Alex grins when Noah steps backward and follows along. "I was going to say I get to choose now. But it seems like you have a plan of your own."

"Only so far as getting you in my bed," Noah says as he stops at his door. "You can choose after that. If you're still capable."

"God," Alex huffs, his gaze scorching as he opens the door and pushes them through. "I cannot believe"—he squeezes Noah's waist as he steers him toward the bed—"how much it does it for me when you're a bitch."

Noah hits the edge of the bed and Alex stops. He cups his hand along Noah's jaw. "I want to see you." He rucks up Noah's shirt and his palm is unbearably hot as he runs it along Noah's oblique. "Can I take this off?"

"You first."

Alex grins, twists his fingers through Noah's curls, and tips his head up for one quick kiss before taking his shirt off. Noah doesn't even have time to take in the broad expanse of Alex's chest before he's lifting the hem of Noah's shirt and stripping it off him. He runs his hands down his ribs and dips his thumbs below both waistbands. "These too?"

Noah flushes all over but manages to nod. Alex's grip tightens around Noah's hips and for a brief, terrifying moment, Noah thinks this is it, this is when it becomes too real. Instead, Alex's eyes widen, a little awestruck, and his composure snaps. He whispers, "Fuck, okay, yeah," in a rush, then everything is a frantic scramble of hands and clothes and Alex's burst of laughter when their teeth clash on a kiss as he tips them over onto the bed.

Noah shifts up the bed and Alex knocks one bent knee to the side, making room as he leans in and kisses Noah slow and thoroughly. Alex's tongue is hot when he opens for it, but when Noah tries to pull Alex in closer, he leans away.

Noah huffs and amusement cuts through the hot, hungry way Alex looks him over. His question gets lost in a groan when Alex faintly scratches his fingernails up Noah's inner thigh.

"I said I wanted to see you."

Noah wants to roll his eyes, but he feels pinned down, frozen in place by how pleased Alex seems, his frenetic desperation from moments before slowed to a simmer as he trails his fingertips across Noah's abs, his collarbones, his throat. He smirks when he thumbs across Noah's nipple and his breath hitches; his awestruck satisfaction, like Noah's giving Alex something by letting him touch his body, grows with every noise he draws out of Noah, and by the time he's made his way back down his sternum and across his other hip, Noah's desperate.

He can't take it anymore, his patience and will to stay still gone, and he surges up for a kiss. He pulls Alex down and the two of them groan into each other's mouths as their dicks finally touch. Noah wraps his legs around Alex's waist, rocking their hips together, and Alex laughs into the crook of his neck. His lips are warm against Noah's skin as Alex mumbles, "I see being demanding wasn't a onetime thing."

Alex doesn't even let Noah finish saying, "Goal oriented," before he's back on him, their hips lined up and his mouth hot and insistent as Alex grinds down and the frantic desperation boils over, and Noah loses himself to the sensations of his body moving with another. He's burning up from the inside out, thoughts lost in a haze, inhibitions seared right out of him, so when Alex reaches between them and thumbs across the head of Noah's cock and says, "Tell me about your unserious thoughts," Noah doesn't hesitate.

Broken up by the moans he can't quite keep in when Alex licks his palm and takes them both in hand, he tells Alex how he fingers himself and thinks about how much he'll enjoy getting fucked, how hard he's tried not to let his mind wander to Alex while he's jerking off, how much harder he comes when he fails, how he's the only person Noah's ever thought about fucking into him and taking what he's been so desperate not to give away. He comes with Alex's name caught in his throat, and his fingers digging into Alex's shoulders to keep him close, desperate to keep the heat of Alex's skin all over him.

They're hot and sweaty, but Noah doesn't want to move. He breathes out a content little sigh when Alex presses a kiss that's more of a smile to the corner of his mouth. He buries his face in the crook of Noah's neck, idly tracing his fingers along Noah's ribs as he muffles a laugh against his skin.

Everything is still syrupy and slow in his mind, but he recognizes the hint of embarrassment in the laugh and moves to run his fingers through Alex's hair. He scratches at the base of his skull and says, "Whatever you just thought, say it."

"It's bad."

"It's a hockey reference, isn't it?"

"No... Only a little," Alex says, still laughing when he shifts to look at Noah. "I was thinking 'that's one way to put the rivalry to bed.'"

"You're so—" But he loses it to laughter before he can think of the right words. Alex dips down to catch his mouth in a kiss and, for the first time since he said it, Noah gets what Alex said about making him feel like hockey—kissing Alex tastes exactly like winning.

# Chapter Thirty-Nine

WHEN NOAH SAID "all in from the jump or not at all" Alex wasn't expecting Noah to fall into a relationship with the same dedication he gives hockey. But he does, and it's quite a trip for Alex to be the recipient of Noah's intense determination and commitment. It's like a switch flips the moment Noah decides being with Alex is something he wants to try, and instead of dedicating the same single-minded focus to denying himself what he wants for the sake of hockey, he turns the weight of all that onto making things work with Alex. And just like hockey, Noah makes it all look so fucking easy.

It doesn't change a thing about how he plays against Alex and even though Alex knew it wouldn't, relief washes through him when the puck drops on their last matchup of the season, more than a month into this thing of theirs, and Alex sees the same insatiable hunger to win reflected in Noah's eyes as always. He's elated by how much he still wants to *beat Noah* specifically, how much delight he still gets from winning a board battle and catching Noah's frustrated swear as he skates away.

The Hellions have already clinched, and they don't need this win like Alex and Brett do, but Alex would hate it if Noah went easy on him, even subconsciously. But it still sucks just as much as always when Noah sets Hendrickson up for a go-ahead goal and Alex's hopes of clinching the first wildcard wilts. But it reignites in the last three minutes of the third when Casey ties it up—all they need is to make it to overtime and when Alex jumps the boards for his next shift, he knows they can keep them from scoring again. When the buzzer sounds, the certainty of being playoff bound zaps through him, sending wild energy coursing through his veins that barely wanes when Noah forces a turnover a minute into overtime, and the Hellions still end up winning.

Alex catches Noah's eyes as he joins the celly, his cocky grin infuriatingly hot even here, when Alex has just lost. Usually he'd wait him out, make Noah break first, but Alex wants to kiss him so badly, he has to look away before he does something stupid like joining the goddamn celly. He wants to get out of here and get his hands on Noah as fast as possible tonight, but an overtime loss that secured their playoff berth still requires celebration and there's no way he's missing it.

They'd already talked about the possibility, so it's surprising when Noah meets Alex outside the visitors' locker room, anyway; even more so when he slips Alex a key to his place and tells him to use it in case Noah falls asleep before he's done celebrating.

The pink of Noah's cheeks is the only mention he makes of it, but the knowledge Noah made him a key makes Alex giddy. Mixed with the success of the night, it leaves Alex floating the entire way to the bar. His time passes in a blur of the boys yelling and drinks pressed into his hand and hours go by before he's calling a car. He's giggling, and more than a little drunk when he stumbles into the backseat of the car, warmth seeping through him as he thinks about slipping into Noah's bed to sleep.

*

ALEX WAKES TO the press of Noah's lips on his bare shoulder and he blinks up at him blearily. Noah is watching him with a small, soft smile. He's shirtless and under the comforter, but his hair is damp, and Alex can smell the mint of his toothpaste. "You didn't wake me up last night or for your shower. Brutal."

Noah ducks his head and laughs against Alex's shoulder. "How could I?"

"Exactly, how *could* you?" Alex pouts.

Noah kisses his shoulder again, feather light, but he feels it like a brand. It makes him shiver, goosebumps blossoming across his arm, and Noah makes a pleased noise, eyes bright and smug when he asks, "Do you want me to make it up to you?"

The simmering heat of arousal he's had since waking spikes. Noah's gaze is heavy on Alex when the comforter falls around Alex's hips and heat floods his veins. "Yeah, I think maybe you should."

Alex kisses Noah's cheek, then throws the blankets off. He bites down on a grin when he gets out of bed and Noah whines, "Now who's being the brat?"

"Still you!" Alex calls over his shoulder. "Gotta keep you happy, baby, and I'm not the one who's uptight about morning breath!"

Noah's quiet laugh warms Alex all the way through and when he gets back, he expects Noah to be at his dresser or rifling through his closet for fresh clothes, so really, it's not Alex's fault that his brain whites out and he can't think when instead, he walks in to find Noah sitting cross-legged at the edge of the bed, running the flat edge of a foil packet back and forth across his palm.

"Um." Alex's tongue is thick in his mouth. He can't think. He's on fire, blood rushing in his ears, heart hammering against his ribs too hard, too fast. "Noah...?"

Noah looks up, pink-cheeked and *determined*, and Alex is free-falling, stomach bottoming out, breath catching, mind nothing but static as Noah sets the condom down next to the bottle of lube that was definitely not on the nightstand when Alex left.

"Are you just going to stand there?" Noah asks, an amused slant to his mouth that sends a rush of affection through Alex and kicks him back into gear.

"I dunno." Alex steps into the space between Noah's legs, drops a hand to his knee, and squeezes. "Is there something I need to get back in bed for?"

"Well," Noah says, gaze hot and challenging as he drops back on the heels of his hands. "*I'm* not getting out of bed, but I guess you can fuck me from there if you want."

Alex swallows and runs his hand up Noah's thigh. Heat burns through him as Noah's breath hitches and his muscles tense when Alex dips his fingers beneath the hem of his underwear. "This isn't you making it up to me."

"No," Noah confirms, gaze unwavering even as his flush spreads. "I did all the prep in the shower, so I'd be relaxed and ready to go when you got up."

"Holy—" Alex's fingers twitch against Noah's thigh. "Fuck. Noah, are you—"

"Don't—" Noah snaps Alex's waistband, his expression serious as he scoots up the bed. "I'm sure."

"That's not what I was going to ask." Noah arches an eyebrow and Alex huffs out a quiet laugh as he climbs onto the bed to kiss Noah until the tension bleeds out of his body. When he pulls back, Noah's mouth is slick and so distractingly pink it feels like a monumental feat when Alex resists letting his body do the talking. "I was going to say, 'are you kidding—that's so fucking hot.'"

"Oh." Noah swallows. "No, I wasn't kidding."

"Okay." Alex sits back on his haunches. "How do you—"

Noah squeezes Alex's bicep. "Like this."

Alex nods, tongue thick in his mouth as they strip down. His thoughts go hazy as Noah lies back against the pillows and tosses him the lube before dropping the condom by his hip.

Alex catches the bottle and kneels between Noah's bent legs. "Don't rush me."

Noah nudges Alex's side with his knee. "Kiss me again and I won't have to."

The demanding pout of Noah's mouth sends a thrill up Alex's spine, and he can't resist. He drops a kiss to Noah's cheek and laughs when Noah makes a low, frustrated sound and hooks his arm around Alex's neck to keep him from leaning back.

"You didn't specify," Alex says, affection swelling in his chest as Noah's mouth twitches in a tiny smile before he hauls Alex in for a kiss, deep and wet and unhurried, just like he said. When Alex pulls back, lips tingling and lungs burning for air, Noah chases after him. He grins against Alex's mouth when he lets him take one last kiss.

Noah's eyes are bright, his cheeks are red, and he's so fucking beautiful it makes Alex's chest ache just looking at him; so, he doesn't. He kisses him again, rough and hot as he rocks his hips forward, the slow drag of their cocks and the way Noah wraps his legs around Alex's waist bringing the heat of arousal to a boil until white-hot desperation burns through the last remnants of his nerves and he can stop second guessing himself and just *move*.

"Okay." Alex drops his head to Noah's shoulder to catch his breath, then scrapes his teeth across Noah's pulse point, mumbling, "I still wanna finger you—is that okay?" as he trails kisses down his neck.

"Whatever you want," Noah says, breath hitching and hips bucking when Alex sinks his teeth into the meat of his shoulder. "As long as you don't make me come before you've got your dick in me."

Alex laughs and takes Noah's nipple between his teeth. He bites down until he gasps then soothes the sting with his tongue. Noah whimpers when Alex moves to the next, his muscles jumping beneath Alex's mouth as he sucks biting kisses down his chest.

"I would never dream of it," Alex says as he settles between Noah's legs and slicks his fingers up.

"Sure," Noah gasps as Alex closes his lips around the head of his cock. "Not like you've ever said you could finger me all day and never get bored."

Alex hums in agreement as he takes Noah in further, then meets Noah's eyes and does it again just around the tip while slipping the first finger in with little resistance. True to his word, Noah is ready, and Alex doesn't waste time before he pins Noah's hips in place with his forearm and adds a second. Noah shudders when Alex finds his prostate, his body tensing and releasing as Alex slowly strokes his fingers back and forth until he's squirming.

Alex really loves this part, and it doesn't take long to lose himself to the sounds and sensations of Noah coming apart beneath him. He loves the hot weight of Noah on his tongue, the way he whines when Alex pulls off and out at the same time, the way he touches his thumb to the corner of his stretched lips, strokes along his jaw, curls his hand through Alex's hair but never urges him forward, and holds himself impossibly still as he tries not to fuck up into Alex's mouth.

"Alex," Noah gasps, fingers tightening in his hair. "You gotta—you said—"

Alex pulls off and Noah grabs at him until they're kissing again, his mouth hot and demanding, as Alex fumbles around for the condom.

Alex's breath catches when he pulls back and sees how wrecked Noah looks—hair a mess, mouth slick, swollen and red, flushed chest heaving. But it's the look in Noah's eyes that has Alex's fingers slipping as he works the condom on and slicks himself up. Noah's looking at Alex like—shit. He doesn't know how to describe it, can't even pinpoint something in hockey to make sense of it. There's an unbearable tenderness cutting through Noah's arousal that makes Alex's heart swell and his blood thrum with wild delight as he realizes he'd give Noah anything as long as he looked at him like this.

So when Noah smiles, soft and gently teasing as he says, "I know you need to go slow, but you do actually have to use your dick to fuck me, babe."

Alex lines himself up and gives Noah what he wants.

He watches Noah's face for discomfort as he rocks his hips forward excruciatingly slow until he bottoms out. He stays put until Noah shifts his hips and nods, breathless as he says, "You can move now."

Alex's mind goes syrupy as he pulls back and rocks back in with slow rolls of his hips over and over as he swallows each sound Noah makes until their kisses turn sloppy and uncoordinated.

"More. I need—" Noah whines as he clenches around Alex's cock. "Please, Alex. Harder."

Noah's desperation, and the soft, broken sounds he makes as he works his hips in time with Alex's thrusts, is all Alex needs to let go. He loses track of time, fucking into the tight clutch of Noah's body hard and fast until he stops begging for more and gasps that he's close and holy shit, Alex has had sex before but it's never felt like this, he's never felt so overwhelmed and unmoored as he does when he closes his hand around Noah, and jerks him off until he loses his rhythm. His thrusts turn erratic as he barrels toward the edge and the long line of Noah's throat as he spills between them is what pushes Alex over and makes him come.

It's hot and sticky between them and Noah surprises Alex when he kisses him, slow and thorough, instead of wrinkling his nose about the mess. When Alex pulls away, Noah looks fucked out and beautiful, and so unbearably soft that Alex dips down for another kiss, quick and chaste, before rolling out of bed. Noah's wearing the same tender expression when Alex comes back with a warm washcloth to wipe him down, and the kiss he gives Alex in thanks is slow and sweet and mind-numbingly good.

Noah doesn't linger in bed with Alex—he's already laid around longer than usual—and when he joins him in the kitchen, Noah is sitting on the counter sipping his coffee while scrolling through his phone. It's nothing he hasn't seen before, but Noah looks unbearably content and relaxed in the moment, so different from how he carried himself even two months ago, and it unlocks something in Alex's chest and the warmth of affection and the overwhelming sense of *right* rushes through him and leaves him giddy.

"Anything new and exciting happen on the 'gram while we were asleep?"

Noah snorts. "Have no idea. I was checking last night's west coast box scores."

Alex blinks as he grabs his own mug. "Really? You don't do that first thing after waking up on nights you don't stay up late enough?"

Noah takes another sip of his coffee before mumbling, "I usually do but..." He flushes as he motions noncommittedly with his mug. "You know."

"Aww bud, that's so sweet," Alex says, throat tight with a sudden influx of emotion. "You fucked up your morning routine for me."

Noah grins, just a tiny thing at the corner of his mouth. "Don't get used to it."

They lapse into a comfortable silence as Alex makes his coffee and when Alex drops a kiss to the extra dense constellation of freckles on Noah's shoulder and settles in by his side, Noah breaks it to say, "I didn't think it'd be that different playing you last night."

Alex raises an eyebrow. "If you're about to say a couple of shared orgasms fucked up your need to win—I'm calling bullshit. You were not even *close* to going easy on me last night."

"As if." Noah rolls his eyes. "You know I love to beat you more than anyone else."

Alex grins, a rush of excitement sparking through him. "That's mutual."

Noah's eyes are bright and amused. "It better be."

Alex takes another sip. "How was it different, then?"

Noah draws his eyebrows together thoughtfully, quiet for a moment, then says, "Like, I knew you needed to make it to overtime to clinch, right? And even though you weren't involved in the tying goal, I was still happy for you."

The joy bubbling through him is overwhelming, and he's relieved it comes out in a laugh that masks the emotion in his voice as he says, "And then you forced the turnover that won the game. That's love, baby."

Noah purses his lips, a little snappish as he says, "I think there's a little more to love than being pleased your boyfriend made the playoffs."

Alex is glad he's leaning against the counter because he feels like he's crashed headfirst into the boards when he realizes what the look from before was. Noah's flushed and uncomfortable, his gaze flickering everywhere but Alex, and that just won't do.

Alex nudges Noah's thigh with his hip, a silent reassurance as much as a plea for attention. It takes a moment, but Noah gives it to him. "Of course there is, but I think it's really cute, and *very you,* that being happy about my team's success just for me was your 'oh shit, I'm in love' moment."

Noah's face lights up with amused annoyance. "Oh my God, shut up, that's not what I said."

Alex smirks. "Oh? It was earlier?"

Noah's mouth twitches. "I've said nothing, and I will continue to say nothing."

"But you're not denying it, that's basically saying it." Alex buzzes with delight as he moves between Noah's legs and kisses the laugh right out of his mouth.

He gets sidetracked by the wet heat of Noah's mouth, the taste of coffee and honey on his tongue, and the demanding way he curls his fingers around the back of his neck. When he pulls back, Alex's cheeks hurt with how hard he's smiling.

"I figured," Noah starts with a mischievous glint in his eyes. "You should get to go first for once."

The laugh bursts through him and Noah looks so proud of himself and *holy shit,* this is Alex's moment. Alex has known he's loved Noah for a long time. He knows for some time that he's been barreling headfirst toward something bigger, different, *more* than he's ever felt for anyone else but right now, in Noah's sunlit kitchen, it knocks into him with rib-cracking clarity that he's *in love* with Noah.

"Oh babe, do you know what you've just done?"

Noah grins, sharp and challenging. "Think I have an idea."

Alex sets his mug down and takes Noah's too. "And what do I get when I once again go second?"

"Which you won't," Noah says, that same fierce determination dancing behind his eyes as he crosses his legs behind Alex to keep him in place. "But if you do, I'll give you whatever you want."

Noah cups his hand behind Alex's neck and pulls him in. An unspoken confession and the thrill of competition buzzes between them as they kiss, and win or lose, Alex knows he already proved it.

# Acknowledgements

This book wouldn't exist without the unwavering support of the people around me. I am forever grateful to Kenny for always being my sounding board. To Kim and Sarah for being two of my loudest cheerleaders. To Janee, who read this book when it was something almost entirely different, and never let me give up on Alex and Noah's story while I reworked it into what it is now. To Chloe, who came in at the end and identified where I could pack a little more punch. To Gina, who always encourages me in the kindest, most thoughtful ways.

A special thanks to Rae and Elizabeth for the work they put into polishing this book, and to Victoria, for knocking it out of the park with her illustrations and bringing my guys to life.

# About the Author

Stephanie Hoyt loves chaotic bisexuals, happily-ever-afters, and stories that blend the melancholy of self-discovery and self-acceptance with the delights of friendship and falling in love. She lives in Houston with her husband, her two children, and her very neurotic dog. She loves reality baking competitions, hockey, and rearranging the living room in times of stress.

# Other NineStar books by this author

*The Magic Between*
*Love Blooms*
*A Holiday Ruse*

www.ninestarpress.com

www.facebook.com/ninestarpress

www.facebook.com/groups/NineStarNiche

www.twitter.com/ninestarpress

www.instagram.com/ninestarpress